Advance Praise for *At the Mercy of the Queen*

"Ms. Barnhill's engaging style harkens back to the lovely, richly textured writing of Jean Plaidy and Kathleen Winsor."
—Diane Haeger, author of *The Secret Bride*

"Just when I think there's nothing really new to say about Henry VIII and Anne Boleyn, along comes this fresh and absorbing view through the eyes of little-known and certainly underrated Madge Shelton, the queen's cousin. Barnhill casts new light on the mysterious figure of Madge—who may really be an amalgam of two sisters, Margaret and Mary Shelton. But inevitably it is Anne herself who bestrides the narrative, continuing, as she always does, to fascinate."
—Sara Poole, author of *Poison*

"Reading *At the Mercy of the Queen* evoked for me the first time I stood on Tower Green and contemplated with a thrill of horror the spot where Anne Boleyn lost her head. I was scarcely older than Madge Shelton, Barnhill's innocent young heroine, and just as thoroughly captivated by the dark-eyed, ill-fated queen. Just when you think the telling of this tragic but familiar tale has surely been exhausted, suddenly there is this fresh, new voice that makes it new again."
—Brenda Rickman Vantrease, bestselling author of *The Illuminator*

"Fresh and dramatic, *At the Mercy of the Queen* gives us a different side of Henry VIII and his infamous second wife, Anne Boleyn, as well as an intriguing heroine in Madge Shelton herself, a cousin and confidante of the queen who is thrust into the heart of Tudor machinations and forced to fight for her own safety."
—C. W. Gortner, author of *The Last Queen* and *The Tudor Secret*

ALSO BY ANNE CLINARD BARNHILL

At Home in the Land of Oz: Autism, My Sister, and Me
What You Long For

At the Mercy of the
Queen

A NOVEL OF ANNE BOLEYN

Anne Clinard Barnhill

St. Martin's Griffin

New York

AT THE MERCY OF THE QUEEN. Copyright © 2011 by Anne Clinard Barnhill. All rights reserved. Printed in the United States of America. For information, address St. Martin's Press, 175 Fifth Avenue, New York, N.Y. 10010.

www.stmartins.com

Design by Anna Gorovoy

Library of Congress Cataloging-in-Publication Data

Barnhill, Anne Clinard.
    At the mercy of the queen : a novel of Anne Boleyn / Anne Clinard
Barnhill.—1st ed.
        p. cm.
    ISBN 978-1-250-00519-9 (hardcover)
    ISBN 978-0-312-66213-4 (trade paperback)
    ISBN 978-1-4299-2554-9 (e-book)
    1. Anne Boleyn, Queen, consort of Henry VIII, King of England,
1507–1536—Fiction.   2. Great Britain—Court and courtiers—
Fiction.   3. Great Britain—History—Henry VIII, 1509–1547—
Fiction.   I. Title.
    PS3602.A77713A94 2012
    813'.6—dc23

                                        2011036004

First Edition: January 2012

10 9 8 7 6 5 4 3 2 1

For Frank,
my own "Sir Churlish"

"... thy sweet love remembered ..."

Acknowledgments

So many hands come together to create a book, some visible, others invisible. I'd like to thank my agent, Irene Goodman, whose faith in this story made me a believer and without whom the book might be sitting in a box, still not finished; my parents, Dr. Jack and Virginia Clinard, for the use of their garage apartment during the completion of the manuscript, their understanding of my need for solitude, and the delicious meals they kindly provided; my three sons for their unwavering support and encouragement; and my husband, Frank, who has believed in me for a long time now.

Having a wonderful editor and other "book experts" on board is a great gift. Thank you, Charles Spicer, for your enthusiasm and probing questions, both of which prompt me to write better. I am also extremely grateful for the passion you have for history and historical fiction. Allison Strobel has been patient with my numerous questions; her expertise and insight are very much appreciated. NaNá Stoelzle's and Lauren Hougen's meticulous work helped get the book in shape for printing.

Even the world's greatest book would languish on a shelf if people didn't know about it. Thanks to Joseph Goldschein, Joan Higgins, and Rachel Ekstrom for such a thorough job in getting the word out. And to Paul Hochman for leading me into the twenty-first century through social networking.

Though writing is in many ways a lonely vocation, my fellow writers have been a great source of inspiration and example. My writing friends in various places, including Facebook, continue to show me how to put words together and have faith in the process.

Thank you all.

Preface

When I was fifteen, two life-altering events occurred. First, I read a forbidden book I'd discovered on my mother's bedroom shelf, a tattered paperback with a cover that showed a woman wearing a very low-cut dress and a crown. The title and author I still remember: *The Concubine* by Norah Lofts. It was, of course, the tale of Queen Anne Boleyn and her famous husband, King Henry VIII of England.

As I began reading, I was immediately enthralled by the love story. I knew the book was based on facts, but, for the first time, dry facts became so real I could imagine the events happening before my eyes, as if I were, somehow, a part of sixteenth-century England. I was taken with the grandeur and the greed, the pomp and the pretension, the loyalty and the lechery, and, most of all, the daring and the danger of those times, especially for women. At fifteen, I was slowly becoming aware that the pre-scribed roles for men and women in our society were deeply etched in the collective psyche. I realized it took an extraordi-nary woman to break those traditional bonds of expectation and venture into the wider world. Anne Boleyn had the intelligence and the courage to navigate her way to the top of a society that regarded women as little more than breeding stock. Through her strength of character, her feminine allure, and her sheer gumption, she refused the role of mistress. Instead, she insisted on the role of queen. Anne Boleyn was everything I wanted to be: attractive, powerful, bright, and in control of her destiny—at least for a while.

The second life-changing moment came while I was visit-ing my maternal grandmother, Helen Gwendolyn McCaul Bal-lard in Lincolnton, North Carolina. In between shelling peas and canning apples, she told me about our genealogy, showing me bits and pieces of our family's tree gleaned from scraps of paper she kept in a small wooden box. I listened politely, but suddenly, my ears perked up. She was talking about a queen, one who shook the world. I realized she was speaking of Anne Boleyn. Somehow, our family was connected to Anne Boleyn and her daughter, Elizabeth I. As it turned out, our ancestors, Sir John and Lady Anne Shelton, were quite close to the queen. Lady Anne Shelton was the sister of Sir Thomas Boleyn, Anne's father. Our ancestor was the queen's aunt!

From that moment, I began reading everything I could find about Anne Boleyn and her Shelton relatives. I discovered Sir John and Lady Anne had large roles to play in history—large enough that we read about them five hundred years later. I dis-covered they had a daughter, Lady Margaret Shelton, who is one of three named mistresses of Henry VIII. In some books, it is even suggested that Queen Anne put forth her young cousin to catch the king's fancy.

I wanted to tell this story and have imagined it for thirty years. I hope I have done justice to that amazing time when England was just beginning to recognize itself as a nation and the church was being turned on its head. And two young women from common British stock, cousins in the first degree, could capture the heart of a king.

At the Mercy of the
Queen

I

1533

The Moost Happi

QUEEN ANNE'S MOTTO

One

lready the grassy fields surrounding Hever Castle were greening, though Easter was several weeks away. The nearby forests had put out tender buds and the barley fields sprouted fresh green shoots. Though the gray sky still shrouded the land, one could feel a hint of warmth, the first indication that spring would come, after all. This, along with the birth of her favorite bitch's puppies, made Madge Shelton frisky that morning, able to shake, finally, the feeling of dread she had carried since her arrival in the south of England. Although she could not know it yet, this was the last morning of her old life, the first morning of the life she'd hoped would never come.

"The fat one, the one with a bit of red on his chest," said Madge, leaning over the roughly made pen that housed ten setters, her uncle's newest stock of hunting dogs.

"He's already been spoken for. Master Boleyn left word that the biggest and best pup was to be trained for the hunt," said Ben Whipple, the son of the yeoman who managed the Boleyn farm.

"We'll see about that. My birthday's coming soon and I shall ask my uncle about the hound. I'm likely to get him, you can be sure of that. My uncle gives me whatever I fancy these days," Madge said. She held the pup to her bosom and stroked behind his ears.

"You'll be mine, pretty boy. And we'll roam the fields together. I'll teach you to point. We'll show my uncle how a good dog and a brave girl can hunt with the best of them," Madge said.

"Master Boleyn's a-wanting to groom the biggest pup for the queen. He knows how she fancies a smart cur. You won't get your way this time, mistress," said Ben. He picked up the runt of the litter, a pitiful-looking setter with only a spot of white at the tip of its tail.

"Shall I drown this one? It's only a bitch," he said.

"Don't you dare," said Madge.

"Master Boleyn told me to get rid of the runt and spare only the smartest, healthiest ones. He can't afford to keep the whole passel," said Ben.

"Give me that little one, then. I'll keep her safe," Madge said. She put the fat pup back into the pen and wrapped her hands around the small black one. The pup nuzzled against Madge and licked her hands. "She knows I'm saving her from a watery grave. Look at how grateful she is."

"Tell you what. I'll let you keep her if you give me a kiss," said Ben.

"You'll let me keep her, Ben Whipple, kiss or no!" Madge stood up abruptly, still clutching the puppy. She smoothed her skirts with one hand while holding the dog against her chest.

"Why won't you kiss me, Madge? You did once, down by the creek. Let me again," said Ben.

"I'll never kiss the likes of you again, Ben Whipple. I am cousin to the queen and must act according to my new station. In a few short weeks, Queen Anne will be crowned, and then you won't dare speak so in my company," said Madge.

"Pshaw. Nan Bullen's no better than a whore and everybody knows it. Catherine's the rightful queen and Old Harry can't change that. Nan Bullen's as common as these pups," said Ben.

Madge pushed Ben out of her way, still holding the black pup. She stomped across the barnyard. Halfway, she stopped, turned toward Ben, her cheeks flushed and her red hair flying every which way in the early morning breeze.

"You'll live to regret those words. My family's no longer simple wool merchants. You'll see—the Shelton name is something these days and you, Ben Whipple, better watch your tongue!" Madge turned again on one heel and headed for the main house where her nurse would have hot tea ready and maybe a tasty bit of raisin cake.

Margaret Louise Shelton, Madge as she was known to the servants and farmers on her uncle's manor in Edenbridge, Kent, was fifteen years old and already a handful for her nurse, Cate. Tall and thin with a smallish bosom, a delicate waist, and flaring hips, Madge was quickly becoming a beauty and she knew it. Her green eyes were wide and expressive, showing every nuance of feeling a young woman could experience. When angry, her eyes narrowed and actually darkened. When happy, her eyes seemed lit from a secret sunshine within. When sad, her eyes turned watery and red-rimmed, much to her chagrin.

Though she gave her nurse, Cate, a good deal of trouble, Madge was happy to have Cate with her, for she was unused to living with the Boleyn family, especially now that Sir Thomas's daughter, Anne, was married to the king. Unlike her own family, where she was the youngest of five children and likely to find a partner in any devilment she could think up, at Hever Castle, Madge was younger than the Boleyn children by fifteen years or more. No one laughed at her jokes or her funny faces. No one wanted to act out the story of Punchinella, and Madge couldn't find one person who would sing duets with her in the early evenings after supper.

Cate was all Madge had to remind her of Great Snoring, her home far away. Madge longed for the fields of the family lands in Norfolk, where she spent summers cavorting with the new lambs. Cate's presence wasn't enough to make up for the familiar life Madge longed for. Besides, Cate insisted Madge practice her best behavior all the time. She could never relax at the Boleyn residence. There was too much at stake for that.

"What have you dragged in this time?" Cate said when she saw Madge carrying the pup into the elegant rooms they shared.

"Ben was going to drown her," said Madge. She sat on the low stool near the fireplace and warmed her hands, allowing the pup to make a nest in her skirts.

"That's your good wool, girl. You don't want to be smelling of dog when you meet the king, do you?" Cate grabbed the pup and held it up for examination. "Nothing but a runt. Not even interesting in its markings."

"Give her back. I don't care what I smell like when I meet the king. Give me my dog," said Madge.

"And what makes you think Sir Thomas will allow you to keep this mutt? He's known for killing off what's weak and small," said Cate, handing the dog to Madge.

"I'll keep her whatever way I can. I'll hide her in our rooms and Sir Thomas won't find her," said Madge. She gathered some rushes from the floor into a small bunch and set the pup in the center of the reeds, near the fire.

"I'm warning you, my Maddie, you mustn't anger Sir Thomas. He's grown powerful these last ten years and your family's fortunes ride on him. And now, they're riding on you, too," said Cate.

"I know, good Cate, I know. I will try to please Sir Thomas as best I can. But I can't live for his good pleasure—I have a life of my own." Madge slipped her feet from the stiff leather boots and stretched her toes toward the warmth of the fire.

"A woman's life is never her own, Maddie girl. We must make our way as we can. Your father sent you here to serve Sir Thomas in whatever way he so desires. Thus far, Sir Thomas has allowed you much freedom but that may pass. You must have it in your mind to obey Sir Thomas and serve the queen." Cate stood behind Madge and took the pins from her thick hair. Red curls snaked through Cate's fingers. The red was flecked with gold and smelled of lemongrass. Cate combed through the locks and scratched gently at Madge's scalp. The girl's shoulders dropped a bit.

"I'll make Mother proud, don't worry. So far, Sir Thomas hasn't said two words to me. If I'm lucky, things will stay as they are and I can go back home by All Saints' Day," Madge said as she nudged the sleeping puppy with her big toe. "Now, what shall we call this black runt of a dog?"

"Better call it Nothing. That way, if Sir Thomas drowns her, you'll have Nothing to miss and Nothing to cry about," said Cate.

"A cruel Cate you are! No, I'll call her Shadow. She's black and she'll have to hide away in shadows if she's to survive. And she follows me as if she were my very own shadow," said Madge.

"Shadow it is, then." Cate twirled the rope of Madge's hair into a bun and secured it with pins. She covered the bun with a plain white cap and sat on the stone floor next to Madge, leaning her head against Madge's knee.

Both nurse and girl were almost asleep when a loud knocking jerked each awake. Madge looked at her nurse, then at the pup. She scooped Shadow from the floor, then hurried to place the dog inside the chest that held her modest jewels—a small brooch her mother had given her covered with seed pearls, a painted comb for her hair, a long chain of gold to wear on her wedding day, and a miniature of her father.

"Why so long to answer, Nurse?" said Sir Thomas, a tall, slender man with a reddish-gray beard and thinning hair of the same color. He wasn't exactly smiling, but he looked as pleasant as Madge had ever seen him. His features, sharp and hawk-like, were usually pinched together as if he were in deep thought or as if he had enemies to smite. Seeing him storm along the walkways in the beautiful gardens of Hever Castle made Madge hide for cover. She avoided him when at all possible, curtsying to him when they processed to church and at formal dinners. She kept her head down and never dared look him in the eye. She behaved exactly as her mother had taught her and so far, she'd escaped his notice. Or so she'd thought.

"Let's have a look at you, niece. Ah yes, you'll do nicely. A pretty one, eh George?" Sir Thomas strolled into the apartments, his son, George, trailing behind him. George was handsome with golden hair and softer features than his father's. Both men were dressed in rich-looking silks and Sir Thomas had a red velvet cloak lined with ermine. His undershirt was cloth-of-gold and Madge had never seen anyone look quite so fine. George, fifteen years Madge's senior, was taller than his father and his eyes seemed more kind.

"Father, don't speak of Madge as if she couldn't hear you. Hello, coz. How do you find life at Hever? Hmmm, no answer, eh? I'll talk enough for the both of us! Has anyone taken time to teach you the new games so popular at court? Chess? Cards? No? Well, coz, I shall show you. After all, once the king and queen arrive, you must help us entertain them," said George, his voice full of fun.

Madge felt her cheeks burn as her cousin chucked her under her chin. She did not know what to make of him; he seemed too full of life to have come from the same stock as Sir Thomas. She kept her curtsy, wondering if Sir Thomas would ever allow her to rise. Her legs trembled.

"Enough, George. Margaret, I asked your father and mother to allow you to come to Hever Castle for a reason. As you know, your cousin, Anne, is now queen of England. This position has been a hard-fought one and will be hard enough for her to hold, even though she sits prettily now. But there are those who would upset her from the throne if they could—the Seymours; the Dudleys; not to mention the Spanish ambassador, Chapuys; and the Catholics. Anne is sitting on the head of a pin and could easily be toppled. It is up to us to keep her in her position until she bears an heir. Once a son is born, Anne, and all of us, will be safe." Sir Thomas stared down at Madge, never once allowing her to raise herself from the deep curtsy she'd taken in his honor. Finally, he raised her head so that she was forced to look at him. "Do you understand, my girl?"

"Yes, my lord." Madge did not understand, but she dared not say so. She knew better than to ask any questions. Slowly, he raised her to a more comfortable position, led her to a bench, and indicated for her to be seated.

"You will be going to court, Margaret. The king and queen

will arrive at Hever later this week. I don't know how many days they shall stay—"

"God's blood, I hope their stay will be short," said George winking at Madge.

"However long Their Majesties stay is not your concern, young George. What is your concern is to help your sister in whatever way you can. You must remember, our future fortune depends on Anne." Sir Thomas's voice was cold and Madge worried that he might strike George. She shivered as Sir Thomas turned back to her, his small, blue eyes full of anger.

"After Their Majesties return to court, Margaret, you shall follow them forthwith." Sir Thomas bowed and headed toward the doors.

"To court? I . . . I cannot possibly go to court. I have no proper clothes. I cannot dance. I lack the graces for court, Sir Thomas. I'm a mere girl, I—"

"Enough! His majesty has assigned you to be one of the queen's ladies-in-waiting and to court you will go!" Sir Thomas thundered. Then he turned to Cate. "Nurse, see that this girl has the best dresses available. Tell my wife, the Lady Elizabeth, to give you bolts of silk to supply you. Margaret will need at least five gowns. You and my wife will see to the construction of each," Sir Thomas said. "As for your want of grace, I would suggest, for your own sake, that you begin to cultivate those skills you lack. George, after we sup, you will begin to teach the girl." Sir Thomas turned quickly and left them. He stopped in the doorway and stared at his son.

"And George, no spoiling this one, eh?" said Sir Thomas.

"Of course not, Father. Of course not," said George.

Sir Thomas gave his son a hard, curious look and then stomped down the hall, his steps on the stone floor commanding and steady as a clock.

Madge, George, and Cate sat still as relics. Suddenly, a cry-ing sound came from the chest next to the bed. Madge began to hum, trying to cover the noise.

"What's that?" said George as he searched the room trying to discover the source of the sound.

"What? All I hear is my lovely Madge's voice. Tell me, deary, where'd you learn that ditty?" said Cate.

"What's that you are hiding, Nurse? Aha! A pup and one from father's newest litter, I'll warrant. What's it doing here?" George grabbed the puppy before Madge could get her hands on the little dog.

"She's mine! Give her to me!" Madge tried to take the puppy from George.

"So, Mousy Madge has a tongue after all! Good! Good for you, coz. Tell me, what'd you name her?" George gave the pup over to Madge, who carefully petted the dog and held her close.

"Shadow. She's my Shadow and where I go, she'll go, too." Madge stared straight into George's eyes, daring him to cross her.

"Then Shadow will be going to court soon. Best keep her safe, Madge Mouse. And yourself, too," said George. "Court isn't for the faint of heart. You're going, so you better learn to mas-ter yourself and your betters."

"No, no, no! You must hold the string down more firmly, Madge Mouse. See, like this," said George, placing his finger across the neck of the lute and pressing the catgut until the tip of his fin-ger turned white.

"I'm trying! I do not seem to have the strength for it. Perhaps we should explore another instrument—the virginals?" said Madge. Two hours earlier, when the lesson began, she would never have spoken so boldly to the great George Boleyn. But her fingers hurt, her head ached, and she wished to return to her rooms.

"The lute is the easiest to play—any dolt can learn it. All you must needs do is strum a little so you can sing. The king loves music and is quite accomplished, as is my sister. I play and carry a tune rather well myself—even our sister Mary can do such. Surely you have some of the family ability," said George.

"Evidently I do not!" said Madge.

"Dear Margaret, forgive my impatience. I am to prepare you for court in a fortnight, teach you those things my sisters learned over years at the French court. It is a quick study and I fear I forget how many hours I spent teaching my own fingers to press the proper string. Let us put the lute away for tonight and try again on the morrow," said George.

"Thank you, cousin. I am quite ready to retire. But if you would like, I shall sing you a lullaby, one my mother used to sing to us as we drifted off to sleep. I do have a small gift with a song," said Madge.

"That is encouraging. Yes, let me hear you, Madge Mouse," said George. He picked up the lute and waited for Madge to begin.

"Rock-a-bye, don't you cry, for we will go to see Nanny/Up the hill, by the mill, to see the wee little lambie," Madge sang softly, her voice breathy and tender.

George motioned for her to repeat the song and he strummed along with the lute. The sound of the strings gave Madge more confidence and, with George's encouragement, she sang out more forcefully.

"Not the most inspiring words but you sang them very nicely, coz. You do have a lovely, sweet voice. And you carry a tune and sing with feeling. All this will delight the king. We shall work more on the lute in the morning," said George. "Make not that dour face, Madge. If you do well, I shall reward you with a sweet from the cook! Now, off to bed!"

Madge curtsied and hurried to her room, ready for sleep and filled with dread of her next lesson.

Two

*H*ush, Shadow, hush. We shall be there soon." Madge cuddled the pup against her chest as the carriage bumped along, sending Madge, Cate, and the dog flying off their seats, then landing again with a loud thud.

"It does not serve my backside well to travel the road to London in the spring. Bloody potholes are so big I'm surprised we don't fall in, carriage and all," said Cate as she rearranged her new skirts.

"At least the rain has stopped for a while. The constant drizzle was enough to send my spirits even further down. That patch of sun is most welcome, isn't it, Shadow?" Madge held the puppy up to the carriage window so Shadow could smell the fresh air of the English countryside. The air within had become stale over the three days' ride from Hever Castle to London, even though Madge and Cate wore pomanders filled with lavender and dabbed rosewater on their faces.

"What think you, Cate? Will we be able to survive at court?" Madge hadn't spoken of the lump of fear that seemed to be stuck right beneath her ribs. That area ached every time she thought of serving Queen Anne, being in the presence of Good King Harry. Two weeks earlier, when the king and queen had finally arrived for their stay at Hever Castle, Madge had been allowed to eat in the main hall only once, the day of the hunt. Henry was dressed in the finest hunting clothes Madge had ever seen. The green velvet outer shirt set off his ruddy complexion and his red hair almost glowed against the black silk cloak lined with matching fur. Even at the hunt, Henry's doublet was covered with garnets, emeralds, and pearls. When he spoke, his tenor voice rang throughout the hall and his laugh was like the waterfall Madge had found in the forest that surrounded Hever—deep and rumbling. Everything about him terrified her.

Queen Anne was as vivacious as the king. Though she was gay, her voice sounded ragged to Madge, a rough, sandy timbre that seemed almost mannish, yet sultry. But the queen didn't allow the huskiness of her voice to stop her from guffawing as loudly as the king. Her dark eyes were full of happiness, but Madge thought she could see something behind the mirth, something almost like fear.

But what could the new queen have to fear? Her belly was already plump with Henry's child and the king obviously adored her. Together, they spread merriment wherever they went, but Madge hoped their eyes wouldn't fall on her. For the first several days, Madge got her wish. The king and queen were too busy to notice a young cousin from the poor side of the family.

Then came the day of the hunt and the breakfast before-
hand.

Madge had been summoned early that morning and Sir
Thomas had told her she was to be presented to the queen immediately. Sir Thomas brought Madge the most sumptuous
dress she'd ever seen, its tiny pearls embroidered fresh from the
hand of his wife, the Lady Elizabeth. The silk was a rich golden
color that set off Madge's eyes. She had never seen anything so
lush, so beautiful.

"Take care not to soil this one—it's the best you'll have for
court. But the queen will meet you this day and you must present well. And see to your hair, girl. It travels over your head
like the hair of the Medusa," said Sir Thomas as he tossed the
gown to Madge.

"Yes, my lord," Madge replied, careful not to raise her eyes.
Instead, she inspected the beautiful gown before her while trying to tidy the wild strands of her hair. Although as an unmar-
ried young woman Madge was allowed to wear her hair flowing
loose, it was obvious Sir Thomas thought she should cap her
head when meeting the queen for the first time.

Madge shuddered in the carriage and stroked Shadow's
ears as she remembered that day, the day she first met the king
and his queen. Her red face and trembling fingers gave her fear
away as she walked slowly to the queen when Her Majesty motioned for her to approach. The queen's fingers were long and
graceful, though the lace of her sleeve hung lower than Madge
had seen before. She'd heard rumors about the queen's extra little finger but Madge couldn't see anything unusual in the queen
except a small, black wen on the hollow space at the base of her
neck. Madge had heard whispers that the mole was the mark of
the devil and Queen Anne had used magic to seduce the king.
His Majesty did seem bewitched, gazing at his wife with such

tenderness and warmth that Madge couldn't watch them for long without feeling the need to turn away.

The carriage jolted her again as it rounded a curve, forcing her thoughts to return to the present moment. The fresh green of the trees had grown deeper as the weather continued to warm the countryside.

"Ah! The little lambs, Maddie. How white they look, scampering beside their dams. Makes me long for home," said Cate.

"At Great Snoring, I was the one to make certain each lamb was well-tended. Father would let me nurse the littlest ones with a wet rag slopped with milk from the cow, those tiny ones who were so small their own mothers refused them. Remember Blackie?" said Madge.

"Aye, such soft wool I never felt before. And Blackie followed you everywhere, just as if you were her own mother," said Cate.

"We mustn't speak of home. It is too sad," said Madge. Her eyes filled and she forced herself to look out the window into the one patch of blue she could find. She blinked quickly until the tears went away.

"Look! Over there, Maddie! It must be London. I see a huge cluster of towers and buildings. Or maybe they're trees," said Cate.

"Your eyes are weak. Those aren't trees. It is London, after all. Oh Cate, I hope we're not to meet our doom."

"Hush, girl. You're the cousin of the queen. You'll be treated as one of the royals yourself. And, if anything goes wrong, you'll have me to protect you. I promised your father and mother I'd give my life, if it comes to that," said Cate.

"Good Cate, I believe you would. But don't worry, I intend to melt into the very walls. No one will bother with me because I shall become invisible. I shall be like Shadow," Madge said.

"Rest a bit, my little lamb. We've the afternoon to spend

before we arrive at court," said Cate as she stroked Madge's head and massaged her shoulders.

Closing her eyes was a welcome relief and the tender caresses across her neck and shoulders helped Madge relax. But she couldn't drift off to sleep. She kept remembering the afternoon she had come face to face with the king.

Madge still felt shame when she thought of how foolishly she'd behaved when Queen Anne had called her forward. Both the king and his bride had asked her questions and tried to engage her in conversation. The queen was witty, telling little jokes to amuse both Madge and the king. They seemed to enjoy each word that came from the other's mouth and wanted everyone at the Boleyn home to do the same. But Madge couldn't think of one funny remark—she couldn't think of anything at all. She answered "Yes, Majesty" and "No, Majesty" but that was the extent of her conversation. With her face burning and her stomach quivering, she'd been dismissed, though not before hearing the king whisper to his queen, "She's a pretty one, but somewhat dull. Are you certain she's the one you want?"

Madge hurried out of earshot before she could hear the queen's reply.

Three

*T*he carriage slowed to a crawl as they entered London, the buzz of commerce ringing through the air while what seemed like thousands of people milled about in the streets, dodging carts and wagons, horses and carriages, other pedestrians, not to mention free-roaming pigs, dogs, chickens, and a few cows.

"At last, Maddie. London! What you couldn't find here wouldn't be worth having," said Cate as she sat up straighter and smoothed her still-blondish hair. Cate Blanton was a fine-looking matron, never married. Her figure was that of a girl's with none of the soft pillows around the middle that showed on most women her age. She had come to the Shelton family as a girl of barely fourteen and had cared for each of the babes until the boys had gone off to school and the other girls had married or gone to a cloister. Maddie was her favorite.

Madge pulled the curtain to one side so she could get as full a view as possible. She took a quick breath and pinched her nose.

"London smells!" she said.

"Yes, 'tis the scent of life, Maddie. Life!" said Cate.

"What could all those people be doing? They look like the ants that nest in the pigsty, each heading in a direction, not looking left nor right, eyes straight ahead. And so many—ragamuffins, shopkeepers, milkmaids! How can they ever find their way in all this . . . this frenzy?!" said Madge.

"There's a jester! How very short he is and dressed so fine. Must belong to the king. And there! A cutpurse, no doubt. See how his eyes narrow and the way he follows that well-dressed merchant," said Cate.

"I never thought London to be like this—it's beyond the mind of man. How far to Hampton Court, think you?" said Madge.

"A good deal of a ride, I'll wager. We're in Cheapside now. Look at all the shops and carts of goods—apples and violets, chickens and ducks, turnips and over there, cabbages! What food they must eat in London," said Cate, still peeking from behind her own curtain.

"No wonder so many are round as fat sheep. I'll not eat so much, Cate. You neither. We don't want to waddle our way at court!" Madge looked at Cate and they both laughed.

At that moment, the carriage jerked to a stop. The driver swore at a passerby and before Madge could drop her curtain, a young man popped his head inside the carriage.

"Who might you be, missy, riding in the king's own coach?" The young man smiled when he saw Madge and stared boldly into her eyes.

"Your better, that's who," scolded Cate as she tried to pull the curtain from the young man's grip.

"I doubt it, old Nurse. Come on, missy. Don't let the cat hold your tongue. You won't get far at court with no wit." He continued to gaze into Madge's eyes.

"I . . . I am cousin to the queen, niece of Sir Thomas Boleyn," Madge said with as much strength as she could deliver.

"Well then, I am wrong—you *are* my better. I am merely the bastard son of the king's brother-in-law. Sir Charles Brandon is my father and I am called Arthur, after the king's dear, dead brother," he said as he swept the hat off his head and bowed with a grand flourish.

"I call you Sir Churlish, for though you carry the name of a great king, your actions here prove you share none of that king's manners," said Madge. She turned her face away from the young man as the carriage lurched forward once again.

"Call me what you will, my lady. I shall be your humble servant!" he called after them.

"Humph. I have heard tales about this—the shame of London! All the young men presume so upon the young ladies. We must take great care, my Maddie. Great care indeed," said Cate.

Madge rested her head against the back of her seat and breathed several deep breaths. She dared not speak for her blood seemed about to burst from her veins. She wasn't sure why. Sir Churlish had angered her, yet there was something beneath the anger, a feeling new to her. When she closed her eyes, she could still see his brown beard, not full and stiff like her father's but soft-looking. And his hair, also dark, the exact shade of his eyes. Those eyes seemed to have laughed at her and she couldn't figure out why. Was she so much of a country bumpkin? Were her features so ill arranged? Why should he mock her?

"Pay him no mind, my girl. London's filled with hundreds like that—all swagger and strut. You won't have to settle for such as he. The queen will match you well enough, you can count on that," said Cate, settling into comfort again. She reached down into a burlap sack at her feet and pulled out a rosy apple. Then a small knife seemed to appear from nowhere and Cate began to slice.

"I care for no match. As well you know, I have no interest in marrying. I'd rather go to the convent or live as you do, Cate. I could serve as nurse to some darling child." Madge smiled at her friend.

"No, Maddie. You're too highborn now to serve as nurse to any except the queen's own child. Maybe that is how she wishes to use you. Who can say? But I'll warrant there's a marriage to be arranged in her plan as well," said Cate as she held a slice of apple for Madge to take.

In what seemed a short time, time enough for two women to eat an apple, the carriage pulled past the gates of a grand house and into a large courtyard. The coachman reined in the horses and a footman opened the door and offered Madge his hand.

"Hampton Court, my lady," he said, not daring to look at Madge as she descended the step and her foot hit the cobbled walk.

Madge stared at the graceful lines of the building and understood immediately why Great Harry had taken over the castle from Cardinal Wolsey. The building was immense and the surrounding grounds perfectly manicured as precisely as the jewels sewn to the queen's garments. Servants scurried hither and thither, each on an errand of utmost import, from the look on every face.

Cate descended from the carriage and grabbed Madge's elbow.

"Don't stand there agape, child. We must act as if this is the life to which we're accustomed. Smile and chatter with me," she said as she guided Madge to the enormous wooden door carved with wonderful scenes of shepherds and shepherdesses, trees and flowers, images of the apostles.

The two women entered.

"Welcome, my good ladies. I am mother of the maids, Mistress Marshall. Follow me and all will be well," said the gray-haired woman. She led Madge and Cate to their beds just outside the queen's apartments.

"Her Majesty will greet you in a few days, when she has time. Until then, you are free to wander in the gardens and in the queen's apartments, though stay away from the privy chamber until you are invited inside by the queen herself. Her Majesty instructs all her ladies to be modest in dress and to behave with decorum, remembering always that you reflect the queen's own dignity. Bible reading is encouraged and the queen leaves her very own copy of Tyndale's New Testament in the outer rooms of her apartments for her ladies to read at their leisure. Rest now and come to sup when you hear the bell. Just follow the others and you'll find the Great Hall," said Mistress Marshall as she ushered them into a small room featuring a window with many panes of glass and two small beds.

"Queen's own dignity, indeed," whispered Cate.

"She is full of dignity and good spirits, too, Cate. You must keep your feelings about her and the new religion to yourself. If the king had the least notion that you're a papist at heart, we'd be finished before we got started. Mum's the word, dear Cate," said Madge.

"I'll be mum for your sake, Maddie. I know how important your being at court is—how your family depends upon it. But I don't have to like it. Nor do I have to read books writ by the devil himself!" Cate ran her hands across the lumpy mattress, brushing off puffs of dust. "I intend to continue to worship as always. In secret, on that you can bet. And I am not alone, Maddie. There are many who think the king is wrong and blinded by his lust for Nan Bullen. And many who think her his whore, even though they dare not speak of it," said Cate.

"But she is my cousin and I will honor her. She is young and so full of life. How she laughs and teases the king—and he loves her so," said Madge. "I think it a wonderful story how a simple girl could win the love of a king and he would move the earth to make her his bride. I could only wish for such a thing."

"Take care in what you wish, my girl. Now, let's unpack these trunks. Then we shall stroll in the garden. We have time before supper."

Four

S urely, we shall find the Great Hall if we can but find the door to get back inside," said Madge.

Cate and Madge hurried from the garden toward the first doorway they saw and entered quickly. Ladies and gentlemen filled the hallway, all heading in the same direction. Cate and Madge joined the flow until they came to an enormous dining room. The king and queen sat at the farthest end of the room and they were surrounded by such dignitaries as Sir Thomas Boleyn, Lord Norfolk, and Sir Charles Brandon. At the lower tables other dignitaries were seated: Sir William Coffin, a gentleman of the privy chamber; Sir Henry Norris; Sir William Brereton and others of great import.

"Where are we supposed to sit?" asked Madge.

"Anywhere we can find a spot. That is, until we are formally greeted by the queen," said Cate.

"Here, then," said Madge as she scooted onto one of the long benches in front of a heavily laden table. Never had Madge seen so much food at one time.

"Shadow shall eat well at court, too. We must watch her figure as well as our own," said Madge.

"Yes, but I expect she'll have no bellyaches with *her* meals. She'll never have to mind *her* tongue," said Cate.

A young man scooted onto the opposite side of the table across from Madge.

"But you must learn to mind your own tongue, mistress. And your lady must learn to loosen hers," the young man said. He grabbed a piece of mutton from the trencher and ate vigorously.

"You!" Cate said. She turned sharply away from him and jerked Madge's elbow so that she had to do the same.

"'Tis I, my dear ladies. And I've worked up a mighty hunger. And thirst. Ale! Ale!" said the young man, waving to the servant with the large pitcher.

The servant hurried over to their table and filled every cup to the brim. Then, before Madge could thank him, he scurried to replenish the next goblet. Madge looked at the hundreds of people in the Great Hall, each dressed in satins and silks, jewels and pearls adorning the delicate necks of the ladies, their hair sparkling with gems, their dresses heavy with precious stones sewn into the very cloth. The walls themselves shimmered with gold and silver coverings and, though Madge and those at her table ate from wooden trenchers, she could see the glint of gold on the tables of the king and other dignitaries.

"I wonder how many eat in this hall tonight," murmured Madge.

"Well over a thousand souls, my lady. Most of them grinning

and plotting their way to the king," said the young man across from Maddie.

"More than I've seen gathered in one room," said Cate.

"The king usually takes his meals in his privy chamber, but now he wants to show the world his new bride, so you find them up there on the dais. More fun when he's not here," said the young man.

"How so?" said Madge.

"Well, now that the queen is his *wife*, she must promote her virtue and make the court a decent and suitable place for children. After all, she's to have the king's own child soon enough. Court makes pure the impure and sullies the innocent," he said.

"I'll hear nothing against the queen. You should be forewarned—I am to become one of her ladies," said Madge.

"Watch your step, my lady, lest you trip and fall, as yet Queen Anne may do. Bluff King Harry may seem jovial but he can let fly more heads than you can count," said the young man.

"Enough of this bold talk—let us finish our meal, Lady Margaret, and be gone from this place," said Cate.

"It's unlikely we shall dine again together, my lady. Sorry if my words have offended you. I'll warrant you'll be eating with the queen in her own chambers soon enough. Just remember, nothing is quite as it seems at court. 'Tis a dangerous, lively place," the young man said.

"I can take care of myself, sir. You are the one with the loose tongue. You should take care not to lose it," said Madge.

Master Brandon grabbed a warm hunk of bread and stuffed it into his pocket as he scrambled over the benches and out of the hall. Madge and Cate relaxed their shoulders, looked at each other, then laughed.

"What a strange young man! Full of mutton and ideas! I

hope the queen greets us soon so we can join her for our dinner. Such company sours my stomach," said Cate.

"Master Brandon *is* upsetting," said Madge. "But listen, the musicians are tuning their lutes. The trestle tables are being taken down and the king and queen are walking down to the open floor. Oh Cate, we shall see our first dance!"

"Not tonight, my dear. It would be unseemly for us to dally here before we've yet been welcomed by Her Majesty. We are allowed to dance only after the queen has accepted you as one of her ladies. And then we dance with those gentlemen she selects," said Cate.

"I do not wish to dance, merely to watch—alas, I do not yet have the skill for dancing," said Madge.

"It's to be a bath for us, Maddie. Then prayers and sleep, for another day beckons," said Cate as she guided Madge out from the Great Hall and into the corridor that would lead them to their room.

When they entered their chamber, Shadow jumped to greet Madge, slobbering kisses on her hands and face.

"Down, girl! You'll spoil my silk!" said Madge as she reached into the muslin sack greasy with food for Shadow. The dog sat, barely able to keep still, tail wagging and front paws kneading the floor. "The smells from the castle alone would feed the hungry. How can the court consume so much? And what happens to that which is left?" Madge asked as she fed Shadow little bits of mutton and boiled carrot.

"I've heard the steward sells the gristle and fat meats to the poor, keeping the better pieces to hawk to the shopkeeps and other such folk. Cardinal Wolsey used to keep a watch on such doings but with him gone, it's hard to stop the trafficking of the king's goods. And the king never knows the waste and business made off his court. He thinks the gold will continue to flow and he'll never have cause to worry. And, the way he's pillaging a few of the monasteries, he's right. Great Harry will not know want," said Cate.

"How do you know all this, Cate? You've only arrived when I did and I know none such," said Madge.

"I listen, dearest. A skill you should develop. And, as your lady, I talk to other ladies who tell me all kinds of gossip—some true, some wild. Besides, at my age, I know a little how the world works," said Cate as she laid out Madge's nightdress and began to comb the girl's hair.

The candles flickered against the well-worn tapestry that hung on the stone wall of their room. On each cot was a plump feather quilt of bright colors; fresh rushes were strewn across the floor. The smell of beeswax sweetened the air with a little help from the sachet of lavender that hung from the belts of both women.

In the candlelight, Madge was beautiful, her skin the color of rich cream with a hint of strawberry at each cheek. Her hair caught the light and glimmered gold and red; her eyes seemed darker in the close room, the green more like the forest that surrounded the castle than their usual light green of new-budding trees.

"When do you think we shall meet the queen?" Madge asked.

"When it suits her, my girl, and not one moment earlier," said Cate.

Cate finished combing Madge's hair, then used the lice comb to be certain none of the bugs had made a home. She rubbed a salve of lemongrass and citrus onto Madge's arms and face to keep the fleas and other bugs away during the night.

"Sleep well, Maddie. Who knows what the morrow will bring?" said Cate.

Five

L ady Margaret! Lady Margaret! The queen will see you. Make yourself ready immediately!" cried Mistress Marshall as she hammered the heavy wooden door of Madge's room.

Cate opened the door and Mistress Marshall barged in looking much like an admiral in the royal navy. Madge pulled up the bedcovers to her chin.

"No room for modesty at court, young miss! Up! Up! Get out her best dress, Mistress Cate, and I'll send for a muffin and cup of ale. She can eat while you fix that unruly hair! The queen will see her sharply after matins!" With that, Mistress Marshall turned her battleship-of-a-self on an impossibly small foot and sailed down the corridor.

"She's taken her sweet time—ten days—and now *we* are to move with all haste. Well, she *is* the queen," mumbled Cate as she pulled out Madge's golden gown, the one she'd worn when she first met the king and queen, the one that set off her green eyes.

"What shall I say, Cate? What shall I do?" said Madge.

"Answer the queen as she requires. Do not make merry; take your cues from her. If she is full of fun, you be so as well. If she is somber, then pull down your mouth. Do not offend her. Make her proud. You are her cousin, remember? That alone will stand you in good stead," said Cate.

"Should I wear the jewels Uncle Thomas gave me, the little pearl necklace?"

"Yes, the pearls speak of purity and wearing them will proclaim your innocence to all the court. The pearls, my Maddie," said Cate.

Cate combed Madge's hair and wet down the unruly curls so they lay flat beneath the French hood, copied from the queen's own, though without the jewels. She pinched Madge's cheeks and lips, then helped her step into her gown. Her stomacher was laced tight, but Madge breathed easily. Though she'd eaten her fill at every meal, her uneasiness led her into the gardens at all hours for walking and playing in the secret hedges with Shadow. Her gown was actually looser than when she'd first worn it.

"You are a vision of delight. The queen will be pleased," said Cate.

"I hope you are right. I want nothing more than to please her. Uncle Thomas has drilled that into my head; he'd do anything to secure the position of the Boleyn clan," said Madge.

"Aye. Even sell his own daughter," whispered Cate as she hooked the pearls around Madge's delicate neck, long and slender, though not so long as the queen's.

"What do you mean?" said Madge.

"Never mind. I hear the bells. Go to the queen. Remember, reflect her own mood back to her and you will be fine," said Cate.

At that moment, Mistress Marshall reappeared at the door.

"You'll do, I suppose," she said with a long face.

Madge curtsied deeply but her face had lost its smile. Seeing that, Mistress Marshall tugged at Madge's elbow.

"You're really quite the little beauty, my dear. But one must never outshine the queen," she said.

The hall leading to the queen's rooms seemed the longest walk of Madge's life. The stones chilled her bones, giving her little shivers as she hurried after Mistress Marshall. The tapestries lining the walls did no good to warm her, though she enjoyed looking at the various scenes portrayed—knights and ladies eating in the deep forest while on the hunt, the Virgin at vespers, lush gardens peopled with courtiers dancing.

At a large oak door inlaid with mother-of-pearl and embossed with gold, Mistress Marshall halted, whispered to the guard on her left. The guard opened the door and led the two women into the queen's chambers.

"Lady Margaret Shelton!" a voice cried as Madge entered the room. She was astounded at the noise: chattering couples playing at cards in one corner; the fool turning cartwheels across the open space in front of the queen's throne; a handsome young man strumming the lute and singing in a strong baritone; laughter ringing out from the queen's own mouth.

"My dear coz, up, up! Let me look at you," Queen Anne said as she stood, then bent to lift Madge's face as she helped the girl rise.

Madge couldn't help but smile at the queen, who looked even lovelier than she had during her visit to Hever Castle. Being with child suited Her Majesty, giving a nice fullness to her otherwise slender figure. At thirty-three, the queen needed the

ripeness of pregnancy to smooth out the furrows that were beginning across her brow. And the lift to her bosom gave her a
womanly shape, very pleasing.

"I am so glad you have come, Margaret. It's nice to have
family around, especially as I shall be shut up in these quarters
soon enough. Let me introduce you," Queen Anne said as she
took Madge by the hand and led her to the bevy of gentlemen
that surrounded the throne.

"Of course, you know my brother, George, Lord Rochford.
His friend, Sir William Brereton. And Sir Henry Norris—ah,
he blushes at beauty such as yours, Margaret. And our poet, Sir
Thomas Wyatt." The queen laughed as each gentleman bowed
and smiled at Madge.

Madge mumbled a "Good, my lord" to each man in turn
and felt the blood rush to her ears. She found she couldn't raise
her eyes to meet any of the gentlemen and would not recognize
a one of them if they were to meet again in the corridor.

"She's a beauty, Anne. Good looks must be part and parcel
in the Boleyn blood," said Wyatt.

"The Lady Margaret does have her charms—those green
eyes could melt my beating heart," said Sir William Brereton.

"Off, you hounds. Leave the girl alone—she's barely out of
swaddling clothes and listen to you. Save your bantering for
one who can banter back," laughed the queen.

"Now, dear Margaret, you are called here to serve as a lady-
in-waiting and I must swear you to my service. The king will
do so more formally at supper tonight but for now, will you
swear unto God to do my bidding, to live honestly and chastely
while in my court?" The queen looked deeply into Madge's eyes.

"Yes, Your Grace. It is my honor to serve Your Majesty until my last breath." Madge stared back into the queen's dark
eyes, the brown so deep as to seem almost black. The queen's

eyes were large and round, with thick lashes that curled up in a most attractive way.

"Then welcome, Margaret. I have a little gift for you." The queen turned and picked up a small package wrapped in blue silk. "You may open it at once."

Madge untied the velvet ribbon and loosened the covering. Inside, a small book, its cover etched in gold, was attached to a golden chain. Beside the book, a ring with three rubies clustered at the center lay waiting.

"Oh, Your Majesty. The ring is beautiful. Thank you." Madge slipped the ring onto her middle finger and watched as the rubies shone against her clear, pale skin.

"This Book of Hours is written in English. You are to wear it at all times and study the works. You will find such admonishments very handy at court. I expect you to guard your virtue at all costs. I cannot afford any unseemly behavior from my ladies. Do I make myself clear?" The queen's voice, until this point warm and friendly, had suddenly turned cool and commanding.

"Yes, Your Grace." Madge felt the blood rise again, not because she had done any wrong but because the queen would mention such things in the presence of so many.

"I'll watch out for her, Anne," said George.

Much laughter from the other men met this comment.

"Yes, brother, but who will watch after you?" The queen's voice had returned to normal and she laughed that low laugh of hers. The others joined in the merriment but Madge felt herself grow redder still.

"Stop badgering the girl, friends. Can't you see she's about to explode!" Sir Thomas Wyatt moved toward Madge and wrapped his arm around her shoulders, guiding her away from the queen. "Pay them no mind, my lady. They are barbarians."

He sat on a low bench near the window and beckoned Madge to join him.

"You will grow accustomed to their ways in time, Lady Margaret. Soon, you'll find your tongue and sally forth to battle with the bravest. Tell me, what think you of court thus far?" Sir Thomas smiled encouragingly.

"I think it unlike any place on earth. Such sumptuous food and drink, the rich tapestries, the fashionable clothing . . . in the north country, we have no such splendor. Why, even the town of London is greater than anything I've known . . . I sound like a silly goose," said Madge.

"Not at all. I can well imagine the change is disconcerting. But I will make you a bargain. If you will allow it, I shall be your friend. I shall show you London and teach you the ways of the court. I am a great friend of the queen's and, as you are her cousin, I offer the same friendship to you," said Sir Thomas.

"I accept. And am happy for it."

"You have never played at cards, milady?" said Sir Thomas. "I find this incredulous. What do you do in Great Snoring for fun?"

"Oh, we do not lack for entertainments, sir. We chase the lambs in the spring and in the summer, we pile the hay in great stacks, then jump onto the stacks from atop the barn. We run our dogs through the fields and follow them, exploring all the wonders of nature as we go. And we dance to the fiddle music of our yeomen, dances as old as the hills themselves," said Madge, happy with remembering.

"Simple pleasures . . . I envy you, Lady Margaret. I fear I shall never be able to enjoy those humble pastimes again. Life at court has cured me of such . . . well, enough of dreary thoughts.

Let us begin. I shall deal out four of the cards—you can see they are all numbered except for the cards with faces—see? The kings, queens, and knaves are the cards you wish to avoid. If you can discard one, do so. Now, you may ask me for one of my cards to match one in your hand—the object is to collect all four of one kind—four of the ones, twos, and on and on . . ."

"And after I ask for one of yours, I then throw off one of mine? Is that it?" said Madge, staring intently at her cards.

"Yes, very good. Methinks you will be sharp at cards, lady. You seem to have your cousin's gift—the queen loves to play and often wins great sums of money from His Majesty," said Wyatt.

"You mean I can win coins for good cards?" said Madge.

"Why else would one play? Now, take your turn and I shall endeavor to teach you all I know about Primero," said Sir Thomas.

"If you are right, Thomas, perhaps I shall be lucky at cards and lucky at love, too," said Madge.

"Lady, with your beauty, I do not doubt you shall have great luck with love—half the men at court are already in love with you," said Thomas.

"I do not know half the men at court—methinks you stretch the truth," said Madge.

"No, lady. I know how a man thinks when he sees a lovely wench full of innocence—I know too well how a man thinks," said Thomas.

"Then thinking should be outlawed, for it sounds like such thoughts are unworthy of fine gentlemen," said Madge, drawing a card from the stack. She reached for her goblet of wine and noticed many of the ladies had withdrawn from the room while the gentlemen played more and more roughly at cards, their talk growing loud and boisterous.

"Dear Thomas, I see I am the only woman left—I shall also retire but I thank you for teaching me this evening. Perhaps on the morrow we can begin again?" said Madge.

"'Twould be my delight, Lady Margaret," said Sir Thomas, standing as Madge rose and bowing to her.

Six

. . . If it be yea I shall be fain,
If it be nay, friends as before.
Ye shall another man obtain
And I mine own and yours no more.

"What say you, Madge? Like it?" Sir Thomas Wyatt sat on the garden wall holding a thick pack of papers.

"It lacks the flowery words of most love poems. But that is what I like most about it. It speaks the truth," said Madge, smoothing her skirts as she sat down beside him. Shadow gnawed one end of a large bone while the queen's little dog, Purkoy, whose uplifted ears and pert face made him look as if he were asking a question, nibbled at the other. The queen's French *"pourquoi?"* had been mangled by the English court into the common-sounding "Purkoy." The queen tried to correct her ladies and Madge had heard the lecture more than once, usually given to the dull Lady Jane Seymour, who had no ear for languages. Though Madge wasn't conversant in French, she could easily mimic the queen's pronunciation.

"I was trying something a little different. I tire of the overblown speech sung out at court. Surely, the ladies must also grow sick from such excess," said Sir Thomas.

"Well, I have not had any such songs sung to me, so I am not exhausted from pretty words. I should like to hear a few," said Madge with a laugh.

"It is only because you keep yourself away from the gentlemen that you don't hear them. Your beauty is the cause for much talk," said Sir Thomas.

Madge felt the blood rise to her cheeks. She certainly didn't feel beautiful, as she had at home where her mother told her often enough she was a beauty. Here, though Cate swore she was the fairest of the queen's ladies, Madge felt out of place and clumsy.

"Then I would not be beautiful. I do not wish talk of any sort about me. I'd much rather disappear," said Madge as she leaned down to scratch Shadow behind the ears. Though still a pup, Shadow was twice the size of Purkoy.

"But you cannot disappear, Maddie. You are cousin to the queen. If you serve her well, you shall be rewarded. I'm sure she'll marry you off to someone rich and you'll be taken care of quite nicely. Pretty as you are, getting you betrothed shan't be a problem. But you must speak to people. Let them know your wit, your merry ways." Sir Thomas smiled.

"It seems I only find my tongue with you, Tom. The others frighten me, especially Sir Norris. The way he looks at me—as if he wished to devour me all in one bite," said Madge.

"Yes, he's a man of appetite, to be sure. But so is our king.

And the king surrounds himself with young men who love to sport as much as he does. It makes for a lively court, don't you think?" said Sir Thomas.

"Lively, yes. And dangerous. My own cousin George is guilty of so much sin I can scarce look at him. I know he goes a-whoring, though the queen has forbidden it. I've heard him brag to Norris and Brereton. And his poor wife. Oh, I'll warrant she's homely and shrewish but I feel sorry for her, the way he ignores her and makes light of the love she bears him. He sees more of the queen than he does his wedded spouse," said Madge.

"How do you know so much, Maddie? Are you a spy?" said Sir Thomas.

"One of the advantages of being a little mouse—I see and hear much," said Madge.

"And say little. Not a bad plan for surviving in these days. But here comes the queen, looking for Purkoy, no doubt. I'll take my leave of you, my lady," said Sir Thomas as he rose, bowed, and walked quickly into the nearby side door.

"Ah, voilà! *Pourquoi est ici, mon cher!* Come, boy!" Queen Anne hurried to scoop Purkoy into her arms.

Madge stood and curtsied low, offering the queen her seat.

"No, no, Margaret, I should like to stand a bit. Henry and I have been cooped up inside all morning planning for my coronation. And the coronation is to be splendid! Would you like to hear?" said the queen.

"Yes, Your Majesty," said Madge, keeping her gaze to the ground. She noticed Shadow had chewed most of the meat from her end of the bone and her mouth was greasy.

"Oh child, do look at me when I speak. I had hoped you would begin to feel more at ease here, Margaret. I know you haven't been here long and life at court can seem a whirlwind if one isn't used to it. But do not be so shy," said the queen.

"Yes, Your Grace. I . . . I shall try," Madge said as she raised her eyes to look at the queen.

"You are a pretty one. I see why all the king's men are agog over you. You could have your pick, Lady Margaret. Have you found any to your liking yet?" The queen was smiling, a light in her dark eyes.

"No, Majesty. I barely know them. I have but one friend and that's Sir Wyatt. He reads his poems to me and he tells me all about the new learning. He is very kind," said Madge.

"Yes, yes, Tom is kind. But he's already married as I'm sure you know. He serves the king and that service keeps him from his little wife. Has he read you any of the poems he wrote for me?" said the queen.

"I don't know. He's read many but he doesn't tell me for whom each is written," said Madge.

"He wrote of his love for me before the king's eye fell upon me. He was my good friend, too." The queen seemed far away as she spoke. Purkoy began to wiggle in her arms, suddenly desperate to return to his bone. Before she could stop him, he leapt down to join Shadow.

"Our hounds are great siblings, though one is huge, the other small. So shall we be, cousin. I shall be your friend and I shall consider it my duty to lure you out of your shell and see you well-matched. Do not let your face fall so, Margaret. You won't be matched for a long while yet. We shall have some fun, first. Now, come walk with me. This babe has begun to flutter and the little prince seems to like it better if I walk each day. From now on, you shall be my walking friend and we'll traverse these paths come rain or shine," said the queen as she grabbed Madge's hand.

Seven

T he queen has told me so herself, Cate—I am to ride
with her in the coronation! Oh, it will be such a splendid occasion—the king spares no cost to make Anne
his queen before all the world," said Madge as she combed
Shadow's coat. The April air was still cool and the fire felt good
against her back as she tried to tease the mats out of her dog's
long, silky fur.

"You are too young for such a spectacle, Maddie. I cannot
think why the queen would want you to accompany her on the
most important day of her life. Why not her sister, Mary? Or
Mary, the king's own sister?" said Cate.

"How could her sister appear on such a day! You know Mary
was the king's mistress long before Anne became queen. It would
not be proper," said Madge.

"And I know the duchess of Suffolk cannot abide your cousin and has refused to appear for the event. Mary Tudor loves the true queen, our Catherine. She will not pay homage to Nan Bullen," said Cate.

"Quiet, Cate! Do you want to get us both thrown into the Tower? You must *not* speak out so against Queen Anne! Who knows who may be listening at the door? Besides, my lord Brandon's wife is ill to death, so I hear," said Madge.

"Sick of what has happened to good Queen Catherine. Oh, don't pout so—I'll mind, I'll mind. Now, tell me more about the coronation," said Cate.

Madge began while Shadow curled up beside her and fell asleep.

Suddenly, loud voices could be heard from the queen's privy chamber along with the shuffling of feet. Cate jumped up and opened the heavy door just in time to see the queen herself, clad in her white linen nightgown, her black hair flying behind her as she stormed down the hall. The king followed after her, his face full of worry. Cate motioned to Madge to join her and watch the scene.

"I cannot believe the willfulness of Princess Mary, your daughter. For her to refuse to acknowledge me as her queen once again . . . It is maddening!" said Queen Anne as she wheeled about and confronted the king in front of Madge's door. Several ladies-in-waiting stood around the couple as if they were watching a cockfight.

"Sweetheart, do not upset yourself so. Think of our little prince—he will not like being jounced around in the middle of the night," said the king, his voice calm but his eyes lively with anger.

"I shall make her a maid in my own household or . . . or . . .

marry her off to some varlet if she will not accept me! She must! She must!" said the queen as she threw herself against the king's barrel chest and sobbed.

"All right, sweatheart. Come to bed—I will see to this in the morning, my love. I promise," said the king, leading her back to her chambers, ignoring the small crowd of women gathered to witness the spectacle.

Cate pushed Madge back inside, closed the door, and bolted it carefully.

"Why does she grow hot about Princess Mary, Cate? The princess hasn't done anything to her. And she's so young, no older than I. It seems unlike the queen to hold such a hatred," said Madge as she crawled back into her bed, Shadow beside her.

"She has to hate what came before her, don't you see? She cannot allow human feeling into her bosom. She cannot think of how poor Queen Catherine is suffering for want of her husband. If Queen Anne thought of those things, all would be lost for her, Maddie. It is an ugly business. I'm glad I'll have none of it," said Cate.

"Aye, her road is fraught with snares, I can see that. But I feel the tug of sleep so I shall nod off, dear Cate. I am happy not to be a queen," said Madge, hunkering beneath the warm quilt that covered her bed.

"Yes, my girl. I have no wish to wear a crown," said Cate. "Now, to bed . . . Tomorrow is Eastertide and you must to church!"

"Aye, the morning will be here sooner than I can catch a wink. But it will be fine to be part of the queen's procession—sixty maids in all I was told—to hear her first mass as queen. I shall be happy to have a new dress."

The next morning, the queen, dressed in robes of estate and

laden with diamonds and other bright gems, processed with her maids to her closet to hear mass. Though the king had not yet been granted a divorce officially, Anne acted every inch the queen. As the ladies left the mass, Madge found herself one of the last to exit the section behind the queen's closet where Madge and the other ladies had stood.

"Happy Easter, lady! You are as lovely as one of the queen's own lilies," said Arthur Brandon, offering Madge a long-stemmed blossom whose scent filled the air.

"Are you the Easter hare brandishing gifts? You have the ears for such a job, Sir Churlish," Madge said, pushing the flower away and continuing to walk toward the group of women heading back to the queen's apartments.

"Ah, yes, these ears of mine hear a great deal, m'lady. And your name comes up frequently. It seems the king's men are most taken with the lovely but mysterious Lady Margaret. Sir Norris is actually quite enthralled, so my longish ears tell me," Arthur said, keeping pace easily with long, loping strides.

"I care nothing for such court rumblings, sir. Now, I must take my leave of you. I'm sure the queen will be asking for me anon," said Madge.

"No, she will be joining the king in his chamber to sup. She must eat for two, you know. But you, m'lady, are only eating for one—would you like to join me for a picnic this warm Easter day?" he said, smiling.

"'Twould be unseemly, sir, to leave my queen's service to go a-larking with such as you. I may know nothing about court but I do know a virtuous lady does not steal away with any fool who asks her. Be off!" Madge spun around to face him, her cheeks pink.

"Ah, my lady blushes—and so beautifully, too. Could that

mean I have touched her heart?" Arthur looked down at her and she gazed into his dark eyes for one second too long. The eyes almost caught her.

"I blush because I must run to keep up with my queen. Unlike some who would loaf their days away, I am at court to serve. And serve I will!" Madge said as she lifted her skirts to run.

"Dignity, my lady. Remember your dignity!" Arthur said as he laughed at her sprinting across the stone hall.

Once inside the queen's apartments, Madge hurried to her room.

"Dear me, Lady Margaret! Why so out of breath?" said Cate.

"Sir Churlish accosted me on my way from mass and I had to flee! He is the most arrogant strutting rooster I've ever seen. I cannot abide him and if I ever have the queen's ear, I'll have him banished," said Madge in a huff.

"Hmmmmm. Such passion hath two springs, Maddie," said Cate.

"What mean you?" said Madge.

"Think on it a while, dearie. But now, we must hurry to sup before all the food is eaten and we have only bones to chew," said Cate.

"Bones, indeed! I could eat a whole figgy pudding by myself!" said Madge.

"I am stuffed as a peacock. Let us do something to ease our bellies," said Madge as she and Cate entered their room.

"I think we should practice your dancing—my word, how the lords and ladies leapt and frolicked! Such movements are not easy—and last time we tried it, you fell flat on your . . ." said Cate.

"You do not have to remind me!" said Madge. "Did you notice a new dance this eve? I am not sure of its name but the gentlemen had to be quite strong, methinks, to accomplish such feats," said Madge.

"As I have observed them, Maddie-girl, the gentleman places his hand like so upon your waist and then turns you about, thus," said Cate as she tried to partner Madge in the galliard. "And then, you leap and I shall lift you into the air—go on, leap!"

Madge did as she was told, but Cate could not hold her and they both fell in a heap onto the floor.

"I shall never learn! It is hopeless," said Madge, laughing at the sight of them covered with rushes and Shadow's kisses.

"Laugh all you will—we shall try again," said Cate. "May I have this dance?"

Madge burst out again, unable to restrain herself. Both women collapsed, falling together onto the cot.

"I shall never fit in at court—oh Cate, you do provoke me—I knew not you had such fun in you!" said Madge, holding her sides.

"You *shall* fit, Maddie! I'll *make* you fit!" roared Cate.

Eight

Quickly Cate! The queen awaits us!" said Madge as Shadow scampered on her leather leash decorated with daisies and violets from halter to handle. "Oh, do hurry!"

"Ready—how do I look?" said Cate as she smoothed her saucy new dress of blue satin.

"Lovely, dear Cate. And how look I?" said Madge as she twirled around in her own gown of green silk edged in cloth of gold.

"Perfect to go a-Maying. You're as pretty as any flower, my Maddie. Take care though. May Day is the day for romance—you might fall into Love's deepest trap!" said Cate.

"I'm not ready for such as that, but I do want to see the queen happy and at play. We have had much trouble these last weeks, too much arguing betwixt king and queen. She is look-

ing forward to this day, where she can frolic with the king to
her heart's delight. And she will bring a return of his good humor," said Madge as she pulled at Shadow to follow her down
the corridor and to the open grounds where stood a large maypole surrounded by ladies in pale shades of silks and satins.
Behind the ladies, the king's men told stories of a ribald sort, so
Madge imagined. She watched as they slapped backs, laughing
with sly glances cast to the queen's ladies. On the outer rings of
the crowd circling the maypole stood the lower folks—cooks
and washwomen, grooms and stable boys, even the lowly milkmaids and pig boys—all looking clean and bright, happy to
have a day of gaming and dancing.

Madge and Cate joined the knot of women waiting for the
queen. Mistress Jane Seymour was there, standing alone as usual.

"Good morrow, Jane. You look lovely in your pink," said
Madge as she curtsied simultaneously with Miss Seymour.
Cate dipped much lower and said nothing.

"Thank you, Lady Margaret," said Jane. She was a plain
woman only a few years older than Madge and she usually
looked miserable. Her pale blue eyes sought the ground most
times and her dour little mouth drooped at the corners, even
when she smiled. Not many of the men noticed her and she
seemed lonely except when her brothers were around.

"Do you look forward to spinning the spider's web today,
mistress?" said Madge, hoping to draw the unhappy Jane into
the spirit of the day.

"No, Lady. Such frivolity seems an unfortunate display when
the queen suffers at Ampthill," said Jane, who then turned her
back on Madge and gave a little cough.

"But the queen is here, Lady Jane. Queen Anne is right here
and soon to join us," said Madge, whirling Jane around to
face her, grabbing her by the elbow. Madge smiled a little to

take the sting from her words, but there was no returning smile from Lady Jane.

"Please remove your hand from my person, Lady Margaret. It is unseemly," Jane said and once again turned her back to Madge.

"Come, Maddie. I think the queen and king approacheth. This way to have a better look," said Cate as she gently led Madge away from Lady Jane.

"Who does she think she is to talk so at the very court where she serves the queen? And when I touched her, you'd have thought she'd come into contact with something loathsome," said Madge.

"Maddie, her family is noble and much older than the Boleyn clan. The court has so many factions, it is hard to keep them all straight but the more I listen, the more I see one for certain— the old nobility cares not a whit for the young people Henry and Anne have invited to court. The youngbloods have the king's ear and he hardly pays heed to what the Seymours or even the duke of Norfolk has to say. He likes the beauty and energy of youth around him. He likes the new learning and the new reli- gion. Some cling to the old while others embrace the new—it has always been so, methinks," said Cate as she pulled Madge to the walkway where the king and queen would appear.

"She thinks she's my better, then. And all I wanted was to be friendly. Well, I won't try that again," said Madge, bending to pet Shadow and replace a daisy that had fallen off her leash.

"Just because Lady Jane is ill-mannered, you don't have to join her in it. The best way to get along is to be kind to all God's creatures. Try to forgive the poor girl. She has enough to fret her—with her woebegone looks, I can't imagine what kind of marriage she will make—if any," said Cate.

At that moment, the horns blared and the king, with the queen happily on his arm, strode into the yard. The men bowed and the ladies curtsied. Shouts of "Long live the king! Long live the queen!" rose as the happy couple advanced to the maypole.

The king stopped at the maypole and grabbed the queen's hand, raising their clasped hands into the air. "My good people, today we go a-Maying. It is the time for the grasses to bloom and the crops to begin. The time for nesting and mating. I already have my sweetheart, as you can see! And she is on the nest proud as any robin." He patted Anne's belly in front of everyone. Madge could see her cousin blush, then smile as the courtiers laughed. "But as for those who have no lover, find her in the weaving of the ribbons and garlands! Let the circling begin!"

With that, the musicians began to play a lively tune. Madge noticed the lead musician, the one playing the lute, was extremely handsome. His hair was the color of burnished gold and his eyes reminded her of the does she'd seen at home— long thick lashes and enormous soft brown eyes.

"Who is that handsome singer? I have never seen such a pretty man," whispered Madge into Cate's ear.

"I am not certain but methinks 'tis Master Mark Smeaton— he is one of the most talented at court, so the women have said. Aye, he has the looks of a god—but he is common-born so do not think of such as he. The queen will match you, have no fear," Cate said quietly.

As the music played, courtiers hurried to grab hold of one of the ribbons with which to circle the maypole. As the men wove one way, the women wove the opposite. Madge was one of the last to grab a garland and she wasn't sure which direction to go until she felt a hand on her waist.

"Ah, my lovely Lady Margaret! I was hoping you'd pick up a strand. This way," said Sir Henry Norris as he ushered her to follow the other women. His thin, dark blond hair blew back to reveal a high, glistening crown of a head and his narrow blue eyes leered at Madge. He was older than she, in his early thirties, she guessed, with a sheen of sweat always covering his face and hands. His voice oiled its way into her ears and made her shiver with disgust.

"I hope as the strings wrap 'round, I shall meet up with you, my lovely lady," he whispered to her as they passed each other.

"Why?" Madge said.

"When the music stops, you must kiss the one you face, dear lady. And I've thought of nothing else since I first saw your lovely lips," Sir Norris said.

Madge spoke not a word but tried to smile at him. Cate's words about kindness had gone to her heart. But she couldn't stand the thought of him kissing her. The music kept going, faster and faster until the young people were spinning around the maypole, tripping over one another and laughing.

"So sorry," said Madge as she stepped on someone's foot. Her head was spinning and the sun bore down on her, making her even dizzier.

"Oh, you may step upon my foot anytime, Lady Margaret. Better you than fat Bessie Henshaw," said a familiar voice. Madge looked up into Arthur Brandon's face. His brown eyes always seemed to be laughing at her, but he smiled kindly.

"Sir Churlish—I'm surprised to see you here. I thought only the true nobles would be at court today," said Madge.

"I'm a natural noble, m'lady. Are you trying to hurt me? Because if you are, such taunts do not work. I've heard the like most of my life. Besides, nothing could bother me on a day such as today," Arthur said.

"I do not care enough for you one way or the other to try to hurt you, sir. Why is today so jolly?" said Madge.

"Because the music has stopped and I'm facing the loveliest lips at court," Arthur said. With that, he grabbed Madge around her waist, pulled her to him, and kissed her full on the mouth. When he let her go, the music had started again with instructions from the king to unwind the mess they had made.

Madge dropped her ribbon and extracted herself from the crowd of young people twisting around the pole. Her face flamed and she was so angry her heart beat hard in her chest. She hurried to Cate where she picked up Shadow's leash and stalked off in the direction of the rose gardens.

"My lady, what is wrong? Maddie? Where are you going? Maddie?" Cate called but Madge made no answer. She continued on her way.

The hedges gave a little shade as Madge and Shadow headed for their favorite bench. Madge could not believe the impertinence of Arthur—to kiss her like that in front of all the court—without her permission! Of course, she did realize that all the court was kissing, too, and probably didn't notice one thing Lady Margaret Shelton was doing. She laughed a little at her vanity—no one cared what Lady Margaret did or didn't do. She was a poor cousin of the queen, here only at the queen's request.

"Something amuses you?" Sir Thomas Wyatt seemed to appear from nowhere.

"Oh, Tom. The most terrible thing happened at the May," said Madge, relieved it was her friend.

"What could be so terrible? It is a day for dancing and making eyes at everyone," he said.

"But you weren't there, Tom. Why?" Madge said.

"I am married, my girl—you know that. And not to one of my liking. So, I decided to spend a few quiet moments gathering my thoughts and writing a poem," Thomas said.

"Dear Tom. You are so kind and good. I am sorry you cannot find happiness in your wife. Such a case is very sad indeed. But perhaps writing a poem can ease your pains," said Madge.

"Enough of that. Why are you so blushed and out of breath?" Thomas said.

"Sir Churlish! He had the very nerve to kiss me at the May!" said Madge.

"Sir Churlish? And who, may I ask, is that?" said Thomas.

Madge turned a deeper shade of red. She hadn't meant her pet name for Arthur to slip out.

"Just a rogue I met on my very first day in London. And he hasn't let me alone since. His name is Arthur Brandon and he's a . . . well, he's a bastard," said Madge.

"I know Arthur well, dear lady. He's the natural son of Sir Charles Brandon and a finer man you'll not find. He's honest and hardworking. Seems he's one who can't be bought and doesn't care a goatshead for who is what at court. He is the son of Sir Charles's youth before Sir Charles was married to the king's sister," said Thomas.

"I don't care what you say about him—he's not much more than a brute!" said Madge as she sat on a nearby bench. Shadow hopped up to join her.

"Don't let such things upset you, Lady Margaret. On the May, it is expected that kisses will go round the maypole along with the ribbons," said Thomas, smiling.

Madge breathed easier. She was glad to hear good words about Sir Churlish, even though she wasn't sure she believed them. And she was happy to find her friend.

"Well, at least it wasn't Henry Norris who kissed me!" Madge said.

"That *is* something to be thankful for—that rake is one I'd never want to kiss," laughed Thomas.

"I should hope not, sir!" said Madge, laughing, too. "Will you be at the coronation next month? I shall be riding with the queen. It's all so exciting! And Her Majesty has sent bolts and bolts of silks and satins for at least four new dresses! She's even promised me a necklace for each dress—I can hardly wait for the festivities!" said Madge.

"I fear I shall not be there. I'm being sent to France for some business," said Thomas.

"France! Oh no, what shall I do without you? You are my only friend," said Madge.

"You will take the greatest care, lady. And become more friendly with the queen. If she is fully in your corner, you will be safe once she delivers the young prince," said Thomas.

"Safe. Yes, that's what I'd like—to be safe and back home," said Madge.

Nine

T he few days before Queen Anne's coronation were filled with excitement as the entire city of London hurried to prepare for the second coronation of an English queen in less than thirty years. Many in the city went about their tasks with less than enthusiastic faces and there were murmurs against the "goggle-eyed whore" who had bewitched the king and placed good Queen Catherine in banishment. But Madge saw little of the disgruntlement. Instead, she was called to the queen's privy chambers early Friday morning.

As Madge went through the outer apartments of the queen's side, she noted how many new dresses adorned the ladies of the court. The queen had about one hundred ladies with only ten who cared for her person and were allowed into her privy chamber and inner bedchamber. Most of these were older, wiser women than Madge, though Madge had dreamed about serving the queen in this way. She admired the lush wall hangings and tapestries that adorned the walls of the queen's apartments. The painted cloth of her own room suddenly seemed tawdry, though when she'd first arrived at court, she'd thought it quite splendid. She was glad she'd left Shadow with Cate, for the king had just banned all dogs from court with the exception of women's lap-dogs. Shadow was still a puppy and could fit on a lap but she would not do so for long. Poor Shadow. Madge hoped to ask, if it please the queen, for Shadow to stay.

Madge entered the privy chamber looking for the queen, but Her Majesty wasn't there. She saw Mistress Marshall stand-ing in the center of a group of young ladies and walked over to join them. She bowed a slight nod of greeting to Mistress Mar-shall.

"Lady Margaret, the queen will see you in her bedchamber immediately. Mind your manners and don't gawk," said Mis-tress Marshall.

"Yes, milady," replied Madge.

As Madge walked through the privy chamber, she noticed the sumptuous carpets on the floor, along with the finely wo-ven smaller rugs covering the enormous walnut chest where some of the queen's plate was displayed. Madge went through the heavy wooden door that led from the back of the privy chamber to the more intimate rooms that lay within. She fol-lowed the narrow hall to the next room, knocked once, but no one replied. She hurried down the corridor once again and didn't stop until she heard the unmistakable laughter of the queen herself. Taking a deep breath, Madge knocked on an over-sized oaken door. She was relieved there was no guard at the queen's bedchamber; she did not like to hear the sound of her name blared aloud by the Yeoman who stood at the outer door to the queen's apartments.

"Enter," said the queen.

Madge pushed open the door and saw the queen lying in what was the most enormous bed Madge had ever seen. It must have been long enough and wide enough to fit a horse. Madge approached the queen and made a deep curtsy.

"Come here, my girl. I've missed our walks—we must take them more often after the coronation—I've been so busy in preparation, I've had no time to spare for walking, except, of course, to walk with His Majesty," said Queen Anne with a proud smile on her face.

"I, too, have missed circling the gardens with our dear pups. How is Purkoy?" Madge said.

"Ask him yourself! He's under the covers somewhere! *Venez ici*, Purkoy!" said the queen. "And here is Urian, as usual, asleep by the fire. He is almost like a bear rug—never moves, never even shudders—and he takes up a great deal of room!"

Hearing his mistress's voice, Purkoy burrowed out from beneath the beautifully embroidered coverlet and greeted Madge with several happy licks on her hands and face.

"And how is Shadow, Lady Margaret?" said the queen as she held Purkoy.

"Not as well as Purkoy, I fear," said Madge.

"Not ill, I hope," said the queen.

"Oh no, Your Grace. Shadow is full of spark. But the king has forbidden all dogs, except the lapdogs of ladies. Shadow will grow to be a hunting dog. I fear she shall be too large to be at court," said Madge.

"I shall talk to His Majesty this very day. You shall keep your dog, of that you can rest assured," said the queen, her low voice understanding.

"Oh, thank you, Your Grace. I shall be ever so happy to have Shadow with me. She reminds me of home," said Madge.

"And you miss your home a great deal?" said the queen.

"Well . . . I do miss the sheep running across the fields and the little stream that flows through the nearby woods. And I miss my mother," said Madge. She didn't want the queen to think she was unhappy where she was, however, so she added, "I like the court very much, too. Especially when I can walk with Your Grace. And the food at court is beyond anything I could imagine. Here, time seems to have sprouted wings—it flies so quickly. Jousts, dancing, gaming, cockfights, tenes, bowles, more adventure than any back home could have in a lifetime."

The queen rose from her huge bed, Purkoy still in her arms. She walked to where Madge stood and raised Madge's chin with her bejeweled hand. The queen looked straight into Madge's eyes and Madge understood how the king might fall in love with her by gazing into those lovely brown-black orbs. Madge felt mesmerized under the queen's stare.

"I miss my mother, too. And you, little cousin, are the sweetest kinswoman I have. I would have you by my side all the time. And Shadow, too. I would like for you to become one of the ladies of my bedchamber. If you agree, you shall be given lots of clothes, for the ladies of the bedchamber are closest to me and must reflect my majesty at all times. And we shall read poetry—Sir Wyatt tells me you've been writing a little and that you have a great appreciation for fine works. And I shall teach you all about the new faith. In time, dear Lady Margaret, I shall find a man for you to marry—one who is worthy of your beauty and intelligence," said the queen.

"Your Grace, I am too young for such a high honor. I wish my mother could see the high esteem in which Your Grace holds me," said Madge.

"Your mother has her hands full now, child. She is with the Lady Mary, the king's daughter. Fear not—your mother serves me well as she has always. As I know you shall," said the queen.

Madge did not know if the queen's new appointment meant she would have to leave Cate. Madge couldn't keep the thought of losing Cate from moving across her features.

"Lady Margaret, Sir Wyatt tells me he calls you by another name—Madge, is it?"

"Yes, Your Grace."

"I shall not call you by that name—it lacks refinement. You look a little sad about your new appointment. Shall you bring your nurse, Cate, to visit anytime? She can even sleep here for the first few nights of your new service. She is certainly welcome," said the queen.

Madge sighed.

"I imagine Mistress Cate will enjoy having a room to herself—most in her position would relish such luxury," said the queen.

Madge couldn't help the smile that brightened her face. Her green eyes lit up and her cheeks turned a light shade of pink.

"Thank you, Your Grace! You are the kindest, dearest queen in the entire world!" said Madge, hugging Anne without thinking. "Oh, I am sorry, Your Grace! I forgot in my happiness that no one can approach Your Grace in such a fashion. Please forgive me!" Madge curtsied low.

"Dear child, I am still a woman, still your cousin. You may embrace me but only when you cannot help it—as just this moment! I'll have no hugs that aren't genuine—but I think yours will always be so, good coz," said the queen.

"Now, let us discuss the coronation and where you will be placed and what you will wear, shall we?" said the queen. She took Madge by the hand and dropped Purkoy to the ground. He followed, steering clear of the many skirts that surrounded him.

The queen led Madge outside into the gardens, shooing away

the other ladies-in-waiting and telling the guard at the door not to allow anyone else to join them, unless, of course, it was the king. The sky was clear of clouds and the queen bent to smell the wild roses that climbed the arbor, beneath which a stone bench perched conveniently for intimacies and perhaps a kiss or two. Madge watched as the queen hummed a lively tune, lifted her skirts, and began to dance gently. She looked so young and beautiful that Madge almost forgot Her Majesty was six months with child. Her dark hair hung loose and swayed back and forth as she moved. She seemed to be, at that moment, every good thing a woman could be in this world. Madge sighed.

"Good Margaret, why such soul-rendering sighs on this sunny May morn? I would have thought becoming a lady of the bedchamber would have brought a blush of pleasure to your cheeks," said the queen.

"Oh, such an honor has made me very happy, Your Grace. I sighed because you look so lovely, so like the roses here in the garden—beautiful and wild and free," said Madge.

The queen laughed that coarse, low-throated laugh of hers.

"Free? Oh my child, I am anything but free! I have never known a moment of freedom in my life, except, perhaps, when I was young, your age. And at the English court for the first time." Madge watched as the queen hugged herself, her hair almost black under the shade of the trellis.

"What was it like for you, Your Grace—your first time at the English court?" Madge said as she plucked a rosebud for herself and inhaled the still-tight fragrance of it.

"After the French court, there was little excitement for me here, dear coz. I served the princess dowager Catherine and she knew nothing but sewing the king's shirts, mending clothes for the poor, and reading her Bible, in Latin, of course. It was dreary, I can assure you," said the queen, laughing.

"You were on everyone's mind, I'll wager. You must have seemed so wise and full of good graces that all the lords must have wanted a betrothal with you," said Madge, sitting at the queen's feet on a little stool set there for such a purpose. The queen had motioned for her to sit and Madge was glad; one more minute on her feet and she would have almost had the nerve to ask for such a favor.

"I did have suitors," the queen said, a sudden sadness moving across her face.

"Oh, do tell me, Your Grace! I am so anxious to learn of love and court and how to behave. There are two bothersome fellows I'd like to know how to handle—and you are so good at managing the king in all his moods," said Madge.

"Hush, child! I do *not* manage the king. Nor let anyone hear you say such a thing! His Majesty wouldn't like to think himself managed by any lady. He is the master here!" said the queen.

"I am sorry, Your Grace. I meant it as a compliment to your charm and beauty only," said Madge with her face downcast.

"Let me tell you how to succeed here, my gentle girl. If you will but follow these laws, engraving them into your heart and mind, you will do well. First, never forget the king is our sovereign lord and holds the power of life and death over us! Second, don't show your true heart to anyone unless it be your queen. Finally, turn to the Lord God for succor," the queen said, suddenly serious, her brown eyes arresting Madge's once again.

Madge broke the lock on her own green eyes, lowered them, and bowed to the queen.

"Your wisdom is as great as your beauty, my queen. I shall do my best to obey you in all you desire," said Madge.

"Well, enough of such talk. I shall tell you about Lord Henry Percy, the love of my youth, and you shall learn what a young girl should never do," said the queen, laughing again.

Ten

Two days prior to the coronation itself, the traditional festivities for the rare anointing of a queen were observed. Madge had ridden with the queen as part of her entourage on the royal barge that had once belonged to the former Queen Catherine, up the Thames to the Tower where the king had appointed sumptuous new apartments for just this occasion. The river was filled with gaily decorated barges and music floated through the air in celebration of the new queen. The queen's own barge was hung with cloth of gold and heraldic banners. The king greeted Anne at the Tower with a welcoming kiss and there they spent two nights. However, on the day of the coronation, Henry kept his royal person hidden; this was Anne's day and he did not want to steal any of her glory.

The day before the coronation, when Anne would receive

God's own anointing, making her the chosen representative of God on this earth, a queen no one could question or dislodge, Madge marched in the parade following the queen's litter, watching in awe the pageants set before the queen on Saturday as she processed through the City of London dressed in a surcoat of white cloth of tissue and a matching mantle furred with ermine. Her thick black hair hung loose down her back, a stark contrast to the virginal white of her clothing. She rode a litter of white cloth of gold drawn by two palfreys caparisoned in white damask, and on her head, a coif and circlet set with precious gems. Madge stared as the entire City of London came out to gawk at their new queen and her entourage, which extended over half a mile, filled with the most noble persons in the country. Most citizens were quiet, with a few shouts of "Whore! Great Whore!" reaching Madge's ears. However, the queen wouldn't have heard such harangues because her musicians surrounded her on foot. Madge noticed Master Smeaton walking very close to the queen and singing out in a strong voice. She could not help but watch him, his face like an angel.

At various posts, the assemblage stopped to see a pageant or to hear a choir. Anne followed the same route that Queen Catherine had followed twenty-four years earlier. The pageants, which were very costly events to the citizens of the realm, followed the traditional themes, proclaiming the queen's virtue, chastity, and fecundity. Wine ran free throughout the city and people drank their fill. Madge was surprised to see all the houses of Cheapside had been hung in cloth of gold and red velvet. Gracechurch Street displayed arras, tapestries, carpets, and tissue. Madge particularly enjoyed the pageant of "The Progeny of St. Anne" performed at the Cornhill by Leadenhall. There, a series of children spoke verses, the first child comparing the queen to St. Anne, grandmother of Christ. The queen rewarded the children by tossing gold coins to them.

After a long day of presenting and exchanging gifts and receiving the homage of her people, the queen finally arrived at Westminster where the king greeted her with looks of great affection. Madge stood close to the royal couple as they surveyed the city with the throngs of people still watching the parade and enjoying the wine that flowed freely from the king's pipes.

The queen reached out her hand to Madge in order to bring her beside herself and the king. Madge looked out into the crowd. Just below her, a young man waved at the queen with his hat in his hand. His dark hair stood out among those with their hats still on. His large frame was well-formed and his face, though not clear at such a distance, appeared quite handsome. The queen and king walked a little farther onto the balcony but the young man didn't follow them. Madge continued to stare at him. Finally, she realized he was waving and shouting at *her*, not the queen. And then she realized who he was—Sir Churlish! She turned on her heel and fell in pace a few steps behind the queen.

"How liked you the look of the city, sweetheart?" Madge heard the king say.

"I liked the look of it well enough, but I saw a great many caps on heads and heard but few tongues!" said Anne, sounding a bit disgruntled.

"Ah sweetheart, such things take time. The people must get used to your kind ways, that's all. And once you've given them the son we all long for, you'll hear shouts enough so that you shall have to plug your dainty ears," said the king. Madge turned away as he kissed Anne full on the mouth.

"Must I ride and then sit and then eat with Sir Norris, Your Grace? I like him not," said Madge as she folded Her Majesty's coverlet back so the queen could crawl into her lavish bed. Her large belly made climbing into the bed difficult, even with the little stool the king had sent to her for such purposes. When she was finally settled in, Purkoy in her arms, she answered.

"It is the king's desire, Margaret. I'll not brook the issue with him, not tomorrow. Nothing shall mar my day of becoming an anointed queen. Who could have dreamed such a thing would happen? Oh Madge, it seems so unlikely that I, daughter of a lowly ambassador, should tomorrow become queen of all the land!" Her Majesty hugged Purkoy and the little dog licked her face.

"I would not wish to ruin your day, Your Grace. I only hoped to ride with my friend, Sir Wyatt," said Madge, pulling the coverlet over the queen's belly and much-risen bosom.

"Tom leaves for France soon and shall ride with his wife. He *is* married, you may recall. I'll have no scandal among my ladies," the queen said.

"Your Grace! I have no such ideas about Sir Thomas! He is my friend and that only. But I'd prefer his company to Sir Norris's—that's all," said Madge.

"And what is wrong with Henry Norris?" said the queen.

"I like not the way he looks at me. And I like not the way he talks to me. Cate says he visits the bawds at least once every week and I see how he tries to touch the ladies of the court, a sneaky sort of touching," said Madge. "I like him not!"

"I know, dear Madge. He is that sort of varlet—you have judged him well enough. But he is the king's boon companion.

You and I must learn to be friendly with him, you more than I. You have caught Sir Norris's fancy, I fear," said the queen.

"What shall I do, Your Grace? I cannot encourage him in his suit. Please intervene for me, my queen," Madge felt her cheeks burn as she spoke so boldly.

"I shall do what I can, dear coz. But some things are beyond my power. Let us wait until the little prince is born—I shall be able to ask anything of the king then," Anne said as she patted her belly and smiled.

"Thank you, Your Grace. And now, to bed," said Madge as she pulled out the truckle bed from beneath the queen's own and covered herself. She tried to ready herself for the long Coronation Day to come, made even longer by her proximity to Sir Henry Norris.

"How fortunate for me that His Majesty, in all his wisdom, hath yoked us together, Lady Margaret. You could not be more lovely—much more of a beauty than our new queen," Sir Norris whispered as he circled his horse close to Madge's steed. They rode side by side in the queen's procession into Westminster Abbey.

"Kind sir, the queen is our sovereign as well as my own dear cousin—say nothing to her detriment, I beg you," said Madge in what she hoped was a haughty voice. All morning, since they were paired together, Henry Norris had pawed, pinched, and otherwise tried his best to touch Madge in a variety of inappropriate places. Her patience was wearing thin. But there was little she could do or say in such an esteemed company. Almost every important person in England was gathered to celebrate Anne's coronation, with a few exceptions: Lord Stafford had paid a fine rather than attend; and the marquess of Exeter, the king's first cousin, was absent primarily because he had been rusticated from court for his support of Queen Catherine. But most of the nobility were present, making it impossible for Madge to cry out or complain just because she couldn't control a frisky companion of the king's.

Of course, Henry Norris was well aware of his opportunity and was not dissuaded by her discomfort at his advances.

"I did but whisper my appraisal of your beauty, Lady Margaret. I do not believe any could hear but yourself," Sir Norris said as he reached over, putting his hand upon her knee.

"Sir, we are supposed to be marching behind the queen in a dignified manner. Do not place your hand on me," said Madge, trying to dislodge him without making too much of a movement. He disengaged and laughed.

"I think you like me not, my lady. How have I offended, pray tell?" Norris kept a smirk on his face, a look that told Madge he did not care a fig whether he had offended her or not.

"I would like you well enough if you did not try to paw me at every point! And if you did not look at me as if to eat me alive! And if you could do more than chatter about my beauty!" said Madge in a huff. She realized she may have gone too far in reprimanding this randy fellow, but she had not been able to stem the tide of words that flowed from her mouth.

"Ah, you prefer a more subtle approach—wooing with poetry and flowers and declarations of eternal love? Much like our vaunted queen, I suspect. Does that mean you wish me to marry you and take you up a step higher than you already are, my scheming Margaret?" said Norris.

"I prefer not to be wooed at all. And no! I care not to marry. As for raising me, sir, I am cousin to the soon-to-be anointed queen of England. I need no further height," said Madge as she tried to ride faster to avoid further conversation. He grabbed the reins of her horse.

"You may not care to be wooed, my lady, but I will woo you. And, God's blood, I'll win you," Norris said, his arm firmly around her wrist.

At that moment, Madge heard a scuffle behind them and turned to look. A man was approaching their steeds on foot.

"Lady Margaret, may I have a word?"

It was Arthur, his face flushed and his rich velvet doublet, a deep turquoise, stretched to show his robust chest as he reached for her hand.

"Certainly, my lord. If you'll excuse me, Sir Norris? I shall meet you inside at table," said Madge as she gave Henry Norris a short nod.

"But . . . but you are to pair with me, my lady. The king commands it . . ." mumbled Norris.

"I shall be with you anon," said Madge.

Norris shrugged his shoulders and continued on his way. Madge dropped back to allow Arthur to catch up with her.

"I never would have believed I would be glad to see such as you!" said Madge.

"What a kind sentiment, lady. I have rescued you from a true rascal and all you do is insult me. Little repayment for my trouble," said Arthur, grinning up at her.

"If you expect payment for chivalrous deeds, you are no better than Norris," said Madge, turning her face from him.

"You misunderstand me. I expect nothing. What else could I expect, given my parentage? I can neither expect nor offer . . . anything," Arthur said with downcast eyes.

Madge hadn't expected to feel regret for her harsh words, but that is exactly what stabbed her heart as they progressed toward the great door of the abbey.

"Forgive me. I am truly grateful for even a few moments away from Norris. I must spend the entire day with him and I can only hope to escape with my honor intact," said Madge as she scanned the lane ahead, looking for Norris.

Arthur touched her slightly on the arm. She turned her face down to him as he whispered, "Should you need help in protecting your honor, you have only to send for me. I am in earnest, my lady."

Madge looked into his eyes and knew he meant what he said. Perhaps Arthur, too, could be a friend. She smiled at him and said nothing. Then, she caught a motion from the corner of her eye—Sir Norris waving his arm to her.

"I must go. Thank you for your kindness," said Madge as she dismounted her horse, handed the reins to a stableman, and made her way to the place Norris had saved for her. At that moment, the trumpets began to blow and the ceremony began. Madge could barely see the queen dressed in her crimson gown, rich velvet edged in ermine. Her long black hair hung freely once again to her waist and a caul of pearls covered her head. She marched in beneath a canopy of cloth of gold, followed by a great train of lords and ladies. Madge and Norris walked in at the end of this line and moved solemnly to their places. Next came the Yeoman of the King's Guard, the bishops and abbots, and finally, the children of the Chapel Royal and the two archbishops. All processed upon red carpet, which extended to the raised platform where Anne sat at the high altar enthroned in all her glory.

The ceremony seemed to last forever as each man of import acted his part. The solemn high mass was sung by the abbot of Westminster but it was Archbishop Cranmer who anointed Anne with holy oil and then placed the crown of St. Edward upon her head, a scepter of gold in her right hand, and a rod of ivory in her left. After the Te Deum was sung, the crown of St. Edward was replaced with one of lesser weight. Anne then took the sacrament and prayed at the altar of St. Edward.

Sir Norris kept stealing glances at Madge and tried several times to hold her little finger. She thought she could not remain standing for another minute, as she had been on her feet for at least three hours, when, finally, it was over. The trumpets played their fanfare and the entire assemblage prepared to return to Palace of Westminster, where a sumptuous feast would take place. Madge noticed how silent the lords and ladies were through these events. Even the London crowds outside gave no shouts or cheers for their new queen. Few hats were tossed and even fewer calls of "God save Your Grace," as were heard every time old Queen Catherine appeared in public, even now, when she was merely the dowager princess.

Madge and Sir Norris marched outside into the warm June air. Madge gazed into the sky and noticed what had started as a balmy, clear day had turned overcast. She felt a sudden sense of danger for herself and the new queen.

"Tired, Lady Margaret? Shall you to bed?" said Norris with a leer.

"No. I am hungry. It is a long time since we supped," said Madge, not wishing to share anything as private as a feeling with Norris.

"That want shall be satisfied soon—I'll warrant the banquet has food enough for the whole city," said Norris, taking her hand and leading her into the Great Hall.

At the coronation banquet, Anne was seated alone at the center of the top table while all the important people were arranged according to the order of precedence. The countess of Worcester and the dowager countess of Oxford stood beside the queen, each holding an embroidered napkin that would be used to shield the queen if she needed to spit or do otherwise. Two other women sat at her feet under the table, ready to do her bidding.

Madge looked around and found it hard to believe that as the trumpets blared and the Knights of the Bath served the queen course after course of rich food, there remained eight hundred people still seated, waiting for their own tasty meal. On horseback, overseeing the entire festivity, sat the duke of Suffolk, who as high steward was responsible for the overall dinner. Madge thought he looked as Sir Churlish might look in another twenty years—handsome and regal with his doublet and jacket studded with pearls. Lord William Howard was also on horseback and his duty was to see to the serving of the food. For the first course, the queen was served twenty-three dishes, of which she ate three. The second course consisted of twenty-four dishes and there were thirty for the third. Each course was heralded by the king's trumpets and much singing.

The king himself was seated on a hidden stage where he could watch the festivities through a lattice and eat his fill. At the end of the meal, the kitchen had prepared many subtleties and Madge was particularly impressed with the wax ships. By then, the hour had struck six and the queen, along with Madge and all the other attendants, had been on parade for nine hours. And there were still the closing ceremonies to endure. Madge hoped all this pomp would not overtire the queen, especially in her delicate condition. She plopped a sugared plum into her mouth and swore she would never forget this day, this feast, this triumphant moment.

Eleven

T he weather of mid-July was warm with plenteous rainfall so that the royal gardens bloomed with all sorts of flowers: roses, gillyflowers, columbines, and lavender. Madge and Cate strolled daily in the various gardens at Hampton Court, taking Shadow out so she would not soil Cate's room. Though the court usually went on Progress in the summer months, because of the queen's condition, the king had decided to stay in London so his wife would not be jostled over the countryside. The king took no chances with his future son's welfare.

Madge had heard no words about Shadow's being in the palace, though by now, Shadow had exceeded even the king's lap. The queen must have arranged things. Madge was beginning to relax, learning the queen's moods and enjoying their frequent talks. The queen was teaching Madge a little French,

how to apply lotions and powders to her skin to be more beautiful, though the queen had told her these tricks were not to be
used now, but for Madge's "older years." Her Majesty also instructed Madge on how to do fine needlework, which the queen
intended all her ladies to learn so they could sew clothes for the
orphans and the poor. Madge soon discovered that the queen's
view of religion was much more like those of the reformers
than the old faith itself. The queen saw mankind as a good and
natural part of the creation and was not so concerned with beliefs about original sin or the evil lodged in the human heart as
the priests and monks were like to describe. Madge found the
queen's faith unshakable and her concern about the virtue of
her ladies oddly prim for one who had a seven-month belly in a
five-month marriage. Nevertheless, Madge remembered hearing one of the poems spoken to the queen during her progress
for her coronation:

> *This gentle bird*
> *As white as curd—*
> *In chastity*
> *Excelleth she.*

Madge had stifled a laugh when she heard it, but the queen
seemed very pleased by the verse and gave the child who read
the lines a gold coin from her purse.

Madge had discovered much about her queen, now that she
was a mistress of the bedchamber, information known only to
the queen's intimates. She saw the strain across Her Majesty's
brow at the end of the day and often Madge rubbed oils and
rosewater over the queen's face and shoulders to ease the tension.
And Madge watched as Henry often turned beet-red while his
wife complained about her growing waistline. The king rarely

replied to her grumbling, but Madge could see his patience was wearing thin.

Cate took every chance to warn Madge of the king's change of heart.

"They say he has already taken up with another young maid, this one pretty as a peach," said Cate, her voice not at all unhappy with this news.

"You are wrong, good Cate. The queen will hold him—you'll see," said Madge as Cate helped her out of her sleeves and into a clean nightdress of soft linen. Dressed in her shift and nightbonnet, Madge sat near the fire.

"Has Norris bothered you of late, my Maddie?" said Cate.

"He's been made Groom of the Stool and is in much demand from the king. Luckily, I see him rarely," said Madge.

"And Sir Churlish?" Cate asked.

"Humph. I care not a whit to see him—he, too, has absented himself from court these last three weeks. Fears the sweats, I'll warrant—probably running like a scared rabbit!" said Madge.

"Or like the king," said Cate.

Both women laughed. They knew how the king loathed disease and how he paced and worried these summer days, stuck in London during the season of plague and sickness.

On her way to the queen's bedchamber, Madge caught sight of movement in the queens's privy chamber. The ladies had bedded down in their rooms and Madge knew the queen was already in her silk nightdress, a glass of warm goat's milk by her bed. Her Majesty had dismissed Madge for one hour while she made her prayers and read from her Book of Hours. Late at night, though it was against the usual rules, the queen often sent Madge from her side, saying she needed a respite from the demands of being in sight of everyone all day long. Because of her condition, the king allowed it, giving Madge a warning that if anything befell the queen and the unborn prince, Madge would be held responsible. Madge remembered the cold look in his eye as His Majesty growled the words at her.

She strained to see who was in the chamber as all the candles had been snuffed for the night. She could hear movement, the rustle of silk skirts, a masculine murmur. Suddenly, she spied a large shape by the windowpane. Even in the darkened room, she could tell it was the king. He was the tallest, most muscular man at court and there was no mistaking his size or shape. A much smaller figure was pressed up against him, a woman. Madge could not see who she was. Madge hurried through the chamber into the queen's inner rooms. Her head spun.

Could Cate's gossip be true? Could the king have tired of the queen so quickly? And the queen, ready to give birth to the prince? Madge could feel the heat rush to her face. He was a monster! A beast!

When she arrived at the queen's bedchamber, Madge was glad Her Majesty was asleep. How small she looked in that massive bed of hers! Even grown heavy with child, the queen seemed no bigger than a young maid. Madge crawled into her truckle bed and pulled up her coverlet. She would not speak of what she had seen. Best for the queen to rest easy until the young prince arrived.

As the court frolicked during the warmth of summer, though the weather was never so warm as to be without one's overcoat, lords and ladies staved off boredom with various sports and games. After a brief day of mourning for the death of Lady Suffolk, Brandon's wife and sister of the king (who had died on the day of Anne's coronation, though weeks passed before the king got word of his sister's demise), the frivolities resumed easily. Almost daily, the king and queen attended jousts at the tilt-yard, with the king often participating. His favorite jousting partner, the excellent Sir Nicholas Carew, broke many a shield and suffered various cuts and bruises. The king wore green and white, the Tudor colors, and carried his wife's token as he strove valiantly against Sir Nicholas.

Like Catherine before her, the queen watched as the king performed his wondrous feats of skill in various sports. His Majesty was particularly good at tenes and the joust. He loved archery so much he made it a law that every man in the land should own and practice with a longbow in case of foreign in-vasion. Wrestling and hawking amused him, especially hawk-ing, which he had just started to enjoy in his midyears. Of course, the hunt was everything for the king. For indoor enter-tainments, which Henry could play with the queen, games of dice such as Hazard, Trey, Gobot, and Quenes were the favorites. Her Majesty and Madge loved to play at cards together and Madge had become especially good at Primero, a game for which the king cared nothing. The queen excelled in All Fours and gambled much money, which the king supplied.

"Come, Lady Margaret, let us go to the lists and watch the king, my husband, unseat that long-legged, dour-faced Nicho-las Carew!" said the queen as she clapped her dainty hands to-gether, the long lace of her sleeve fluttering like a tiny flag.

"Must we, Your Grace? I tire of the king's breaking of lances. Would you not rather stay here for a quick game of Noddy or Trump?" said Madge as she stood at the queen's gaming table and shuffled the gilded playing cards.

"I tire of the king's mock battles, too, little one," the queen whispered in Madge's ear. Then she said loudly, "Tire of the king's fun?! How dare you even voice such a thought, you slovenly wench," the queen said as she slapped her hands together so it would seem as if she had disciplined Madge severely. It was a frequent charade played out by the queen when the two cousins were alone in the bedchamber. To the court, Her Majesty had one face; but to Madge, the queen was more of her true self, much as she was when her brother, Viscount Rochford, came to court.

"Yes, my queen," said Madge, smiling at Her Grace.

Madge picked up the queen's train and together they proceeded from the bedchamber. Madge knew the king, though he visited his wife nightly in her private rooms, no longer shared her bed. The queen had explained that such behavior was seemly because both she and the king desired the birth of the young prince more than anything. Neither would risk jeopardizing a smooth, timely delivery. Madge imagined the king knew his wife's temperament well enough to realize she must be shown great attention as her lying-in approached.

As the queen proceeded to the tiltyard, the other ladies-in-waiting followed her. Madge thought them all lovely and smiling this midsummer day with the exception of Lady Jane Seymour, who looked as if she smelled a sour odor.

As Madge passed by the lonely looking girl, she smiled at her. Lady Seymour did not return her smile but lifted her chin a bit higher. Though Madge had tried several times to befriend Lady Seymour, all her efforts were rebuffed. Still, Madge pitied the young woman who hadn't yet married, though she had a large dower and fine family. It was her plain face that drew no suitor, and her quiet way—it seemed the life had gone out of her. The gentlemen at court often called her "Plain Jane" behind her back, but Madge heard them. Henry Norris had said the rhyme boldly to Madge, as if his wit could help him press his suit. Madge thought him merely cruel and lacking in any true wit.

As Madge and the queen took to the stands, the king rode out on his favorite mount from Governatore's bloodline, Trojan. Henry trotted to the queen's booth, doffed his helmet, and bowed.

"My queen, I carry your colors today and would win for your honor and beauty," said the king.

"I shall be your sweetheart, Your Majesty, as always," answered the queen, smiling down at him with what seemed to be true affection. She patted her belly and added, "Our son wishes you care and Godspeed."

The king then kissed Anne's blue-and-purple kerchief and tucked it inside his armor next to his heart. As he did so, Madge caught sight of a flash of yellow within his suit, a silk rag already next to his heart. She knew then Cate's gossip was true—the king had a lady love and it wasn't the queen.

As the queen bade her ladies to sit, she grabbed Madge's hand and squeezed until Madge thought her fingers would pop.

"Did you see that token already near my lord's heart? Yellow, it was. The king has taken one of my maids, I'll warrant. He shall not! He shall not!" whispered the queen.

Madge said nothing but looked straight ahead as the jousting began. Secretly, she hoped the king would topple off his mount and break his faithless neck! He had been struck before and suffered grave injury. Why not this day? But as the queen seemed to cool her ardor, Madge realized the king was the only person alive who could keep the queen safe. She had made enemies and too many lords and ladies supported old Queen Catherine, though not so boldly as before. Madge kept her ears to the wall to discover how the queen fared at court and was dismayed to find even her uncle, the duke of Norfolk, had become irritated with the queen's sharp tongue and willful ways.

Madge considered the queen and why so many hated her. To the men at court, especially the old guard, the king had married beneath himself when he wed Boleyn's daughter, whose family had been part of the new merchant class before the meteoric rise of their clan. Because the queen espoused the new religion and was well-read in such matters, Madge could see the queen's own erudition stood against her. She dared to argue points of theology with the king himself—Madge had heard such discussions from her truckle bed. Her Majesty often won the battles, leaving the king huffing and in haste to leave the queen's side. The noblemen and commoners in the north hated the destruction of a few abbeys and monasteries, though many people agreed with the king's reforms. An equal number desired the old religion. Changes of all kinds shook the country and Queen Anne was blamed for everything.

The horns trumpeted as the king and Sir Nicholas faced each other in the tiltyard. The king looked resplendent in his armor, carrying his long spear and shield. He was a large man, though no taller than Sir Nicholas. But Sir Nicholas was thin and wiry—the best lancer in the land except the king himself. Madge felt sorry for the horses, carrying not only the men with their armor but also draped in armor of their own. Madge glanced at the queen. She was smiling, waving at the king, though her hands were clenched together and her eyes looked glassy as if she'd been crying. Madge knew the queen would never cry. She couldn't afford for her enemies to guess anything was amiss between her and His Majesty.

Madge thought of the queen's gaiety among the courtiers, the beautiful way she sang and played the virginals. She looked completely royal with her French hood and stylish clothes. When she danced, all eyes were on her. In the flickering torchlight, she moved with the grace of an angel and her dark hair flowed freely down her back. Not a man could resist such charm; even her enemies swayed under her spell, even Ambassador Chapuys, Catherine's own man.

But though the queen held men enthralled, some seemed to resent even this. Her allure made them hate her all the more, Madge thought.

The thundering of hooves, the striking blows, the sound of splintering wood and shouts from the crowd as Sir Nicholas fell to the ground woke Madge out of her dream. The king rode toward them, his visor up. He was smiling, breathless.

"My queen, I have slain a villain in your name. I give you his life," said the king, bowing courteously from his mount.

"Spare him, my lord," the queen answered, her voice tight. She did not smile. "But remember, Your Majesty, that I may not always be so merciful."

The king seemed confused by her tone and Madge watched as his cheeks colored. But he said nothing and rode over to speak with Sir Nicholas.

"I tire of this. Come along, Lady Margaret—I shall nap a while," said the queen, smiling at her ladies and the few gentlemen standing among them. Her retinue stirred, ready to accompany the queen to her apartments. She raised her hand, saying, "No, no. Please stay and enjoy the merriment here. The little prince must rest but you need not stop your fun. Lady Margaret will fetch for me." With that, the queen turned and Madge lifted her train. Together, they returned to the queen's bedchamber.

Twelve

I shall box his royal ears! I will not be used thus!" said the
queen in an outraged whisper once they had returned to
her chambers. She paced the floor, her tiny body seeming
to shoot out fire with every step.

"Your Grace . . . Anne . . . you will upset your humors and
those of the prince if you don't calm yourself," said Madge, trying to hold onto the queen's arm to slow her furious stomping.

"I care not! I care not for anything but scratching out the
eyes of the maid when I find out who she is! How dare he! How
dare he betray me!" the queen said. Then, suddenly, the queen
flung herself across her enormous bed and cried. Madge sat on
the edge of the mattress and rubbed the queen's shoulders.

"Majesty, calm yourself. If His Majesty has taken a maid, it
has nothing to do with you. I see how he comes to you each

evening, saying good night and kissing your mouth. I see the tenderness in his eyes, dearest Anne. He loves you still," said Madge in a soft voice.

"The king loves no one but the king," said Her Majesty. She turned onto her back and looked at Madge. "There is no room for love at court, cousin. Remember that."

"But His Majesty does love you—think of all he has done to have you as his wife," said Madge.

"He has done it for this little prince I carry. He may have loved me once, but that love is gone—gone forever!" said the queen, crying once more.

"Perhaps the king finds a maid to satisfy his odious lusts, Your Grace. In your condition, this you can no longer do," whispered Madge.

The queen paled. Her ladies knew better than to speak of such personal matters, though these concerns were common knowledge.

"That will be all, Lady Margaret. I will to bed," said the queen, her tone imperious and angry. Madge curtsied and bowed low.

As Madge hurried down the stone hall to the great door leading to the rose gardens, she heard footsteps behind her. Then, a rough hand grabbed her elbow and whirled her around.

"It *is* you, coz! I thought that pretty red head must belong to someone I knew!" said George Boleyn. Madge gazed into his face, smooth shaven with even, well-formed features. His large blue eyes, so unlike those of the queen's, bored into hers. He smiled as he bent to kiss her full on the lips.

"Lord Rochford, welcome," Madge said, curtsying after she wrenched herself away from his eager embrace. "Has my favorite poet returned with you?"

"Really, Madge, George will do. I want us to be the best of friends. No, Wyatt tarries in Paris—the City of Lights suits him. And where is my lovely sister?" he said.

"Resting, my lord. She has not been well this afternoon. I would not disturb her," said Madge.

"Is it a bumpy ride for her?" George whispered, pulling Madge to him so he could speak into her ear. She could smell his man's odor of dust and sweat and horse. She knew he had just returned from France, doing ambassador work much as Lord Wiltshire, his father, had done.

"'Tis, my lord," said Madge as she tried to distance herself from him.

"The king?" said George. "Up to his old tricks?" He released her and studied her face.

"I know not of any tricks, my lord. But Her Majesty has suspicions of His Grace," Madge said softly. She wasn't certain how much she should divulge to him. She knew Lord Rochford was loyal to his sister, but she also knew he was one of the king's men as well.

"He's taken a maid then," said George, more to himself than to Madge.

She remained quiet, waiting for him to dismiss her. Without another word, he grabbed her waist, pulled her to him, and kissed her once more, a lingering kiss. She felt his tongue probing her pursed lips, trying to gain entry.

"You make me glad to be back at court, Lady Margaret. I shall see you again," he said as he hurried toward the queen's apartments. Madge gave a quick curtsy and headed outside into the fresh air.

Her mind seemed to rattle around in her skull as she searched for Cate. George's kiss seemed unlike the friendly peck on the cheek she got from her brothers or her father. And his tongue.

Never had Madge imagined such a thing. The act seemed unchaste.

Suddenly, Madge saw Shadow galloping toward her, Cate running to keep up. Shadow was now loping in that ungainly manner of young hunting dogs. Madge fell to her knees and embraced the slobbering hound, letting her lick her on the face, hair, and mouth.

"Would that I were a cur, mistress," said the slimy voice of Henry Norris who had popped out of the hedges behind Cate. He doffed his cap and bowed with a flourish. Madge remained kneeling, tucking her head in a small nod.

"Perhaps that is a wish already granted, sir," said Madge, still not looking at him.

"Ha! You have a wit after all, my lady," Sir Norris said.

"Barely, my lord. But a little wit is all I need to battle you, sir," said Madge, surprised at herself. She had not wished to make enemies at court, but Henry Norris was too full of himself and she could not withstand the temptation to whittle him to size.

"This parry could mean only one thing, my lady—that you wish for me to be your knight. I hope it is true, for I want nothing more than to belong to you, body and soul," said Norris with particular emphasis on the word *body*.

"I have no such wish. I was only being rude on the hope you would leave me to speak with my nurse," said Madge, rising to her feet and glaring at him.

"My lady's wish is always my command," Norris said without emotion, though Madge could see a flush cross his face. He turned on his heel and headed away from the two women.

"You go too far, Maddie. He is a powerful man, not one to meddle with, I'll warrant," said Cate, embracing Madge.

"I am not far from the queen. I have a little sway as well," answered Madge. "Good Cate, I have missed you. The queen keeps me at her side continually," said Madge.

"It is said the queen treasures you above all the other ladies. And your conduct has been without flaw from what I hear. You remain chaste, though there are several who would change that!" said Cate.

"That rogue, Henry Norris, is one—even I can see what he is thinking," laughed Madge. She linked her arm through Cate's and the two women ambled down the garden path.

"The king has another lady—I have seen them together," whispered Madge.

"Do you know who she is?" Cate said.

"No—I saw only a shadow. No, not you, girl. Down!" said Madge, pushing Shadow back onto all four paws.

"Does the queen know?"

"She has seen the lady's handkerchief tucked into the king's armor at the joust. She is beyond herself with grief and anger. And fear," said Madge.

"She will have nothing to fear once she delivers the young prince. That will set her on firm ground. And you, too, Maddie. Then she'll find you a fine husband," said Cate.

"I have not yet found one man I should wish to marry at this court. They are all lechers," said Madge.

"I fear you are on the mark, Lady Margaret," said a hearty voice Madge knew well.

"Your Majesty," she said, bowing her head low and curtsying to the ground. She felt Cate move beside her, almost in unison.

"Rise up, dear cousin! No need for such formality," said the king, raising Madge up by the elbow. She looked at him briefly, then diverted her eyes.

"How like you living at court, then, if I were to discount all the lecherous men from your consideration?" said the king, a smile about his lips.

"The court is the finest in the world, Your Majesty. Though I have not ventured from England's shores, Her Grace, the queen, has told me much of the French court. And though the courtiers may be amorous here, they are absolute devils in France," said Madge, recalling a few of the ribald tales the queen had told her of Francis I and his many love affairs.

"Some are devils here, my lady," said the king with a strange look on his face.

"Perhaps such men are always drawn to goodness, sire. You have gathered many learned and true-hearted men. Thomas Wyatt for one," Madge said.

"Humph. Wyatt seems to warrant praise from all the Boleyn clan," said the king.

Madge realized he was referring to Wyatt's famous love for the queen prior to the king's suit. She reddened.

"It matters not, pretty Margaret. I know I have the queen's heart. And she has mine," said the king.

He laughed and gently touched Madge's chin, guiding it until she faced him and gazed into his eyes, which were pale blue and very small. Yet, he towered over her and she realized she was trembling. He was smiling down at her, his little bow-mouth turned up in a grin.

Madge did not know what to say to the king. She could not call him a liar, though she believed he was one.

"Would that you had your cousin's wit, lady. Your beauty is beyond reproach, fresh as a new egg. But you never speak! Well, I'm off to greet the queen, then to the hunt! The cat will keep your tongue, mistress!" said the king, laughing as he strode from them toward the queen's apartments.

Thirteen

I will not abide such goings on, sire! I am your lawful wife! You should keep faith with me! Such is the sacrament of marriage!" said the queen, her face, usually quite pale, reddened all the way down to her collarbone. Madge hated that the queen had chosen to confront the king while Madge was still in the room, though she was somewhat hidden behind the door of the great walnut wardrobe. She had been removing the queen's last outer garments when the king burst into the room with a bouquet of roses. Madge decided to duck into the wardrobe once she saw the queen's look as she grabbed the roses from His Majesty. She knew a squall was brewing and it was best to keep as far from it as she could.

"Madame, I do not need you to tell me about the sacraments! Nor do I need you to point where I should go and with whom! You would do best to shut your eyes to what I do, as your betters have done. Do not forget that it was I who raised you up and it is I who can cast you down again!" shouted the king, his words hard and cold.

"Cast me down as you wish, my lord. And cast your son down with me!" said the queen, her voice loud and high-pitched, sounding nothing like her usual low tones. Such noise hurt Madge's ears, the caterwauling of the queen set against the king's blustering shouts. Madge closed her eyes, trying to make herself disappear completely. Obviously, both the king and the queen had forgotten she was there. Or perhaps they didn't care. She was so far beneath them, she scarcely could have mattered.

At the queen's words, the king softened as if he suddenly realized any suffering on the part of the queen might affect his little son, the one for whom he had moved heaven and earth. Tenderness for both Anne and the prince flooded into his heart. Such changes were not unusual for this man, Madge observed. One minute, he could be full of laughter and joking; the next, his face would become cloudy and his voice thunderous. Getting along with such a man was akin to walking on eggs from the poultry yard, trying not to break a single one.

"Now sweetheart, let us not quarrel. You know you have my heart—you've the proof right there in your belly—big and round as it is," said the king, tenderly caressing the queen's stomach, his hands fitting all the way around the circumference. The queen's face seemed frozen, her mouth turned down and her eyes looking off into the distance. Madge watched as the king fell to his knees and kissed the queen's belly, cooing to the prince as he did so. The queen sighed, seeming to release her anger. A rueful smile played across her mouth. She stroked the king's hair almost absentmindedly.

"I have no wish to quarrel, my lord. I wish only to be loved by you as once I was," said the queen, her shrill voice now quiet as a whisper.

"You shall always be my queen, my beloved," said the king. Madge noticed he did not say he loved her as before. She wondered if the queen also noted this omission. The king rose and embraced his wife, patting her back and holding her in his large arms, much the way a bear might hug its mate. Or its prey, thought Madge.

"Sweet, I must off to bed now. The lists have tired me this day and there is much work of state to be done on the morrow. Kiss us now, there's a good lass," said the king as he pressed his smallish mouth against the queen's full lips. He did not linger but turned and headed for the door. He then glanced once more at the queen and blew her another kiss. "Rest well, my love," he said.

"And you, my lord," said Her Majesty, that faraway look still in her eye. Madge kept as still as she could; she barely breathed.

"You may come out now, cousin. You have weathered the worst," said the queen, collapsing on her mattress.

"Majesty, how do you bear it? How can you make do with such a man?" Madge asked as she pulled the queen into a sitting position and began rubbing her narrow shoulders and thin back. Madge could feel the small bones moving beneath her hands and marveled again at how tiny the queen was, almost frail. She seemed too small to survive the ordeal of birth, Madge thought. And such a thought terrified her.

"We bear what we must, Margaret. I made this bargain with the devil. I went into the whole affair with my eyes open wide. I knew what he did to my sister—tiring of her once he'd been invited into her bed. Marrying her off to William Carey, a mere nobody. Of course, once the sweating sickness claimed

Carey, poor Mary has had to beg her bread. God knows, my father, the great Lord Wiltshire, refuses to help her. And her boy, Henry? What is he but another Fitzroy? Another royal bastard! No, I could not face a fate like Mary's. So I tried to create something different. I tried to find a way where there was no way," the queen said as she lay down on her side so Madge could rub the whole of her back and a bit of her belly, too.

"I know, Your Grace. You have achieved greatness. But I fear to tread on the path you've carved out. I fear where it leads," said Madge.

"All our paths lead to death, cousin. Mayhap mine will come in a scarce two months when I'm brought to bed with the child. The prince could easily be my end," said Anne.

"Think not these thoughts. Look instead to the king's proud face as he holds his long-awaited son! Think how his love for you will flow then," said Madge. She said these words, but in her heart, she did not believe the king would ever love her cousin as he had before he had come to her bed. It seemed to Madge Henry loved the hunt evermore over the kill.

July turned to August and Madge found herself enjoying the warmth, though the light didn't linger in the heavens as long as it had in July. Already, she sensed the change of seasons. Fall was coming and with it, the birth of the prince. The king had continued his romance with the mysterious lady, though Her Majesty said nothing more about it. However, Madge noticed the queen was more and more complaining with the king, concerned with the loss of her figure, worried that he no longer loved her, fussing about her ladies and how they vexed her at every turn. The king laughed and smiled with the queen, but

Madge noticed his eyes did not light up the way they had in the past. He was humoring her because of the child. Madge feared what the queen had said was true—the king no longer loved her.

Madge tried not to imagine what the loss of the king's great affection would mean. Instead, she put all her efforts into pleasing the queen and easing her burdens. As the time for her confinement approached, Her Majesty seemed to need Madge more and more. Often, days passed before Madge was allowed to walk in the gardens or join the rest of the ladies for supper in the Main Hall where she might laugh and talk, live easily in the freer air of the court rather than always breathing the stale air of the queen's apartments. Mostly, Madge did not mind being with the queen when Henry was not around. After supper, the queen would clap her hands, call her musicians, bring the ladies and gentlemen into the privy chamber, and all would frolic, kicking up their heels and leaping. The queen often made up her own steps and those jigs would soon become the most popular in court. Though she was large with the child, Anne still enjoyed the attentions of the king's men: Sir Brereton, Norris, and the rest. She could move them with a laugh or a flash of her dark, dark eyes.

One evening, Madge sat near Mistress Seymour, who looked more dour than usual.

"Lady Jane, why so glum?" said Madge kindly.

"I have no heart for music. Such a waste of time. All I can think of is how the king has betrayed the true church as well as the true queen," whispered Lady Jane.

"You know such talk is treason . . . why not enjoy the singing and the dancing? You are yet young. Look there at Master Smeaton—how handsome he is as he plucks the lute," said Madge.

"Humph. A pretty boy, I'll give you that," said Lady Jane.

"See how he gazes so adoringly at the queen. He sees much to love in our esteemed sovereign. Perhaps you could learn to love her, too," said Madge.

"You truly are without insight, Pretty Madge, as I've heard you called. Smeaton's gaze is filled with ardor but not for the *queen*," said Lady Jane.

"What mean you, milady?" said Madge.

"I mean that if the priests of old could have their way, dear Mark would burn like a faggot of wood," said Lady Jane.

Madge turned away from Lady Jane and stared at Master Smeaton. She did not understand what Lady Jane was talking about. Mark surely loved Their Majesties; one had only to look at him as he stared at the king and queen. Lady Jane had once again turned a friendly gesture into an opportunity to humiliate Madge.

This August day, the queen had sent Madge out to gather some berries in the nearby woods. Blueberries, blackberries, raspberries, and flowers, especially the lacy white flower the queen loved so well that many were calling the bloom "Queen Anne's lace." Madge had quickly found Cate and Shadow strolling through the herb garden off the royal kitchen. Soon, the small party was on its way to the green wood.

"What will the queen have made with the berries? A pie? Jellies?" asked Cate, always interested in the queen's doings.

"I know not, Cate. Perhaps Her Grace wanted her chamber to herself for a few moments during the warmth of day. Or perhaps she knew I longed for the out of doors and found a suitable errand for me," said Madge, her small pail in one hand, Shadow's leash in the other.

The two women approached the bushes that edged the

deeper forest and Madge saw dark, plump berries scattered there. Birds perched along the small branches and Cate ran at them, shooing them away.

Madge reached for the nearest cluster and plucked as many as she could.

"If anything were to happen to the queen in childbed, what would become of us, think you?" Cate asked softly. Imagining the death of a sovereign was treasonous, and expressing such thoughts dangerous business indeed.

"Do not speak of such things. We pray she will be strong in childbirth. Any other event will bring us back home to Mother, a fate which would suit me fine. I tire of the court. The Boleyns, the Howards, the Seymours, that horrid Cromwell—all bickering and shoving their way to the king and his blessings. I want none of it!" whispered Madge. Her hands kept a steady rhythm as she picked the berries, hearing the satisfying plop as each landed in the pail.

"Yet, childbirth is the most dangerous time in a woman's life, Maddie-girl. I've been told by the serving women that the king will order his own doctors to tend to the queen. You must not let that happen. Those men know nothing of birthing a babe," said Cate.

"What should I do? I can't overrule the king," said Madge.

"When the time comes, go to the kitchen and ask for Dame Brooke. She is the best midwife in London. She has saved many a babe and mother, too. I'm told she's the one you want," said Cate.

"Dame Brooke. . . . When the time comes, Cate, I shall heed your words," said Madge.

At that moment, Madge noticed two men swaggering up the small knoll toward them. She could not tell who they were but she nudged Cate.

"I hope Sir Norris has not followed me here. If it is he, we shall hurry back to the castle," said Madge.

"I do not believe that lively gait belongs to Norris, dear. I know those legs and that jaunty cock of the head. 'Tis my lord Brandon and his whoreson."

Madge shaded her eyes to get a better view of the men. She recognized Sir Churlish's confident stride as the men made their way to the edge of the green wood. Part of her wanted to run deeper into the shade of the forest while another part seemed unable to move. The men covered the distance quickly and before she knew it, Madge found herself in a deep curtsy to the duke of Suffolk, Charles Brandon.

"Your Grace," she whispered as she stared at the weeds and brambles at her feet. She noticed the fine leather of the duke's boots.

"Lady Margaret. Please arise. You as well, Mistress Cate. Marvel not that I know your name—my son has told me much of the Lady Margaret and her lovely nurse," said Brandon as he gently took Madge's hand and helped her to her feet. He was handsome with dark hair and eyes, the same coloring as his son. Though a little older than the king, Brandon retained much of his fitness and youthful manner. His eyes gave no hint of the sorrow he must have felt after losing his wife, the king's sister. Madge had not known Lady Mary, but the whole court talked of her beauty and how Brandon seemed lost without her.

"The day is full of sunshine and the bushes fat with berries. The queen has a taste for these, I suppose?" said Sir Churlish as he reached for one and popped it into his mouth.

"Yes. Cate and I are almost finished here. We must return very soon as Her Majesty may have need of me," Madge said. She couldn't help but remember his kiss on May Day, though she had not seen him since.

"But lady, your pail is not half full," he said. "Methinks you seek to deceive."

Madge had no response and felt her cheeks begin to burn. Cate quickly dumped the contents of her own bucket into Madge's.

"'Tis full now, sire," she said and grabbed Madge's hand, pulling her toward the downward slope. "We must be off!"

"Wait but a little, Mistress Cate, I beg of you. I would you walk with me and help me fill your bucket. I will happily pay for the berries," Brandon said as he guided Cate by the elbow, taking her toward a large hedge filled with blackberry canes. Cate had no choice but to release Madge's hand and allow herself to be drawn away.

"My father is at a loss without his wife. He must have company from any fair woman he meets," said Sir Churlish, smiling.

"My Cate is still fair, though no longer young. But she will have no truck with any man, no matter how high he has risen. She has told me thus," said Madge, plucking a berry almost as big as her thumb.

"You, milady, are fair and young. What say you to men?" he said.

"To my friends, I say much. To scoundrels, nothing," said Madge, turning away from him.

"Then I would be your friend, mistress," he said. "Now, to other matters. The whole court awaits the birth of the prince. How does Her Majesty?" He plucked a handful of berries and ate them, one at a time.

"Well enough. She will soon go into her confinement, I'll warrant," said Madge, still turning away from him.

"She has already made merry much longer than most queens. Many wag their tongues, saying she takes no care for the babe she is about to birth. Queen Catherine went to her confinement a full six weeks before the babes came," he said.

"Such care did her little good. My mistress will be delivered of a prince, one she has done all she can to protect and love, in spite of His Majesty's doings," said Madge, her voice tight, full of anger. "And she has not waited longer than any other anointed queen—the babe will not come yet for weeks."

"His Majesty's doings? Ah, I see," he said, smiling gently at Madge. "You cannot think the king would not take his pleasure while the queen is with child! He has always done so," he said.

"Then he has always done wrongly, Sir Chur—" Madge caught her tongue. She did not want Arthur to know she thought of him often enough to have had his pet name stick in her mind. Though she had called him by that name several times, he might imagine he heard a fondness when she said it to his face after their kiss, which she could not get out of her head.

"So, you still think me Sir Churlish, eh? Madame, I am your friend and defender. I wish you could see that," he said, staring intently into her eyes.

"How so? I need no defender. I am safe enough in the queen's company, her chamberwoman, no less." Madge gazed up at him, daring him to disagree.

"Madame, no one is safe at court. I fear for you if the queen does not bear a son," he said.

"Best look to yourself, sir. You will not go far on the coattails of your father," Madge said. Just then, she heard Cate's girlish giggle and saw Brandon and Cate hurrying to them, blackberries spilling as they ran.

"Tell your Cate to watch herself. My father is noted for his ways with women. And Mistress Margaret, will you please call me Arthur? I long to hear that name upon your lips," he said.

Madge was appalled at the look of Cate, for her hair had come undone and her bodice was stained with small droplets of purple juice. Charles Brandon's hands were also purple, sticky with blackberries.

"Oh, Maddie—I am worn out with running! His Grace has tried to eat all the berries in my bucket—a hungry rascal he is," she said, her face pink and covered with a light sheen of sweat.

"That I am, madame, hungry indeed!" replied the duke and there was no mistaking his meaning.

"We must away at once, Cate! Her Majesty will be expecting us. Come, quick now!" Madge said, pulling at Cate's hand just as Cate had so recently pulled at her own.

Before she could object, Cate found her feet fairly flying down the hillock, the men standing above them, laughing and yelling.

"Good-bye, fair Cate! I'll see you anon!" shouted the duke.

"Lady Margaret, remember me as your friend," shouted his son.

Madge and Cate continued toward the castle, their hair blowing free and their hearts pounding.

"Good Cate, you must know the duke is a rogue! And newly a widower! And as close to His Majesty as a flea," said Madge. She and Cate sat in a nook on the far side of the knot garden, hidden by a surrounding hedge of boxwood.

"Maddie-girl, I have not had so much fun these many months at court as those few moments with the duke. He made me laugh," said Cate, reaching down to pet Shadow, who curled at their feet.

"But you are my nurse! My maid! And I must be above

reproach! The queen has told me thus many times," said Madge. She felt her heart beating against her frame. She had never imagined she would have to give instruction to Cate; since childhood, Cate had helped *her* navigate the world.

"I shall be more circumspect, Lady Margaret. You will have no need to reproach me or my conduct," said Cate, her face serious and full of anger.

"Cate, dear Cate. I am only worried for your sake. They say the duke had three wives at once before he married the king's sister—and only much later did the pope grant dispensation. He got Sir Churlish on some poor maid; God only knows how many more there are with his blood. I wish only your good," said Madge.

Cate looked at Madge and smiled. At that, Madge took Cate's hand in her own.

"We tread dangerous ground, good Cate. Many would do us harm. The queen's enemies surround us, as well you know. Have a care," Madge said.

"Ah, Maddie, fear not. I know what Brandon is—but he awoke something in me I did not know was there. With you secluded in the queen's apartments so often, I am lonely," said Cate. At this, Shadow sat up and licked her hands. "You understand, don't you, Shadow? You miss our Maddie, too," she said.

"After the babe is born, I shall have more time for leisure," said Madge.

"I shall keep His Grace at arm's length—of that you may rest assured," said Cate.

"Good Cate," said Madge as she leaned her head against Cate's shoulder.

Fourteen

"Your Grace does me great honor to sup with me privately this night," said the queen as she sat across a small table from His Majesty. Madge stood behind her, waiting to serve as was needed. Sir Henry Norris stood behind the king, keeping his eyes on Madge's every move. They were the only people in the queen's apartments. The king had sent the rest scurrying away.

"Where else would I be, sweetheart? On the morrow, you travel to Greenwich for your lying-in. After the procession to your rooms, when next we meet, I hope to see you holding our bonny boy in your arms," said the king.

"Pray God it shall be so, my husband. Has the dowager princess sent the christening robe for little Prince Edward?" Anne asked gently. Madge was surprised the queen would mention Catherine at such a time. She knew how the former queen, now referred to as the dowager princess since her marriage to the king had been annulled, hated to part with anything that once proclaimed her his "lawful" wife.

"I fear she has not, my sweet. But do not worry—I have ordered the finest of my silkwomen to stitch our boy a gown for all time," said the king tenderly. Madge was glad the queen's remark had not upset him. She wanted the queen to enjoy her time with His Majesty, untroubled by the obstinacy of her predecessor.

"I hope the apartments will be to your liking, lady. I have had the tapestries replaced and have placed several beds within for your ladies. The groaning chair has been prepared and there is but one window to be opened, so no evil airs will enter to sicken you or the child," said the king.

"Thank you, Majesty. I am grateful for all your care," said the queen, smiling. She motioned for Madge to refill her wineglass.

"Won't you have more meat, lady? The pheasant is quite tender," said the king, his mouth dripping with grease.

"I have little appetite these days, my lord," said the queen.

"Humph . . . too early for that sign. You have at least another month to feed our boy, bring him fat into the realm." Henry patted his own belly, which had grown a bit along with the queen's.

"He will be fine, fat, and fit, husband. I have taken every care, as well you know. I long to return to your arms," she said.

Madge glanced at Henry Norris and blushed. He smiled at her, then licked his lips.

The procession into the queen's lying-in chambers in Greenwich was impressive, with many prayers said for her health and the safety of the little prince. Madge and the other women knew the dangers of childbirth and an air of anxiety filled the apartments.

Every dignitary from the realm crowded into the rooms to pray for the queen and to hear the blessings for the new prince. Madge saw her uncle, Thomas Boleyn, now Lord Wiltshire, the queen's father. Beside him, his son, George. Norfolk, Cromwell, Sir Nicholas Carew, Brandon, Norris, and other members of the privy council all jostled for space as the king knelt at Anne's bedside, holding her hand, tears in his eyes. Madge stood on the other side of the queen's enormous bed with her own pallet laid out on the rushes.

"God bless you, sweetheart. And pray God give us a prince," whispered the king as he brushed his lips across the queen's cheeks.

"I shall do my best, my husband. God willing, I shall see you again," she whispered back to him. He smiled, took his big hand, and cupped it around her face. He shook his head back and forth, put his finger to his lips to shush her, then knelt to receive the prayers and blessings of the archbishop of Canterbury, Thomas Cranmer.

"If it please God, bring this realm a hearty prince and a speedy return to health for our good Queen Anne, she who loves the holy Gospels and has helped bring our land to the truth. Long live our beloved sovereign, King Henry the Eighth. Amen." The archbishop then spoke soothing words to the queen and took his leave. One by one, the dignitaries left their good wishes and blessings with the queen. Her brother kissed her on the cheek and Madge saw him wink his eye at her.

As the men withdrew, the queen's women entered the chamber. Madge followed directly behind the queen. It would be perhaps six weeks before the birth of the prince, then another thirty days before the queen would be churched. None of the women would be allowed back into the world for as long as nine weeks.

"I shall go mad, methinks! How can it be that I should wait in these stuffy rooms until he is born! No wonder queens die in childbirth! Who can abide this . . . this tedium!" the queen whispered to Madge as she made her toilet in the private chamber pot.

"Your Grace, it has been only three days—do not despair so. There is much time to pass yet," said Madge as she faced the tapestry to give the queen her privacy. She thought the queen looked pale and the hot August air pressed upon them both.

"You are right, cousin. I must endure everything. All depends upon it. I fear to think what may befall me if I do not deliver a prince. Henry does not hesitate to rid himself of those who thwart him. He has already strayed—I cannot hold him as I did before we were wed," said the queen quietly. "I tire of the chatter of the others, Margaret. I shall send them into the outer apartments. But I would you stay with me."

"Of course, Your Majesty. It shall be my *delight*." Even though Madge tried to say the words as if they were true, she could not hold back her laughter. The queen laughed, too.

"No one's *delight*, my girl! Would that it were!" chuckled the queen. "Ah, dear Madge. How heavily this child weighs upon me! I do not know how I can carry him another few weeks."

"You will do it, my queen. You must. Would you like for me to sing you a ditty? I can strum the lute a little now, thanks to Master Smeaton. Your brother believed me hopeless but I have improved since then. Mayhap it will lull you to sleep," said Madge.

"Begin with 'Greensleeves.' 'Tis the song the king made for me—very long ago," said the queen.

The next day, Madge found herself once more alone with the queen in the queen's innermost room. Madge could feel sweat roll down her sides, in spite of the ivory fan she used to keep herself and her queen as cool as possible.

"Your Grace, tell me a story of love. I hear of love at every turn. But alas, I have never loved," said Madge, hoping to distract the queen from her wretchedness.

"Love will find you, of that you can be sure," said the queen with a little laugh.

"But how will I know when I am truly loved? I know graceful words fill the mouth of Sir Norris when he speaks to me, but there is something else there as well. Methinks it is not love at all," said Madge.

"How right you are, girl. Norris is filled with filthy lust for you—as most men would be. Men are not governed by anything but such lusts, it sometimes seems. Yet, there can be love between men and women," said the queen, the familiar faraway look again crossing her features. Her face seemed to relax.

"Tell me, Your Grace. Tell me about love," said Madge.

The queen lay against the pillows of her bed, surrounded by sumptuous satins and silks. Madge wished the king could see her as she was this moment: serene, gentle, and filled with warmth.

"I shall tell you a tale that does not end well," said the queen quietly. Madge continued to fan her as the queen spoke.

"Once a young girl came to court—she was just a little older than you, Margaret, when she arrived. But unlike you, the English court did not frighten her, for she had been brought up in the finest court in the world. While there, she became fluent in French and Latin, and was taught to read and write. Many learned men spoke with her. She heard Erasmus lecture and actually met Leonardo da Vinci, the great artist and thinker. She danced with much grace and played the virginals and lute," said the queen.

Madge noted the queen seemed to be in a dream, her voice low and soft as a butterfly wing.

"Her father wanted to give her every advantage, so she could rise in the world," said the queen. Then, she paused.

"What then, Your Grace? Did this young girl rise? Did she make a good match?" asked Madge, unable to contain her curiosity.

"Some would say so, yes. But that part of the story is for later. You asked of love, did you not?" said the queen.

"Yes, Your Grace," said Madge.

"Then listen," said Her Majesty as she turned on her side, her back to Madge. "Rub a little, will you, child?"

Madge began to knead the flesh and found it supple and warm. She waited for the queen to continue.

"She was not a beautiful maid but handsome enough. It was her style, her wit, her laughter that drew the lords of the court to her. And there was one, a great lord, who took her heart," said the queen.

"What was he like, Your Grace?" Madge imagined such a young man and when she did so, a picture of Sir Churlish appeared in her mind.

"He was kind and gentle, not much tall and pale. His eyes were as blue as the petals of the cornflower and when he looked at the young girl, his eyes seemed to catch fire with love. He was from a great family in the north of the country, serving an evil priest who had risen far beyond his station. When this same priest came to see the king, the lad would get him to the queen's apartments to see the young woman for whom his eyes were ablaze." Again, the queen fell silent.

A long while passed and Madge thought her royal cousin had fallen asleep, so quiet were they together. Then, as if awaking from some dream, the queen continued.

"The lady and her knight walked often in the gardens, learning of each other, stealing a kiss now and again. It was near the great wood when this brave knight asked for her hand in marriage and she gave it. They were plighted, though neither had breathed a word of it to anyone. Their secret—their secret delight," said the queen.

"And did they marry, Your Grace?" said Madge.

"No. Their love was found out. The great cardinal of days gone by discovered the betrothal and snatched their love away as if it were but a fly he could catch in his fat hand. She was sent packing to her father's house and the young lad, he was married immediately to someone of the cardinal's choosing. They never spoke a word together thereafter," said the queen.

"'Tis indeed a tragedy, Your Grace. Such love is rare at court," said Madge.

"Rare as hens' teeth—but enough of sadness, my girl. Let us read from Tyndale's Bible about Our Lord and His suffering. Let us humble ourselves before God and pray for the prince to arrive soon—before we both succumb to an ill humor," said the queen.

"Lady Margaret? Lady Margaret?" said the queen, her voice tight with fear.

"Yes, Majesty. What is it?" said Madge as she rubbed her eyes, trying to see in the dark of night.

"I fear the babe is coming—my belly is gathering itself into a hard ball, just as my mother told me it would. And my sheets are soaked—I fear to light the candle to see what the liquid is—I fear it may be my life's blood," said the queen.

"But Majesty, isn't it too early?"

"That may be so but I fear the babe does not know it. For again, he tries to come—ahhhhh!" The queen emitted a low groan and Madge was on her feet in a matter of seconds. She ran to the outer door and opened it.

"Bring a torch—quickly!" she said to the ladies. Soon, Mistress Holland appeared and lit the tapers and sconces in the queen's bedchamber. In the dim light, Madge inspected the queen's sheets and found there was no blood, but the sheets were indeed wet.

"Your water, madame, has broken. I will fetch Dame Brooke," said Madge.

"Do hurry, Margaret. I don't think we have much time," said the queen, her face pale in the golden light.

"Madame, the king ordered me to call Dr. Linacre the moment your time came. I must find him immediately," said Mistress Holland.

"Do as you will," said the queen, holding her breath as another contraction gripped her.

Madge hurried down the back stairs, one, two, three flights until she entered the cavernous area where the cooks and bakers and scullions spent most of their days. All was quiet in the dead of night and Madge was not sure where Dame Brooke might be. She began shouting into the gloomy kitchens and soon, she saw candles flickering beneath the doors in the servants' quarters.

"What's all the caterwauling? Who's in here?" rang a gruff voice. Madge watched as an old woman in her nightdress made her way down the corridor from the left.

"The queen is in her labor. I need Dame Brooke immediately!" said Madge, trying to keep the terror out of her voice.

"She's at the end of that hall," said the old woman, motioning to another corridor. Madge hurried, her bare feet slap, slap, slapping against the stone floor. She found the last door and banged her hand on it.

"Dame Brooke? Dame Brooke? The queen has need of you— *now!*" screamed Madge, feeling the panic rise in her throat.

The door opened and a middle-aged woman emerged, carrying a bag of various implements and cloths. Her reddish-gray hair was pulled back tightly in a bun and her clothes were clean and crisp. She moved with purpose and authority.

"Has her water broken?" Dame Brooke asked.

"I think so—her bed was wet but there was no blood—I checked. But her belly is gathering up hard and she thinks it's time," said Madge.

"Sounds like it *is* time," said Dame Brooke. "Grab those cloths and that long feather on my cot—hurry girl!"

By the time they had returned to the queen's confinement chamber, Dr. Linacre was already there and the queen was still abed.

"Get rid of him, missy. He'll kill the queen with what he don't know," whispered Dame Brooke.

"How can I? The king has sent him to help," said Madge.

"Help her into the grave, most like," said Dame Brooke. She walked over to the queen's bed and whispered into her ear. The queen sat up as best she could and looked at Dr. Linacre.

"I believe, Doctor, I have been mistaken. The pains have stopped. I am sorry to have disturbed your sleep but . . . ah, I will no longer need your services this night," said the queen, struggling to keep her features from a grimace as another pain seized her.

"If Your Majesty is certain, then I shall be happy to return to my home. I shall check in soon if Your Majesty would like," said Dr. Linacre as he bowed to the queen and left the chamber.

"Ahhhhhhh for the love of heaven, help me!" screamed the queen.

"That's why I'm here, Nan Bullen. Now get up out of that bed! No child can be born with you abed. Walk a little while I unpack my things and then, take a seat in the groaning chair. We'll let the pull of the earth help bring the bonny prince into this world," said Dame Brooke.

Madge helped the queen to her feet and took her arm as she walked around the room. Dame Brooke had laid out clean strips of linen, what looked like the catgut strings of a lute, a long knife, a feather, and several vials of powders and liquids, none of which Madge could identify.

"Take a seat, Your Grace, in the groaning stool. I'm going to lie down and will be looking up at you as you sit. That way, I can see how far along you are and from this position, I'll be able to catch the babe when he comes," said Dame Brooke as she lay down on the clean rushes and put her head under the heavy damask curtain that skirted the stool. "Aye, you're pretty far along. I'll warrant this babe will be here within the hour."

As the queen sat on the groaning stool, her ladies stood around, helpless.

"I would be alone with Dame Brooke and Lady Shelton. Mistress Holland and Lady Boleyn may stay. The rest, leave immediately!" said the queen, looking in great distress as she sat upon the groaning stool.

To Dame Brooke's surprise, the labor continued, with the queen's screams growing in intensity.

"How much longer?" said Madge.

"I don't know. She's pushing out all her strength, I fear, but 'tisn't enough," said Dame Brooke.

"Can you do anything to help her? I cannot bear her to be in such pain," said Madge.

"If you think you can help me, I'll quill her," said Dame Brooke.

"I'll do whatever you say," said Madge.

"Bring me that vial, the last one in the second row. And the peacock feather," said Dame Brooke. "Now listen with care. When you feel her belly harden, tickle her nose with this feather. But not until you feel the belly draw up. Understand?"

"Yes. How will I know when the belly is drawn up?" said Madge.

"Mother of God—you put your hand on it and wait. In the meantime, Nan Bullen, you can pray to St. Margaret and take a sip of this," said Dame Brooke as she took the vial, uncapped it, and lifted it to the queen's mouth. Madge could smell the contents and was happy she was not required to drink such swill. But the queen's pain seemed to have eased a bit after a few minutes.

"Now, Nan Bullen, when I tell you, you sniff this powder into your nose as hard as you can," said Dame Brooke.

"What is it?" asked the queen.

"Never you mind what it is—*you* must obey *me* now! Or you will die in your arrogance," said Dame Brooke.

"Yes, yes, I'll do whatever you say," said the queen as another pain came upon her.

Madge took her hand and placed it on the queen's belly. She could feel the lump harden beneath her fingers and waited until it seemed to reach its zenith.

"Now—it's hardened now!" she cried.

"Sniff, Your Grace, sniff hard. Now, Madge, get that feather and tickle her nose. Come on, woman, tickle!" said Dame Brooke.

Madge kept one hand on the queen's belly and with the other, ran the peacock feathers under the queen's nose and even up inside. Suddenly, the queen sneezed hard and the sneezes kept coming until she'd sneezed four times in a row and then she yelled once again, a prolonged scream that sounded as if she were being torn asunder. Then, Madge heard a slap and a small, mewling cry.

"Someone take the babe!" commanded Dame Brooke as she handed up a bloody, wiggly thing from beneath the groaning stool. Madge motioned for Lady Boleyn to grab one of the clean towels from the bed. Lady Boleyn did so and took the squirming babe from Dame Brooke's hands.

"Here comes the afterbirth—take it, Madge, and bury it in the courtyard—that will protect the babe from the evil eye," said Dame Brooke.

Madge received a bloody bundle. She wrapped it in a clean cloth and set it beside the door. She would bury it later. The queen was pale but still seated as the midwife treated her from below.

"Is it a boy? Do I have my prince?" said the queen.

Madge had hardly thought to look. She glanced at Lady Boleyn who shook her head.

"You have a fine, healthy daughter, Nan Bullen," said Dame Brooke. "A fine girl with the king's own red fuzz atop her head."

"Oh no! It cannot be! I have promised Harry a son—I have failed him," said the queen. "No, no, no! He'll put me away! He'll put me away!"

"Now, now, dearie, calm yourself. You can get into your bed now, Nan Bullen. You are all fixed up. Love that yonder babe—for, though sons be fine for fathers, there's nothing better than a daughter for a mother," said Dame Brooke.

The queen rose slowly, awkwardly, and crawled into her bed. Lady Boleyn had bathed the child and anointed her with almond oil, then swaddled her tightly in the strips of cloth made for such purpose. She then lay the babe on the queen's chest, next to her heart. The queen held her daughter and patted her, cooing soft words. Soon, mother and daughter were asleep.

In a mere ten days after entering her confinement, the queen had given a relatively easy birth to the child all Christendom had been awaiting. To her complete disappointment, the baby was not the much longed-for prince, but a princess. The king visited her immediately after the baby had been cleaned and swaddled, blustering into the hitherto forbidden rooms, waking his sleeping family.

He had been so confident of a son that announcements and invitations to the christening had already been printed, and extra S's had to be added so that the documents were changed from "prince" to "princess". When he came to the queen's apartments, he immediately cleared the room of everyone but Madge, who sat on her pallet beside the queen's bed.

Madge could feel the energy in the room when he entered. She saw the queen's quick intake of breath as she awoke and heard the scurrying of feet as the king ordered everyone to leave.

"You may stay, Lady Margaret. Your tongue never wags, I'll warrant," said the king as he gazed not at Margaret, but at his wife.

"Sweetheart," he said kindly.

"Oh my love, I am so sorry," said the queen, tears coming in a rush.

The king sat down beside her and held both her hands.

"No matter, no matter. We are yet young. There will be more babes. A son next time." He gave her tender looks that Madge was happy to see—it seemed there was still love in his heart for his queen.

"We shall name her Elizabeth for my mother. And yours," said the king. At that moment, a small cry came from the nearby cradle. "Ah, she likes her name!" The king gently lifted his daughter and brought her to his burly chest. She cried a bit louder. He patted her, then touched the tuft of red hair on her head. "You are your father's daughter, sweetheart. Yes, you are!" he said. The baby cried even louder.

"If Your Grace will hand her to me, I shall feed her—I believe she is hungry," said Anne.

"Feed her? Woman, surely you know queens do not feed their young! Lady Margaret, go to the other ladies and find a suitable wet nurse," ordered the king. Madge got up immediately, smoothing her dress as she did so.

"But Your Grace, I am her mother—surely it is I who should give her nourishment?" said the queen.

"Madame, you will need to get her a brother as soon as you can. This, above all else, is your concern," said the king in some anger. "You promised me sons, a castle full of boys ready to carry on the Tudor dynasty. Your mission from God is to get them! If you die trying, you must give me a son!" The king's voice had risen as had his color. He turned to Madge. "Go, Lady Margaret! Go!"

Madge did not need to be told again. Off she ran, out of the innermost rooms to the outer chambers where the women gathered, playing cards, reading, stitching, and passing the time as best they could. She found Lady Bryan who went to fetch the wet nurse, for Lady Bryan had already made proper arrangements. She knew the king's mind in such matters as she had been in charge of the other princess years ago. Madge returned to the ladies' chambers and moved to an open window, a welcome relief, the air fresh and cool.

Fifteen

*M*adge enjoyed more and more freedom from the queen's presence as the weeks prior to Her Majesty's churching passed. The queen was busy with the princess, Elizabeth, and His Majesty, who visited them daily. Often, the queen sent Madge out on some pretended errand so that the family could enjoy one another without the eyes of the court upon them.

Madge sought out Cate and together they would walk in the gardens or take Shadow to the grazing fields nearby, though getting to those open places took half an hour or longer.

"How does Her Majesty?" Cate said as the two of them found a hidden spot in the garden.

"Happy—in love with her new babe and the king. She has never looked more comely and she has had a change in spirit, too. No longer ill-tempered but sweet and full of smiles. Of course,

she worries that she has disappointed His Majesty and she often says strange things—like the king will rid himself of her if
she does not produce a son. I try to soothe her but oft times, in
the lonely night, I hear her crying," said Madge, reaching to
scratch Shadow behind the ears.

"And the king?" asked Cate.

"His Majesty makes merry with the little princess. His eyes
are for the queen and no one else, though I have heard him sigh
and moan when the queen talks about the princess. His longing
for a son is not abated. What of you, Cate?" said Madge.

"If you ask of Lord Brandon, as your smile tells me you do,
he has proven himself, indeed, a scoundrel," said Cate.

"How so?" said Madge.

"Have you not heard? He has stolen his own son's plighted
wife and married her himself! And she not much more than a
child—twelve or thirteen, I'll warrant. They say his son is heart-
broken. Humph—it had not been five months since the king's
good sister died, yet off goes my lord Suffolk as if he were a
young buck. Humph," said Cate.

"I had not heard this news! Bad blood—those Brandon
men—bad blood!" said Madge.

"I am evermore glad I did not succumb to the duke's wishes.
Oh, he did try me, Maddie—more than once! But I held onto
my virtue. Take that as a lesson," said Cate.

"Good Cate, I never doubted your virtue—I can only hope
to follow," said Madge. "I begin to see that few leave court with
virtue intact—I intend to be one of them, if I must grow finger-
nails as long as spikes!"

In early October, a few days before the queen was to be churched,
Her Majesty invited several of the king's favorites, along with

His Majesty, to dine with her and her ladies in the outer rooms of her apartments. Madge was in charge of procuring music and selecting the dances for the occasion while Lady Jane Seymour and Lady Rochford, wife of George Boleyn, made the rooms beautiful with bouquets of colorful leaves and late-blooming flowers. Madge had met Lady Rochford only once and found her arrogant and aloof. It was said that she and her husband were often at odds. Madge could see why this might be so—her cousin, George, was full of life, loving to play at cards and to carouse the streets of London. But Jane Parker, his wife, had a dour expression and listless eyes. She and Mistress Seymour made a hapless pair—sad, gray turtledoves sitting fatly on the branch while the queen, a bright cardinal, twittered and chattered with great liveliness.

Madge discussed dances and songs with Master Smeaton. They had devised an order of song that would tell the story of the king and his lady love, something they hoped would please both king and queen.

"Your ideas are clever, Lady Margaret. I did not know you had such a head upon your pretty shoulders," said Master Smeaton.

"'Tis easy when I work with you, sir. Your own knowledge of music and the dance are considerable," said Madge. She smiled up at him and felt the warmth of his brown, brown eyes. "Tell me, sir—have you a mistress here at court?"

"Nay, I am the son of a sheepherder and only my talent keeps me here. I first came to the Royal Children's Choir as a small boy. Because I could sing and learned to play the instruments with great speed, the choirmaster recommended me to His Majesty and here I have been since," said Master Smeaton.

"Is life here to your liking then?" said Madge.

"Oh lady, there is no place on earth I would rather be. I love to sing for the king! I love the food and the pretty people, the rich tapestries, the gold plate as it glitters—all these things have I grown to cherish. The king himself has given me fine clothes and he gave me this," said Master Smeaton as he held up his hand to show a small garnet ring. He kissed the stone and looked lovingly at the king. "'Tis my most prized possession."

"I am glad you have found a home here, Mark. Many would not find such a welcome," said Madge.

"I have no property, no rank, no gold—nothing but the king's delight in my music. There is safety in that. I do not meddle in the intrigues of the court. I only wish to sing and please my king," said Smeaton.

As the chamber ladies made ready for the evening, the queen's apartments bustled with activity. Even Jane Seymour's pasty cheeks took on a peachy tone as she arranged and rearranged the table settings and centerpieces. Madge made certain the rushes were fresh and the center of the floor clear of tables so if the queen and king wished to dance, they would have room to do so. Finally, all was in readiness, and Their Royal Majesties entered from the queen's privy chamber.

Madge curtsied low and watched as silk slippers with golden embroidery passed on the floor in front of her. She noticed the king's feet were twice the size of his wife's. To her dismay, they stopped in front of her. She kept her lowly position.

"Dear cousin, arise," said the queen as she took Madge's hand to help her stand.

"Your Majesty is lovely this eve," stuttered Madge, aware of the king's presence just a few inches away.

"Aye, that she is, Mistress Madge. We shall have a new prince soon, God willing," laughed the king, his eyes never leaving his wife's face. His face was flushed with wine and desire. Madge felt her own heart beat faster. He filled her with fear and awe.

"God willing, my love—yet you must be patient a little longer! I am still unchurched!" said the queen, a strange smile on her lips.

"Vixen," whispered the king and Anne turned to him, grabbed his meaty hand, and kissed it, giving it a lick with the tip of her tongue as she lowered her great eyes, then raised them to his. Madge could hear the intake of his breath.

The royal couple continued down the row of maids and groomsmen, greeting each warmly. At the very end of the line, closest to the door, Madge heard the queen welcome Master Arthur Brandon. Madge could not believe her ears—she could not imagine how Sir Churlish could have wormed his way into this private affair. Before she could ponder on it, however, she felt a rough hand on her elbow, guiding her to the corner of the room where few people were congregating.

"Milady Margaret, your hair is a shimmering halo—the modest covering of an angel. Will you join me in a game of trump?" Sir Henry Norris held onto her arm so firmly she had no choice but to accompany him. He reeked of something sour, yet sweet, a heavy scent that almost made Madge ill. She stopped in front of a small gaming table and turned away from him, looking at the ladies and gentlemen milling around the chambers. Master Smeaton was tuning his lute while servants brought in sweetmeats to tempt the appetite.

"I play not well, milord. Another would give you better sport," said Madge, still not looking at him.

"Nay, nay, lass—you will do quite nicely. Come. Sit," he said as he pulled out her chair and almost shoved her into it.

Madge tried to sit gracefully but the force of his arm caused her to teeter for a moment. Finally, the chair settled firmly on the floor. Madge watched as Sir Norris took the seat opposite from her and began to shuffle the large cards.

"You will note, mistress, I am quite adept with the cards. You should be on your guard," he said, his thin lips pressed in a smile.

"I am always on my guard with you, sire. And with every man at court," said Madge, trying to keep her voice pleasant, though this man, above all save the king, made her uneasy.

"Ah, you cousins—such *virtuous* women," said Norris. His voice oiled its way into her ears and she felt somehow violated.

"My queen instructs all her ladies to have a care of their chastity, for to lose such is to add insult to Her Majesty, who wishes to have good ladies at her court," said Madge, looking at the cards in her hand. She could hear the strumming of the lute and she knew Master Smeaton would begin to sing anon.

The room grew quiet, all in readiness for the music. No one spoke except Sir Norris, who continued, despite evil looks from the others.

"Virtue is overvalued, mistress. If you would be my lady, and I had your virtue, I would make you my own—shower you with jewels and other meaty tidbits," he whispered loudly. At this, Madge rose abruptly and joined Lady Rochford and Lady Seymour on the outer edges of the group surrounding Master Smeaton. Soon, his strong sweet voice took her away from the castle, back, back to the open fields of the north country. She closed her eyes. Her breathing loosened and she could feel the tightness around her throat release a little. When the song was finished, Madge opened her eyes.

"Would that my voice could carry you such a ways, mistress," said Sir Norris in her ear. His hands encircled her waist and pulled her back against him. She could smell wine on his breath and noticed both Lady Rochford and Lady Seymour had moved away from her, staring as Sir Norris continued to caress her. Madge felt the blood rise to her cheeks. She looked to the queen, who was also staring at her, one lovely eyebrow raised. The king, too, watched as Sir Norris held her tightly from behind.

Madge could not think of how to escape him. To wrench herself free would be unseemly, disrupting the graceful manners of the court. Yet, by forcing himself on her in so public a place, Sir Norris had already broken the etiquette of courtly love. Oh, she did not want to shame the queen. Yet, she was taking disgrace upon her own person by allowing such behavior. All the court would think Sir Norris was her lover. She shuddered.

Suddenly, Master Smeaton struck up a lively dance, not the one they had planned but something completely unfamiliar. At that, Master Brandon appeared in front of her and held out his hand.

"Lady Margaret, if I may have this dance?" He simply stood, waiting.

"Delighted, Master Brandon," Madge said, "though I do not recognize the tune." Master Smeaton played handily, the lute strings vibrating quickly, the notes plucked faster than the usual court dances.

"Oh, 'tis the Dompe, mistress—a dance of the yeomen! Come, I'll teach you," he said, taking her hand and leading her away from Sir Norris. He wrapped his arm around her waist and they began a lively jig, round and round, her long curls whipping in circles as Master Brandon moved faster and faster to keep up with the music. Madge never knew she could fly so quickly, her feet barely touching the floor and Arthur's strong right arm holding her steady as they whirled around the chambers. Soon, other ladies and gentlemen whirred with them and all was flash of color and bright movement. Master Smeaton kept playing faster and faster until Madge was breathless. She realized as they came to a quick stop that Arthur had guided them to a private space behind an arras that hung near the outer entrance to the queen's quarters. He pulled her by the hand and she ducked into the alcove, glad of the open window.

"You may not know the Dompe, mistress, but your legs most certainly do. You are light as air on my arm," said Master Brandon.

"The queen has had many weeks to teach me a few things—the dances of France, some music, skill with my needle," said Madge, looking out the window onto the torches lining the walkways below. "Aye, 'tis a warm night for such a time of year."

"Mayhap you are warm from the dance—or Sir Norris's love-making," said Master Brandon.

"Just when I believe you are my friend, you say such impudent things. I will ever be cold to Sir Norris; he chills my blood whenever I am near him," Madge said.

"No one will believe you after tonight, dear Lady Margaret. He was much too familiar with your person," said Master Brandon.

Madge looked into his eyes and they held no laughter. He meant his words.

"Think you so? I did not know what to do when he fondled me as though I were a mere cur. I did not wish to upset the queen's entertainments with protest. I could do nothing but stand and stew, smelling his foul breath and feeling his hands around my waist," said Madge, her cheeks growing even hotter as she remembered her humiliation.

"Milady, I know you have not been long at court and you are young—innocent. But you must learn how to handle men such as Sir Norris. You must forget what you know of manners and give him a rebuff he cannot mistake. I won't always be able to rescue you, Margaret," said Master Brandon, standing closer to her than was necessary, even in such cramped space.

"Rescue me? Is *that* what you did? Ha! I thought you wanted to dance with me—Master Brandon, I have no need of such rescuing from you. How did you even get into the queen's apartments? I know you were not on the list of guests," said Madge, looking away from him, again casting her gaze to the night sky.

"My father is the king's boon companion. But my father is still feasting with his bride and did not wish to come to court during his honeymoon. He sent me in his stead. Even a son born on the wrong side of the bed can represent the family well enough, I'll warrant," said Brandon. "Now, will you walk with me a while in the gardens below? The night air will bring on good humors for us, I'll wager." Master Brandon took her hand and kissed it tenderly, unlike the way Sir Norris touched her. Madge felt something give in her chest. She smiled at him. Surprising herself, she said, "Arthur, I would love to take some of this sweet night air—but we mustn't be gone from the queen for long—she will, perhaps, have need of me."

He poked his head from under the tapestry, motioned for the guard to open the outer door, and ushered Madge into the corridor, their steps tapping lightly on the stone as they rushed into the gardens below.

Sixteen

A few days after the queen was churched, Madge found herself alone with Her Majesty for the first time since Arthur and Madge had walked in the garden. How often she had thought of that night, the way the stars blinked in the sky, the moon's pale light bathing everything in a sort of fairy shimmer. Suddenly, a turn around the garden with Arthur seemed magical. He talked of court, matters abroad, his father and new "mother." He told her how to escape men like Sir Henry Norris and before they returned to the queen's apartments, he kissed her full on the lips, not in fun as he had at the May Day. No, this kiss was gentle but firm. He kissed her as if she were his alone.

"Lady Margaret, I would speak with you," said the queen as Madge unpinned her hair, readying her for bed and another visit from His Majesty.

"Yes, Majesty?" said Madge, alarmed by the cool tone of the queen's voice.

"My husband, the king, made remark upon your obvious fondness for Sir Henry Norris the other eve. Sir Norris has asked for your hand and the king has sent a message to your father, Sir John. He expects a reply on the morrow. I have no doubt but the response will be favorable to the king's wishes," said Anne.

Madge could not hide her dismay.

"Tut, tut. I know this is not what you want, dear cousin. Norris is a scoundrel of the first sort, but he is the king's own man, Gentleman of the Stool. My dear Harry trusts him and believes he will make a good match for you. He has a good income from his lands. Don't look so glum, child. It is pointless to pout—the king has declared for it, so you might as well look on the good side," said the queen as she removed her stomacher.

"But Your Grace, I like him not. He is . . . he is . . . oily as goose livers!" said Madge.

The queen laughed her husky laugh, stepping out of her farthingale and petticote to put on the black silk gown the king had given her for a wedding present. The dark fabric brought out her eyes and enhanced her deep brown hair. Madge laughed, too, for who could resist a beautiful queen such as Anne, standing in her bare feet in a loose shift of silk, awaiting a visit from her king.

"Well you know, dear cousin, that the women of our blood know how to keep a man waiting and wanting! So, do not fear. Make Sir Norris woo you, accept his tokens of love and esteem, flatter him with one of your innocent smiles once in a while. You may be able to outlast him. Who knows what the future may bring?" said the queen as she waited for Madge to brush her hair until it shone.

"Wise words, milady," murmured Madge as she slowly

counted the one hundred strokes. She wondered if she should confess her growing fondness for Master Brandon. Suffolk's bastard would hardly be a fine enough match for the queen's cousin; at least, so Madge believed her uncle would say. Thomas Boleyn cared for nothing but his fat purses growing ever fatter.

"Why so quiet, Lady Margaret? Is my hair so full of fascination?" said the queen, a teasing smile on her lips.

"I beg Your Grace's pardon—I . . . I was thinking," said Madge.

"About a secret love perhaps?" said the queen.

"No! No, Majesty—I have no such secret love. I was remembering the story you told me once—about love and how it rarely ends well. Was that your story, Majesty?" said Madge.

"That shall be my secret, dear coz. For now, I am happy with my king and hope this night to get him a son! So, off with you, girl!" said the queen as the guards marched down the chamber, escorting the king to the queen's apartments.

"And Lady Margaret, walk all you will with Master Brandon. Just remember, in my court, virtue is demanded—keep him at bay along with Norris!" said the queen, again smiling.

Though the sky was deep blue with nary a cloud, the air nipped at Madge and Cate as they hurried from the chapel to the Great Hall. The weeks had been growing colder through late October, though not so cold as to keep Madge inside.

"I cannot marry Sir Norris, Cate. I will not!" said Madge. "He is a smelly cur and I will not have him!" Madge hurried down the stone corridor with Cate barely able to keep up.

"Maddie-girl—slow down! You'll give me apoplexy. And keep a quiet tone—'tis All Saints' Day and many are remembering those who have gone beyond us to the heavenly court. Whew! I am no longer young, child—here, come in here and let us sit a moment—you can tell me all about it," said Cate, lifting her skirts so she could settle onto a stone bench by a window in a niche of the hallway. A fine tapestry covered the bench, keeping the cold from her.

"I will not sit down! I must needs run and run until I cannot bear to run any longer!" said Madge as she flung a velvet-covered box on the ground, unlocking the contents. A single pearl on a golden chain rolled across the flagstones and stopped at Cate's foot.

"Aye, what is this? A love token! From Norris?" said Cate.

"Who else? Since my father gave his permission for us to wed, I have had three such gifts, each richer than the last. He follows me everywhere—he sits across from me when I sup and I cannot enter the gardens without him showing himself, eager to shield me from the cold, he says! Ha!" Madge knelt and put her head into Cate's lap.

"There, there, Maddie-girl. You are barely sixteen—the queen will not forsake you. She will help you keep the marriage at bay, at least while she can," said Cate.

"She rarely calls for me these days—mayhap she forgets my plight. She and the king and the princess Elizabeth spend hours together. And I am free to do as I please, so long as I can avoid Sir Norris," said Madge.

Cate and Madge fell quiet as they heard approaching footsteps.

"What-ho! Who are these lovelies hiding in the corner? I should have known—my little Mouse. How now, cousin?" blustered George, his face flushed with wine, though the day was young. His fingers were burdened with rings of all sorts—rubies, sapphires, emeralds—and about his neck were gold chains. His sleeves were slashed showing cloth of gold beneath the blue velvet and Madge had never seen him look so fine.

"Viscount Rochford," said both ladies, curtsying low.

"Arise, lady—you, too, Mistress Cate. Now, Lady Margaret, let me see you—I am so often away from court on the king's business I cannot keep up with your beauty. You look older, girl. I'll warrant you have found the court to your liking, eh?" he said as he studied her carefully.

"The court is the most exciting, commodious, beautiful place on earth," said Madge. She wanted George to know she was grateful to have been chosen to serve the queen.

"Indeed, indeed. I'll warrant much is happening," said George with a leering grin.

"How can we help Your Grace?" said Cate.

"More, ladies, how can I help you?" said George. He kept smiling at Madge. "I believe I can help you most by giving you a few juicy tidbits of gossip, Mistress Mouse. Hmmm. Where shall I begin?" He plopped down where Cate had been sitting and pulled Madge down next to him.

"I don't have time for idle gossip, sir. I must be to the queen's apartments as I still have shirts to sew for the orphans and widows," said Madge with as much haughtiness as she could muster.

"Tsk, tsk, my proper little Mouse. You will like this news. My sister won't mind if you miss a few stitches at her sewing party," said George, putting his arm around her shoulders, scooting closer to her while patting the vacant spot on the other side, indicating a seat for Cate. For a moment, Cate remained standing, then relented and took her place next to George.

"Won't I be the envy of the court—one rooster surrounded by two plucky hens," he said.

"If you have news, cousin, I do wish you would let it spill from your lips," said Madge, laughing. Suddenly, George didn't seem so frightening, all of them crowded on the bench. He seemed like a schoolboy intent on nothing but mischief.

"Ah, that is what I like to see—a woman full of mirth and happiness! But, to my news! Your dear friend, Wyatt, is returning to court—on his way even now!" said George.

"Happy tidings, indeed!" said Margaret, thinking of all they had discussed. Wyatt had encouraged her to write her own verse and she had shown him her feeble attempts, which he had praised overmuch, she thought.

"That is not all, dear cousin. I understand a certain young lovely is to marry the king's own man, Sir Henry Norris," said George, smiling.

"How I wish that *were* idle gossip," said Madge, her face showing her disdain.

"Maddie, watch your tongue," said Cate. Madge saw Cate's warning look.

"What I mean, Lord Rochford, is that I have no desire for marriage yet—I am still quite young. Sir Norris is kind to offer me his name, but I am not yet eager to change my own," said Madge.

"Yes, yes. Dear cousin, do you think you are the only one who has tested Norris's character and found it shallow and weak? I was sorry to hear of the match and broached it with Anne but she cannot prevail against the king until she bears his son. I will help you keep him at arm's length if I can," said George.

"For that, cousin, I shall always be your friend," said Madge with a smile. "I know you understand what it is to be unevenly yoked."

"Aye. Only too well. But, we do as we are ordered, eh my

lovely?" he said as he chucked her under the chin. He arose abruptly and bowed to both ladies.

"I must be off. I understand I have other relatives in unhappy states—my dear sister, Mary, so recently widowed, is back at court and I need to pay my respects. Adieu, ladies," he said.

"Maddie-girl, you must watch your tongue. Even with George, you cannot tell your heart. Keep your feelings close. Learn to dissemble as does every other person in this palace of liars," said Cate, taking hold of Madge's hand and rubbing it tenderly.

"But George seemed so like a boy sitting here beside us! I felt he would understand since his own wife is distasteful to him. I could see his compassion for me in his eyes," said Madge. Madge considered what Cate had said and linked her arm in her nurse's. "As always, you are wise, Cate. I shall heed your words."

"Not that Lord Rochford might not have such tender feelings—but he is a Boleyn to the core and would stab his own mother if it might advance his position. Let us walk a while and speak of happier things. I know you are filled with joy to think of Wyatt's return," said Cate as the two women walked toward the herb garden. Madge could smell the basil and sage as her skirts brushed against the bushes. The lavender with its stiff brushy stems caught at her hem, too, and she inhaled the fresh fragrance.

"Nothing could make me so glad! Except a romp in the fields with Shadow. Shall we rescue her from your room and escape these cold palace walls?" said Madge.

Seventeen

As Christmas drew nearer, the court grew. People from every station made their way to London to see the pageantry and partake of the food and wine King Henry provided. Gifts had to be given to the royal couple and gifts received. The excitement of Christmas Eve was made greater in that on that special night, the Advent fast was over and revelry could begin in earnest. Yet, at present, such revelry was well over a fortnight away. The queen had sent for Madge after supping privately with the king in her apartments.

"Lady Margaret, would you be so kind as to rub my shoulders as you did when I was filled with the princess Elizabeth?" said the queen late one evening after the king and his musicians had left.

"Yes, Your Grace," said Madge as she sat on the queen's enormous bed and began to massage her thin shoulders. She could feel the tenseness of muscles, bunched like knobby grapes along the queen's spine. Suddenly, she heard the queen emit a sob and saw tears running down Anne's cheeks.

"Your Grace, did I hurt you? What is the matter?" said Madge.

"No, no, dear cousin. I am bereft. It has been almost a fortnight since the king had the princess Elizabeth off to Hatfield with Lady Bryan. My arms ache for her . . . I fear I shall not see her again," said the queen with new tears flowing.

"Majesty, surely you will see her—Hatfield in Hertfordshire is not so very far. And I know Lady Bryan is a good and kind nurse—she cared for the princess—I mean, the lady Mary, did she not?" said Madge.

"Yes, yes. But my heart is breaking for Elizabeth. She is mine! She is mine!" said the queen.

"I cannot imagine the pain you must feel, Majesty. And I am very sorry you must bear it. But think of how you might see the princess as often as you like—you have your own hobbies and your own saddle—could you not ride to Hatfield when you so pleased? You *are* the queen, after all," said Madge, still kneading the queen's shoulders.

For a moment, all was quiet.

"You are right, Margaret. I *am* the queen," said Anne. Madge noticed the flickering tapers and how lovely they looked as they made shadows on the tapestries that hung on the walls. The soft light cast the queen in a golden glow and, though her face was puffy with crying, Madge thought she looked as beautiful as ever.

"Your Grace, I hope you do not show your tears to His Majesty. 'Tis close to Christmas and I have heard it said that His Grace is always merry at that time. It would not do for you to be sad in his presence," said Madge with hesitation.

Without warning, the queen began to laugh, that high-pitched laugh that seemed so unlike her.

"Dear coz, oh dear coz! You telling me how to manage the king! It is rich—it is too rich!" said the queen, now laughing to tears.

"I . . . I hope I have not offended Your Grace," said Madge, surprised at the quick change of mood.

"No, no. I am merely surprised! You look so innocent but now you have learned how we must dissemble to live—liars, we are liars all. Wyatt has it right in his poem—enough of this, enough. Bring me my bowl and cloth so I may wash away these tears and put on the face of joy," said the queen.

"Come, Cate, the feast is almost upon us—we do not wish to be late! Hurry woman!" said Madge as she pulled Cate by the hand toward the Great Hall where the Christmas dinner was to be served. Madge could not have imagined all the guests who were squeezing into the hall, nor could she have guessed so many could have fit. And all dressed in their finest clothes. Madge wore a new gown the queen had passed along to her—green silk with tiny pearls sewn across the bodice. There was a French hood to match and the rich color set off Madge's green eyes.

"You shall cause my heart to burst its cage, Maddie. Slow down!" panted Cate.

"I am starving! I don't want to miss the delicacies!" said Madge.

"Ah, milady, have no fear—I have vittles enough for two in the king's apartments," said a familiar voice.

"Sir Norris," said Madge as she curtsied slightly.

"I have not seen you for such a long time, my lovely. Where

have you been hiding?" he said, his arm encircling her waist and pulling her to him.

"Sir, you saw me two days ago in chapel. I remember well how you pinched my arm when I withdrew from your presence to follow Her Majesty to her chambers," said Madge.

"It was merely a love touch—you are my betrothed after all. Come, let us find a seat together as our sovereigns have no need of us this night," he said. "Madame, you may find a seat elsewhere—I will take charge of Lady Margaret."

"Yes, sire, as you wish," said Cate. Madge watched as Cate threaded her way to the other side of the room, casting a glance back to the couple as she walked farther and farther away. Madge felt her appetite diminish as Sir Norris motioned for her to sit down at a corner table crowded with people she did not know. He crammed himself tightly beside her and put his arm around her shoulders.

"Now, my pretty girl, I have you to myself. For once," he said. Just then, a servant brought a large platter containing the traditional boar's head, trimmed with bay and rosemary. Behind him was another, toting an enormous bread basket. Both placed their burdens on the table. At that moment, arms reached out from everywhere and hands stabbed at the meat and grabbed chunks of bread. Madge wriggled out of Norris's grip and took a hunk of meat.

"Sir Norris, could you cut this for me?" she asked and smiled up at him.

"It would be my honor to do you any service, milady," he said with a leer. He took his knife and stabbed a small portion of meat, then placed it on her trencher.

Then, she began to eat in earnest, not that her appetite had returned but by eating, she would not be forced to converse with Norris. After the pork, servants brought in roasted swan and seethed brawn. The spicy smell of the meats mixed with the holly and ivy scent of the decked hall. In the torchlight, everything glittered.

"My lady eats her fill—I like a wench who is not ashamed of her appetites," said Norris. He had not eaten a mouthful but watched Madge, his small eyes gobbling up everything about her.

"Our fast was broken only yesterday, Sir Norris. Are you not hungry?" Madge said, scanning the room for Wyatt, hoping to see him fresh from Paris.

"Your beauty satisfies all my hunger, mistress. I can only hope one day to be as close to your lips as that tidbit of meat— for they would be sweeter to me than any marmalade from the king's own confectionary," said Norris. He rested his hand upon her knee, slowly idling his way toward her thigh, pulling the satin of her farthingale up along with his fingers.

"Unhand me, kind sir," said Madge, her voice icy and her eyes directly on his. The look she gave him could not be mistaken.

"You can forestall me, lady, for now. But when we are wed, I will have my way," said Norris, taking his knife and stabbing a great slab of pork onto his trencher. The tone of his voice chilled Madge. She ate silently.

Before the serving of the tarts and subtleties, the Lord of Misrule marched into the Great Hall, musicians and dancers following him, all dressed in fanciful costumes. Lions for the king, leopards and falcons for the queen, fearful dragons and colorful birds all processed in, coming to rest at the king's table. Madge saw one of the royal favorites, Master Smeaton, playing his lute and singing a carol with a loud, happy voice as he gazed at the royal couple seated on the dais. The king's fool, Will Somers, leapt upon the king's table wearing a great gold crown twice his size. Elbowing the king to leave his throne, the fool plopped down on Henry's lap and pretended to eat the royal food. Madge laughed at the sight, as did Their Majesties. Soon, a mummery began and the whole court guffawed at the antics of the fool and the Lord of Misrule.

As the servers poured more mulled wine, the Lord of Misrule matched dancers—first, he paired the king with one of the serving wenches and the queen with the fool; then, as the music started, he continued picking and choosing partners. Madge tried to hide her face, but the Lord of Misrule seemed determined to find her out. He took her by the hand and grandly presented her to a lion whose mouth was filled with sharp-looking teeth. Though she knew better, she was almost afraid of the beast.

The lion bowed gracefully and placed its paw upon her waist to lift her high in the air, as was the custom for the galliard. Setting her back down, he jumped higher than any of the other dancers. She then curtsied and they began to leap together. He twirled her around and around. The lion did not speak, nor did Madge. From the corner of her eye, she caught sight of Cate dancing with Lord Howard, duke of Norfolk, her uncle. Cate looked terrified but the duke seemed amused.

The music stopped and once again the Lord of Misrule started creating mayhem. Madge curtsied again to the lion and started to return to her table. The lion's paw caught her hand.

"Mistress Shelton, thank you for the honor of your company," said a familiar voice.

"Arthur? Can it be you behind this great mane?" Madge said.

"'Tis I, milady. And I will never tell you how much silver I had to pay the Lord of Misrule to lead you to me," he said. "I must say, it was worth every sovereign."

Madge said nothing.

"Come with me into the garden—I have a surprise for you," said Arthur.

"To do so would be unseemly, Master Brandon. Have you not heard? I am betrothed to Sir Norris," said Madge, her tone colder than she had intended.

"I have no will to dishonor you, milady. But I think you will be happily surprised if you would but follow me. We shall be gone but a moment. No one will miss us, I'll warrant," he said.

"Doth this beast upset you, dearest Lady Margaret?" said Sir Norris, who had somehow found his way to them, weaving through the crowd of dancers leaping and frolicking in the hall. He wrapped one arm around Madge's waist, as had become his habit.

"'Tis a tame lion, sir—only my good cousin, Lord Rochford. He has an early gift for me in the garden and we were just heading outside," said Madge. The lion bowed slightly but said nothing.

"I hope you will pardon my intrusion, Lord Rochford. I have no desire to spoil your sport. Would you like me to accompany you, dear Lady Margaret?" said Norris.

Madge gave him her sweetest smile, patted the arm around her, and disengaged herself.

"No, dear Norris. George and I have much to discuss. I will see you anon," Madge said.

"As you wish, milady," said Norris, his voice full of acquiescence and honor for Lord Rochford.

The lion took Madge by the hand and led her quickly outside.

"Well done, milady. You are, indeed, growing accustomed to life at court. The lie came as easily from your lips as if it were the truth," said the lion.

"My aversion to my betrothed teaches me all manner of

subtlety. I do what I must," said Madge, finding it easy to con-
fide in the furry beast at her side. "Where is my surprise?"

"Here, dear Lady Margaret," said a low voice to her right.

"Thomas? Could it be?" she said, still holding the lion's paw
and hesitating.

"It is I, milady, come back from Paris and waiting to kiss
you," said the man.

Madge ran to him, hugged him, and kissed both his cheeks.
He stepped into the light of the torches and she could see he
was thinner and looked worn from his journey.

"When have you come? Where did you go? What have you
seen? Who have you met?" she asked.

"Ah, so many questions! I shall answer all of them in time,
dear lady. Shall we sit for a moment?" he said and offered her
his cloak for her shoulders. She wrapped up in the luxurious
velvet and began to warm herself. She sat on the bench and
motioned Thomas and Arthur to join her.

"I must away, Lady Margaret. Another mumming will begin soon for which I am to play a part. Happy Christmas!" said
the lion as he bowed to her and kissed her hand. She could feel
his lips warm and moist against her fingers.

"Thank you, Arthur," she said. She was almost sorry to
watch his furry mane disappear back into the castle.

"So, dear Thomas, why such secrecy? Why meet me out here
when surely your return will make the king and queen even
merrier this happy season?" said Madge.

"I wanted to see you first, dearest Madge. I wanted to hear
how you fare, and what news you hold," said Thomas.

"You see I fare well. Court life agrees with me thus far. Except for one horrid event," said Madge.

"I have heard it already, lovely lady. That scoundrel Norris has got himself betrothed to you—the cur! Is there nothing to be done?" said Wyatt.

"The queen cautions me to keep him waiting. When she is again with child and brings the king his long-awaited son, she will ask His Majesty to release me from my troth. Until then, I must endure Sir Norris and his slimy hands," said Madge.

"He is notorious for such—I have heard it said that he forces his way with any kitchen wench that claims his fancy. Though he dare nothing of that kind with the queen's cousin, I'll warrant," said Wyatt.

"What of you, Sir Thomas? Tell me all," said Madge.

"I have written many a verse whilst in France and have read much, especially the evangelism books of which our queen is so fond. I am proud that England has shaken off the shackles of the pope and all the bishops, the foul priests and carnal cardinals! Our Henry and Anne have shown the world the corruption of the old religion and now must lead us into the ways of the new. Shall I show you some of my verse?" Wyatt said.

"Nothing will please me more. And I shall show you some of mine so you will not think me idle in your absence," said Madge. "Shall we meet after matins?"

"I shall be here, dear friend. And now, I will make my way to Their Majesties. I have a token of a poem for their pleasure. Adieu, dear Margaret," said Wyatt.

The twelve days of Christmas passed in revelry and pleasure, yet the birth of the Savior was in no way overlooked. Daily masses were said with all in attendance, alms and shirts were distributed to the poor, with special attention paid to women with small children who were in distress. Queen Anne herself

saw to the needs of the poor and with her own hands gave gen-
erously. Madge had grown to admire the way the queen prac-
ticed the Lord's charity among her lesser brethren. When the
queen went among her people, though they did not love her as
they had Queen Catherine, she was ever kind to them.

"Oh, what a lovely little girl you have, madame! What is her
name?" said the queen as she held a dirty street urchin by the
hand.

"Catherine, Your Grace. After the former queen," said a
woman whose clothes were tattered and covered in filth.

The queen ignored the slight and Madge watched as she
took a small bag of gold coins from her girdle and handed it to
the woman.

"Buy food and warmth for your child, mother. Keep her safe
and yourself as well," said the queen with a smile.

On New Year's Day, gifts were exchanged. Madge and Cate
had embroidered a delicate cap for the queen with a matching
one for Elizabeth. The queen was well pleased with the gift
and, in turn, handed Madge a new dress and a strand of pearls.
Her Majesty gave Cate a set of cards for the many hours she
spent alone. The king gave each a silver goblet with the Shelton coat of arms on Madge's cup while Cate's was plain. Madge
and Cate gave the king a silken shirt, roses stitched in silver
and gold thread. He was greatly pleased.

Finally, the queen presented Henry with a magnificent table
fountain of gold, which held three naked women from whose
breasts issued water. Studded with rubies, diamonds, and pearls,
the fountain was a symbol of fertility. Nothing pleased the king
more and he rewarded his wife with several caches of jewels as
well as much gold plate. As he led her onto the floor for the last
dance of the evening, Madge wished she could find a man to
look at her in such an adoring way.

"Lady Margaret, may I have this dance?" said a man near her. She turned to see Arthur dressed in his finest clothes. His brown eyes seemed full of laughter, as if he found her endlessly amusing. Somehow, this infuriated her.

"I care not to dance, sir. I . . . I was going to retire anon," she said until she saw Sir Norris approaching her. "But, one more dance will not harm me, to be sure."

Arthur took her hand and smiled.

"You will even dance with the likes of me to avoid your intended, Margaret. I am not at all flattered," he said.

"Sometimes I feel as if you are laughing at me. It brings on my fury," she said.

"I do not laugh, milady. Indeed, where you are concerned, I am most serious. What think you of the queen's gift to His Majesty?" said Arthur.

"It is not like anything I have set my eyes upon. Master Holbein designed it, I am sure," said Madge.

"Yes—his hand is on it. Do you sift out its meaning?" said Arthur.

"Of course. The ladies in the fountain represent the king's beneficence. His bounty," said Madge.

"Mistress Margaret, surely even you are not that innocent! The queen is with child again! The women are flowing with milk—the only time this can happen is after the birth of a babe. Her Majesty has just announced to the court and the king that she is once again carrying the royal issue," said Arthur.

The queen had said nothing of this matter to her. But then, why should she? Of late, Madge had been sent out of the queen's bedchamber and had slept with the other attendants. Only the queen and, upon occasion, the princess Elizabeth slept in the bedchamber. And Her Majesty had complained of the peacocks screeching about in the gardens, so the king had instructed

Sir Norris to house them at his manor some five miles away. There had been the tears shed for Elizabeth and then tears for other events. It all made sense—the queen was again with child.

"Wonderful, wonderful news!" said Madge. She could not help but think of ridding herself of Sir Norris.

In her enthusiasm, she clung to Arthur so tightly that he swept her away from the other dancers into a corner. There, he kissed her once again. This time, she kissed him back with a fervor that surprised her. Who knew what the new year would bring?

II

1534

Vertuous Demeanor and Godly Conversation

QUEEN ANNE'S INSTRUCTIONS TO HER LADIES

Eighteen

T hough the new year started off well enough for the king and his queen, old troubles soon reared up like angry stallions. The dowager princess Catherine wrote her nephew, Charles V, the emperor, of her continuing trials and suggested he take whatever action he deemed necessary to help her. If this meant launching an attack against the king, so be it. Her daughter, the lady Mary, was settled at Hatfield with the princess Elizabeth, yet failed to acknowledge her half-sister's place and refused to give up her own title as princess. That his own child refused to obey him infuriated the king. That his subjects also refused to accept his will in the matter of his marriage and his church, raised his ire to the boiling point. He forced several more closings of monasteries, though the queen wanted them to be reformed rather than confiscated as royal property. Madge watched as the tensions of the court made their way to the queen's own heart. Once again, Madge was required to serve the queen as her intimate lady of the bed-chamber.

"Majesty, how long until we depart for Eltham? Shall I pack your green gown? Will the yellow silk be needed as well?" said Madge as she took out the dresses and laid them on the queen's large bed to sprinkle them with rosewater and lavender.

"The king hath told me 'twould be five days hence. Yes, take the yellow—it has a loose skirt which will suit me well as time goes on. Lady Margaret, know you that Master Brandon will accompany us?" said the queen.

Madge felt the blood rush to her cheeks as she sorted through the silks and satins, checking them for stains and odors.

"No, Your Grace," said Madge.

"I asked for him especially as I needed a strong man to han-dle my horses and Sir Carew advised me he could use the help. Sir Nicholas is not young, as you know, though he still serves His Majesty well as Master of the Horse," said the queen.

Madge said nothing, though she could not keep her heart from pounding to think Arthur would be going with them to Eltham, and then on to Easthampstead Park in Windsor For-est.

"Have you nothing to say of this?" said the queen.

"I am sure Master Brandon will be a fine choice, madame," said Madge, keeping her face turned from the queen, pretend-ing to study of the queen's wardrobe.

"Come, come, Mistress Margaret. I expected a better thanks than this!" said the Queen.

"Thanks, Your Grace?" said Madge.

"Hmm. Mayhap I have misjudged. Would Sir Wyatt have suited you better?" said the queen.

"Whatever suits Your Grace suits me, Majesty," said Madge, "though I do count Thomas Wyatt as a dear friend."

"Yes, as do I. Come here, Lady Margaret. Look at me. I have wagered much on my wisdom, my woman's wisdom, and thus far, such inklings as I have had have not failed me. I cannot believe I have so misconstrued what is before my very eyes. Do you not love Master Brandon?" said the queen.

Madge had not thought of love, though her heartbeat quickened each time she glimpsed Arthur and she could feel her cheeks begin to burn when he was near. She had returned his kisses at their last meeting and had felt sad yet relieved to be joining the queen on the modest Progress for which they were now preparing. The Progress had been the queen's idea and the princess Elizabeth was to meet them in Eltham. The queen intended to take her daughter along for the rest of the journey, then bring her back to London for a long stay. Given her condition, the king had agreed.

"I . . . I do not know, Majesty," said Madge.

"Have you not kissed him? Nor he you?" said the queen.

"Well . . . yes. We have kissed—once on May Day, once in your apartments before you were churched, and then again at the New Year," Madge said. She had not told anyone about Master Brandon, not even Cate.

"Your Majesty, how did you know about Master Brandon? We have not been indiscreet as I have taken your instructions to my very heart. My virtue has not been broached, I swear by the Blood of the Savior," said Madge.

"Please, Lady Margaret, make no such pledges to me. I know because I have a woman's heart. I see how your eyes brighten when they light upon Master Brandon. And how your cheeks grow rosy. I know much of love, lady. Though I am now married, 'twas not always so. But have a care. If I have discovered your secret, there are others who may know it as well. Cromwell has spies everywhere, though I cannot imagine that he would find your little love affair of interest. But believe me, if he roots out your case, he may find a use for it. I trust him not. The king himself would be angered if he knew you and Master Brandon were stealing away together like thieves in the night—His Majesty would control the lives of all his subjects and you know what happens when he is not obeyed," said the queen as she looked through her wardrobe closet, selecting other gowns she would take on Progress.

"We shall take more care, Your Grace. Are you not going to chastise me about loving another though I am betrothed to Sir Norris?" Madge asked.

"Tut, tut. I hope in a few months to relieve you of that promise. Of course, Master Brandon will not be a suitable husband. You are, after all, my own blood and will need a superior person to wed. But surely we can find one more to your liking than Norris. In the meantime, enjoy your Arthur as well as you can. I do caution you to guard your virtue for it is a rare jewel. Be that gem guaranteed, I will make you a fine match indeed. It was I who placed our cousin, Mary Howard, with Henry Fitzroy, the king's own son. I can do almost as well for you, dear cousin," said the queen.

"Your heart is kind, Your Grace. I shall follow your wise words," said Madge.

"How far now, Master Brandon?" said Madge as she rode beside him. He looked handsome wearing the king's livery. They rode splendid horses and were placed close behind the queen's litter, which was used at the king's insistence. He was not happy with this small Progress taken in the dead of winter. There would be no hunting for him and the weather was disagreeable. Madge had heard him plead with the queen to return to Hampton Court, but Her Majesty was determined to see Elizabeth and bring her back to London. Madge could see that His Majesty wanted to please the queen, but also feared for the queen's health and that of the new babe.

"We should arrive in time to sup, I'll wager. This cold brings out the roses in your cheeks, milady. Would that I could warm you," he said. She smiled at him.

"Sir, you do warm me. You have made this cold and cloudy journey most pleasant," she said. She looked at the countryside, which seemed wild and dismal. The trees were covered with a thin film of snow and the sky was the color of pewter. Madge wondered what dangers might be hiding in the wood. She had heard of bandits and madmen haunting the forest.

"Think you, Arthur, we be safe traveling at such a time of year?" she said.

"Milady, I would die to preserve you. You must know that," he said.

"I would prefer you live, sir," she said.

"Do you not see all the king's men, armed with swords and spears? Who would dare attack His Majesty? You fret for nothing," he said.

"Yet, I have heard it said that many outside of London hate the queen and wish Catherine yet wore the crown. And I have heard that some would see Her Majesty dead," whispered Madge.

"There are those who dislike her, to be sure. Yet, to strike against the king would be certain death. Few will relish that, I'll warrant. Let your heart be at ease," he said.

On they rode until Sir Nicholas motioned for the entire caravan to stop. As the guards let down the queen's litter, Madge dismounted her own horse, ready to assist Anne should the need arise. She watched as Lady Jane Seymour brought the chamber pot into the litter and was glad it was Jane and not herself who performed *that* duty while they traveled. Arthur hopped down beside her and soon, most of those on horseback had dismounted and were scattering in the woods. Arthur took her hand and led her into the darkness of the forest. He excused himself for a moment and stepped behind a large oak tree. She was happy she had no need to relieve herself and waited for him, slapping her arms to warm them.

"Come here, dearest, let me keep you toasty," said Arthur, embracing her. He leaned to kiss her and for many minutes, they continued. She could hear his breathing become shorter until he was panting in her ear, his lips nibbling the lobe and then her neck. He placed his hand on her breast and she gasped with surprise.

"It is unseemly for us to be so long in the woods. Someone will take note of it. And if Norris searches for me and finds me not—what then? Arthur, we must take great care—we do not wish to offend the king," said Madge.

"No one is paying us any mind—they are all busy. Come, let us kiss while we have a chance. Who knows when we will be alone again?" said Arthur.

"No. I am returning to my horse," said Madge.

"Will you not declare your love for me? Will you not give me my heart's ease by letting me know that I mean something to you—that what I feel is in some small way given back to me?" he said, his breath still short and hurried.

"I do not know what love is—so I cannot say that I love you. Besides, I am betrothed. Until the queen bears a son, I belong to Norris. Then she will make me a better match," said Madge.

"A better match, eh? So, I am good enough for you to kiss

but not fine enough for you to marry. I am, after all, only the bastard son of Lord Suffolk," he said as he released her. "You should remount your horse, Lady Margaret. I am certain I can find Sir Norris to ride beside you."

"Wait! Arthur, I didn't mean . . . wait!" She hurried after him but when she located her horse, his mount was no longer beside it. She saw Sir Norris making his way to her.

"Ah, my Lady Margaret. Master Brandon told me you longed for me. I would have joined you earlier but Her Majesty insisted I ride with Countess Rochford. I have never met a more disagreeable woman! I heard her complaints until I thought I should go mad or wring her scrawny neck!" said Norris. "Thankfully, I now have entered heaven."

"My lord, you are too kind. How like you this Progress?" Madge said.

"I like it not, mistress. A foolish thing to make such a journey in winter. I know the queen wishes to see her daughter, but surely there must have been another way," he said.

"Her Majesty is with child, sir. The king conforms his wishes to her own. Such is seemly when love is involved. I would hope my own husband would do the same for me," said Madge.

"I shall tell you what your husband will do for you, lady. He shall get babes upon you, one each year, until our house is full of sons and daughters. He shall not play the fool for a mere woman, as does our king. I shall rule my own house, mistress. Any other notions should be shaken out of your pretty head," Norris said.

"If such is the case, though your house be full of children, you shall not know my love," said Madge, her voice as cold as the wind that blew around them. She turned her face away from him and took secret delight in Arthur's kisses.

At dusk, Madge could see the outline of Eltham Palace against the evening sky. Though not as large as Richmond Palace or Hampton Court, the castle was commodious enough to house those on Progress, boasting carefully tended grounds now covered with a light blanket of snow. She watched as birds flew over the towers and onto the gardens to pick seeds and suet left there for them by the kitchen scullions.

When they arrived in the courtyard, the queen's litter was placed on the ground and the queen emerged, her hair tucked beneath her snood. She clapped her hands together twice and Nicholas Carew went to her immediately. She whispered to him and he headed toward Madge.

"Lady Shelton, Her Majesty would have you join her," said Sir Nicholas with a short bow.

"Yes, Your Grace," replied Madge with a brief curtsy. She knew this member of the privy chamber was no friend of the queen's, thus no friend of hers, either. Carew continued to support the dowager princess Catherine and her daughter, Mary, though he had signed the Act of Succession along with most of the king's men.

Madge took her leave of Norris and hurried to the queen, her skirts growing damp and cold with snow as they skimmed across the yard.

"Will you walk with me to the Great Hall? I have much to ask of you," said the queen. The king joined them.

"Of course, Your Grace," said Madge.

"Lady Margaret, well met," said the king, smiling, his red beard flecked with snow and his blue eyes taking her measure.

"Your Majesty," she whispered.

"Come, come, lady. Stand and let us walk together. My dearest queen hath a favor to beg of you," he said.

"I am always happy to serve Your Majesties," said Madge.

The king wrapped his arm around his wife and led her into the entranceway. Servants took their dampened cloaks to set them by the roaring fires and brought them mugs of wine. The king, the queen, and Lady Margaret found a private corner and the king indicated for Madge to be seated on a cushion at the queen's feet.

"We shall tarry a while here—the rest of you move on to your supper. The ride has been cold and long—to the tables and stuff yourselves!" shouted the king to other members of the progress. Then His Majesty turned to Madge. He continued to take stock of her until she felt her face grow quite warm.

"The Boleyn blood bakes pretty women, eh Anne? Though she cannot hold a torch to your beauty, she is a lovely girl," said the king.

"Aye, Harry, that she is! And one we can trust for she says naught and hears everything," said the queen. She wrapped herself in a coverlet of velvet and silk one of the servants had brought. "Lady Margaret, I have something I would like for you to do—if you succeed, you will be mightily rewarded. If you fail, well, you will not be the first—brave men have tried and failed."

"How can I please Your Grace?" said Madge, keeping her eyes cast to the floor.

"As you know, the lady Mary is here. I would like for you to tell her if she will but accept me as her queen, she can be reunited with her father's love. Entreat her tenderly, for I would treat her as mine own, if only she would obey the king's command," said the queen.

"And tell her I'll see her head separated from her shoulders if she continues to defy me," said the king, his face puffed up with anger. "I will tame her obstinate Spanish blood!"

"Harry, dear, have you not heard it said more flies are caught with honey than vinegar? Be gentle with her, Margaret. She has suffered much and is only a little older than you. Come to me after you have obtained her reply, even though the hour be late," said the queen. "Dear Margaret, I regret your mother and father were unable to accompany the princess Elizabeth to Eltham. They remained at Hatfield—I know how you would like to see them," said the queen as she patted Madge's hand.

"Lady Mary will see you now," said Lady Bryan, curtsying slightly to Madge as she entered the rooms of the young woman who had been a princess for most of her life. Madge made a deep curtsy to the small woman seated on the thronelike chair. She thought her legs would go numb before the lady Mary bid her rise.

"Why have you come?" said the lady Mary in a voice that sounded more like a man's than any girl Madge had heard. Madge stole a quick look at her face and saw blue eyes and thin lips pressed together as if she had eaten something sour.

"My lady, I . . ." Madge began.

"I am the princess Mary and you will address me as such or I will send you away immediately," said Mary.

Madge did not know what to do.

"Your Grace, I apologize for misspeaking. If you would but hear my poor plea, you will, perhaps, have your heart's ease," said Madge.

"Go on. But first, tell me your name," said Mary.

"I am Lady Margaret Shelton," said Madge.

"A cousin to the concubine, am I correct?" said Mary.

Madge felt her humor begin to change, anger simmering in her belly.

"I am cousin, yes." Madge tried to keep her voice warm and inviting, sweet like the honey of which the queen had spoken.

"What is your purpose with me?" said Mary.

"The queen wishes for Your Grace to accept her position as your loving stepmother by signing the Act of Succession and regaining your father's love. She says that if you will but do this, you will find her a kind and loving mother and your father will allow you to come again to court. You will be afforded all honor due to the daughter of the dowager princess Catherine and your life will be rich with food and music and dance. Happiness is yours, if you would but accept the queen," said Madge, as gently as she knew how.

Silence.

More silence.

Madge became troubled as the quiet grew between her and Lady Mary. She began to wonder if Mary had heard her at all.

Finally, Mary stood. She was short, not nearly up to Madge's chin. Madge could see her neck was pulsing and quite red.

"I know of no queen except my mother, who is far away from here, so she could not possibly have sent you. As for reconciliation with my father, the king, if his mistress would intervene on my behalf, I would be most grateful. You may leave our presence now," said Lady Mary and turned her back on Madge.

Nineteen

S he said what?! That horrid girl! That cursed bastard! Oh Harry, what shall we do with her?" said the queen after Madge had made her report.

"By heaven, she will do as I command! She will do it or she will pay the price as others have done! I will not have her and her mother raise an army against me! They must accept you, dearest, and they must accept our boy! Zounds! I will break her!" shouted the king. Madge watched as the king hit his fist against the serving table, shaking everything that had been set upon it. Then, she observed how the king, as if suddenly reminded of his wife's tender condition, gained control over his wrath and became gentle. He turned when he heard sobs from the queen.

"Tut, tut, what is this? Sweetheart, do not shed such tears. We will bring Mary round, takes but time. Now, now, dearest.

Do not take on so. Remember our boy—for his sake, desist from your cries," said the king with more tenderness in his voice than Madge had heard recently.

"I know, I know. She must obey her king. But I am cut to the bone by her coldness, her hatred of me. And I have not yet seen Elizabeth. Why haven't they brought her to me? Do they not know how my arms long to hold her? And those wretched women who lined the road in that last little village—shouting those awful words about me! It is too much, Harry—just too much!" sobbed the queen.

Madge wanted to go to Her Majesty and rub her shoulders, but she dared not. Instead, she turned her face away from such an intimate scene.

"There, there, my love. You are overwrought. The journey has been long and you are tired. There were only a handful of women along the road and I shall find them out and send someone to speak with them. They don't know you, dearest. If they did, you would win them easily. No one really knows you as I do and you will always have my heart," said the king.

"Will I, Harry? Will I?" said the queen.

"Yes, my love—always," said the king as he leaned over to her and kissed her for a long time.

"Oh Harry, can you not come to my bed tonight? I have need of your strong arms around me," whispered the queen.

"Oh madame, how you tempt me! But no, I would not meddle with you now. I might disturb our little prince and neither of us would want that. No, my sweet—the boot must needs be on the other foot awhile—*I* must now keep *you* at arm's length—until our son is born. But then, woman! You can look forward to my love, which I shall keep as a precious jewel for you alone," said the king, rising to his feet.

"Lady Margaret, go find that confounded Lady Bryan and

tell her to bring the princess to us! Immediately!" shouted His
Majesty.

"Yes, Your Grace," said Madge.

"Now, madame, what say you to some music to calm your
nerves? I'll have them bring in Master Smeaton and I shall
sing to you myself! Does this please my dearest?" said the king.

"Yes, my love!" Anything that pleases you doth make me the
'moost happi,'" said the queen.

Madge hurried out of the chamber to find Lady Bryan. The
first person she found, however, was Wyatt.

"How now, mistress? Why such hurry?" said Wyatt, bowing.

"I am sent to find Lady Bryan so she might fetch the princess for the queen," said Madge, continuing her brisk walk.

"Whoa! Whoa! Mistress! You will never find her that way.
The princess is housed down this hall—I shall show you," said
Wyatt.

"Always my friend, Thomas! I am glad you are with us on
this Progress—it shall be more pleasant!" said Madge, her
skirts rustling as she rushed to follow Wyatt.

"The queen bade me come—I would have been as happy in
London, roasting by the fire in the king's privy chamber. Tell
me, Madge—have you been writing any poetry of late?" said
Wyatt.

"Not more than a few accursed lines—I am kept too busy
by the queen. When she is with child, she has great need of me.
She seems to prefer my company to that of her other ladies,"
said Madge.

"I understand her preference. Your loyalty is true and there
are few here the good queen can trust. She has many enemies.
It is easier to fault her than to cast a shadow on the king," said
Wyatt.

"And safer, too," said Madge with a smile.

"Madame, here is the princess Elizabeth's chamber. I will see you anon," said Wyatt.

"Oh Thomas, won't you come to the king's bedchamber? Master Smeaton will be singing as will the king himself. I will inquire of the queen if you may join us," said Madge.

"Milady, I would be most honored," said Wyatt. "I shall wait outside until you motion me to enter."

Together, they took turns carrying the princess Elizabeth to the queen. Madge noted the bright reddish-gold hair and thought that, though the king could claim her by her locks, her face mirrored that of the queen's.

By the time Madge brought Elizabeth to the king and queen, a small group had gathered in the privy chamber—Master Smeaton, Sir Brereton, Lady Jane Seymour, Sir Francis Weston, Countess Rochford, Lady Margaret Douglas, Sir Norris, and other favorites of the king. Madge immediately asked if Sir Thomas might join them.

"Do bring in our favorite poet, Lady Margaret. He shall entertain us with his verses and Master Smeaton shall accompany him on the virginals," said His Majesty, his blue eyes filled with happiness.

"Yes, invite him in—I would so like to hear something about true love," said the queen, gazing into the king's eyes for a long moment, then turning to the babe that lay between them.

Elizabeth had awakened in a good humor and was smiling and giggling with her parents as they lay upon a large bed. The queen looked serene and happy, nuzzling her daughter, giving her many kisses and caresses. The king, too, took pleasure in the babe, holding her up for all to see. Madge took her place among the courtiers and was surprised to see a solitary man standing back from the others, almost hidden in the corner.

"My lady Shelton. You look quite lovely after such a hard ride," said Arthur quietly.

"Do not speak pretty words to me, sir. Not after your little trick this day," said Madge.

"Pretty words for a pretty lady—what is wrong with that? Is that not the way of the court?" said Arthur.

"I do not give a fig for such things as well you know. Why did you leave me in the hands of Norris? Do you now hate me?" said Madge in a sudden fury.

"Mistress, I could never hate you. You told me in the wood that you needed to find a superior person to marry. You are betrothed to Sir Henry Norris. I felt you should ride a ways with your lover, so all the court could see. And, after all, I'm merely Brandon's bastard. I am too low for such as you, milady," said Arthur in a whisper.

"I stung you with my words. What would you have me do? The queen has told me I cannot marry you—she has told me she will find me an appropriate match. Would you have me go against her wishes? Even if I loved you, I could not do such a thing," said Madge.

"Then you do not love me. I shall withdraw from your presence, mistress, in that case. Though to be away from you will break me," said Arthur.

"Do not withdraw, I beg of you. Just understand that I cannot accept you as husband," said Madge.

"If you will not marry me, then will you give yourself to me, body and soul?" said Arthur.

Madge laughed at his forwardness. If such words had come

from Norris, she would have slapped his face for them. But somehow, coming from Arthur, she welcomed them.

"Kind sir, though your offer of service is quite tempting, I must remain chaste until my marriage. I have told you this. Try to remember it," said Madge as she touched his arm.

Just then, Norris approached them.

"Master Brandon, what are you doing in the king's chambers? You are not a groom," said Norris while he pulled Madge by the elbow away from Arthur.

"I am here at the queen's command, Sir Norris," said Arthur, giving him a short bow from the waist, but not lowering his head. Instead, he kept his eyes on Norris.

"Ah. Do you mind if I take Lady Margaret from you for a moment? The king is going to make a speech and I would she stand by my side for it," said Norris.

"The Lady Margaret is yours, sir," said Arthur.

Madge and Norris moved closer to the king's bed where His Majesty stood, holding Elizabeth. He clinked his knife against his wineglass and all grew quiet.

"As you can see, the princess Elizabeth is healthy and beautiful—perfect in every way. I wish to announce that I have ordered a new cradle made for the bonny prince who is on his way to us. Cornelius Hayes, our renowned goldsmith, is to craft the cradle and it shall be of purest silver, inlaid with many precious stones and shall have the Tudor rose carved therein. A splendid cradle for a splendid prince!" roared the king. At that, he carried Elizabeth back to her mother and kissed the queen with great passion. Madge could not hear what the queen said to him, but her face was all smiles.

By the end of March, the Progress finally returned to Hampton Court where the queen and the Princess spent much time together. When he was not busy working on state business with Master Cromwell, the king joined them.

Cromwell had fashioned another, more strident Act of Succession for all the king's subjects to sign. Actually, several acts were passed around the same time. These documents recognized Elizabeth as the only legitimate heir, should anything happen to His Majesty. They also made a law that any words spoken or written against the king's new marriage would be considered treason. The confiscation of church property for the king's coffers continued, under Cromwell, to go beyond reform of the monasteries to simple pillage. Those who refused to sign the papers were arrested and executed with marvelous speed.

Madge heard grizzly stories circulating around the court upon her return, and she noted how the atmosphere had changed. Before Cromwell's new legislation, the court had been a place of pleasure; the king had enjoyed all the good things offered in the earthly realm. But now, fear and gossip filled the air. No one spoke their thoughts, for to do so might prove deadly. Before the latest laws, those who kept the old faith, such as Cate, did so in relative ease, judging they would be tolerated by His Most Gracious Majesty. But now, with Cromwell hunting them down with his network of spies and henchmen, the papists were forced to worship in utmost secrecy, fearing for their lives. Support for the dowager princess Catherine, which had once been widespread among certain courtiers, dissipated into the air. Lord Suffolk and Sir Nicholas Carew retired to their manor houses far from London, as their loyalty to Catherine remained unchanged, though they had signed all the papers they were asked to sign. Danger lingered in the air. The plague, a rainy season that sent much of the land into famine, hangings and burnings of holy men who refused to acknowledge Henry as head of the church, hangings and burnings of anyone who might be labeled "heretic"—these evils bedeviled the country. At the center, cursed for all that was raging around the country, was one name and one name only—Queen Anne, Henry's "goggle-eyed whore."

Madge began to have fears for the queen and for their family. Norfolk, the queen's uncle, was becoming more and more aloof with Her Majesty, and Madge had heard the queen say harsh words to him. He was part of the old world—the old faith, the old order.

Lord Wiltshire, the queen's father, as well as her brother George, were in France, trying to convince Francis I that one of his sons should become betrothed to the princess Elizabeth. Such a match was pleasing to the queen as she considered the French king her friend.

The new Spanish ambassador, Eustace Chapuys, refused to recognize the queen or any of her ladies and caused trouble at every opportunity. There was nothing he would not do or say to help the dowager princess.

Yet, through all the turmoil, the king kept his queen daily by his side, though he insisted she rest frequently and he took care not to let his difficulties reach her ears. For her, he was all smiles and pleasantries.

As for the queen, she had recalled Madge as mistress of the bedchamber and kept her close. During the long afternoons, they played cards, usually All Fours or Primero. Sometimes, they rolled the dice in such sport as Hazard or Quenes. Frequently, Her Majesty called for Master Smeaton to play for her while she rested. Often, she and Madge fell asleep on the queen's bed, the cards and die scattered between them, Master Smeaton playing the virginals softly in the background. On just such an afternoon, the queen received more bad news.

"Madame, the lady Mary, your sister, would speak with you," said Mistress Marshall herself. Madge was immediately on edge as Mistress Marshall rarely came into the queen's bed-chamber and only when there was trouble among the queen's ladies.

"Admit our dear sister to us at once, Mistress Marshall," said the queen, rising from her bed and sitting in one of the nearby chairs. Madge stood behind the queen, ready to be of service. She watched as Lady Mary Carey entered and curtsied deeply to the queen. She was not certain, but it seemed the lady Mary had a small belly.

The queen did not seem to notice but rose to greet her sister with a hug.

"Dearest sister, what brings you to my bedchamber on such a cloudy afternoon?" said the queen, motioning for Mary to sit down in the chair opposite her.

"I came to receive your good and generous blessing," said Mary in a small voice.

"Then I bless you with all my heart, dear sister. How can I help you? Our father is sending adequate money and food for you and the children, I hope. The king himself instructed him to do so," said the queen, smiling.

"Yes, Majesty. Father is faithful to send exactly the amount the king requires—no more, no less. Little Henry and Mary are growing nicely and have enough of everything," said Mary.

"Good, good. How then, may I be of assistance to you?" said the queen.

At this, Lady Mary fell from the chair to her knees and held the queen's hands in her own. Tears fell onto the queen's lap.

"What is this, Mary? Why these tears? Nothing can be this bad, sister. Come, tell us your troubles," said the queen, lifting Mary's chin so she could look into her large blue eyes.

"Oh Anne, I have done something you will not like. I fear the king will be filled with anger when he hears it," said Mary.

"Tell us, sister. What have you done?" said the queen, her brow beginning to wrinkle.

"I have married William Stafford, a Yeoman of the Guard," said Mary and then burst into sobs.

Madge watched as Anne's entire body stiffened. For a moment, the queen said nothing. Then she pushed Mary from her and stood.

"I cannot believe you to be such a stupid cow! For you to marry, without the king's permission, to a . . . a . . . commoner when you are sister to the queen! What have you done, Mary! What have you done! Get out! Out of my sight!" screeched the queen. Before Mary could rise, the queen grabbed her by the hair and pulled her to the chamber door. She threw her out with a mighty shove.

"Am I to be ruined by my foolish sister? Oh, Margaret, what will the king say—he will be sorry he wed me, a mere English woman, when he could have married a princess from France. Oh, he will find me low and common now. What has she done!" The queen cried as she flung herself across her bed. Madge hurried to her side.

"Majesty, no one could take the dignity of your royal person from you. You are a consecrated queen and what your silly sister does is of no consequence. His Majesty may be angry, but this will not touch his love for you. Be of good cheer! You carry his son and when the prince is born, the king will forgive all, even such as Mary," said Margaret as she stroked the queen's back.

"Think you so, Margaret? Think you the king's love can withstand so much?" said the queen.

"Madame, I can see how he looks at you—his eyes wet with love. He is yours and always shall be. There, there. Do not dismay. Let us refresh ourselves with some wine and cherry tarts. They are delicious, I am told," said Madge.

The queen began to laugh.

"Oh Lady Margaret, if only all problems could be solved with wine and cherry tarts! You amuse me, child. I am glad you are with me in these frightful days," said the queen.

Madge did a little dance for the queen's pleasure as she prepared their repast.

Twenty

Madge hurried to Cate's quarters to see if she and Shadow wanted to go for a long walk into Cheapside where Mary and William Stafford were living. She was on a mission from the queen herself. The day was sunny and the air was warmer now that the end of March was near. She knocked on the door and heard great shuffling from inside the chamber. Cate opened the door, struggling to hold onto Shadow's collar.

"Maddie, come in, come in. It has been long since I have seen you, my girl. What of the queen?" said Cate.

"Her Majesty is well and getting fatter by the day. We think the bonny prince to come in early August. I have an errand to run and I hoped you and Shadow might accompany me," said Madge.

"What sort of errand?" said Cate.

"I am to go to Cheapside to Braxton's Inn to find the queen's sister, the lady Mary and her new husband, William Stafford. I have news for them," said Madge.

"I have heard the king rusticated them without a penny, with nothing but His Majesty's mighty wrath," said Cate as she wrapped her cloak around her and tethered Shadow.

"Master Cromwell took up their plight and went to the king on their behalf. He told the king that Lady Mary had said to him that her "heart overruled her head" in this matter. When he said that, His Majesty began to laugh, saying, 'Of her, we would expect nothing else—she always was a silly wench.' And then the queen asked if she could give them a manor house in Norfolk with a goodly income. The king cannot refuse her these days. With only one condition—they are never to come to court again and Mary's son, Henry Carey, must stay here under the queen's guardianship. He had previously been declared her ward, but the queen had allowed him to stay with his mother. Now, he is commanded to live at court," said Madge.

"With his father," whispered Cate.

"Speak not a word of that—yet, we know 'tis true," said Madge. "Are you ready, Shadow? Will thou walk into the great city of London? Here is a bit of lamb I saved for you," said Madge as she gave the dog the tidbit she had kept in her sleeve.

As Madge and Cate left the order of Hampton Court for the mean streets of London by the west gate, Cate lost control of Shadow, who pulled and pulled against her until the dog gained her freedom and ran at high speed into the city streets.

"What shall we do, Maddie? I'll never catch the cur in these skirts," said Cate.

"We must! She'll be lost in no time—or worse, some poor

man will make her his supper!" Madge said as she headed in the direction Shadow had taken. Before she had gone more than a few steps, however, a pleasing sight greeted her eye.

"Shadow! And Master Brandon! Oh, thank you for catching her—we feared she would be gone for good," said Madge as she hurried to them. Arthur wore dark brown breeches and was in his linen shirt, his doublet folded across his arm. His hair was mussed and he panted almost as heavily as did Shadow. Madge knew capturing Shadow had been no easy task.

"At your service always, Mistress Margaret. And the lovely Cate is with you I see," said Arthur. "Where, may I ask, are you ladies going this blustery afternoon?"

"We are on an errand for the Queen. We must find Braxton's Inn in Cheapside," said Madge.

"Then allow me to escort you. London can be a rough place for two fine ladies walking alone. Besides, I can keep Shadow on her tether," said Arthur.

"We really don't need . . ." said Madge.

"We would be delighted if you would accompany us, Master Brandon," said Cate with a stern look toward Madge.

"Then let us be off," said Arthur, smiling.

For the first time, Madge and Cate witnessed the daily hurly-burly of the city on foot. Stalls lined the streets with a variety of merchandise, the men and women calling out their goods. "Apples here! None rotten!" "Fish, caught this morning! Fish, fresh fish!" "Hot chestnuts! Hot roasted chestnuts!" "Cherry tarts and meat pies! Tarts and pies!"

They passed apothecary shops and tailor shops with bolts of pretty satins and plain muslins stacked against the walls inside. Housewives hurried to buy what they needed while gentlemen of various degree went about town, some puffed up with pride of rank, others looking hither and yon as if they planned thievery. The queen had warned Madge against conies and crooks, cutpurses and pickpockets, which she called "nips and foists," much to Madge's surprise, as she would not have thought the queen would know such terms. Though Madge had asked directions to Braxton's Inn, and received a detailed account from Sir Nicholas Carew, who had returned to court at the king's command, she became addled as she witnessed the confusion and noise around her. She was glad to have Master Brandon's guidance.

"Turn here, ladies. We have just a little ways to travel ere we arrive," said Arthur as he took Madge's arm and guided her down a narrow, cobbled street. Cate followed behind them.

"Watch yourselves. You never know when some good wife will toss out the contents of her chamber pot on your heads—or peelings or rinds or any other garbage. The streets are filled with such, as you can see and smell," said Arthur.

"Aye, 'tis enough to make my nose itch," said Cate.

"I thought it was the 'smell of life,' dear Cate—that's what you told me when we first arrived," said Maggie.

"That it is, my girl, that it is," said Cate.

"Up ahead, that white building on the left—that is Braxton's Inn—I have delivered you safe and sound," said Arthur.

"Won't you come in with us? You might be interested in our little errand—we can sup here together," said Madge.

"I cannot refuse such a request, milady. Will Shadow behave herself or shall I tie her to the rail?" said Arthur.

"She will be a good girl if we but feed her scraps while we eat," said Madge. "Bring her in."

Arthur, Madge, Cate, and Shadow climbed the wooden stairs and entered the inn. The interior was dark with a sitting room to one side and behind that, a large dining area with a table that would seat at least a dozen. The innkeeper, a burly man with a full beard and small eyes stood behind a bar where he kept a large book and quill pen.

"Sir, we are looking for Master William Stafford and his wife. We were told they are staying here," said Madge with authority.

"And who is it wants to see 'em?" said the man, his eyes narrowing.

"My name is Lady Margaret Shelton and I have come from the queen herself," said Madge, drawing herself up to her full height, hoping to impress the man with her importance.

"From the queen? And I'm Cardinal Wolsey. Now if you want a room, you and your handsome fellow, there ... two guineas will get you a few hours," he said and winked his eye at Arthur. At that, Arthur stepped up to the bar and gently pushed Madge behind him.

"Sir, the lady has explained that we are about the queen's business—I suggest you give us the information we desire," said Arthur. His voice was level and he did not puff himself up the way some men do in order to look menacing. However, there was something about the look in this eye that Madge noticed and found frightening. The innkeeper must have seen that same look, for he scratched his head and then told them where to find Mary and William.

They once again climbed rickety stairs and found the proper room. Arthur knocked on the door and Master Stafford opened it, inviting them in.

"Mistress Mary, I bring word from the queen," said Madge, curtsying low and waiting for Mary to bring her to her feet.

"Arise, coz. You have no cause to make such obeisance to one who is banished from court," said Mary with a slight smile.

Madge had always thought Mary pretty in the conventional sense—blond hair, blue eyes with a pale complexion. It was hard to believe she and the queen were of the same blood, their coloring as different as their manners.

"You may be banished, milady, but the queen sends comforting news. She has given you a manor house and lands in Norfolk, with the king's blessing," said Madge, pleased to be the bearer of such generosity.

"William, do you hear? Anne has not abandoned me! She has saved us!" said Mary as she jumped into her husband's arms. He kissed her well and Madge could see how they loved each other.

"Master Cromwell did his part, too. There are only two conditions placed by the king," said Madge, suddenly uneasy about telling Mary she must leave her son, Henry, at court.

"Here 'tis," said Master Stafford. "The axe."

"Not so bad as that, but you may not find it to your liking. First, you are never to return to court. With the gift of lands comes banishment for a lifetime," said Madge.

"I'll not be sorry to leave such a place as this," said Mary quietly.

"Nor I, my love, nor I," said Stafford.

"The next condition will be more difficult to bear, I fear," said Madge. "You must leave your son, Henry, with the queen, to be raised at court under her wardship. The girl you may take with you," said Madge.

"Oh cruel, cruel man! For I know it is His Majesty who has demanded this sacrifice! Anne would never be so hard!" said Mary as she clung to her husband.

"Yes," said Madge. "But the queen wanted me to say these words to you—she will love little Henry as though he were her own. He shall be brought up with the princess Elizabeth in Hatfield. She will direct the Progress to the north country as often as the king will allow. You can see the boy hence. Her own heart is broken every time the princess Elizabeth is returned to Hatfield, so she understands the love you bear little Henry. She wishes you all happiness and hopes these arrangements will be agreeable," said Madge.

"Your sister has honored the bonds of family, my love. We are lucky to be as well off as she has made us. We shall have our own boy, my darling. Far away from the court and all danger," said Master Stafford. He pulled her to him, his arms strong around her. "You have been brave, madame, for many years. You have suffered much. Let us take this chance for happiness and trust in the goodness of your sister that our boy will be well looked after."

Silence filled the room. The two children, who had been sitting on the trundle bed, playing games of string and fingers, said nothing. Mary sobbed for a few moments, then looked into her husband's eyes. She seemed to find strength there for she nodded her head.

"Thank my sister for her mercy and generosity. Shall I bring Henry to court on the morrow?" said Mary.

"Yes, Her Majesty would take her leave of you then, as well. She sent this, too," said Madge and handed Mary a purse filled with gold coins.

"At least we will be able to pay our bills here and on the journey. Tell Anne once again I thank her," said Mary.

"We will take our leave of you so you may spend your last evening together. May God bless you on your journey home," said Madge, moved at the thought of Mary giving up her child so she and her new husband could start a life of promise together. Pain and joy mixed quite thoroughly at court, she thought.

"I do not wish to eat here, Master Brandon," said Madge as they made their way down the steps.

"Then we must hurry to reach Hampton Court in time to sup," said Arthur as he and the women emerged from the inn.

"Yes. I know you must take care of your stomach, young Brandon," said Cate haughtily.

"I take excellent care of my stomach, milady, for I have much I must stomach," he said with a grin.

"Humph," said Cate.

"Mistress Mary seemed pleased with the news from the queen," said Arthur as he took Madge's elbow to lead them back to Hampton. There were puddles of water and mud in the cobblestone streets.

"Of course, she was saddened at the thought of leaving her son, but seemed heartened to know she and Master Stafford now have a place to live. She was touched by the queen's kindness and mercy, I think," said Madge.

For the remainder of their journey, Arthur was oddly quiet. He did not respond to Cate's taunts, nor to Madge's murmurings about how wrong it had been for Mary and William Stafford to follow their hearts.

They arrived at Hampton Court with a few minutes to spare before time for supper in the Great Hall. Arthur walked Shadow to Cate's room, where he handed the dog's leash to Cate. He stood at the entranceway.

"I would speak with Lady Margaret, Mistress Cate, with your permission?" he said, indicating with his arm that he would like to enter Cate's room.

Cate looked at Madge who nodded her assent.

"Take care, Maddie," muttered Cate as Arthur's large frame seemed to take up all the space, making Cate's quarters seem even more cramped than usual.

"Lady Margaret, if we could be alone for a moment?" said Arthur.

"It would be most improper." said Cate.

"Leave us," said Madge. "I am very much mistress of these circumstances—you have naught to fear," said Madge.

"Yes, Lady Margaret," said Cate and with that, she took Shadow and left them.

"What do you have to say to me that could not be stated when Cate was in the room, Master Brandon?" said Madge.

"Pretty Madge—that's what they call you, you know—the men in the king's apartments, the grooms, everyone—Pretty Madge," he began.

"This is what was so important as to dislocate my Cate— what men say about me?" said Madge.

"No, milady. I have been thinking all the way from Braxton's Inn. Your cousin Mary and her ill-conceived marriage bodes well for us," said Arthur.

"How so, sir?" said Madge.

"The queen is merciful and generous to those she loves. And there is no doubt she loves you, Lady Margaret," said Arthur.

"What does that have to do with you?" said Madge.

"Mistress, as you must know by now, I love you. I want to serve you all my days. I would marry you this very day if you would but have me. Do you love me?" said Arthur in a low voice.

"I have told you before—I am too young to know love," said Madge, her heart beating against its cage.

"If you have no love for me, then I am going to walk out this door and you will not see me again. I am entirely sincere in this, lady. I will not display my heart for you to walk over without regard. Do you love me?" he asked, staring into her eyes.

Madge couldn't speak.

"I see I have misjudged your ardor in our kissing. Perhaps you kiss Norris in the same way—or Wyatt. Good-bye, Pretty Madge. You will not see me again," he said, turning toward the door.

When Madge saw that he meant his words, she was overcome.

"No wait! Arthur, do not go! I do love you—I must! I am undone to think of you gone from me," she said as she flung herself into his arms. She kissed him, then, not waiting for him to kiss her first. And in that moment, she knew he had her heart.

After several minutes of sweet kisses and tender touches, Madge heard Cate's knock. She cracked the door open.

"Anon, dear Cate, anon. We will be but a moment," said Madge.

"Maddie-dear, remember your upbringing," said Cate.

"I am as I ever was, Cate—have no fears. We need just a moment and then you may join us," said Madge as she closed the door once again.

"I believe after the queen has her son, she will forgive us if we marry, just as she has forgiven her sister. She loves you much, Margaret. She will want you with her, and I believe my father can still persuade the king of some things, though he is not in favor as he once was. We can marry, Margaret. We can be happy," said Arthur.

"Perhaps you are right, dearest. The queen does seem to forgive those who act on the impulses of love. We must wait until the prince is born and lives. No one must know about our love. We can meet here, in Cate's room, secretly," said Madge, suddenly carried away with the idea of marrying Arthur, giving herself to him, body and soul, as he had said. She shivered.

"As you wish, my pretty Madge. I shall always obey you in these matters," said Arthur.

Just then, another knock at the door.

"One more kiss to carry with me," said Arthur, pulling her to him. Madge kissed him, following the play of his tongue in her mouth, feeling him against her. She almost lost her breath and in that moment, Cate opened the door.

Twenty-one

W hat knavery is this? And in my very room!" hissed Cate as she entered the chamber.

"No knavery, dear, dear Cate. I love Arthur and he loves me. He has asked for my hand in marriage and I have given it," said Madge, smiling.

"Have you gone mad? Have we not just seen what happens to those who marry without His Majesty's permission?" said Cate, pulling Shadow in behind her. Her face was puffed up and red as a plum.

"Yes. We have seen the queen give her sister a tidy manor house with enough income to take care of her for life. To be banned from court would be a godsend, if one has one's love. 'Tis a good end to a bad beginning," said Madge.

"You are playing with fire, Maddie. The king is not one whose courses run steady. He flies with the wind and his humors are changeable. You cannot expect Her Majesty to control his tempers," said Cate.

"I know, dearest Cate. But if we wait until the little prince is born, strong and healthy, we can marry in secret, then go to the queen and gain her blessing. She will persuade the king to forgive us, though he may punish us a bit to soothe his bruised feelings. But he will grant pardon. I just know he will," said Madge.

"Yes, that is one way it could go. He could just as well separate your heads from your bodies. In case you have not noticed, many have lost their lives these bloody days, aye, and for less than a spurious marriage," said Cate. "Need I remind you of the Carthusian monks? And Wolsey, whom the king had loved? And the most noble Sir Thomas More? You play with fire when you dally with our sovereign."

"Mistress Cate, I assure you I would never put the Lady Margaret in danger. I would lay down my life for her," said Arthur.

"Aye, that I do not doubt, sir, for you are as smitten as ever I've seen a young fool. But even you cannot prevent the king from acting in a rage," said Cate.

Madge took hold of Cate's hands and dropped to her knees in front of her nurse.

"Will you not help us, dear Cate?" Madge said.

For a long moment, Cate looked into Madge's eyes, no doubt seeing the babe and then the young girl, the many moments of friendship that had passed between her and her charge.

"Aye. God help me, I'll do what I can," said Cate.

"I knew you would not fail me," said Madge as she rose and hugged Cate to her.

Arthur bowed to Cate and kissed her on the cheek. She gave him a slight smile.

"Now begone with you—out, out, you have sullied my room long enough," she said as she shooed Arthur out the door.

As the spring equinox approached, all the gardens began to green, the trees to bud soft silky leaves, and the earliest flowers to nudge out of the cold earth toward the warmth of the still-pale sun. Daffodils and hyacinths, crocuses and forget-me-nots, all slowly peeked out, coaxed by the warmth, at first hesitant and then, finally, fully open. The queen's belly was full and both she and the king were merry, walking in the gardens, laughing as they supped. Madge joined them often, along with Norris and a few favorites. When she was not with the queen, she often sought Wyatt for his quick wit and his friendly advice on various matters. When they could, she and Arthur met in Cate's rooms, kissing and fondling one another, each enjoying the temptations of the flesh.

One day, the queen asked for Madge to walk with her in the gardens. Her manner was serious, or so it seemed to Madge.

"Lady Margaret, this winter hath lasted long and now that warmer weather has arrived, I think it be time to make merry with His Majesty. What think you of a special supper to be served in my apartments for the king's new men and a few select ladies of the court?" said the queen.

"Whatever Your Majesty desires suits me. I am at your service," said Madge as they strolled arm in arm.

"Good. Then I would like for you to make up a list of entertaining friends—Thomas Wyatt and the other ladies who scribble in that booklet of poetry I see being bandied about—" said the queen.

"I did not know Your Majesty knew of my feeble attempts to write verse. Thomas has encouraged me, along with Lady

Margaret Douglas as well as Lady Mary Howard, in our rhymes," said Madge.

"I have seen it, mistress, and there is much more there than poetry. Of courtly love and base carnal desires, I have read. But no matter, such is life—I'll warrant Lord Surrey and Thomas Clere hope to gain more than good verse!" said the queen with a laugh.

"Your Majesty, I assure you I have no such desires! I simply like to see what I can make, whether it be a jest or a love poem of some meaning—it is a good pastime when the winter winds blow cold," said Madge.

"Does Norris write you love poesies, too?" said the queen.

"Sir Henry could not do such, as he hath no gift for goodly words. His mouth is full of foulness and filth. I will be relieved to be rid of him when Your Majesty brings forth the bonny prince!" said Madge.

"And so it shall be. But remember, Lady Margaret, we have long to go," said the queen as she stooped to pluck a daffodil. "I shall ask Master Smeaton to gather goodly musicians, you bring the wordsmiths to read their best compositions, and we shall welcome the spring," said the queen.

"Must I invite Sir Norris?" said Madge.

"Of course. He has the king's love," said the queen as she added another bloom to the few she held in her hand.

"Yes, Majesty," said Madge.

"I know how His Majesty lacks good company when I am indisposed, waiting impatiently for the birth of the babe. This time, he has kept me by his side at all times and has showered me with love and affection. No taking another lady, not even in innocent courtly love. I would that he find some merriment while we wait," said the queen.

"Then I shall endeavor to make the evening one he shall not forget," said Madge.

The queen set the king's surprise for two days hence and Madge spent many hours helping Wyatt and the other writers decide which poems to read for Their Majesties. She and Lady Douglas, along with Lady Jane Seymour and Countess Rochford, prepared a dance to celebrate the queen's large belly. The queen ordered special delicacies, favorites of the king's including orange marmalade and roast goose, dried cherry tarts and sweet cream. The best ale was brought in barrels to the queen's apartments and Madge hung green boughs across the arras, gathered flowers into vases, and had fresh rushes scattered on the floors. She had no time to see Arthur, though he had sent a note.

Servants lit the wall sconces and the tapers. Slowly, the ladies filed in, their gowns and jewels sparkling. Though Lent was only halfway through, on this night, the feeling was festive rather than funereal.

When the queen entered the outer apartments, she looked radiant. She wore a dress of crimson lined with ermine and her long hair hung to her waist. Her face glowed with happiness. As the king's men arrived, she, more than any other woman in the room, captivated them with her beauty and charm.

Finally, the king himself arrived without fanfare, as he had expected a private dinner with his wife. When he saw all his favorites before him, bowing in their best fashion, he smiled and bellowed out, "What is this?" Then he moved to the queen and bowed low.

"Wife, have you forgotten the season?" he said, though smiling at her.

"No, my lord. But I know how long the winter has drawn itself out and how dreary such gray days make you feel, Harry.

I know how hard Your Grace has worked during these difficult times. I know Cromwell brings you bad news after bad news," said the queen, smiling up at him.

"These are tedious times, it is true. Master Cromwell also brings me wealth, lady. Do not forget that," said His Majesty, a caution in his voice.

"Let us not speak of Master Cromwell this eve. Instead, come sit with me, my love. Our friends are here—there is fine food. Let us enjoy our fellowship together," said the queen.

"Well said, lady," said the king as he sat beside her at the table. The queen clapped her hands and servants began to bustle over the king, bringing him ale and food, then serving the rest of the gathering. The king fed the queen from his own plate, spooning good things into her mouth, sometimes placing bites there with his large fingers. She often licked the grease from his hand and Madge could see his breath quicken.

After all had eaten their fill, Madge and the ladies began their dance, while the musicians played. Madge was nervous, not having danced in front of others in quite this way, but she was graceful and she knew it. Soon, she lost her fear and moved with the other ladies until the dance was over. They bowed to Their Majesties and found their seats, Madge on a large pillow at the queen's feet.

"Your little cousin has the Boleyn grace, Anne. She is becoming quite the beauty," said His Majesty, staring at Madge.

"Yes. Court life agrees with her, methinks," said the queen.

"Step up here where I can see you, Lady Margaret," said the king. Madge rose as gracefully as she could and curtsied to the king until she felt him pull her hand to rise.

"No wonder they call you Pretty Madge. Where's Norris? Come here man!" roared the king.

Norris bowed and smiled.

"This is your intended, eh? Tell me, sir, why do you sit over there with that plain young Seymour woman when you could dine with this beauty?" said the king.

"Though we are betrothed, Your Grace, milady told me she would be much too busy this eve to be bothered with the likes of me," said Norris.

"Never let it be said that I kept lovers apart. Master Smeaton, music! A dance for the lovebirds!" blustered the king, smiling.

Madge had no choice but to dance with Norris, feel his hot breath on her neck, his sweaty hands around her waist. She tried to avoid his glance but every time they stepped toward one another, he was staring at her as if he would ravish her at that very moment. Finally, the music stopped and the king clapped his hands. The rest of the company followed suit and before she knew what was happening, Norris leaned her back and kissed her in front of all, his hands roaming over her person with obvious ownership. She tried to straighten up and push him away, but she could not move. He reached for her breast and pinched her nipple. Everyone saw.

"Many's the babe to come from those loins, eh Norris?" said the king. Norris stood her up and smiled at the king.

"My lord, I can barely wait to begin. But she won't have me yet. She keeps me waiting until I must burst!" said Norris.

"I know what it is to wait, man. But I tell you, the wait is worth it for one such as she. As it has been for my lovely queen," said the king.

Madge was able to wriggle away from Norris as Wyatt stepped forth to present poems for the king's delight. At some, His Majesty laughed and at others, tears formed in the corners of his eyes. Madge was relieved to be seated once again at the queen's feet. Her Majesty smiled at Madge and patted her arm in sympathy. Madge felt at that moment that Arthur was right—the queen would always be on the side of true love, especially when she considered how horrible it would be for Madge to marry Norris.

After much entertainment, the queen grew tired and His Majesty ordered everyone from the rooms, except for Madge. The three of them retired to the queen's bedchambers where the king and queen sat up, talking quietly. Madge lay down on her cot, giving them privacy.

"Harry," said the queen gently, "what of the monasteries? I am concerned that Cromwell is not using the property for good. I had hoped to secure money for our universities and help for the poor after the monasteries were dissolved. Reform rather than destroy."

"Meddle not in such affairs, Anne. You attend to your business—bring us a son! I shall manage Master Cromwell—I like my coffers to be full and he is making them so. All he does, he does on my command," said the king.

"As you wish, my love," said the queen. "I only want for you to be the greatest of all kings. It has pleased God to set you on the throne and to set me here beside you. I want to be your helpmeet and dearest friend."

"Give me my prince and you do me all the good in the world, lady. And now, to bed, shall we, my love?" said the king.

With that, he rose to leave. Madge also rose.

"No need, Lady Margaret. You must needs rest, too. Take good care of my queen," he said.

"Yes, Your Grace," said Madge.

"Come dear, help me into my nightdress. I am quite exhausted by this night's festivities," said the queen.

"As am I, Your Grace. Though I believe the king enjoyed it immensely," said Madge.

"Yes. I had hoped to persuade my dear Harry to curb Cromwell's excesses but to no avail. I am, after all, a mere woman!" said the queen.

"Frail and weak," said Madge with a smile.

"Yes, frail and weak though I be, I can still manage this royal lion. At least, some of the time—never forget your power, Margaret. Even though Norris acted a lout tonight, the king does not like such a display. Though he laughed, I know him. He is courtly and wishes to treat women well, with dignity. 'Tis his royal upbringing. He likes neither the crude nor the obvious," said the queen.

"I like it not, either. If I must marry Norris, I wouldst as soon die," said Madge.

"Do not fear—I will stop it somehow. Now, to bed, Pretty Madge," said the queen.

Twenty-two

B y the end of May, though the king had intended to meet King Francis I at Calais, he had reason to cancel the trip. He told the French ambassador he could not attend because of the queen's delicate condition. But that was only part of the reason. His ambassadors to France, Lord Wiltshire and Viscount Rochford, the queen's father and brother, were not making good headway in arranging a marriage for the princess Elizabeth to one of Francis's three sons. The latest news was that Francis had doubts about Elizabeth's legitimacy, in spite of Henry's various laws proclaiming it. As a result, Henry was not as anxious as he had been to meet Francis. Madge overheard him tell the queen that Francis could be left to stew in his own juices for a while.

"Let him wonder about our friendship—I am king of England and he should beware!" roared Henry.

Though it was too early for the queen to retire to Greenwich for the birthing of her child, Her Majesty required Madge's presence daily. The queen needed foot rubs and back rubs; Her Majesty desired a cherry tart; Her Grace wished for fresh flowers to fill her rooms. Whatever the queen's fancy, Madge was the one person she counted on and Madge was determined never to fail her dearest cousin and friend.

"Lady Margaret, I am tired this afternoon and would nap a while. Will you go to His Majesty and tell him thus—I am sorry I will not be able to play cards with him as he requested," said the queen, laying back against her many pillows.

"Yes, Your Grace. Would you like some ale, perhaps some dainties before I leave you?" said Madge, aware of Her Majesty's cravings for sweet foods.

"No, dear. Rest is all I need. Do give Harry my dearest love," said the queen.

Madge was happy for an opportunity to escape the queen's bedchamber. She stopped in the outer rooms of the queen's apartments and smoothed her hair, checked her dress, and lined her mouth with olive oil, a jar of which was kept in the ladies' rooms. Madge hoped to see Arthur.

As she made her way to the king's privy chamber, she heard boisterous voices, much laughing and shouting. She gave her name and the nature of her errand to the guard at the door and waited until he returned to give her leave to enter. When she walked into the privy chamber, she was surprised to see Norris, Brereton, Wyatt, Francis Weston, and several other men gathered around the king. They made way for her as she passed through, Norris bowing low and smiling at her, trying to catch her eye. She walked past them all and curtsied before the king.

"Pretty Madge, you have a message for us from the queen?" said His Majesty.

Without rising, Madge answered, "Yes, Your Grace."

"Come, come. Stand and tell us what word from our most beloved wife," said the king.

"Her Majesty regrets that she is unable to keep her engagement with Your Grace for playing Primero this afternoon. She is tired and has taken to her bed," said Madge, with her head bowed.

"Aye, 'tis probably a good thing—the queen needs to build her strength for the birthing of the babe. But tell me, Pretty Madge, would you like to join me at cards?" said the king, smiling.

Madge felt her face flush. She was surrounded by the king's men.

"I have no such skills, Your Majesty. Playing with me would be no challenge," said Madge.

"'Tis never a challenge when I play with any but my queen— she is the only one who will not let me win! But run along, Pretty Madge. I can see you like not this company of men— were I a lovely young maiden, I, too, would feel as if I had walked into a den of lions," said the king, who laughed heartily to see Madge back out of the chambers, her face red and her eyes filling with tears. The other men joined the king in his merriment and Madge heard the king say to Norris, "You'll have your hands full making that one care for the likes of you, Norris. She's skittery as a kitten."

"I have ways to tame a puss, sire. Many ways," said Norris, again to much laughter.

Madge hurried to Cate's room. She knocked and before she could calm her breath, Cate opened the door.

"What is it? What is wrong?" said Cate.

"Why think you something is the matter?" said Madge, still struggling to settle her heartbeat.

"You are white and red at the same time. You breathe as

though you have run the length of the castle and you look as if you might burst into tears at a moment's notice," said Cate.

"The king and his horrid, horrid men! I had to deliver him a message and was not well treated. My own intended husband mocked me—I cannot abide him! I cannot marry him!" said Madge.

"There, there, Maddie. Soon the queen will bear her son and you can be released from Norris once and for all. You and Arthur can marry, just as you have planned," said Cate.

"Have you seen him?"

"Aye. This morning he was in the garden and he told me he was going to the horse stables to help break a new steed for Suffolk," said Cate.

"Think you he is still at the stables?" said Madge.

"Let us walk together and discover him," said Cate.

Cate and Madge made a circuitous route to the stables, lest they be seen by Norris or his spies. When they arrived, Madge heard Arthur singing inside the enormous stalls. She walked in while Cate kept guard at the door.

For a moment, she watched him brush down a huge stallion, pure black with a noble brow and sixteen hands high if not more. Arthur was working along the flanks, singing jovially. She loved how he looked at that moment. His brown hair was mussed and he had removed his jerkin so that his shirt hung loose about him. She watched as he took long, steady strokes across the horse's body, his own form as firm and fit as that of the stallion. She could have watched him forever, but she had little time.

"Arthur . . . my love," she whispered.

He turned around at once, dropped the brush, and hurried to her.

"My pretty, pretty Madge! What are you doing here?" he said, sweeping her up and kissing her hungrily.

"The queen sent me on an errand and she is resting. I have a moment and wanted to find you. Methinks it has been long since I have seen you," said Madge, kissing him all over his face and neck.

"Soon, we can hope to have every hour of every day, dearest," he said. He drew her to him, kissing her deeply. "I do not know how much longer I can wait."

"Wait we must, sweetheart," said Madge.

Instead of pulling away from her, Arthur took her by the waist to a clean pile of hay, fell to his knees and patted a place for her to sit beside him. She did so and soon, they were kissing once again. He laid her back against the hay and she could smell the sweetness of it. She brought her arms around his neck and kissed him once again. She felt as if she could kiss him forever. His hands moved over her body, lingering in various places. For once, she did not resist him but allowed him free rein. They continued thus until she felt ready to step out of her clothes and become his once and for all.

"My dearest, we must stop while I am still able to gain control over my senses," said Arthur. "We dare not be as man and wife until our plan is complete and we have the queen's blessing. We dare not . . ." he said as he stood and pulled her up beside him.

"You look like a scarecrow! Covered in straw!" said Madge, brushing him off and laughing.

"You look no better, milady!" he said, while he did the same for her.

"I will come to Cate's door on the morrow about this same time. Mayhap her Majesty will require another nap," said Arthur.

"If Her Grace releases me, I will be there—if not, keep this to remind you of me," said Madge as she kissed him fully and took his hand to press against her bosom. She heard him sigh and broke away from him once more.

"Until we meet—you are ever my dearest," said Arthur.

"And you mine," said Madge.

As the weeks passed, the queen did, indeed, take to her bed each day. Madge noticed how drawn and pale Her Majesty looked and how she lacked desire to do the smallest deed. The king visited her every evening, brought her special treats and gifts that often made her smile. But Madge saw the worry cross His Majesty's brow at times when he thought the queen was not looking.

She and Arthur met at Cate's most afternoons, talking and making plans for their secret wedding. They both insisted Cate remain with them as they feared their passion might overrule them. No one could afford such a mistake. And though Cate kept them chaste and pure, neither of them believed such a state of grace could last. Arthur and Madge longed to tell the queen of their plans; they longed for one another as the days grew warmer.

In late June, the queen seemed weaker than usual. She called Madge to her and whispered, "Margaret, I fear the babe is coming sooner than we expected—too soon. Tell no one but do not leave me this day. Close my bedchambers to all but yourself and Dame Brooke, should we have need of her. I am unwell . . . unwell."

Madge did as she was commanded and sent the other ladies from the queen's apartments. She sent for Dame Brooke, who arrived speedily with her satchel of implements. She brought warm broth to the queen, but Her Majesty ate no more than a few spoonfuls. Madge rang for willow bark tea but the queen refused it. By nightfall, Madge was terrified as the queen began to bleed. Her Majesty said not a word, just lay on her bed, her lips moving in silent prayer.

"'Tis not a good sign, this blood," said Dame Brooke as she examined the queen in her intimate places.

"Should I send for Dr. Linacre? I am no midwife—I know not what to do," said Madge.

"Aye, mayhap that be good. For I fear things will not go as they should. I'll need all the help I can get," said Dame Brooke in a low voice.

"Yes, yes, send for him and for the lady Mary, my sister. I would have her with me," said the queen.

"Mary is in the north country, Your Grace, remember? I shall send for Dr. Linacre," said Madge.

"Yes, yes. Hurry, dear Margaret—I fear the babe is seeping away even as I lie here," said the queen.

Madge ran from the bedchambers and grabbed the first maid she saw in the outer rooms.

"Fetch Dr. Linacre—now!" she said, hurrying back to the queen's side once she was sure the girl was well on her way.

"Your Grace, I fear the babe must needs come out. I'm going to rub this sweet almond oil on your belly and on your womanly parts—do not be ashamed—I have seen a thousand such parts," said Dame Brooke as she poured warmed oil on the queen's belly and rubbed it into her private areas. "This will ease the babe's coming."

Madge watched as more blood gushed onto the bedsheets. She glanced up at the queen.

"I fear for Her Majesty," whispered Madge.

"With good reason. . . . Ah, here comes the babe floating out in a river of blood," said Dame Brooke.

Madge watched as the babe washed out easily, covered in his mother's blood. He was still, too still. Dame Brooke cleared out his mouth and pinched his nose several times. She swatted his bottom and when that did not work, she massaged his chest, warming his little body with her own heat. But nothing brought life into the limp body.

"'Tis no use. He has gone back to heaven," said Dame Brooke as she made the sign of the cross on his tiny chest with the still-warm almond oil. She then sprinkled him with a pinch of salt and baptized him in the Catholic way; Madge supposed it the only way she knew.

The queen lay motionless on her bed and Madge could not see her breathing.

"Is the queen to die as well?" she said.

"Not if I can help it. Here, get rid of this," said Dame Brooke as she handed Madge the afterbirth. "No need to bury it this time. Now, wrap the babe in the usual cloths and place him beside his mother. Then, bring me that catgut along with those smaller pieces of linen, the packing cloths. And bring the knife," said Dame Brooke.

Madge did as she was told and watched as Dame Brooke took a needle and threaded the catgut. She then stitched the torn places on Her Majesty's person and packed the area with clean cloths to staunch the bleeding. The queen did not flinch or move a muscle during the procedure. She looked at the little bundle beside the queen—the babe was as cold and blue as ice.

"Will the queen live?" Madge asked once again.

"Methinks she will. But she has lost a great deal of her life's blood and she will be weak for some time. I don't know if she will be able to bear more children. But speak not of that to a living soul—our work here is sacred and our secrets are sacred as well," said Dame Brooke. "If she stirs, give her this sleeping draught. She will need rest for at least a fortnight. Do not let her fret overmuch about the bairn—such sadness will delay her recovery."

At that moment, Dr. Linacre and Mistress Holland entered the chamber.

"How does the queen?" said Dr. Linacre.

"She fares well enough. But the boy is lost—born dead. I did all I could," said Dame Brooke.

"I am sorry for it—I should have arrived sooner—perhaps I could have helped in some way," said Dr. Linacre.

"Nothing more could have been done, sir. I have delivered thousands of babes and this one was gone before he had a chance to live. I have done the necessaries to preserve his wee soul," said Dame Brooke.

"Does the king know?" said Madge.

"He is on his way here now—ah, I hear the Yeomen of the Guard marching to us," said Dr. Linacre.

A moment later, the king burst into the bedchamber, his face flushed and filled with fury and grief. He looked at his queen, white with pale lips and a now-flattened belly. Beside her, wrapped in the softest lamb's wool, lay a small bundle. Henry knelt beside the babe, uncovered the child, and saw it was a boy, a perfectly formed baby prince, his blueish skin waxy and his head covered in soft, reddish down. The king picked up the child and clutched him to his large chest. Henry sobbed.

No one in the bedchamber moved. Dr. Linacre stood as if struck by a magician; Dame Brooke kept still as she hugged the far wall; Madge froze at Anne's side, afraid to look at the king, afraid to make a sound, afraid to breathe.

Carefully, with great tenderness, Henry placed the bundle beside the queen. He touched her face with his meaty hands, cupping her cheek as one might touch a butterfly wing. Then, he rose, gained mastery over himself, and spoke.

"No one is to know of this. We will not speak of it again. On pain of death, there is to be no talk of what has happened here this day," said the king. He then turned on his heel and stalked out of the queen's bedchambers. No one moved for several moments. Then, as Madge was rising to her feet, she heard an enormous howl, a sound so loud and so filled with pain she thought at first it was a bear let loose among the dogs. Then, she realized it was the king himself.

The queen slept all night and Madge stayed by her side, barely sleeping herself. She did not want Her Majesty to awaken alone, or be by herself when she examined the babe still by her side. Madge did not know what to expect after such an event, but she knew her queen and she knew the days ahead would be difficult.

"Margaret . . . Margaret . . . are you here?" said the queen.

"Yes, Your Majesty. I have been with you all night," said Madge.

"I cannot remember . . . is the prince yet born? My head feels as if it has been stuffed with cotton. I know I feared the prince would come too soon but I cannot remember . . ." said the queen as she struggled to sit up.

"Your Grace, you delivered a son but he came too early. He is . . . he is . . ." Madge could not finish.

"He is dead," said the queen, her voice dull.

She then turned to the bundle at her side and picked it up. Slowly, with utmost care, she unwrapped the blankets and gazed at the little one within.

"Perfect . . . he is perfect . . . see his little fingers, long and slender like my own. And his hair, the color of his father's. So tiny he is. So frail and helpless . . . I cannot bear it! I cannot bear that he never even drew a breath on this earth. Why send him? Why send him to me when he cannot draw one breath?! Oh, *mon dieu!*" said the queen as she continued to hold the baby to her breast, cradling the head in one hand, patting the small back with the other.

Madge said nothing while the queen held her baby through the morning and afternoon. No one disturbed them and the queen spoke not a word to Madge. She cooed and sang to the boy, rubbed his chest and kissed his entire body. Finally, she swaddled him again in the blanket and lay back against her pillows.

"Does the king know?" she said.

"Yes, Majesty. He came immediately. He has seen the babe and yourself," said Madge.

"How did he take the sad news?" said the queen. "He shall put me away! He shall be rid of me for I have once again failed him! I fear for us, Margaret. I fear for all of us! What will become of me? What will he do?"

The queen's voice has become quite strained and she thrashed about in the bed. Madge knew she was quickly losing control of herself and Madge needed to say just the right words to comfort her.

"He shed many tears, Majesty. He touched your face very gently, a touch full of love," said Madge.

"He cannot know . . . he cannot know how my heart breaks. He cannot . . ." The queen melted into sobs and Madge stood by silently. Dr. Linacre had told Madge to remove the babe from the queen as soon as she could do so without upsetting Her Majesty, so a proper Christian burial could take place. Master Cranmer was waiting in the chapel to officiate.

"Majesty—cousin, may I take the babe to the chapel now? They are waiting," said Madge softly.

"No. I do not ever want to let my little Henry go. I would keep him with me always," said the queen, her eyes blurry and strange-looking.

"Dearest, you must let him go to God. You will have another. . . ." said Madge.

"I care not a fig for another! This is my boy! Here, right here! I cannot let him go from me—he will fear the dark and he will need his mother!" said the queen. "Leave me! At once!"

Madge made her way from the bedchambers, confused and sad. She did not know what to do, so she hurried to Dr. Linacre. He sent her to bed with the other ladies and said he would give the queen another sleeping tonic. Madge did as she was told. By the next morning, the babe was gone from the queen's chambers and Her Majesty was sleeping unperturbedly.

Twenty-three

For the next fortnight, Dr. Linacre mixed his potions and the queen slept. Each time she awoke, she asked for her son and seemed muddled and confused. When she asked for the prince, she received another dose of the sleeping medicine. Madge stayed with the queen the entire time. The king did not visit.

By mid-July, the queen seemed to have accepted her loss, though she made no motion to arise from her bed. She refused the daily draught of medicine from Dr. Linacre and began to sip the broth Madge procured for her. Slowly, the color returned to her face but there was no light in her dark eyes. The king kept his distance from her until the forty days passed, those days in which she would have been churched, if the prince had lived. The king still believed a woman "unclean" after a birth, even a miscarriage, until the allotted time had passed. Dr. Linacre told her this one day when she asked why the king refused to visit his queen, who was so full of sorrow.

As harvest time approached, the king sent word that he would come to the queen's apartments to sup. Madge and the other ladies of the bedchamber worked hard to prepare for His Majesty's visit, ordering his favorite foods and arranging for pleasing music as well as having the scrubwomen give the apartments a good airing and cleaning. During the business buzzing around her, the queen remained in her bed, listless and without smiles.

About an hour before the king was to arrive, Madge asked the ladies of the bedchamber to leave, giving Madge a private moment with the queen.

"Who does she think she is, ordering us away from Her Majesty's presence?" said Jane Seymour, who refused to move an inch from where she stood.

"She has lost her senses—thinks herself the queen," said Lady Douglas.

No one left the room until Madge begged the queen to send them all away.

"Yes, yes, begone, all of you! I would hear what my cousin has to say," said the queen wearily.

At her command, the ladies scattered, their silk and satin skirts rustling against the fresh rushes. The queen sighed heavily.

"What is it, Margaret?" she said.

"Majesty, I have spent every moment with Your Grace since . . ."

"Speak not of it, not one word," said the queen.

"And I know the grief in your heart. I have heard you sobbing in the night and seen how you ache. I also saw the king's own sadness when first he came to see how you fared, whilst you slept. He loves you still, though his disappointment is keen.

You must arise from your bed and greet His Majesty with fair looks and soft words. There are those who would see you fail, Your Grace. And those who hope His Majesty will tire of you soon. You must get up from your bed, put away your sorrow, and become the lady for whom the king moved all the world," said Madge.

She had not meant to give such advice. She had merely wanted to suggest that the queen try to give succor to the king, as Arthur had told her many tales of the king's wild talk in his own bedchambers—that he had been bewitched, that he would never get a son, that God frowned on his new marriage. Such talk struck fear into Madge's heart, not for herself so much as for her beloved queen. Madge had seen enough into the king's own character to know he would not blink at putting a once-beloved wife away, perhaps even striking her head from her shoulders if he deemed it necessary. And if the queen did not soon give him a prince, the king would, no doubt, deem it so.

"Dearest cousin, I thank you for your wisdom. A better woman would heed it. But I simply have not strength to fight an entire court. I care not . . . I care not . . ." said the queen and broke into weeping.

"Madame, please. Please do not cry. The king has not seen you in weeks and you must present a pretty face and a happy countenance. All depends upon it!" said Madge.

"I would pray a while before His Majesty arrives. Please send for Cranmer," said the queen. "I would have the comfort that my helpless, innocent boy is in God's hands now."

Madge sent for Master Cranmer and left the queen and her minister alone in the chambers. She waited with the other ladies.

"So, Pretty Madge is among us now, ladies," said Jane

Seymour. "Has the queen put you away, too? Or is she cooking up more witchery to blind the king to her evil ways?"

"Lady Jane, I know you favor the old religion but surely even you have signed the king's laws. There is more evil in popery than in any part of our blessed queen," said Madge as she stared into the pinched eyes of Lady Seymour. "I would remind you of the power in an anointed queen," said Madge, her ears burning with anger. "You should mind your tongue."

"I have no fear of the whore. I hear that the king has set his eyes on a new mistress, one of great beauty and charm. Some say he will put this new lady on the throne," said Lady Jane.

"You speak treason—you should be thankful I am not one to spread malicious lies or tell tales. You might find your own head on a pike at London Bridge," said Madge.

At that moment, Archbishop Cranmer opened the door to the queen's apartments and emerged. He crooked his finger toward Madge, beckoning her to go to the queen.

"Her Majesty will dress now, Lady Margaret," he said.

Madge hurried into the queen's bedchambers and found her sitting up, trying to brush out her hair.

"Madame, allow me," said Madge, taking the brush from her hand. While she brushed with one hand, she pulled out a lovely green dress for the queen's approval with the other. Then, with the queen's permission, she recalled the ladies and, together, they dressed the queen. Though Anne felt as flimsy as a rag doll in her hands, Madge was happy the queen was at least out of her bed.

"Make way for the king! Make way for the king's majesty!" shouted the yeomen as they marched into the queen's outer apartments where Anne sat on her velvet throne, regal in her green dress, her long dark hair hanging to her waist. The gentlemen accompanying the king placed themselves at various posts around the rooms and then the king entered, smiling at the queen's ladies. He immediately bowed before his wife and took her hand. She started to rise to give him obeisance, but he quickly put his hands on her narrow shoulders and kept her in her seat.

"How does my queen?" he said softly as he took the large chair next to hers. Madge stood behind the queen, ready to assist if need be.

"Well enough, Harry. I have missed you these long weeks," said the queen.

"And I you, my love. I . . . I am sorry about . . . our boy," said the king.

Madge watched as the queen's hands began to shake. She knew the queen was close to tears and saw quick plashes fall onto the green silk of Anne's gown. The king drew Anne's face close to his and Madge could hear him whisper, "My heart is broken, too, my love. But, we shall have more sons. He was perfect—we shall have another."

The queen said nothing for a moment. Then, in a voice as flat as the horizon, she said, "I care not for any other. I want my son! The boy we have lost! My whole body aches for him."

Madge did not want others to hear such words from the queen so she motioned for Master Smeaton to play a lively turn on his virginals. Soon, the ladies and gentlemen were dancing around the room, no longer attuned to the queen's deep grief.

"Thank you, Pretty Madge. I see our queen is not yet herself. I would help her if I but knew the way," said the king, looking at Madge with begging eyes. Madge shrugged her shoulders at him—she did not know how to lighten the burden the queen carried.

"Anne . . . dearest . . . 'tis the season of the sweats now. What say you we go on Progress to the country. The fresh air will do you good and we can get away from the things that sadden us," said the king, his mouth moving against the queen's ear.

"I have no wish to leave my rooms, Harry. I have no wish to sing or dance or play at cards. I would pray and take the Sacraments each day. I would sew for the poor widows and orphans who no longer have the monasteries to help them," said the queen.

Madge saw the king's face grow rosy at the mention of the monasteries.

"Madame, you would do well to forget the plight of the poor and homeless and think of your own danger. Though I raised you up, I can just as easily cast you down again," hissed the king, though quietly.

His remarks seemed to reach something in the queen. Her eyes focused on his mouth and she brought her hand to his face for a gentle caress.

"Ah, Harry, would you strike me down so soon? My dearest love, would you frighten me when I am only sorry to have disappointed you so? My heart breaks for our son and for you, too, my king. I have failed you—perhaps I am not worthy of the honor you have given me," said Anne. Her brown eyes were moist and enormous-looking. Madge thought she had never looked as fragile or as pretty. She could see the king's face lose its harshness, love flooding his features once again.

"I would have you in my bed once more, sweetheart. I would have you happy and gay, dancing and singing as you did before," said Henry.

"Then all shall be as you command, my lord," said the queen. She clapped her hands to stop the music and rose.

"Dear friends, thank you for being so jolly and spry. And

Master Smeaton, thank you for the lively song. I will now play and sing for the king's good pleasure and would ask that you leave us," said the queen.

Madge started from her post behind the queen but the queen turned to her.

"Lady Margaret, if you will stay with me—I need your strength. Lie on your pallet and be still as a mouse—Mistress Mouse, as George calls you," said the queen. She was smiling at Madge, though it was a sad smile.

The room emptied, Madge lay on her side facing toward the king and queen, though she had no clear view of them. The queen began to play and hum, a slow song. Madge thought she recognized it as a ballad from her childhood about a lady who was forced to marry against her will. Rather than give herself to her husband, she walked into the sea where she had watched her lover sail away. When the queen had finished the song, the king spoke softly.

"Madame, you have not lost your charm—I could listen to you sing all this night," he said. He rose and indicated the queen was to rise also. Then, he took her in his arms and began to dance with her, gently, around the room. He sang himself, his strong tenor voice lilting this way and that, singing a love song. When the song was over, he kissed the queen on the mouth.

"Come away with me, Anne. Let us start anew. A Progress would take us far from here, far from our pain. Come away . . ." he said, kissing her face, her hands, her neck.

Her Majesty stood perfectly still. She seemed to allow this lovemaking but was not participating in it. It seemed to Madge that the queen's inner heart was far, far away.

The king stopped his kisses and looked into the queen's eyes.

"I cannot, Harry. I do not wish to go on Progress—I need some time to heal my body and my soul. You go ahead, beloved. Go and hunt as you list. When you return, I promise I will be my old self. While you are gone, I will spend my days in prayer and my nights also. I must have this time, dearest, else I may never return to myself," said the queen with dignity.

"If this is what you wish . . . it shall be so. Perhaps it will help to send our daughter to you here. That should cheer you," said the king.

Madge saw Anne's face light up.

"Yes, Henry! Send Elizabeth to me, my love! And when you return, you shall find me ever cheerful and happy once more—then, my dearest, we shall endeavor to make a prince!" said the queen.

With that, she kissed the king on the cheek and clapped her hands for the servants to bring them refreshment. She did not see the dark look the king gave her in her happiness. But Madge saw.

Over the next week, plans and preparations were made for the king's Progress. The princess Elizabeth journeyed from Hatfield with Lady Bryan, while the lady Mary stayed at Eltham with Madge's parents. On the day before most of the court departed with the king, Madge was hurrying to Cate's room, hoping to meet Arthur there. She had received a message from him that morning.

"Come in, Maddie-girl. I'm almost packed. I wish you were coming with me," said Cate as she placed her creams and lotions into a cachet. Shadow sat at her side.

"You must keep your eyes and ears open—so you can report all to me of the king. If there are any who plot against

Her Majesty, you must give me their names as well. With the loss of her son, the queen is in a weakened state, both in her body and mind, but also, I fear, with the king himself," said Madge.

"Aye. It is said he is already enamored of a new beauty. He is a rascal, our sovereign. Barely buries his son until he's on the move to a new love. Granted, I have not loved the queen but I am sorry for Anne now. These cannot be easy times for her," said Cate.

"Indeed, they are not. But remember, Cate, though the queen follows the new religion, it is she who has tried to stop the dissolution of the monasteries and convents. She has made an enemy of Master Cromwell by doing so. And she has great concern for the poor and for the education of our people," said Madge.

"Tut, tut. All well and good, but she has much to atone for—our dear Queen Catherine's misery at Kimbolton for one thing. They say Anne is poisoning her and trying to poison the lady Mary as well," said Cate.

"Surely you do not listen to such idle gossip—my own woman! The queen is as godly a woman as I know and growing more so with the passing of each day. She would be kind to the lady Mary if only the lady Mary would accept her. And 'tis not the queen who has sent the dowager princess to Kimbolton— that order came from His Majesty," said Madge.

"No matter now. We must do our best to preserve her—for in preserving the queen, we preserve the fates of our whole family," said Cate. "And for that reason and that reason alone, Maddie-girl, I will be your eyes and ears on the Progress. Now, methinks I hear the familiar step of Master Brandon on the cobbles," said Cate with a smile. Shadow stood and began to jump around.

Before he could knock, Madge opened the heavy door and Arthur stepped inside.

He swept Madge into his arms, twirling her in quick circles as he kissed her. Then, he set her down and stared into her face.

"Pretty Madge, you do grow more beautiful each day—let's see, it has been five whole days since last we met—that makes you five times more lovely," he said, kissing her full on the mouth.

"Arthur—we are not alone, remember?" said Madge.

"Aye, forgive me, dearest. I forgot my manners I was so anxious to see you," said Arthur. "Mistress Cate, how goeth the preparations?"

"Well enough, young Brandon, well enough. We leave on the morrow and will not return until the birthday of the princess," said Cate. "I will hate to leave Shadow here." Cate patted Shadow's head and took her small cache of herbs and medicines out to the wagons below. "I shall be back in a few moments. Mind your manners, Master Brandon."

"At last! We are alone," said Arthur as he held Madge once again, Shadow nudging between them with her cold nose.

"Yes, my love! It has been far too long since mine arms have held you," said Madge, resting against him. For a moment, they were silent. The whole court bustled outside Cate's door.

"All this fuss and going about! 'Tis trouble indeed! I am glad to stay here," said Madge.

"But think of the adventure you shall miss, my love! Hunting and feasting, tilting, dancing, and riding through the wild north country! I wish you were coming—I shall be miserable without you!" said Arthur.

"By the sound, you shall be quite happy—hunting and dancing and singing! You shall not miss me one whit!" said Madge.

"Ah, let me show you just how much I shall miss those pretty dukkies!" said Arthur, fondling her playfully.

"None of that, sire. We must be more careful than ever. Now that we have lost our prince," said Madge.

"I will not give up, Pretty Madge. I will have you yet—as my wife, of course!" he said as Madge swung her small fists at his chest.

"Dearest, do be careful while you are traveling with the king. There are dangers," said Madge.

"Yes—the biggest being the king himself! Fear not! I shall endeavor to please His Majesty in all things," said Arthur.

"His wrath is a fiery furnace these days. I fear what may happen if the queen does not regain her pluck soon. She still mopes and cries, though having the little princess with her seems to help. Sharpen your ears and eyes, my darling. We must keep the queen informed on all the moods of the king. Her safety is our safety," said Madge.

"You speak more and more like a true courtier, mistress. I like it not," said Arthur.

"I would survive, sir. You should seek to do the same," said Madge.

Twenty-four

During the six weeks of the king's Progress, Madge, the queen, and Princess Elizabeth enjoyed a peaceful time. Each day, the queen and Madge attended the Mass given by Matthew Parker, the newly appointed bishop. Often, Parker would accompany the queen to her apartments afterward and they would discuss ways to bring the English Bible to the people. Madge sat at the queen's feet, her sewing in her hand, and listened as the queen and Master Parker discussed theology and God and death and salvation. The queen seemed to change before Madge's eyes. She was no longer the young woman who had conquered the most goodly king in all the world; no longer the laughing, dancing maiden without a care in the world but to comb her dark hair and flash her dark eyes; no longer the one who gambled with cards and rode into the hunt with the enthusiasm of the king himself. The queen now seemed more dignified. She had grown serious and desired above all things to see virtue and goodness at court. Her ladies and their religious lives concerned her, as did the king's health and well-being. She and Master Parker talked about the bloodshed that tainted the kingdom and how the queen might spare more of those labeled heretic as well as those who labored in the monasteries. The princess Elizabeth and her well-being worried the queen, too, though Master Parker assured Her Grace that Elizabeth's place was secure.

Madge listened and learned. Slowly, as the days gave way to one another and the sky turned that brilliant blue of autumn, the queen regained much of herself, though she was no longer young in either looks or in spirit. Madge thought her to be the most beneficent, wise, and kindly of queens. The stresses and strains had taken their toll on her beauty, yet Anne still possessed the kind of charm men found alluring. At least, Madge believed this to be true.

"Here Purkoy! *Ici, mon chienne! Vitement!*" cried the queen. Purkoy ran to his mistress's arms, jumped up, and licked the queen on the face, his fluffy tail wagging and his bright eyes happy at the almost constant attention the queen had bestowed upon him while the king and the court had been on Progress.

"*Bon chienne! Bon!*" said the queen. Princess Elizabeth reached for Purkoy's ear, grabbed it, and held on while the dog settled into the queen's lap, next to the princess.

"The princess likes Purkoy, methinks," said Madge, laughing as the two played, rumpling the queen's nightdress.

"*Mais oui! Naturellement!*" said the queen as both pup and baby crawled over her.

"I have not seen you this happy in some time, Your Grace," said Madge.

"It is pleasant, is it not, to have our rooms to ourselves. Surrounded by those we love and those who love us—'tis a rare moment at court. No one here is scheming; the king isn't stealing a glance at some young maid—well, he may be doing thus but at least not before my very eyes!" said the queen.

"Yes, Majesty—I, too, have enjoyed our time away from the fuss and bother—why, 'tis noon and we are still frolicking in our nightclothes!" said Madge. "The only unpleasant sight is Master Cromwell, who scowls at me when I am forced to walk the corridors on Your Majesty's business—what a man is he!" said Madge.

"He is not pretty but he does his master's bidding almost as well as Wolsey did. Though I trust him not—he is ruthless against the monasteries and wouldst take from the church to fill the king's coffers," said the queen.

"Let us not think on such things today—the sun is high in the sky and the birds are winging across the gardens. Shall we take the princess and our dogs out for a walk?" said Madge.

"A grand idea. Come, Elizabeth, let us dress you—the blue silk, I think—it matches her eyes, eh Lady Margaret?" said the queen as she began to remove Elizabeth's nightdress.

Madge helped dress both the queen and the princess, slipped one of her older dresses on as she would be handling the dogs. Soon they headed for the gardens and the fields beyond, where Shadow and Purkoy chased hares and fetched sticks.

The early days of autumn passed with a continuing sense of peace and contentment for Madge and the queen. One glorious day melted into another and as the weeks passed, the queen's face became more relaxed and her youth seemed to return, along with her fiery spirits. Madge, though much younger, could hardly keep up with the queen, such was her energy and happiness. Though there were still moments when Madge found the queen in tears over her lost child, those instances grew more and more infrequent. The presence of the princess Elizabeth seemed the best medicine for the queen's broken heart.

At the Feast of St. Michael and All Angels, Bishop Parker said a special Mass for the queen and those few ladies left in her service. After the Mass, the queen invited the bishop to her apartments for the midday meal. Madge served them both.

In the middle of the meal, Madge heard a commotion outside the queen's rooms and instructed the guard to allow her into the open hall so she could see what was causing the stir.

"I would see the queen or her bedwoman, Lady Margaret Shelton! It is of urgent import!" said a man's voice.

"Arthur! What are you doing here?" said Madge. She hurried to him, nodded a quick greeting, pushed the guard's arm away, and led him just outside the queen's door.

"Mistress, I have news which you must hear—you and then, the queen," said Arthur, his eyes full of concern.

"Come," said Madge as she led him down the hall to Cate's room. Once inside, she kissed him but he pushed her aside.

"Mistress, though I have missed your kisses, what I have to tell you must come first," said Arthur, tossing his cap onto Cate's bed.

"Well? Speak man!" said Madge.

"It is the king, Margaret. He is at Wulfhall, Sir John Seymour's manor near Savernake Forest," said Arthur.

"'Tis the right time for His Majesty to be so—'twas planned in his Progress," said Madge.

"You do not understand—I believe the king is interested in the Lady Jane Seymour. They dine together each evening, often alone with only her parents to chaperone. They hunt of a morning, then the lady retires to her sewing while Great Harry bowls or naps. I fear the king's heart is going out to the quiet, ever-gentle Lady Jane," said Arthur.

"This cannot be true—it is uncharitable for me to speak thus, but the lady in question is . . . well, she is . . ."

"Plainer than dirt? Aye, that she is and almost as muddle-headed. She is nothing like our queen, who shines and glitters with wit and style. How the king can think of Lady Jane, I do not know—I like my women fair and lovely to behold," said Arthur, grabbing Madge's waist and kissing her quickly on the tip of her nose.

"Perhaps this is the reason for his attraction—perhaps he tires of the sparkle of the diamond and longs for the softer look of a . . ." said Madge.

"Plain polished stone? I know, I know, give me not that stare! I should not poke fun at the poor lady because she has no beauty—after all, not everyone can be a beauty," said Arthur.

"Are you sure of this, dearest? Is there no room for doubt?" said Madge.

"It is what my eyes tell me, my love. I wish it were not so. There are some who say the king fancies a pretty lass, one full of life and dancing. But no one can say her name and I have not seen His Majesty press any such girl in particular. The one His Majesty spends time with is the Lady Jane Seymour," said Arthur.

"We must go to the queen at once," said Madge as she led him into the queen's privy chamber.

"Such news does not surprise me, Master Brandon. I am, however, quite taken aback that you should ride all this way to tell me about it," said the queen, sitting at her gaming table with Arthur and Madge standing in front of her.

"I am sorry to bring such tidings, Your Majesty, but I would serve you honestly," said Arthur.

"But your father, my lord Suffolk, holds no love for me. Why do you care about my case?" said the queen.

Arthur did not speak. For a long moment, silence hung in the room like a thick cloud.

"Majesty, Master Brandon knows of my great love for Your Grace. I asked him to keep me informed about the court while on Progress. My nurse, Cate, has the same instructions," said Madge.

"Mistress Cate is your servant—naturally she would bring news and would be loyal to you. This does not explain the actions of Master Brandon," said the queen.

"It is because, though I love Your Majesty, there is another I love—my lady Margaret, your dear cousin," said Arthur. Madge noticed he looked pale and his hand trembled at his side.

"Ha! My eyes told me thus some time ago, sir. I wanted to see if you had the nerve to say the words here, to me. It pleases me that you have such courage," said the queen.

"What shall we do, Your Majesty? What's to be done?" said Madge.

"We shall go on Progress ourselves, Lady Margaret! We shall join the king at Wulfhall and then we shall see who captures him!" said the queen, her eyes lit with sparks of anger and will and determination. "I will not give up so easily that which has cost me everything," the queen whispered under her breath.

———

The queen rode in a litter covered with the Tudor colors and Arthur led the small procession on an enormous white steed. Lady Margaret rode on a palfrey beside him and the journey itself was full of laughter and sweet lovers' words. The queen brought her most sumptuous clothes and her most valuable jewels. She also packed her lute, her virginals, a dancing costume, and a small harp as she intended to entertain His Majesty as she had done when first they met. The nip in the air brought out the roses in Her Majesty's cheeks and her weeks of rest and play had done her much good. She was ready to win back her king and Madge had no doubt but that she would do so.

They arrived at Wulfhall after three days of travel and were announced to Sir Seymour and his wife immediately. Lady Seymour arranged for their rooms, with the queen's room right next to the king's, a situation for which the queen was thankful. Madge and the queen shared a look of bemusement after the queen had been announced, and they watched with mirth as the Seymours scuttled around to make room for them. When they arrived, the king was at the hunt and Lady Jane was resting. Madge followed the queen into her room and began unpacking. She had left Arthur at the stables seeing to his horse.

"I would bathe, Lady Margaret. And do bring that oil of lavender to me—also the vial of cinnamon. His Majesty has always loved the smell of it—the odor alone should remind him of . . . well, our happiness," said the queen as she prepared for her bath. Madge directed the servants to bring the warm water to the large tub she had ordered brought to the queen's room. Once the queen was inside, Madge bathed her with soft cloths and washed her long hair in rosewater. She added a special oil to make the queen's hair shine.

"What gown, Your Grace?" said Madge as she placed the queen's undergarments on the bed.

"What think you, Margaret? Which will hold most allure for the king?" said the queen.

"I have always loved the crimson gown—it goes well with your eyes and your hair," said Madge, holding the gown up for Her Majesty to see.

"Well enough! Now, help me out of here, lady," said the queen.

Madge heard the heralds announce the return of the king's hunting party and felt her heart skip as she thought of him lumbering up to his rooms to change for the evening meal. He would know, of course, the queen had arrived. But would he come to her door? Or would he wait for her to be announced at supper? Suddenly, Madge felt frightened. What if His Majesty were angry about the queen's unexpected presence? What if he turned ever more to Mistress Seymour?

The queen had arranged to enter the Great Hall without fanfare or announcement. Instead, she wished to sit before the king as a lady-in-waiting would. She intended to sing and play for him while he ate.

"God save the king!" rang the heralds as Henry entered the hall. He was larger than Madge remembered, bigger than life. His ruddy cheeks and pale blue eyes squinted around the room. When they lit on his queen standing with the other ladies, a tiny smile played about his smallish mouth. He sat at the center of the head table and indicated the food was to be served. Dozens of men and women brought platters and bowls of steaming food and the sounds of the feast clattered and clanged through the hall.

Without a word, the queen moved to a small stool set before

the king and began to play her lute, a gentle tune. The room grew quiet and as it did so, the queen began to sing. Her voice was always lovely, Madge had thought. But this night, it seemed she sang with the skill of a nightingale. She sang of a poor maid's love for a most noble knight who was high above her station. The maiden gave herself to this noble knight and had a child by him. Though he was pledged to another, he broke this arrangement, much to the dismay of his people, and married the lovely maid, who gave him many sons. At the end of the music, the king had tears in his eyes. Anne arose and stood before him at the table. She curtsied as deeply as possible and said in a strong voice, for all to hear, "Most beloved husband, I have come to you because I could not bear to be apart from Your Grace a moment longer. Though we have had a time of great sadness, such grief is now behind us. I am again ready, like the moon around the earth, to encircle you with my love."

Madge watched the king carefully. He wiped the water from his cheeks and rose. He held out his hand to Anne and told her to come to him. Great Harry embraced his still-beautiful wife, kissing her long and on the lips, for all to see. Madge stole a glance at Jane Seymour. Her usually pale cheeks burned and those dull eyes cut away from the intimate scene to stare at the food in front of her. Madge caught Arthur's eye and they exchanged a victorious look.

The rest of the evening, the king had eyes for no one but his queen and she for him. She danced with him and for him, sang more, played more, laughed more, and charmed more than she had in some time. It was easy to see how Great Harry had fallen in love with such a woman, Madge thought. She truly was a queen among queens.

Later that night, as Madge prepared for bed, she heard a knock on her door.

"Cate, dear Cate! I am glad you found me—I spied you not when we supped," said Madge as she hugged her servant and drew her into the room.

"I am glad you and the queen are come! There is much I have to tell you," said Cate.

"Then sit, dear friend, sit on this stool and tell me all," said Madge, her loose shift slipping off one shoulder. Her hair caught the light from the fire and she rubbed her arms for warmth.

"Winter comes soon, methinks," said Cate as she sat down on the stool beside Madge's pallet. She was glad the rushes were fresh and that Madge had been given a small, private room next to the queen's.

"Yes, yes. What news?" said Madge.

"The king loves another! The news runs all around Wulf-hall. They say she is a beauty—young and lithe with golden hair and rounded bosoms—much like Bessie Blount," whispered Cate.

"Have you seen this inamorata?" said Madge.

"What's that?" said Cate.

"The new love—have you seen her? Do you know her name?" said Madge.

"No, 'tis a mystery. Yet, that is the news I have heard," said Cate, sipping a mug of ale Madge handed her.

"What about Lady Jane Seymour? What of her and His Majesty?" said Madge.

"Pshaw! They have danced a little—only because 'tis her father's house and His Majesty is a gracious guest. Lady Jane has little to catch the king's eye, I fear. Poor girl, she'll be too old to marry off if Sir Seymour doesn't make a match for her soon," said Cate. "And such a match will be hard to secure if any young man gets a proper look at her."

"I heard His Majesty loved her not a little," said Madge.

"Nonsense! How could he be fond of such as she when he has been married to the proud Queen Catherine of Spain! Even Queen Anne is beautiful and witty, though I will never approve of her or her haughty ways," said Cate.

"She is not haughty, Cate. She is vexed at the king's unfaithfulness and her heart is broken over losing her son. She has much weighing on her thin shoulders," said Madge.

"That I'll warrant. Great Henry is a hard man to hold. Better than she have tried," said Cate. "Now, I must be off to bed—I am in the ladies' main bedchambers downstairs—if you should want me."

"I'll find you, dearest. I am most happy to see you again!" said Madge.

During the remainder of the king's Progress, the royal couple spent their days on the hunt, with the king and his men slaughtering many stags and roes for their evening meals. The queen rode beside the king and killed a buck and more than one coney. Madge usually withdrew to her rooms during the hunt, though she enjoyed the out of doors, especially the autumn beauty of Savernake Forest with the cloudless blue sky, rust-colored leaves, golden late-blooming flowers, and the cool fresh air. The air was a welcome relief from the humid winds and often unsavory smells about London. When she could find a way to creep out by herself, she often walked over the hills and valleys of the forest. On many such days, she sent word for Arthur to meet her at a designated spot, say the large boulder atop the second hill or the curve to the left in the little river that meandered through the fields. Those stolen moments with Arthur were the sweetest part of the Progress for Madge. Unfortunately, the king kept most of his men busy with cleaning hunting gear, tacking the horses, and preparing the carcasses for cooking.

Sir Henry Norris always rode next to the king and, when the queen rested with the ladies, Norris and Sir Francis Bryan, the "vicar of hell," made merry with Great Harry. Bowls, tenes, games of darts, and cards kept them happily occupied. Though Madge had seen Norris a few times, she had not been forced to spend time with him. He seemed happy enough with the pretty serving girl Madge had seen coming from his room.

The day before the Progress was to depart Wulfhall and return to London, the king and queen called all the ladies and gentlemen of the Court together in the Great Hall.

"Dear friends, at the suggestion of my dearest and most beloved wife," said Henry, looking at Anne with great fondness, "there is to be an archery contest between the ladies of the court and their gentlemen friends. This is not to be any ordinary contest but one in which a true hunt is to occur. First, the ladies will go about with bows and arrows to shoot what prey they can—rabbits, squirrels, deer, hedgehogs, chickens, snakes, wild boar—whatever the ladies wound will count for them. This afternoon, the gentlemen will face the same challenge, with one exception. They must tie one arm behind them!" said the king, laughing heartily as the men protested the conditions.

"Look to, gentlemen! We must give the fairer sex a solid chance to best you! After all, you have hunted since boyhood and I'll warrant many of the ladies have never held a bow!" said the king. "When the horns blow, the hunt will begin. Ladies, you may ride or go on foot. May the sharpest marksman win!"

Madge stood beside Lady Seymour and Lady Rochford.

They were making plans to hunt together, but neither looked her way. It was clear she was not welcome in their party. She searched the crowd for a possible friend, but the ladies were dispersing with great speed. She decided she would hunt alone. She picked up a small bow and a quiver of arrows, slung them over her shoulder, and made her way toward the forest. She noticed many of the ladies were heading into the sun so she decided to go in the opposite direction. She hoped she would find more possibilities with fewer hunters nearby.

As the sun shone down on the meadow ahead, Madge noticed the greens of the grasses were fading to brown and some of the brush had already turned crimson and ochre. The air smelled of cut hay and Madge watched as a V of geese flew overhead, honking and squawking like screaming children. She marched along, not looking where she was going. Instead, her eyes were on the sky, following the birds and the clouds. Such excursions reminded her of home, though by now Great Snoring would be cooler and she would be wearing her heavy cloak. She was heading for a large stand of oaks at the edge of the forest where she felt sure she would find a hare or weasel she could snare. With her steady stride, she reached the wood fairly quickly. Beneath the trees, shadows gathered and a great silence enveloped her. She felt as if she were entering some sort of holy ground, a place of unknown age where something very ancient still lived. Whether it be wood sprite or a saintly hermit she did not know. But she felt a presence in the forest.

She continued to travel into the trees, her skirts snagging on the underbrush and the rocks bruising her feet. She found a large boulder covered with lichen and decided to sit upon it so she could quietly wait for an animal to venture into view. She lay her bow and quiver beside her, keeping her breathing even and her movements to a minimum.

After a good while, the birds suddenly stopped their twittering and the wood grew more quiet. Madge did not move. She thought she heard the bushes rustle behind her, but she did not turn for fear of startling the prey.

"Guess who?" said Norris as he placed his hands over her eyes.

"I can tell 'tis you, Norris! Your voice gives you away," said Madge, trying to remove his hands from her eyes.

"Lucky guess, milady—but it is I who am lucky in finding you so alone in this dark wood—I like the queen's game. Indeed, I find it much to my heart's desire," he said, still keeping his hands over her eyes and refusing to allow her to face him.

"You have given me quite a fright!" said Madge as she pulled at his hands. He refused to budge so she decided to try another tack. "Dear Henry, please allow me to see you. Allow me to turn toward you and greet you properly," said Madge, her voice soft and whispery.

"All right, dearest—I will release you if you will promise me a kiss," said Norris.

"I will kiss you, I do so swear," said Madge.

At that, he let loose of her and she faced him. His face was flushed and she could smell wine on his breath. Indeed, his shirt was stained with it as were his lips. He grabbed her waist and pulled her to him.

"For that kiss, milady," he said as he yanked her hair so her head fell back slightly. He kissed her upturned lips, forcing his tongue deep into her mouth. He tasted of vomit and she could not help pushing away from him with all her strength.

"Like you not your betrothed's kisses, my love? Then mayhap you will like this better," he said as he threw her against the boulder and stood over her, his foot against her chest so she could not rise. He began to unlace his codpiece and his breeches.

"You and your haughty ways! I'll teach you a thing or two,

milady. I have offered you my name—I, groom of the stool and the king's boon companion—and you treat me as if I have the pox! I will not abide it!" he said as he began to raise her skirts, lowering himself on top of her while she struggled against him.

"I beg of you—Norris, please! How will I ever learn to love you if you take me like this!" said Madge. She tried to keep her voice calm, hoping that if she remained that way, she could reason with him.

"Any kitchen slut could teach you a thing or two about love, milady. A slut would know to shut her mouth and open her legs when I say," said Norris.

With that, he hit Madge across the lips and she felt warm blood at the corner of her mouth. At that moment, she realized her calmness would not stop him. So she began to scream.

"Shut up, you whore! Shut up! Or I'll stuff something in that mouth you will not like!" said Norris.

Madge fought him, slinging her hands and fists against him as hard as she could. She could feel his manhood pushing against her skirts, which, thankfully, were many and full. She tried to kick him but he was too heavy.

"Witch! You bit me! You shall pay for that, milady—I'll take you frontways and back!" he said.

She felt his hands pull and tear her slips. He was almost to her private self when suddenly, she saw someone behind him, someone enormous, carrying a drawn sword.

"Sir Norris, arise!" said a blustering voice.

Norris leapt up and bowed to the king. He quickly laced himself back together and tucked in his shirt.

"What mean you by this?!" said the king.

"Your Grace, forgive me. I wanted to consummate my betrothal, which is my legal right as Your Grace well knows," said Norris.

"Such consummation is usually accomplished with the lady's acquiescence, sir. It would be unseemly to behave otherwise, especially with the queen's own cousin. I will not have such goings on in my court!" said the king. His Majesty took Norris by his doublet and shook him until Madge imagined his teeth rattled in his skull. The king continued to upbraid him.

"If I hear or see such things again, you will be sent from our presence forever and will lose those many appointments I have given you. Leave us at once and return to London this hour. You may see to the cleaning of the great house of easement—and see to it immediately upon your return—before you eat, before you sleep! Consider yourself lucky with this mercy, which is given only because you have been my friend!" roared the king.

"Yes, Your Majesty," said Norris as he bowed low.

"And Norris, apologize for your unmanly behavior to the Lady Margaret," said the king in a steely tone.

Norris rose and turned to Madge, who was busy rearranging her skirts.

"Mistress Shelton, I am truly sorry for my boorish behavior. I will not act the rake with you again," said Norris. With that, the king waved him away. Then, His Majesty knelt down to comfort Madge.

"Pretty Madge, I fear Sir Norris was in his cups. He is a knave but I have loved him long. I am very sorry he has allowed his lower nature to rule him. May I help you up?" said the king very gently.

"Thank you, sire. Thank you for saving me," said Madge as she rose.

The king put his great arm around her shoulders. Though she tried to contain her tears, she could not. She leaned against the strong chest of the king and cried. He held her to him and stroked her hair with his meaty hand.

"'Twill be all right, Lady Margaret. I will not let any varlet harm you. 'Twill be all right. Come now. Let us return to Wulfhall," said the king.

Twenty-five

Madge's tussle with Norris in Savernake Forest had frightened her completely, but she told no one about it. She also begged the king to keep her secret as she would be humiliated if the news ran round the court. His Majesty gave his sacred promise and allowed her to ride behind him and the queen as they traveled back to London. Many times during the journey, the king gave her kind looks and often sent her tasty morsels from his own plate. The queen said nothing but seemed happy that the king was taking notice of one of her cousins.

As for Arthur, Madge dared not tell him about Norris—she feared he would run him through and be tossed into the Tower as a result. So, she bore her fear and her anxiety and her deep hatred of Norris in silence. And, though she was filled with fear at seeing Norris again when the Progress returned to London,

she did not share her woes with anyone. Secretly, she hoped the
king would relent and allow her to break her troth, after having seen what a churl Norris was.

Though the Progress had gone well after the queen had
joined the king at Wulfhall, Madge took note of how often
the king visited the queen's apartments to sup with her after
they had come home to London. For on those days His Majesty
supped with Anne, he usually bedded her as well. Madge could
only count one time when the king attended his wife since their
return to court.

In the queen's outer apartments, Madge kept watch over
Lady Jane but could find no fault in her behavior, which remained haughty and circumspect. Madge began to believe that
perhaps Arthur had been wrong—perhaps the lady who had
briefly captured His Majesty's attentions was someone other
than Jane Seymour.

By the Feast of All Saints, Madge had started to worry in
earnest that the king had not come again to the queen's apartments. Anne spent her days sewing, debating theology with
Bishop Parker, going to the Mass, and gambling at cards and
dice. She brought in musicians when she wanted to dance and
dance she did—with her ladies and several gentlemen who
visited the queen's apartments regularly: her brother, George;
Brereton; Weston; Wyatt; Richard Pace; and, occasionally,
Arthur. Norris often proved busy on the king's business when
the queen invited him to join them. Madge hoped it was his
shame that kept him away.

"Lady Margaret, I would speak with you," said Arthur, coming up behind her in the queen's outer rooms where the ladies
had gathered for games of cards and tables.

"Certainly, sir," said Madge.

He led her to a small alcove where they could speak in some privacy. He kept his voice low.

"You should warn the queen there is another lady—one of her maids—a Mistress Eleanor of Northumberland. She is new to court and already the king has spied her and wishes to make her his own," said Arthur.

"She is a beauty—I have played Noddy with her many times and have lost not a little. She plays her hand well," said Madge.

"Aye, a treat for the eye she is! I have already come upon her sitting on the king's lap, giving him kisses, and running her tongue around his ear—His Majesty seemed quite taken with the lady," said Arthur.

"Is she so very pretty? And so much so that she has caught *your* eye as well as the king's?!" said Madge.

"Never so pretty as my Pretty Madge—there could not be as fine a woman as the lady Margaret Shelton!" he said.

"Humph. Now you try to soothe me. Are all men like the king? Does the sacrament of marriage mean nothing?" said Madge.

"I do not know all men. I can only say for one—myself. And, for myself, I will tell you that when I take a wife, I shall cleave only unto her—that is, if the lady is your own dear self," said Arthur.

"You say those words now, before we are wed. I'll reckon the king said much the same to the queen ere they married. And now look! He breaks her heart most cruelly!" said Madge.

"He hides his lusts from the queen and always shows her the greatest respect. But he is a man used to getting all he desires—he is the king! For him, to bed a wench is nothing more than drinking a fine wine or eating a tasty sweetmeat. But his wife, she is the one who can give him a son and for that, she remains his one constant love," said Arthur.

"'Tis silly to think of love, then. For queens especially," said Madge.

"Queens are lonely women, I'll warrant. And sad," said Arthur.

Madge did not know whether to tell Her Majesty of the king's new interest or to keep mum. Anne had seemed quite happy on Progress, laughing and making merry with the king so that things seemed almost back to normal. Madge did not want to disturb the veneer of peace and calm that enveloped the queen now that she had regained her allure and had vanquished the threat coming from Jane Seymour.

Though Madge kept Arthur's news to herself, the queen had other gossips who were eager to tell her of the king's new lady love. Soon, Madge noticed how worn and tired the queen began to look. When she combed Her Majesty's hair, she noticed several strands of gray, which the queen commanded she pluck out. One such evening, quite unexpectedly, the guards trumpeted the entrance of His Majesty. Madge dropped her hairbrush and curtsied. The king entered the queen's bedchamber with a smile and a hearty greeting.

"Wife! I have been too long away from you, sweetheart! Come, give us a kiss!" bellowed the king.

Madge watched as Anne rose slowly, her hair hanging around her face and down her back, the soft shift of her nightdress clinging to her delicate frame, the neck loose, showing her throat and shoulders. In the torchlight, the queen still retained her beauty. She curtsied low to the king, then rose and kissed him fully for all to see.

"Your Grace does me much honor," Anne said. "Will you command your men to leave us, dearest?"

"Be gone! All of you!" shouted the king, his face flush with pleasure.

Madge started to leave as well, but Anne took hold of her arm.

"Lady Margaret, I wish to speak privately with His Grace but I may have need of you in a moment. Would you please step inside the garderrobe and stop up your ears?" said the queen, pointing to the small room that housed Her Majesty's sanitary facility.

"Yes, Your Majesty," said Madge quietly.

She entered the stall that was home to the chamber pot and the cistern for washing away the royal wastes. Though every effort was made to keep such places within the castle clean and sweet-smelling, after a few days, all such areas grew a stench. Madge pulled down the wooden cover so she could sit. She looked around the tiny cubicle and had to smother a laugh— how had she come to this? Hiding in the queen's garderrobe, trying not to gag on the smell. Arthur would find this scene rich indeed. However, she lost the humor of the moment as she heard nothing but silence in the queen's bedchamber. She obediently put her fingers in her ears, just in case Their Majesties began to speak. Though the queen had remained calm upon His Majesty's entrance, Madge sensed a storm was coming. She had seen the clouds in Her Majesty's eyes.

"How dare you come to me, Henry? After you have been kissing and fawning over one of mine own ladies?" said the queen.

Madge could hear quite clearly, even though she held her ears.

"Madame, I do not get your meaning," said the king in a calm voice.

"*'Madame, I do not get your meaning!'*" mocked the queen. "Well, dear husband, let me make it plain enough so that even Your Highness can understand it! I will not have you courting my ladies! 'Tis unseemly and I simply will not abide it. I have sent the lady Eleanor from court! You'll have to satisfy your filthy lusts with me or with a kitchen scullion!"

For a moment, there was silence. Then the mighty lion roared: "How *dare* you send anyone from *my* court without *my* word! Madame, you have gone beyond the most foolish monk in the kingdom!"

Madge could hear movement and crashing of gold plate against the walls and floors.

"I have borne you children and I have loved you, Henry! I cannot look away as Catherine has done—the love I bear for you is too great!" screamed the queen.

"Madame, you have good reason to be content with all I have done for you—for if it were to begin again, I would not! Do not forget from whence you came!" growled the king.

Again, there was silence and then Madge heard the king shout for his guards. Within a moment, he was heralded out of the queen's bedchamber. Madge did not move. She waited several minutes until the queen opened the door, her face streaked with tears.

"Oh Margaret, I have made a mess of it once again. Why does my temper come so easily? Why can I not hold my tongue?" said the queen.

"Dear cousin, I can see how much love you bear the king. If I were in your place, I, too, would be grievously vexed! When I think of Arthur in another woman's arms, well, my mind grows muddled and all I can think about is scratching him and wounding him. Not to mention what I think of doing to the wench! 'Tis a natural wish to do violence to those who harm us," said Madge.

"But I cannot do such things—as a Christian wife, I should be obedient and worshipful of my husband," said the queen. She flung herself across her bed and sobbed. "I am not made in such a way—I have held the king's love since he first saw me dancing in a masque—all those years ago. I was but a maid. I played Perseverance and Harry was Ardent Desire. How he loved me then! How he loved me!" cried the queen.

In the days following their argument, the king and queen appeared together in court. Few would have noticed the coolness between them: the king smiled at Anne and she, in turn, spoke softly to him. With the lady Eleanor gone, there was no one to steal the king's glances.

The Advent season came and with it, the cold snows of winter. On the first day of the snows, the king and queen frolicked, throwing snowballs and building snowmen. Some of the palace craftsmen started a contest for the best-carved snow creature and Master Holbein won a silver cup for fashioning the king's lion and the queen's leopard. One night, while Madge was attending her, Anne began to speak in quiet tones.

"Lady Margaret, I have been thinking," said the queen.

"Of what, Majesty?" said Madge.

"I have been thinking of the king and Elizabeth and my little dead prince. The soothsayers have predicted that soon a queen shall burn. I have no doubt it is I about which they prophesy. I tell you this, cousin. And I spoke these words once to the king himself. Though I were to burn a thousand deaths, it would not move my love for the king one jot. How strange to think it true! After all the years of waiting for the crown, what I most long for now is my husband's love. At the beginning, I cared nothing for His Majesty, though he were comely and well-proportioned. Lord Wiltshire, my father, begged me to become the king's whore, like my sister before me. But I would not!"

said the queen, staring into the fire. Madge sat on her trundle bed and looked up at the queen.

"Madame, I believe you still have His Majesty's love. But the harsh words you sometimes speak cool him. He forgets how much he loves you. If you could but sweeten your voice to the king and to his courtiers—and yes, even old Uncle Norfolk—the king would warm to you again and again. You are still young and beautiful—you have borne him a perfect daughter and can still conceive a prince. You must forget your own feelings, Your Grace. Tame your tongue and play the game you know so well. You shall win, I will gamble my bag of sovereigns on it," said Madge.

"Perhaps you are in the right, Lady Margaret. I will promise to be to him ever loving and kind—I wrote a verse once, saying something like that to Harry. He found it charming and amusing, as he used to find me," said the queen. "But enough pining over what has been—let us plan what shall be! I shall invite the king to my bedchamber on Christmas Night. I will try all the tricks of love I learned in France and I will make him mine again!" said the queen.

For over an hour, Madge and the queen planned the night, what foods to bring into the bedchamber, which wines. Madge promised to spend the whole afternoon helping the queen prepare herself—bathing her, combing her hair until it glowed, spraying her with lavender and cinnamon, making certain the bedclothes were aired and brushed and the rushes fresh and sweet-smelling. Together, they wove a dream of love so that the queen slept peacefully and Madge felt the warmth of hope bloom in her heart.

Every night thereafter, through the Advent fast until Christmas Day, the queen made merry with the king. She laughed and pulled the king to his feet, clapping when he leapt and pranced through the galliard. She designed masques and selected music, inspired good talk with learned theologians and philosophers, read poetry by Wyatt and the other verse-makers, including Madge. The king seemed in high spirits, though he did not come to the queen's bedchamber. Finally, Christmas Night arrived and Madge had everything prepared.

The king did not arrive as early as Madge and the queen had hoped. But when he entered the bedchamber, his guards clearing the way before him and announcing his presence, His Majesty was full of good cheer. He sent the guards away and began to drink the fine wine Madge had set in an ewer. Then, as if he had suddenly noticed her, he motioned for Madge to leave the chamber also.

Sometime in the early morning hours, Madge felt a hand on her shoulder.

"Lady, wake up. I would see you," said the queen.

Madge arose quickly and quietly, surprised to see Her Majesty traipsing about the outer rooms in her shift with her delicate feet bare upon the rushes. The queen held her finger to her lips and Madge moved as quietly as possible. Soon, they were in the queen's bedchamber where the king lay snoring, his nightshirt still open at the neck.

The queen motioned for Madge to follow her to an alcove where a bench was hidden behind a large tapestry.

"I have failed," whispered the queen.

"What do you mean?" said Madge.

"I could not rouse him—nothing I did moved him to the act. He had had too much wine and, though he tried as well as he could, there will be no babe from this night," said the queen.

Madge had no words—she did not know of such matters.

"Le Roi n'estoit habile en cas de soy copuler avec femme et qu'il

n'avoit ne vertu ne puissance. He has never had much skill or virility, especially in the last year or so. He is no longer young and lusty—at least not with me," said the queen. "If I do not have a babe, I am lost. What to do? What to do?"

The queen began to sob softly and Madge watched as her delicate hands shook. Soon, the queen's whole body trembled and Madge could see the fear in her eyes. She put her arm around the queen's thin shoulders and held her, trying to quell the terror that was rising in her own heart. Could the king do away with an anointed queen? Would he?

Twenty-six

In the twelve days of Christmas, the royal couple ate and danced and played at cards, enjoyed the mummery, and the music of the season. At Epiphany, they attended Mass together and dined on venison and peacock for their main courses with syllabub for the void. No one seemed to know the danger that lurked around Her Majesty and her supporters. The king had no other lady and he kissed the queen often on the mouth. Only Madge knew such actions were a sham. The king even made his way to the queen's bedchamber several more times during the season, but the results were always the same. He could not play the man.

Her Majesty was beside herself with worry. She cried and tore her hair after the king left her apartments in defeat. He blustered and bragged about his randy ways with his courtiers, but the queen said he had cried in her arms with frustration. She was at her wit's end.

As if that were not enough, Purkoy fell from a high window and was killed. So much would be her grief that all were afraid to tell Her Majesty. Finally, the king broke it to her. Her sobbing and screaming rang through the stone walls and for six days she stayed in her chambers, refusing to see anyone but Elizabeth. Madge finally convinced her to rejoin the king in the Great Hall for supper, telling her that unless the queen appeared, the king might find interests elsewhere. Madge called the apothecary for a draught that would calm the queen's nerves and Her Majesty was able to face the court, to laugh and jest and dance and sing, in spite of her loss.

As the winter winds blew and the king's moods grew more solemn with the confiscation of more and more monasteries, the queen began to behave strangely. Only Madge knew of her desperation and her fears. At night, Madge often woke to screaming—the queen's eyes would be opened wide and a hoarse choking sound would come from her throat. Madge had to shake Her Majesty to bring her to herself and then the queen would often lie in Madge's arms until sleep returned.

One day, when much snow lay on the ground, after the queen and her ladies had spent the morning sewing shirts for the poor in preparation for the Maundy, the queen took her rest. She commanded Madge to lie on her pallet nearby and began to talk about the Christian duties owed anointed kings and queens by each person in the land. Then, Her Majesty began to talk about how God had ordered everything so that the whole worked together without difficulty, as long as each person obeyed their betters and remained content in the station God had given them.

"Lady Margaret, do you believe the Lord God would

bring me to this high estate only to see me toppled?" said the queen.

"I do not know of such things, Majesty. I believe there are those who would topple you for their own ends. The lady Mary and the dowager princess still have many who support them. They may sign the king's Laws of Succession—they value their heads, do they not?" said Madge.

"Yes, I know. Capturing a heart is much more difficult than forcing someone to sign a document. I would capture their hearts. I would be as kind and generous a queen as any could desire. But they will not give me a chance," said the queen.

"If only they could know Your Majesty as I do, they would love you completely," said Madge.

"Do you love me, dearest cousin?" said the queen.

"You know that I do—have I not served you well?" said Madge.

"Yes. You have served me better than all the others," said the queen.

They fell silent and Madge napped, in spite of her desire to keep watch over the queen. When she awoke, the queen was leaning over the edge of her great bed, looking at Madge.

"You are a pretty girl, Margaret. 'Tis how the king speaks of you—Pretty Madge, he calls you," said the queen.

"I am surprised His Majesty would think of me at all," said Madge.

"He asks about you most solicitously—'How's is your dear cousin, Pretty Madge?' or 'Does Pretty Madge do well these days?'—I wonder . . ." said the queen.

Madge said nothing. She was touched that the king still remembered her plight and wished to assure her safety and happiness. She was thankful His Majesty kept Norris busy and away from her. She had only seen him in passing. He had not acknowledged her.

"Are you the pretty one all the court is buzzing about? Are you the one who has caught the king's eye?" said the queen.

"No, Your Grace. No! I am your woman—I . . . I care nothing for the king!" said Madge.

"Watch your tongue, cousin! Say not such things even when we are alone. Methinks the very walls have ears," whispered the queen.

"Madame, my own spies tell me there is no pretty woman. But the king has returned his fancy to the Lady Seymour," whispered Madge. She hadn't meant to tell the queen about Arthur's observations.

"Jane Seymour? I thought we had vanquished her at Wulf-hall. I cannot believe my Harry would find anything to admire in that creature! She has no gift for music, no wit nor beauty. She is a fine needlewoman, one of my best. But small, even stitches hold no man. Are you certain of this information?" said the queen.

"I have it on most trustworthy authority. I know she follows the old religion and still loves the lady Mary. Her brothers are forward and the king has, of late, rewarded their service," said Madge.

"'Tis true. Sir Edward pushes to be made a member of the royal privy chamber. He has not yet succeeded, but he has never been so bold until these days," said the queen. "As I should know better than any, the king often favors the family of his newest beloved."

"Majesty, what can you do? How can you secure your crown?" said Madge.

"I must have a son! 'Tis the only safety for us. But how, when His Majesty is sick with trying me? How, when the king has returned his favor to Lady Jane?" said the queen. She continued to gape at Madge as if weighing her. After several minutes, the queen spoke with utmost solemnity.

"Arise, Lady Margaret," she said as she herself rose from her bed and took her seat at the throne chair. She sat and spread out her skirts so that she looked completely regal. Madge rose and curtsied to the queen.

"Fall upon your knees, Lady Margaret," said the queen.

Madge went immediately to her knees in front of the queen's throne. She wondered if the queen had suddenly lost her senses and feared what the queen might do next. She felt the tip of the queen's scepter on her shoulders.

"Lady Margaret, this day, do you swear by all that is holy that you are my loyal and true servant? And that you will do as I bid, no matter the cost to yourself, even though it cost your life?" said the queen in her most commanding voice.

"Yes, Majesty—I so swear," said Madge. She could not stop the trembling she felt in her legs and she wondered what the queen was going to ask of her. To her knowledge, no such ceremony had ever taken place in the queen's apartments. This was a new thing and Madge wasn't sure what it meant.

"Arise, Lady Margaret," said the queen as she herself rose and kissed Madge's cheek.

"Come, let us walk in the gardens. There is much I would say to you," said the queen.

The two women, one cloaked in ermine and purple, the other in gray wool, strolled in the colorless garden. The queen led Madge far from the prying eyes and ears of the castle to the outer edges of the finely trimmed hedges. There were no benches, so they stood beneath the sheltering wall of boxwoods to keep the chill winds at bay.

"I swore you to my service for a reason, Lady Margaret. For

I have a plan, a way to win the king back to my bed," said the queen in a solemn voice.

"This is good news, Your Grace. I believe you can easily woo him from Mistress Jane," said Madge.

"I think it is not *I* who shall woo him, Margaret," said the queen.

"I do not follow the thread of Your Grace's thoughts," said Madge as she pulled her cape closer around her shoulders.

"Harry cannot withstand warm looks from a pretty face— and there is none more comely than your own, cousin," said the queen.

"What do you mean, Your Grace? What are you saying?" said Madge, now trembling.

"My darling Henry is going to stray. Of that, I can be sure. Though I find it most humorous that for the eight years I kept him at bay, he did not follow after any scent but mine own. But now that I am his wedded wife, he falls back to his old ways," said the queen. Madge noticed that, though she seemed sad when she spoke, her dark eyes had taken on a flinty look.

The queen walked a few steps farther away from the castle and turned once more to face Madge.

"If I allow him to seek his pleasure with Mistress Jane, she and her brothers will ally against me—others will join them. Catherine and Mary's supporters, those who wish to see England return to the pope, all the old guard who I have insulted or humiliated will band together to push Mistress Jane and the king together," said the queen.

Madge followed close as the queen continued to walk along the edge of the boxwoods.

"What can be done then?" said Madge.

The queen stopped and again faced Madge.

"If I can put one forth to the king who would be loyal to me, one who would speak kind words about me as they lay upon their pillows, this would serve me much better than to allow Mistress Jane and her crew to malign me. If there were some pretty young girl who the king already favored, someone I could trust . . ." The queen then fell to her knees in front of Madge and grabbed both her hands.

"Lady Margaret, you would be such a one, for in all the court, no one loves me more. I know you would be true to me. I also know the king finds you fair—he has told me thus many times. Your youth, your innocence, your mild manner—all these will please the king. What say you? Will you serve me thus?" said the queen, still on her knees.

"Majesty, please arise. Such supplication is unseemly," said Madge as she tried to pull the queen to her feet. "I am not certain I could do as you ask. I lack skill with men and have no desire for the king in that way."

The queen rose and did not speak for a long time.

"He will kill me, Margaret. I know it. I have heard it prophesied that a queen shall be burned and I have seen the dark looks the people give me. You must help me, Margaret, or I will die. I feel it in my bones," said the queen.

Madge took in the queen's words and weighed them. She knew the king was capable of great cruelty and yes, murder. So many had been slain because they would not sign the Act of Succession; others because they refused to give up the old faith. Anyone who crossed the king was at risk, and Queen Anne had surely crossed him by not yet giving him a son. And she had seen hatred flare in the king's eyes for his queen, especially when Anne complained of His Majesty's unfaithfulness.

"Your Majesty, I would give my life to protect you—I will also give my virtue if that is your wish," said Madge, her decision sudden and complete.

"Arthur? Arthur? Are you here?" said Madge as she searched in the great stables. One of the Yeoman of the Guard had told her Master Brandon was feeding the horses and could be found there. She stepped carefully to avoid the scattered piles of dung. The stables were remarkably clean but had to be swept several times each day. As she walked into the dark building, she could hear whinnies and neighs on either side. She saw a figure down at the end of the stalls. She hurried toward the man.

"Arthur?" she called once more.

"Pretty Madge! What are you doing here?" he said, raking up the straw from the floor and placing fresh hay in the manger.

"The queen sent me—we must talk," said Madge. "Is it safe here?"

"Aye. 'Tis no one here but me," said Arthur. "Come, let us sit on this bench. I'll get a blanket from one of the horses to warm us—don't worry, mistress, I'll find a clean one!" said Arthur.

They settled on a nearby bench and he wrapped the blanket around them both.

"'Tis a cold, cold January—methinks my nose will freeze plumb off!" he said.

Madge said nothing. She leaned into him and felt herself grow warm. She loved the hard feel of his chest and his arms around her, the stubble of his beard and his strong, square hands holding her own.

"I wish we could sit so forever," she said.

"Away from court and all its dangers," he said. "Now, tell me why you have come searching for me. What service may I do our good queen?"

"You may not think her good after I speak. If you will but hear me out, you will see the good in it—for us both," said Madge.

"Pretty Madge, you sound terrified. What is it, lass? What has you so frightened?" said Arthur.

Madge remained silent for a moment. Arthur held both her hands in his own, waiting.

"I fear most from you, sweetheart," she said quietly.

"Me? You know you have nothing to fear from me. I am your beloved—I would lay down my life for you, Pretty Madge," he said.

"You may not feel so after you hear my words. I may as well begin," said Madge. She took a deep breath and swallowed hard.

"The queen has asked me to take an action which is both dangerous and odious to me. 'Tis also a mortal sin," said Madge.

"She has not suggested murder, has she? The lady Mary or the princess dowager?" said Arthur.

"No, no," she said.

"Then out with it, dearest. Maybe I can help you accomplish this dangerous mission!" said Arthur.

Madge laughed out loud and then became quiet again.

"The queen wishes me to capture the king's eye. She desires His Majesty should turn his attentions to *me* rather than to Mistress Seymour," said Madge.

"But this is whoredom, mistress! You cannot give yourself to the king if that is not your desire—or is it your wish? I know well how His Majesty pays his whores! Jewels and silks and satins—the soul is a costly thing, as well the king knows. He has the means to purchase yours!" said Arthur, his voice cold and hard.

"No, 'tis not my desire to become the king's whore—and I hope to avoid such if I can. But, I will do as the queen instructs me—she is my sovereign liege and I will help her within my power. She has been ever kind to me and has been my true friend since I came to court. She has lost her babe and her little Purkoy. She has lost the ability to bring the king to, well—the king has not virility with her and she fears it is because she is older now and has lost her beauty. She blames herself," said Madge in the faintest of whispers.

"She still has beauty, though I will agree 'tis not as alluring as before. The stresses and strains of court have taken their toll. As for the king, he is in the middle of his years. Often, men who live as he has lived, those who eat their fill and drink their cups, have such difficulties. 'Tis not the queen's fault," said Arthur.

"Do you not see—the king faults her—and is ashamed in her presence. He will no longer come to her. And there are so many rogues who would see her fall from power, would see her put away or worse. Her state is desperate," said Madge.

"That may be, but why sully such as you, dearest? Surely, there is another way!" said Arthur.

"You have not heard all. The queen has promised if I do this for her, she will see that we can marry and she will give us a small manor house near Great Snoring. We shall be away from this den of iniquity forever and shall live in happiness and peace near my own people," said Madge.

"She dangles before us that which we desire above all else. Yet, I would not see you despoiled by such as the king. 'Twould be a stab unto mine own heart," he said.

Madge raised her hands to cup his face. She looked deeply into his dark eyes.

"My love, I do not want to do this thing. But my queen asks it of me. And I believe her when she says her very life is in danger. My allegiance is to her and by following her commands, I follow God's. She is an anointed queen and rules by God's will. If I do not obey her, then I do not obey God," said Madge.

"Is this what she has told you?" said Arthur.

"Yes. 'Tis also in a wondrous book and she showed me the pages. *The Obedience of a Christian Man* by Master Tyndale. This tome tells us our duty is always to obey our sovereign and in doing so, we obey God. Though it seems sin to us, such as the queen requests is really for the common good of all. For if the queen is successful and roots out the usurper, Mistress Seymour, then the king will return to her and, hopefully, get a son upon her," said Madge.

"She has her ways with you, Pretty Madge. Does she tell you that you can avoid the king's bed?"

"She believes this is true—if I but catch his eye and smile and dance and laugh with him before all the court, it will serve well enough. Because of his 'troubles,' the queen does not believe he will try to bed me—he will simply appear to do so in front of the court. Then, though the queen does not conceive, he will look to one and all the most active and virile of men," said Madge.

"And what if it goes another way? What if he does demand you in his bed?" said Arthur.

"Then I shall go and I shall whisper good things about our queen. I will use that time to turn his mind once more to Anne," said Madge.

"I like it not! I will not allow it!" said Arthur.

"You cannot allow or disallow such things, sir. You are not my husband nor have you any power here," said Madge. She immediately regretted her harsh words and sought to soothe him. "I will make a pledge unto you. If it seems the king will have the use of my body, I will give myself to you first. You shall have my maidenhead and my love forever."

"I do love you, Pretty Madge. I will take your pledge and give you one of mine own. Though you go to the king and are his for a while, I will continue to love you and we will marry," said Arthur.

"Yes, my beloved. We shall be man and wife. When we are far away from all this, the memory of it shall fade like a bad dream. Happiness will rule us and I shall bear you many sons," said Madge as she kissed him.

III

—

1535

♛

That Thin Old Woman

DESCRIPTION OF QUEEN ANNE
BY SPANISH AMBASSADOR EUSTACE CHAPUYS

Twenty-seven

The king has taken notice of you already, Lady Margaret. I have seen him smile at you and he often inquires about your health. There is something between you, is there not?" said the queen as she spoke softly to Madge in the late evening. The two women sat across from each other at the gaming table, the queen sipping wine and Madge eating a quince tart and drinking hot milk.

"Yes, madame. Though 'tis not what you think—I had not wished to tell you of this but I want you to know His Majesty is innocent of lusting after such a one as I," said Madge. She felt her cheeks grow hot remembering how the king had saved her from Norris.

"What then? Why this change in His Majesty's manner toward you?" said the queen.

Madge did not know how to begin her story. She hesitated

but the queen did not speak to fill the silence. Instead, Her Majesty waited. After a long moment, Madge gathered her courage and began the tale.

"While we were on Progress—that day of the archery contest between the ladies and the gentlemen—remember? Sir Norris set out to ravage me in the forest. He followed me to the great woods and if the king had not heard my screams, my virtue would be ruined. His Majesty pulled Norris off of my body where he had pinned me against a rock. The king has continued to help me by keeping Norris busy at court, giving him no time to pursue me. His Majesty warned him away from me, though we are still betrothed. At least I know Norris will not take me by force. That is our secret, Your Grace," said Madge, her voice strained with recalling the frightful events of that day.

"Dear cousin, I am sorry for your trials. But for our new purpose, this situation is perfect. Old Harry likes to think himself a hero. For you, he actually *is* one. You can play on this, Margaret. Here is what you must do to bring him round," said the queen, looking at Madge steadily. Madge held her gaze.

"First, when you catch him glancing your way, hold his eyes and then, very slowly lower yours. Then, if you are close enough to him, whisper that he looks especially handsome— make note of his clothing or the way he moves. If, perchance, he asks to partner you in the dance, hold yourself close to him and afterward, touch his arm when you speak. Flatter him and praise him. If you see that you have captured his interest, withdraw yourself and become shy and modest," said the queen.

"Madame, I do not think I can do as you tell me—I am by nature modest and retiring. I am not one to call attention to myself. The king would know I was not myself," said Madge.

"You must do exactly as I tell you—Margaret, you are comely and graceful—the whole court refers to you as Pretty Madge!

Do you think the king does not know this? You would be a shiny coin in his pocket," said the queen.

"But what if he should wish to take me to his bed? You have told me he cannot complete the act but, excuse this, Your Majesty, what if he is able with me?" said Madge.

"Well, then go through with it. All the better!" said the queen.

"But Your Grace, his pate is balding. He hath a bigger belly than your own when you birthed Elizabeth. Indeed, he hath become old since then. And, well, there is an odor about him . . ." whispered Madge. She feared revealing the king's flaws to his own wife, but she could not contain the revulsion she felt when she imagined His Majesty touching her person.

"He is no longer the handsomest prince in Christendom, it is true. Yet, there is much to admire in him—his courtesy and his hearty laugh. You are not instructed to love him, lady. You are instructed to woo him away from Jane Seymour—for my sake," said the queen. "As for the smell, it comes from his leg and is not there always. Only when the leg has an open sore."

"Think you he has the pox?" said Madge.

"No. The pox has other parts which His Majesty does not have. 'Tis his old jousting injury that sometimes vexes him. Pay it no mind," said the queen.

"Madame, Master Brandon wishes me to ask it once more— will we be able to marry after I have done as you ask?" said Madge.

"Yes, yes. If all goes as I plan, you and Arthur will be wed by summer," said the queen.

Toward the middle of February, after the Feast of St. Mathias the Apostle but before Lent, the queen held a gala event in her apartments. She invited several of her ladies including Mistress

Seymour, Lady Rochford, who had just returned to court, and a few others, none of whom were beauties. Indeed, when Madge saw the list of those to come, she thought a plainer gathering of ladies she had not seen. The queen explained that in such a crowd, Madge would stand out even more than usual. The queen also asked His Majesty and most of his groomsmen to attend. Master Smeaton was to provide the music and the queen's fools were preparing a humorous masque.

The queen herself helped Madge dress for the occasion and bathed her with rosewater. They took turns brushing each other's hair until both shone in the candlelight. The queen showed Madge how to redden her lips and cheeks. She also gave Madge one of her most sumptuous dresses, a deep yellow that set off Madge's eyes. Both daubed kohl on their eyelids, a new fashion set by the French. The effect was to widen the eyes and make them stand out.

"Remember, smile at the king. Let him see you laughing. And dance with any man who asks you, keeping him entertained with your wit. Keep your voice low, not shrill and, if the king asks you to take a turn with him around the apartments, take his arm and keep your hand there, caressing him as he speaks," said the queen.

"I will do as best I can, Majesty. I hope I will please you—'tis a rare thing you ask of me," said Madge. Her stomach felt fluttery and her cheeks were tired with practicing her smile.

"We live in rare times, Margaret. You are the only person I trust among all the court. Master Cromwell pretends to be my friend but his goals are not the same as mine—he would pilfer all the church property to give to his master. We have quarreled about the issue several times. Even mine own father would side with the king against me if it were to come to that," said the queen.

The two women looked at their reflections in the long mirror in the queen's bedchamber. One was dark and thin, pinched with worry; the other was buxom with light red hair that shone golden in the light. Of almost the same height, Madge had more meat on her bones and her face was shiny with youth. The queen's face was drawn, though she still used her great dark eyes with some effect. And, when she smiled, the years seemed to disappear.

"When the king enters, there will be no fanfare tonight. The men will be masked. I have partnered you with His Majesty, but you will feign surprise when he unmasks himself. While you are dancing, give him fair words, as if you did not know his royal person. Of course, his girth is a bit bigger than most of the groomsmen—I find it amusing he believes he can still hide himself behind a mask," said the queen.

"He is a proud man, Majesty. Like most, I'll warrant," said Madge.

"Yes, and can easily deceive himself," said the queen. "Come. I hear a commotion! Let us go into the outer rooms. Lady Margaret, you do look quite delectable," said the queen.

"Thank you, Your Grace. You also," said Madge.

"Mistress, I would you be my partner for the dance," said the king, dressed in clothes of earlier times, wearing a feather in his cap and a green mask across his eyes. His suit of clothing looked like what the famous Robin Hood might wear, a plump Robin looking more like the rotund Friar Tuck of legend.

"Sir, I would be delighted," said Madge, taking his proffered hand.

Together, they danced the slow la volta. Madge found it easier to converse with the king in his role of Robin Hood than in his role of sovereign lord.

"You dance with much grace. May I ask your name, sir," said Madge.

"Robin Hood, mistress. And yours?" said the king.

"Lady Margaret Shelton," she said. The king twirled her around, almost lifting her off the ground. "You are so strong, Master Robin! Why, you can pick me up as lightly as a flower." She caressed his shoulder as he led her into the next steps.

"You are a flower of beauty—the prettiest flower in this bouquet," said the king.

"Nay, sir, you but jest. Our queen is the finest flower in all England," said Madge.

"Aye, she is still a beauty. But you are young, a rosebud just opening. Her Majesty's beauty is in full bloom," said the king.

"I find there is much beauty in age as well as youth," said Madge.

"Hmmm. I am no longer young, myself," said the king.

"Oh Master Robin! You jest! With arms as strong as yours and a sprightly dance, you are certainly as young as I," said Madge.

"Perhaps you make me young and strong," said the king.

"'Tis not in my meek power to do such. You must be truly so. Ah, the music has stopped. Shall I bring you some ale? Wine?" said Madge. She held onto the king, though the other dancers had pulled apart. She willed herself to keep close to his person.

"Mistress, such refreshment would be most welcome!" said the king.

Madge went to the side table where ale, wine, sweetmeats, and various delicacies were arrayed with great decoration. A stuffed peacock, with all its feathers fanned out, created the centerpiece and the Confectionery, under the direction of Mrs. Cornwallis, had made one of the king's favorite puddings. Madge put a few bites from several dishes onto one of the golden plates stacked for such a purpose and filled a mug with ale. She returned with these foods for His Majesty. She almost curtsied as she handed them to him, but that would have ruined his surprise. So, she simply acted as if he were Arthur and gave him no extra courtesy.

"For you, Master Robin," she said. The king had taken a seat on one of the many benches the queen had brought into her apartments for the special entertainment. He motioned for her to sit on his knee.

"A sturdy chair awaits you, Lady Margaret," he said, patting his knee.

"A fine seat I am sure. But, even though you be the famous Robin Hood, it would be unseemly for me to accept such a chair, however much I might desire it," she said. Madge forced herself to look at the king; then, as the queen had instructed, she lowered her eyes.

"So you are a virtuous woman—'tis a fine thing to be. Tell me, how do you manage to keep your virtue in such a court?" said the king.

"'Tis not so difficult, Master Robin. Though some would take what is not theirs, most will wait for marriage," she said.

"Rascals and varlets all who would steal such a prize! But must a lady always have a pledge ere she love?" said the king.

"Dear, dear Robin. The game of love is rigged against a woman. If she loses her maidenhead before she is wed, her name is no longer among the good. No man will marry her if she is sullied. There are no such punishments for men who live ungodly lives, giving in to their filthy lusts. No, a woman of good character must protect herself from all harm," said Madge, leaning in close to the king so she could speak softly in his ear.

"Well spoken, lady. I admire virtue in women," said the king.

The queen clapped her hands and the music and talk ceased.

"Now has come the time to strip away the masks of these gallants who have come to our gathering. See your partners!" said the queen.

The king immediately set his plate and cup on the bench next to him and stood. He faced Madge and with great drama, flung away his mask.

"Your Majesty," Madge said as she immediately curtsied. The king pulled her up quickly.

"No need, lady, no need," he said smiling.

"Your Grace, had I known 'twas you, my talk would not have been so free. Please forgive me any forwardness. I was so deceived, I began to think truly *was* Robin Hood I spoke to," said Madge. She looked down, then cast her eyes back up at him.

"Lady Margaret, your king has found you all charm. You did nothing amiss. Would you now like to join me in the pavane?" said the king.

"Harry? Dearest Harry? Would you do your queen the honor of a dance?" said Anne as she glided over to them.

"Madame, it would be my great delight. Lady Margaret, I hope I shall see you again this evening. Thank you for the dance," said the king, bowing slightly to Madge. She curtsied to them both and watched as they began the slow, stately dance. The queen was full of grace and Madge wondered how the king could ever desire another.

At that moment, Sir Norris approached her.

"Pretty Madge, may I have this dance?" he said in his oily manner.

"Of course," said Madge, remembering the queen's instructions to dance with all who asked. She smiled kindly at Norris, as though she had forgotten what had happened the last time they met.

"Mistress, I have not seen you since the unfortunate day in the forest at Wulfhall. I have been severely reprimanded by the king himself and he has kept me from you. He has exacted a promise that such thing will never happen again. I have given my word and asked his permission to speak with you. We are, after all, still plighted to one another and I would ask your forgiveness and seek your pardon," said Norris. Though his words were pretty, his tone was such as to render them false.

"I thank you for your apology and, as a God-fearing woman, I will grant you pardon. Perhaps you can learn tenderness or perhaps time will change our circumstances. Whatever the future might bring to us, I forgive you and wish you well," said Madge with as much warmth as she could muster. She noticed the king and queen danced nearby and His Majesty was looking at her. She smiled at the king and then laughed as if Norris had said something witty.

"Mistress, why do you laugh?" said Norris.

"'Tis nothing. Just a passing fancy—for a moment, I thought of the queen's fool and a little joke she made the other day—nothing at all," said Madge, still smiling at Norris.

By the end of the revels, Madge had danced with every man in attendance and four times with the king. She had followed every instruction the queen had given and noticed the king's eyes did not leave her.

"You did very well, Lady Margaret. I know the king and he was quite taken with you, though he thought he was being discreet. But a wife knows. I am sure he will find reason to see you again. Remember, be warm and then cool. Make much ado about him when you are with him, but also allow him to see you at games with other men. He has already forgotten Lady Seymour, at least for this night. He did not dance one time with her," said the queen.

"I shall do as you tell me, Your Grace. I hope all will end well," said Madge.

"It shall. After the king has finished with you, you and Master Brandon will marry and all this will be forgotten. I will have my son and England will have an heir," said the queen.

Twenty-eight

y May Day, the court was abuzz with rumors about the king's new love, Mistress Margaret Shelton. Her uncle, Lord Wiltshire, along with George, paid her homage as well as did Master Cromwell. Cromwell sent her a dozen dotterels while the duke of Norfolk bowed to her as he passed her in the corridors and sent her some shrimps and carp. The king had given her a strand of pearls on Easter Day and had sent her venison on another occasion. Her father, Sir John, had received monies from a small monastery and both her parents had been given some gold plate by the king, for the "solicitous care" of the princess Elizabeth. All was going as the queen had planned.

"Dearest Arthur, I do not know how much longer I can keep the king from my bed. Daily he pushes me, wheedles and cajoles me. I fear he has more experience in bedding than I do in avoiding," said Madge as she leaned against Arthur in Cate's room.

"I know, my love. You are walking on a wire. One misstep and we are all done for," he said as he kissed her fingers, one at a time.

"Let us talk no more of such things. Let us be merry while we have the chance. Have you seen the book Wyatt carries with him these days? 'Tis a collection of writings by many lords and ladies at court. I have added a few of mine own jottings to it—just verses in jest, declaring admiration and love. Lady Douglas and John Clere make such amusing poems! I have shown it to the queen, thinking to delight her with the rhymes, but she is in no mood for such. Though she praises my progress with the king, she sometimes acts as though she hates me for it," said Madge.

"It must be quite difficult for her, hearing from your own lips the ways in which the king woos you, knowing all the king says and does. Yet, she insists you continue. The king has been treating her with great public affection. He seems to love her still, if outward show be proved," said Arthur.

"I speak of her goodness and her beauty all of the time. Until he puts his fingers to my lips and bids me hush. If I have his ear at all, I will do her what good I may," said Madge.

"Let us speak no more of the king. . . . I would see this great work you and Wyatt have created. Can you get it for me?" said Arthur.

"Yes, 'tis easy enough. We all pass it back and forth, adding our jots and tittles. Perhaps I will write a secret love poem for you, something that only you will understand. A hidden code declaring our love," said Madge.

"That, I would like," said Arthur as he leaned in to kiss her. They were easy with each other now, their bodies familiar, though not as completely known to each other as they would desire. Arthur touched her face and then her neck. Soon his hands were on her breasts and she was breathing quickly. She could feel dampness in the usual place and a tingle sizzled up her spine. She had grown used to those sudden tingles. She sometimes wondered what would happen if she and Arthur continued their fondling and kissing, moving beyond their usual stopping point.

"Dearest . . . we must cease. The queen awaits me. I have been too long away from the prying eyes of the court. The king has asked me to hunt with him in the morning. I will not be able to escape until the afternoon, when His Majesty naps," said Madge, rising from the pallet and straightening her dress.

"I shall be here, my love," said Arthur, running his hands along her waist to her hips. He pulled her to him. "I cannot wait until you are mine! I will make you forget there was ever a King Henry the Eighth of England!"

"When I am with you, my love, I have no sovereign but you!" said Madge.

May turned slowly to June. The king often sought Lady Margaret's company when he could remove from the dreariness of discussing important matters with Cromwell. He told Madge about these issues, though she cared not a fig for such disclosures. While he prated on about how Cromwell would have him now be friends with the emperor Charles V, the nephew of the dowager princess, Madge allowed her mind to wander to Arthur and the way he kissed her. The king explained why he still held out for a French alliance. He tried to make clear how the death of the old pope, Clement VII, and the election of the new, Paul III, had seemed at first heartening news. Paul III had made overtures to the king, suggesting that if he would but put away his concubine and return to his wife, he would rescind the previous excommunication. Madge immediately told the king that he was ruler in England and the head of England's church— Pope Paul should humble himself to Henry, not the other way around. As she often managed, Madge said exactly what the king wished to hear and he became even more bound to Anne, if only to prove his own authority and majesty. And though Madge had very little interest in what he said, she was happy when she could give a response that helped the queen's position.

But no matter what she did to bring the queen back into the king's affections, the queen would undo her work in a matter of days. The strain of having only the king's great appetite to protect her from her enemies played on the queen's nerves. More than once, she screamed at those who would help her if only she could control her temper. First in a long line of those she offended was the duke of Norfolk, who had whispered that the king would reinstate Mary back into the succession if the queen did not bear a son soon. Madge was in the outer room of the king's chambers when Anne rounded on Norfolk in full fury.

"To think, mine own uncle would imply that the Spanish bastard should be in the succession when Elizabeth is the only legitimate issue of the king is beyond my brains. Has he straw in his head? Dost he think Mary will love him because he hath turned against me, an anointed queen? Nay, Uncle, have a care! I can still bring down a knave such as you! Out of my sight! Out, wretched man!" shrieked the queen, laying many curses on the duke as he left her presence. The news of their quarrel rolled quickly around the palace and even the king showed sympathy to Norfolk, having himself been on the other end of the queen's sharp tongue.

That first week of June, the king and Madge strolled in the knot garden. The weather was pleasant, with warm winds blowing fragrant scents from the roses and the bride's veil. The king held his arm out for Madge, which she took with a smile. They walked slowly, as the king's leg pained him, though the wound had finally closed and seemed to be healing. He led her to a secluded spot where they were completely hidden by high hedges. Nestled inside this green alcove was a stone bench. The king sat upon it and pulled Madge onto his lap.

"This is what I like—Pretty Madge sitting on my knee! The sun is shining, the birds building their nests—I feel young and ready to have that which I have desired for so long. What say you, lady? Will you now give yourself to me?" said the king as he kissed her on her cheek and forehead. His beard scratched against her skin, and she knew that later, her face would be irritated and red. She leaned against him, the odor from his person almost overcoming her. She thought of him without his clothes and how he might smother her with his mighty weight. And she thought of Arthur, how she loved him and how she wanted it to be Arthur who took her, his strong lean body hovering over her, love lighting his eyes. She did not think she could stomach bedding the king, but she also knew she must give in to her fate. She must do all she could to save the queen.

"There is nothing I should like better, Your Grace," she said, as the queen had instructed.

"Then let us designate a time and a place. I have a house in London where we shall go. We will sail down the Thames in the royal barge at evening time—'twould seem innocent enough. Master Smeaton will amuse us with his songs—perhaps he would sing one of mine own, for I have often written of the great love I bear you. What say you to this?" said the king, his hands roving over her shoulders, her waist, and her buttocks. He kissed her, his thin lips firm against her full mouth. She thought his breath foul but forced herself to return his ardor. The queen had commanded that Madge bring their love to its culmination and she had sworn to do so. She traced Henry's lips with the tip of her tongue as the queen had shown her. She could feel his heart thudding beneath her hand.

"In three days' time, Your Grace, I shall sail down the Thames with you," she said.

"Oh my beloved! You will not be sorry you have finally acquiesced. I will be your ever-faithful servant, serving only you, sweetheart—of that you can be assured," said the king as he lifted her skirt and began to use his fingers to discover her secrets. For a few moments, she allowed this, feeling the plump hands growing more and more bold. He was not gentle and she cried out.

"Yes, my dearest—I know how you long for my manhood— you shall have it! Upon my word you shall!" panted the king.

At that moment, a small commotion nearby interrupted the king's explorations. Suddenly, Norris stood before them.

"Oh . . . I am terribly sorry . . . forgive me, Majesty! I was merely walking in the gardens when I heard a cry—methought a lady was in distress!" said Norris, his face bloodred and his eyes finding no safe place to land.

"Fool! Miscreant! You heard no cries of ravage here! Not all must take what they desire—for some, such plums are given freely! Be gone! I will speak with you in my chambers!" said the king.

Norris bowed, keeping his eyes to the ground. He dared not look at Madge.

"Lady Margaret, I do beg your pardon for such a gross interruption. I will see to it Norris keeps what he has discovered to himself. I would not impugn your standing at court," said the king.

"Thank you, Majesty. I would hate to hear what rumors Norris might spread about me, though I am still his intended wife," said Madge, running her hands up and down the king's chest.

"I think you love him not, lady," said the king, his breath coming in short gasps.

"I fear you know me too well, Majesty. I love him not one whit," said Madge.

"Then perhaps I shall release you. Not now but later. I will make a better match for you," said the king.

Madge knew he meant he would match her with someone else, once he was finished with her. She kissed him on the cheek, his beard still rough.

"Thank you, Your Grace. I will be happy on that day!" she said.

"I will not see you again until three days hence, milady. Matters of state must have my attentions. But on that glorious day when you yield to me, I will send Sir Weston to fetch you. Follow him to my barge and I will meet you there. Take care the queen does not get wind of this or we are undone," said the king.

Madge hurried immediately to the queen's bedchamber.

"Your Majesty, the king wishes for me to meet him at his barge three days hence. We are to sail down the Thames to a house which he keeps for such purposes. I am sorry to tell you these things, my queen," said Madge as she brushed the queen's hair.

"It matters not. My heart is steeled against all feeling, Margaret. I have set this act in motion and I will not shrink from it because it pains me. You have His Majesty's ear at present. As a result, he is ever kind to me, though he has not come to my bed. Mayhap he has forgotten all about Mistress Seymour by this time, though I know how his mind holds onto a thought once it has been planted. But, if things move forward as I hope they will, he will return to my bed at your own request. And when he does, I will get a prince this time! I know this must be so—I believe our Lord has ordained it. So, lady, have courage. I know I shall," said the queen.

"Are you certain this is the only way to manage the king, dear cousin? I feel like a lamb led to slaughter—he is so unseemly and the thought of the act so distressing to me. I would beg Your Majesty to reconsider, to find another way, for this is loathsome to me," said Madge with as much force as she could command.

"Lady Margaret, please remember you speak not only of my husband but of your king. Such rude sayings I will not tolerate. You may not love His Majesty but I do. And I will not hear him disparaged by such as you. Do you not think I have racked my brains trying to find my way back to His Majesty? Think you this is pleasant for me to contemplate? My husband in your arms? We do this because we are forced to it! If I had my way, Mistress Seymour would be sent forever to Wulfhall and Harry and I should remove from court and live in peace in a little cottage somewhere. But that is not to be—we are at court—the deadliest place in the land. Have courage, girl! We may both survive this yet!" said the queen in a steely voice.

"As you will, Your Majesty," said Madge, once again resigning herself to her fate.

Madge began to rub the queen's shoulders, seeing that she was thinner than before. Such a lack of flesh did not suit her well. Madge saw lines around her eyes and mouth. More gray strands mottled her hair.

"Lady Margaret, there are things I would tell you about the king and his . . . person," said the queen slowly, as if struggling to find the exact words she needed.

"Yes, Your Grace?" said Madge.

"Sometimes, as I have said before, Harry is unable to complete the lovemaking. He loses his stamina. If this should happen while he is with you, do not act unhappy. Remain calm. There are certain things you can do to help revive him. Sometimes these secrets work and sometimes they do not," said the queen.

"What secrets, Your Grace?" said Madge. She hoped the queen would not give her a potion to slip to His Majesty. She did not feel confident she could act with such stealth.

"Certain . . . ways I learned in France . . . the ladies of the court there whispered many such things to me of love, actions a woman can do which the English know not—tell no one of them," said the queen.

Then the queen began to explain what she had learned while serving in the court of Francis I. "There are other places you can receive the king if he fails to gain entry to your womanhood. You can place his person in your own mouth and please him in that way. This usually works, especially if you tease him with the tip of your tongue and take gentle hold of his jewels. He has come around to this technique more than once, though he complains he abhors my French lovemaking," said the queen.

After describing in great detail several other acts the queen wished Lady Margaret to perform, Madge flung down the hairbrush.

"Majesty, enough! I cannot think of doing such to the king's person. I would not have the stomach for it. Nor can I think the king would like such sinful things. He would think me a bawd of the worst sort," said Madge as the queen explained.

"No, no, Lady Margaret! These are the actions that please men most. Such tactics have been used in France for years and are only now coming to England. Besides, he will not tell of their use as he is too modest," said the queen. "We can only hope these secrets will have the desired effect. If they do not, it may mean the end of the king's love for you—he cannot stomach a woman who has known him to fail," said the queen. "His aversion to me began when he could no longer play the man."

The day before Madge was to set sail up the Thames to become the king's mistress, she felt the need to get away from the court and the heavy business at hand. The queen granted her permission to take Shadow for the entire afternoon, and Madge intended to use her free time to ponder all that was happening and garner her courage for what lay ahead. She went to Cate's room to get her dog.

"Maddie-girl, come quickly. I would a word with you," said Cate, her face flushed and her eyebrows knit in worry.

"Good Cate, what is wrong?" said Madge, rushing to pet Shadow and attach her tether.

"I know you love Master Brandon truly but child, what are you doing with His Majesty? Every scalawag in the castle, from scullery maid to the archbishop, is talking about you as if you were the biggest whore in Christendom. This is not how I have taught you, Maddie. You know 'tis wrong," said Cate as she fingered her rosary.

"Sit down, dear Cate. There is more to this than you can know. I ask that you trust me. All I do, I do for our future and our queen," said Madge calmly.

"A fine way to serve the queen, bewitching her king," mumbled Cate.

"I cannot tell you more, Cate. You must hold on to the belief that I treasure your teachings, but I do what I must. It will turn out for the good, I promise," said Madge. "Now, I'm off! Shadow and I will wander the forest and run until we are without breath. Take heart, Cate—I will not disappoint you," said Madge, giving her a kiss on the cheek.

"Humph," grumbled Cate.

The sun was directly overhead when Madge and Shadow hurried through the gardens out into the surrounding meadows toward the king's hunting forest that lay to the west of the castle. A few sheep dotted the hillside with its sweet-smelling grasses, while the poultry yard with its coops lay to the south. Madge could barely see the hens and peacocks, ducks and geese as they pecked at the corn scattered by the young boys who tended them. At the top of the hill, the meadow gave way to forest. She and Arthur had walked this way many times over the winter and spring, taking any chance they could to escape the castle and seek the peace of the trees and sky. Deep in the woods, they had found a creek that bubbled over stones and fallen limbs. At one point, a small waterfall spilled into a deep pool, and, next to the pool was a large tree trunk that had been felled by a storm. Arthur had carved their initials into its bark and encircled them with a heart. He did it in such a way as to conceal their true identities, but Madge knew what the cipher meant. She hoped to lead Shadow to that place where Madge would then trace the lover's knot with her fingers while Shadow drank the cool water.

Madge looked behind her before she entered the wood. She wanted to make certain no one had followed her. The meadow was clear of anyone save the sheep and one shepherd boy.

"Come, Shadow. 'Tis lovely in the woods. And you shall find water soon," said Madge. She leaned over the dog and untied its tether. "Run, girl! Run to your heart's content!" she said as she raced after the dog. Leaping and bounding over trees and roots and boulders, Shadow moved like a spirit set free and Madge followed as best she could. Soon, she was off the trail to the creek.

"Here, girl. This way," she called. After a minute's wait, Shadow leapt back into view and trotted to Madge. Madge then began to run in the direction of the pool. Shadow followed. Finally, they arrived at Madge's favorite spot and Shadow drank from the pool in great gulps. Madge bent down and cupped her hands so she, too, could drink. Then, she sat upon the great tree trunk and found Arthur's heart. She began drawing her finger around the familiar trace. But something was wrong. Someone had gouged out the initials and made a mockery of the heart. Madge felt suddenly afraid.

Who could have found their secret place? And who would have taken a knife to the symbol of their love? Madge looked around. She saw nothing but the new green leaves on the trees and an occasional ground squirrel. A fairly big fish swam across the pool to hide in a shady spot. Shadow sat by her feet, after circling several times. Content that no one was near, she relaxed. Probably some young knave had been walking through the woods and had come upon the heart. Too young for love himself, he thought himself old enough to carve. That was the explanation, surely.

Madge allowed herself to relax and began to ponder her trip up the Thames to the king's house in London—had he called it Miraflore? She hoped she could go through with the deed; she had steeled herself for it. Though the king was gallant and had been generous and kind to her, she did not love him, nor did he stir her feelings in the least. She tried to imagine what he would look like without his luxurious clothing. She thought of an enormous fat chicken that smelled of putrid flesh and had foul breath. She shuddered.

"What shall I do, Shadow? Would that I were a dog and did not care who rutted with me . . . I feel my soul as well as my body shall be defiled. Yet, I must obey the queen—she is God's anointed, as is the king. It seems I have no choice. . . ."

She thought of Arthur and how he might feel, knowing she was giving herself to another. The price seemed too high. But if she could get the king's ear, even for a brief while, and encourage him to seek pleasure once again with his own wife, all would be worth it. Surely, this time, the queen would bear a son and her place would be beyond any threat. Madge and Arthur would be married and well away from court. She thought of them together and lost herself in a dream of love.

Shadow brought her up short when the dog emitted a low growl. Madge scanned the woods, looking for what had her dog's attention. Shadow stood and continued to growl, the fur on her haunches standing up.

"Lady Margaret! Well met!" said Norris.

Madge jumped to her feet and she could feel Shadow's body against her skirts, solid and taut, ready for a fight.

"Sir Norris. I am surprised to find you here in the forest," said Madge, her throat tightening.

"Dearest lady, I come here often—I find the solitude soothes me. I have several times brought along a lady to soothe me as well," Norris said.

"I, too, enjoy exploring these woods. But alas, 'tis time for me to return to the queen—she bid me not stay away too long," said Madge, starting for the path.

"No, Margaret. Tarry a while with me," said Norris, catching her arm.

"Though I would count it a pleasure to do so, sir, I cannot," said Madge, trying to loosen his hold on her arm.

"Have you seen that pretty carving on yon trunk? Methought it was a lover's knot. And that the lovers so immortalized there were you and that Brandon bastard! But I cannot imagine you would lower yourself to love such as he," said Norris. "Not when you have the chance for me, lady." He pulled her to him and tried to kiss her.

"Sir, we have played this game before. I would have thought you a wiser man than to try playing it again," said Madge, forcing her voice to sound haughty and brave.

"Aye, we have—and I was winning until the king began his sport. Now, you are no longer a sweet maid, but the king's whore. A whore with one is a whore with all," said Norris as he pulled her to him again, staring down at her with what seemed a contained fury.

"My virtue is still intact, sir, make no mistake. And if you take it from me by force, the king will hear of it. He will separate your head from your shoulders!" said Madge. Shadow was growling, going at Norris, though not biting him yet.

"No doubt of that, Lady Margaret. I am not foolish enough to sully what belongs to the king and I am sure you serve His Majesty well enough. But he will tire of you soon, as he has all the others. And when he does, I shall then have what I list," he said. He still held her close to him, his grasp on her arms firm and unyielding.

"If you release me and go on your way, I shall not mention our encounter to His Majesty. Unhand me!" said Madge as Shadow continued growling. For a moment, they stood still as statues and Madge wondered if Norris had lost his senses—she thought he might try to take her even yet, though it would mean his head.

Madge heard a slight rustle through the forest, as if someone were making his way toward them. A shudder of fear raised the hairs on her arms. For though the woods belonged to the king, often madmen and murderers sought concealment in the shadows of the great trees that grew so large a grown man could hide in the hollows of their trunks. Robbers and cutthroats were known to accost weary travelers in these very woods, as Arthur had cautioned her many times. But when she was with Arthur, she had not known fear.

"Norris! On your feet, man, and take your blade," said a voice.

Norris grabbed his sword.

"Brandon! You have naught in this," said Norris.

"I have everything in it. You may as well know it now—she is my beloved and has promised herself to me. She loves you not," said Arthur.

"Would you defy the king? He has given her to me—I have his word on it," said Norris.

"I will defy the whole world for her! Now either fight or run, Sir Norris—your choice," said Arthur.

"Your skill with the sword is well-known, Master Brandon. I will get me to the castle and let His Majesty pronounce your fate," said Norris, placing his sword in its sheath. "You have not heard the last of this!" he said as he carefully backed away from Arthur. Once he had moved a safe distance, he began to run toward the meadow. He yelled a final taunt, "Heads have rolled for less!"

Twenty-nine

W hy didst come all alone to our favorite spot? Why not ask me to join you?" said Arthur as he held her against him.

"I thought to have the afternoon to prepare myself—for what is to come on the morrow. I wished to pray for God's help. I needed to consider all that might happen. I longed for a time of peace before I am to give myself to the king," said Madge.

"I have thought of nothing else. My blood boils when I think of you in that old man's bed. My heart has commanded my legs to run and I have been roaming the halls of the castle looking for you—I went first to the queen and she told me she had given you the afternoon to yourself," said Arthur. Madge could hear his heartbeat, fast and hard, against her ear. His body seemed tense, ready to slay dragons. She grew afraid.

"My love, must you go through with this rash scheme?" said Arthur, still holding her as though he would never let go.

"There is no way out. The king expects me to give way. The queen has ordered me to do so. You see how precariously she teeters on the throne. Since the death of the little prince, the king has not been to her bed but a few times. His eye roves where it will and ladies are put before him daily. The Seymours continue to whisper in his ear, no doubt about their virtuous sister. The queen's enemies seek to control His Majesty and bend him to their will," Madge said. She could feel the fear of Norris combine with the fear of what she must do in the trembling of her body. She wanted to make Arthur understand why she must complete the act that the queen set spinning.

"My dearest, dearest Arthur, I despise the thought of the king's hands upon my person—his foul breath and his odious leg. I would not come near him if I did not believe the queen's life depended on my success. I have seen the evil looks he gives her when her head is turned away from him. We both know he is a man of great danger, growing more so by the day, it would seem," said Madge. She felt tears threaten to pour from her eyes. She threw her arms around Arthur's neck and sobbed, "The queen has been ever kind to me. But it is for *us* that I bed the king—for *our* future. You must know that," said Madge, clinging to him, her fingers clutching at his cloak.

"You are shivering. Norris has frightened the death out of you. Come, let us sit on the tree and I shall calm you," said Arthur as he led her to the tree trunk. He spread his cloak out for them to sit upon and put his arm around Madge as he joined her. "After I learned you had the afternoon to yourself, I thought you might bring Shadow to the wood. Luckily, as I was heading up the hill across the meadow, I saw Norris entering the trees, hurrying and looking around to see whether or not he was observed. I knew then you might be in trouble. He has said often that he would take you before he wed you, to see if he could mold you to fit him, you being a maid," said Arthur.

"He is a toad. The king has promised to release me from my vow. And with the queen's blessing, we can marry," said Madge.

They sat on the log for several minutes, kissing and giving each other comfort. The sun was no longer high and Madge knew her time was limited. She sat up and faced Arthur.

"Let us marry now," she said, staring into his eyes.

"What do you mean?" he said.

"I mean to keep my promise—I said I would come to you before the king could lay his hands upon me and I aim to keep my word. Let us marry right now, in our woods, beneath the trees that have offered us their shelter so many times. If we pledge our troth here and you make me your honest wife, who will know? The king will not be able to tell if I am a true maid or no. The queen has told me of tricks I can use to fool him if he should wonder. Let us become one flesh," she said, her breath coming in little puffs.

Arthur stood and drew her to him. They held hands.

"Before God, I marry you, Lady Margaret Shelton, and will give my life for you," said Arthur.

"Before God, I marry you, Sir Churlish, and give my love to you," Madge said, smiling.

"I consecrate this union with water," said Arthur, cupping a handful and pouring it over Madge's hair.

"And I as well," said Madge, splashing him on the head.

They dallied in the water, plashing and spraying each other until their clothes were wet. Arthur led Madge to his cloak, which he now spread on the ground. Slowly and carefully, he removed her damp skirts and her shift. Naked but unafraid, she

lay down upon the soft mossy earth, her pale flesh kept clean
by his cloak. He pulled out a small packet from his breeches
and then let them fall to his knees.

"What are you doing?" said Madge.

"'Tis called a lover's sheath. It is a new thing to keep the
pox at bay—I do not use it for that reason, fear not. I am clean
and I know you are, too. But they say it can also keep my seed
from giving you a babe. We must be very careful," he said.

"But . . . what *is* it?" she said.

"Always the curious Pretty Madge! It is a finely woven linen
cloth dipped in lard and dried in the sun. Dr. Linacre, the
king's own physician, prepares it for many of the men at court,"
said Arthur.

"A marvelous invention—but hurry my love, hurry!" said
Madge.

Arthur lowered himself onto her, kissing her deeply. He then
ran his tongue along her entire body, licking her behind the
knees, on the inner flesh of her elbows, along her thighs until
he came to her womanhood. He looked at her, his eyes glassy
with desire and then he began to kiss and nibble and lick her
most private parts until she was wet enough to accommodate his
member without much pain. Once within, he stirred her slowly,
barely moving at first. She remembered the way her mother
made a sweet pudding, slowly building the ingredients to a
roaring boil. It was the same with Madge. Without warning,
she felt a deep pulsing in her womb. This throbbing then radi-
ated outward to her womanly parts, down through her legs to
her toes while at the same time, skittering along her spine until
her head felt as if it would burst. She groaned with pleasure and
pulled Arthur to her, her hands suddenly alive with purpose,
guided him over and over until she felt once again the building
up of her desire.

She lost all track of time. It seemed she and Arthur went beyond time and space, entered another realm altogether. He continued to move slowly within her, bringing that delicious feeling to her body several times before she felt him thrust more quickly, seemingly without control. She watched his face as his eyes rolled back in his head and he gave a loud sigh. He collapsed onto her, kissing her cheeks and her forehead.

"Oh my love," she whispered.

"My Pretty Madge . . ." he sighed.

Thirty

The next morning, Madge awoke and felt the stickiness between her thighs. She lay back against her pallet and smiled, remembering. She had not imagined such pleasures could be lurking in her own body, like a secret treasure waiting to be opened. Arthur had known every way to delight her and in their short time together, he had proven his virility three times, leaving her exhausted and filled with all the joy she could hold.

Though she would give herself to the king this very day, she was glad that Arthur had taken her maidenhead. She was happy that Arthur had made way for the king, rather than the other way around. She shuddered when she thought of the king having his way with her. Could she complete the act? Or would she run out of His Majesty's arms, screaming her disgust? She looked out the glazed windows of the queen's bedchamber and noted the dark sky. Pellets of rain hit the panes and dripped down in little runnels. Madge glanced up at the queen's bed and saw Her Majesty still sleeping, her mouth open a bit, a soft snore coming from it. The queen had been up long into the night. Madge had heard her walking and murmuring to herself, then tossing in the enormous bed, not able to find a position to her liking. Madge stayed awake, listening, as long as she could, but sleep finally took her away. She dreamed of Arthur's mouth, his tongue, his hands and fingers, his manhood. Such dreams kept her happy until her very waking moment.

She turned away from the queen and pulled the coverlet over her shoulders. She touched the private place where Arthur had been and enjoyed the feel of him still inside her. She could smell him and she did not want to bathe as that would take the scent of him away from her. But she knew she must. The king would know the odor of love and he must be deceived above all else. But for this moment, the scent could linger so she would not forget it.

Soon, the chamberlain entered to set out the queen's clothes, clean the rushes, and prepare the inner and outer rooms for the queen's breaking of the fast. Madge arose and poured water from the ewer into the large bathing bowl. She planned to use the water after the queen had washed her face and hands with it, to clean her private parts. She was to meet the king's barge after Their Majesties had dined, at evening when the first stars crept out.

"Lady Margaret, bring my green kirtle and the green-slashed sleeves. I would look especially fine this day," snapped the queen.

"Yes, Majesty," said Madge. "Madame, you must recall what is to happen tonight . . ."

"Of course I recall it! Think you I have lost all my senses?" said the queen.

"No, Majesty. I wondered what *I* should wear. And if you would wish me come to your bedchamber when the king has returned me in the morning," said Madge.

"Yes. Come immediately to me. As for your clothes, you will wear this lovely blue dress—I think of the color as midnight blue, so dark and alluring. Feel, 'tis velvet and look at the jewels sewn within. The king has not seen me wear it—the tailor made it for you, Lady Margaret. It will be yours to keep after tonight. Now, take this necklace of diamonds and wear your hair down loose. Make a daisy chain to weave in with those curly locks of yours—you might even fashion a crown of daisies for your head. You will be quite fetching, Pretty Madge," said the queen, her tone odd and cold.

"Majesty, I . . . beg of you one last time . . ." Madge said.

"No! Speak no more! What is to happen will happen, grudge who may. Now, quiet! I am to sup with His Majesty tonight and I would be in fine spirits. Take the dress and the jewels to your nurse's room and have her help you adorn yourself. The whole court already tells the tale of the beautiful, young Lady Margaret and her lover, the king! Be gone! I will speak with you in the morning," said the queen.

Madge hurried to Cate's room, carrying what she needed for her meeting with the king. Cate had gone to break her fast at the Great Hall and Shadow leapt up to greet Madge when she knocked, then opened the door. She lay the clothing on Cate's pallet and played with her dog. She was too nervous to eat and thought about the evening to come.

She admired the king; he was brilliant and strong, capable of great kindness and courage; he wrote music, tilted with the most accomplished jousters of the day; he danced and hunted with great skill, yet he could also debate theology until the wee hours of morning. He loved to laugh, yet was easily moved to tears. He sang with gusto and lived with enormous appetite. Such a man Madge had never imagined. As a king, he made her proud. As a man, he left her cold.

She had seen him display great patience, as when the queen was with child and peevish. She had also seen him act cruelly. Recently, when the princess dowager Catherine had been quite ill, His Majesty had prohibited her daughter, the lady Mary, to visit. Spending a few days with her mother would have done both mother and daughter great good. But, Lady Mary would not acknowledge Queen Anne as rightful queen and the king was livid about it, so he refused to allow Mary to give succor to her ailing mother. The whole court muttered against His Majesty's unkindness.

Madge studied the necklace the queen had given her to wear. The diamonds shone in the light, polished cabochons smooth and rounded. She was fortunate to be able to adorn her neck with such jewelry, if only for one night. She picked up Cate's rosary beads, which she usually kept hidden in a pouch of her under shift. Madge thought about what she had done with Arthur. Though they were not married by a priest, she felt as if God Himself had married them. She agreed with the queen that between herself and God, there need *be* no priest. What had happened with Arthur, though many would think it a sin, felt to Madge more like a sacred union.

But what about the events that were to happen this very night? What would God think of a woman who gave herself to her king, not for love, not for money, but because she loved the queen? Would God think such an act a sin? Or is that what Jesu meant when he said to lay down one's life for another is the greatest love? Verily, Madge did not wish to lie with the king but she was willing to do this in order to save the queen. She could see for herself how easily the king could be led astray by a pretty face, the sound of a soft voice, a delicate hand. She would guide him back to his wife and then, the royal couple would get the prince the whole of England longed for. If bedding the king was the only way she could get his ear and help him find his way back to Anne, then so be it.

Though she could work things out thus in her mind, in her heart, Madge felt full of doubts and trepidation. Her love for Arthur weighed on her and she feared he would leave her out of jealousy once she became, in body and soul, the king's own woman. How could he still love her, knowing she had pandered herself to the king? How could he be at court each day, seeing Madge and the king together, wanting her for himself? Would he not begin to despise her for what she had done?

Madge fell onto her knees, holding Cate's rosary. For the first time, she felt herself surrounded by a Presence. She knew God was with her and she told all her troubles to this God, the way she used to confess everything before the priest. Time passed and still she prayed, crying and then laughing and then crying once more. Her eyes rimmed red and her nose matched. She did not care. Perhaps if she were no longer "Pretty Madge," the king would not desire her. She prayed that this cup pass from her lips, but she knew such deliverance would not happen. She thought of herself like a coney caught in a trap of twigs, no escape. No escape.

Exhausted, she ceased her prayers, lay down on Cate's pallet, and slept.

"Maddie, wake up! Wake up, I say!" said Cate, prodding Madge's torso with her foot.

"What time is it?" said Madge.

"Late afternoon! I was called into Mistress Seymour's room to help milady with her sewing—she was stitching a lovely shift of satin, for her wedding night, she said. I let out a bit of a 'humph' and she then said, 'You might be surprised to find me married by next year, dear Cate. Surprised indeed.' I know more than she might think—I knew she meant the king! That prim, dough-faced wench plans to marry the king! Now I know that whatever you do to save the queen is the right thing—we are all safe as long as Her Majesty is safe. But if she were to fall, the Lord help us. I said no more to Mistress Jane but hurried so I could come to you, Maddie-girl. I knew you would have need of me," said Cate, prattling away as she gave Shadow some tidbits of food and straightened the blue gown, which Madge had mussed a little as she napped.

"I must ready myself—I wish some great wind would blow me away from all of this—away from court and the queen and the king! I would fain not do what I must do this night," said Madge.

"I know, I know. I felt that way too, until I heard from my own ears the schemes of Mistress Seymour! She hath nerves of iron. But come, dearie—let us fix your hair and get you ready to meet Sir Weston," said Cate.

"Cate, think you God will forgive what I am about to do— 'tis a mortal sin, well, two, I suppose—fornication and adultery," said Madge.

"I do not know what God might or might not do. But, though it be a sin, if you can save the queen and your family, you should do so. Now, let us sweeten your hair and soften your skin. Take off all your clothes, girl. I know just what you need," said Cate.

Madge obeyed, thinking again about Arthur and God and her mother and the queen and the king. Her thoughts churned about as confused as the golden fish that crowded in the king's garden pond. She could feel each heartbeat throbbing in her head and her ears buzzed. Finally, after fidgeting about, milling around and around Cate's room, and moving every second or two, Cate handed her a glass of fine wine, which settled her a little. But she had no appetite and when Cate brought supper, Madge ate only a piece of bread dabbed with drippings.

"You are the loveliest girl, well, woman in all the court, Maddie. I will pray for you throughout the night," said Cate as she hugged Maddie good-bye.

Madge made her way to the garden and waited by the stone bench near the roses. Soon enough, Weston walked toward her.

"My Lady Margaret! How pretty you are! You will surely please His Majesty," said Weston.

"It is my desire to do so, sir. How far to the barge?" said Madge.

"We shall walk a ways to the river. All is in readiness. If your ladyship will take my arm?" said Weston.

"Yes. Lead on," said Madge.

"I thought the king would be on board," said Madge after she had been seated.

"Aye, such is what he said. But I mentioned it might be more prudent for His Majesty to meet you at the house. The court is full of spies and gossips. His Majesty would not wish the whole world to know his business," said Weston.

The river was crowded, as was usual for a summer night. Lords who lived along the banks of the Thames enjoyed an evening sail with their ladies. Merchants and tradesmen often headed for home by river and Madge could hear lutes being strummed and the sound of flutes floating on the evening air. The king's barge was sumptuous, with large pillows for reclining. His Majesty had sent wines and ales for Weston and her, as well as various meats. There was marchpane in the shape of a cupid and a plum pudding. Madge's stomach felt as if it were in her throat, so she did not partake of the generous supply. Weston, however, ate his fill.

They did not speak for a long while.

"Finally, we arrive, milady. Allow me to help you ashore," said Weston as he poled the barge into the shallow water and set a board for Madge to walk on. He gave her his hand and led her onto the yard in front of a small manor.

"Just follow the path in the grass and you will find the king in the house, waiting," said Weston, who seemed suddenly to grin at her. Once he saw her face, however, he suppressed his smile.

"Thank you, Sir Francis," she said with as much dignity as possible.

Madge walked up the narrow path and knocked gently on the front door. She hoped no one would answer, but was quite surprised when the king himself opened the door to her.

"Pretty Madge! Come in, come in. 'Tis a pleasant night, eh? I see Orion and his bear!" he said, pointing at the sky. "Look there—a good omen for us—Venus, the bright evening star," said the king. Then he ushered her into the front hall of the cozy manor house. Tapestries hung on the walls and there was a small gaming table set with wine and food. Two chairs sat on opposite sides of the table. At first, Madge thought they were completely alone, but then she heard the sound of virginals coming from another room.

"Have some wine, dearest? Mayhap a sweetmeat?" said the

king, offering her a drink served in his own gold plate. Her stomach fluttered.

"No thank you, Your Grace. I fear such spirits would over-heat me," said Madge with the sly smile she had cultivated over the past month, a smile that hinted at what might be in store for its recipient.

"Perhaps you are right, dearest. I should despair if I, too, should become *overheated*," said the king. "Shall we adjourn to the sitting chamber where Master Smeaton is playing his incomparable music?" said the king.

"Yes, Your Majesty," said Madge with a curtsy.

"Mistress Margaret, on this night, I am, simply, Henry. Please do not call me by any other title—unless it be sweet-heart," said the king.

"Of course, Your—I mean, Henry," she said.

He offered her his arm and together they strolled into the next chamber, an even smaller room with two tiny windows covered by heavy damask draperies. Master Smeaton sat in a corner with his virginals, a merry melody tinkling from its keys. He smiled a greeting to her when they entered the room.

Madge walked over to him, trying to mask her fears.

"Mistress, you look lovely tonight," said Master Smeaton, his eyes seeming sad. Madge thought he lacked his usual good cheer.

"Thank you, sir. Are you ill? You seem not yourself," said Madge.

"I am . . . ever in the king's service, though he breaks my heart," said Master Smeaton with a strange smile.

"Has he been cruel to you, Mark?" said Madge.

"No, mistress. He is ever kind—it matters not—I wish you well," said Master Smeaton.

"Give us a merry jig," said the king.

Immediately, Master Smeaton changed his tune to one familiar to Madge from the rolling hills of Great Snoring. Though he played as well as ever, Madge watched as his doleful eyes followed the king's every move.

The king began the familiar steps to the reel and Madge knew exactly what to do. That the king would know a dance common to the poor farmers in the north country surprised Madge. What learning escaped this king?

By the end of the song, Madge was breathless and she and the king were laughing at the whirling and spinning they had completed together. They collapsed upon a bench beset with soft pillows covered in silks and velvets. The king motioned for Master Smeaton to stand near them and told him to lay aside the virginals and bring his lute. He then instructed him to begin an old ballad of King Arthur and his lady Guinevere. The king began to sing softly to Madge in his fine tenor.

Though the king had chosen the song for its tale of love, the sound of Arthur's name over and over brought a great sadness to Madge. She tried to imagine he were with her in this comfortable manor rather than the king. But in His Majesty's presence, her Arthur seemed inconsequential and she was overwhelmed by the king's own person. This, too, made her sad.

"'Tis a lovely tune and most sorrowful," said the king after the song was over. "You have a tender heart, lady, to be so moved by my song."

"Who could not be moved by such a tale? And Your Majesty's—" said Madge.

"Uh, uh, uh, lady. I am Henry tonight, remember?" said the king.

"Yes. Forgive me . . . Henry. Your voice gives such feeling to the music—'tis as if the melody is in your blood," said Madge.

"I have always loved music, Pretty Madge. And I will confess it moves me often to tears. We share so many things," said the king.

"Yes. Our great love for the queen being another," said Madge.

"Speak not of the queen, Pretty Madge. Instead, speak of your feeling for me. This is our first night as mistress and her humble servant. And I would serve you well, lady," said the king.

"I cannot help but speak of her who brought me to court. After all, were it not for the queen, I would not be here with you tonight," said Madge.

"'Tis true, 'tis true. What say you? Shall we send Master Smeaton away and enjoy our little lovers' nest while the night is yet young?" said the king.

"Whatever you desire, Henry," said Madge.

The king wasted no time in paying Master Smeaton with a small bag of gold and hurrying him out the door. Then, after latching it, he returned to Madge.

"Let us to bed, Pretty Madge. I wish no longer to wait," he said, pulling her up from the pillows and into his arms. He kissed her, his small thin lips pecking against hers. There was no tenderness in his kisses and she felt nothing like the passion she knew when Arthur had kissed her. But Arthur's lips were full and soft, and when he kissed her, it seemed their mouths melted one into the other. The king's kisses felt as if a rooster were kissing her. Madge giggled at the thought.

"What amuses you, lady?" said the king in a husky voice.

"Nothing, Your Grace. I am more than a little nervous and when I feel this way, I often giggle. I fear it is a folly of my youth," said Madge. She felt herself blushing.

"No reason to be afraid, my pretty one. I have deflowered many a maid and have been told afterward there has never been a more gentle and kind prince," said the king, lifting her to him until her feet left the ground. He swept her up and carried her into yet another room, this one already lit with tapers and candles. A large bed with much elaborate carving on the headboard filled most of the space and Madge could see that the covers had been properly brushed and arranged. "Come, my dearest," said the king in a soft voice.

Madge felt secure in his arms as she continued to be amazed at his strength. Though approaching his old age, Henry retained some of the physical gifts of youth. He laid her across the bed and began to take his clothing off. He was in his very fine nightshirt when he came to her. She could see his manhood poking at the thin linen, making a sort of tent.

He then began to remove her clothes. He began with her shoes and then her hose. He pulled her to a seated position and removed the sleeves of her dress, then her bodice. As her breasts revealed themselves and fell loose, he began to unfasten her stomacher. Slowly, the midnight blue came apart to reveal her shift beneath it. She started to unfasten the necklace but he caught her hands.

"I am *your* servant this night, milady. Allow me," he said. He took the daisy crown from her hair and kissed each flower. Then he removed the necklace and kissed her neck all around. He quickly moved to her breasts, which he sucked and kissed, first one and then the other, for a very long time. In spite of her coolness of feeling, she did begin to stir within her own person. But she could not allow her lusts to overcome her; she must begin her work for the queen with a clear head.

"Henry, will you answer me a question?" she said as he rubbed her nipple between his thumb and forefinger, very gently.

"Anything, dearest," he said, nibbling her nipple.

"What if . . . what if there is a child?" she said.

"What if there is! What wondrous news that would be! Any woman in the kingdom would be proud to bear the king's seed! I would provide all your needs and our babe would be brought up like a prince," said the king as he rubbed the palm of his hand lightly over her breasts.

"Or a princess?" said Madge.

"Or a princess. Have no worries, Pretty Madge. If you give me a healthy son, you will receive all the homage and honor I can grant to you," said the king.

"But Henry, I fear the queen would not be pleased. And our child would be another royal bastard. This would not lead to peace in the future. It might make for another civil war," said Madge.

"These are not worries for such a pretty head! Let us enjoy each other. Ahhh, see! You are already wet—in just a few more moments, you will moan for me," said the king.

Madge worried that she was not speaking enough good about the queen. She felt she must do all she could before the king had her. Afterward, who knew what would happen?

"Henry . . . beloved, perhaps I will take a glass of wine now," said Madge.

The king sighed. But he rose and bowed to her. "Anything my mistress desires, I shall make it so."

In a few minutes, he returned with two glasses of wine. Handing her one, he raised his own to her and said, "Lady Margaret, to our love."

"To our love," Madge said.

Madge took a couple of sips and rested against the pillows. The king quaffed his glass down and set it on the nearby table. He lay beside Madge and began to fondle her once again.

"I was thinking . . ." she said.

"Of what, my love," he said.

"When I was very young, the queen came to Great Snoring—she was also young, barely a maid, perhaps seventeen, the age I am now. She was so beautiful—her dark hair hanging down her back, her brown eyes like liquid. So lithe and graceful, she danced for my mother and father after our sup. Then she sang and like an angel it was. I have heard it said at court that she is the most beautiful woman in the whole of England," said Madge.

"She is a beauty to be sure. And I remember her when I first saw her . . . if she could but bear me a son, I would love her better," said the king.

"She is still young, Henry. She could still easily give you a few boys to bellow and boast about," said Madge.

"Humph. She could, if I would but plant the seed. Her tongue has grown sharp and her temper foul. Such changes have taken all my desire for her. I would wish my wife more pliant, more supple to my will," said the king as he began to pull up the hem of Madge's shift. He traced hearts on her inner thigh and slowly began to circle around her most private place. She could feel herself wishing to rise to meet his hand, but she did not. To show that she knew something of love might give him suspicions about her purity. She had every intention of convincing the king he would be the first to assail her. On the queen's instructions, she had hidden a needle in the hem of her shift with which to prick herself after the king had taken her and had fallen asleep. The smeared blood on the linens would prove her chastity.

"But isn't a wife supposed to urge her husband to be the best man he is capable of being? Surely, if Your Majesty thought highly enough of the queen to make her your consort, you must have believed she has wisdom and discretion as well as intelligence and beauty. So great a man as you, Henry, would need a woman who could use her brain as well as her body," said Madge, gaining courage as she allowed him to touch her here, then there, then here again.

"Aye, she is not lacking in that way—and she has debated me most satisfactorily, especially when she speaks of the new religion and my role as head of the church. Ahh, how like you this, lady?" said Henry, thrusting his fingers into her slowly, back and forth, back and forth.

She could not stop the sigh that came from her. She found her thoughts more and more difficult to maintain. Suddenly, her desire rose in her body and she wanted nothing more than to yield to the king, to those fat fingers that prodded her so expertly. But she had to maintain focus on her mission—build up the queen.

"Dear Henry, if the queen is such a good woman, why do you wish to be with women like me? Would it not hurt the queen to think of you, her lawful husband, doing such?" said Madge.

"Good God, woman! Are you trying to unman me? Let there be no more talk of the queen!" shouted the king.

Madge snapped to her senses and all the ardor that had been building cooled. The king seemed to sense this and stopped his hands from their work.

"Let us have another glass of wine, shall we?" said the king as he rose to fetch it. Madge noticed that there was no longer a rise in his nightshirt. He brought more wine and they quickly drank two more glasses. Madge was beginning to resign herself to becoming the king's true mistress that very night. She could think of nothing more to say about the queen.

"Now, we shall try again," said the king. It was not a request but a command. Madge lay down next to him and they kissed. However, she did not feel the pressing of the royal person against her, as she had felt earlier. There was no hint of the king's manhood.

Though they continued to kiss and the king fondled her, the act came no closer to being accomplished. Madge realized this was what the queen had warned her about. She decided to use the techniques mentioned by Her Majesty, though the mere thought of putting her mouth on the king was making her stomach queasy.

She began to kiss the king's chest, slowly going lower and lower upon his body. She took her tongue and licked from his belly to his nipples and back again. Then she began to lick beneath the belly button.

"Lady Margaret, what is this? Who hath told you of such things? Hast the queen set you to these actions? Has she pandered you to me?" blared the king, sitting up in the bed.

"No, Your Majesty. I was following mine own desire—my desire for Your Majesty's person. Forgive me if I offend. I am truly sorry," said Madge, terrified.

For a moment, the king sat very still. Madge felt the urge to cry and decided if she were going to do so, this might be a good time.

"Pretty Madge, Pretty Madge . . . do not shed tears. It is I who should be sorry—I know you to be a true maid. It is this French lovemaking the queen brought with her—she is so skilled that it makes me doubt her own virtue. And, after I waited so long to taste of her, I am angered to think of what she may have done ere we met. I do not like her French ways of love—'tis debauchery of the lowest sort," said the king.

"Oh Henry, I do not know if what I was doing was French or Spanish or English or Irish—I only know my body was in command of my better nature. As for the queen, I would stake my life she was a maid when she came to you. She is my cousin and I would know," said Madge.

"Of course. You are right. So many speak ill of the queen,

constantly babbling in my ears 'til I am almost mad! But you have it right, dearest," said the king.

He rose from the bed and began to put his clothing on. Madge sat up and watched him, afraid to speak.

"Pretty Madge, what say you we arrange another night for our love. I have lost all desire and am weary with worry about the problems that plague the land. Would you mind if your servant brought you here another time?" said the king.

Madge rose in her shift, stood next to the king, and kissed him full on the mouth.

"My dearest Henry, we will try again as soon as you wish it. I shall be ready for you here," she said as she touched her heart, "and here," she said as she touched her womanhood. She heard him take a sudden breath.

"Mistress Margaret, you do know how to woo me," he said.

Thirty-one

Though the king promised to steal away again with Madge soon, she did not hear from him in the days that followed. She reported all that had happened to the queen and the queen seemed quite pleased. The gossips had it that the king had lost his love for Madge and had turned his attentions back to Lady Jane Seymour. However, Madge knew better, for the king had invited her once more to meet him at the house on the Thames. This time, Sir Brereton was to accompany her on the king's barge.

In preparation for what now seemed to Madge to be inevitable, she bathed and Cate helped her dress. She wore a silk chemise beneath her gown that was stitched with gold and silver thread and trimmed in Belgian lace. The queen had had it made for herself but decided such an undergarment would help entice the king. The gown she chose was deep green, bringing out her own pale green eyes. She wore the small chain of gold her mother had given her—she thought it would give her courage and help her remember who she was and from whence she had come.

She was to meet Brereton in the late afternoon, before supper. The king explained he wished to sup with her. As they sailed up the Thames, few boats were on the river. The day's business was still being conducted in the streets of London, merchants selling their wares. Perhaps the king knew few would see her as she came to him. Perhaps he wanted to keep her as much a secret as he could. She silently thanked him for it.

They arrived at the house in what seemed like short time to Madge.

"Lady Shelton, the king awaits you," said Sir Brereton, his smiling face handsome in the late afternoon sun.

"Thank you, kind sir, for bringing me. Safe journey," said Madge as she watched him push off with a long pole. She lifted her skirts and strode up the path to the front door of the cottage. Before she could knock, the king opened the door and bowed to her.

"My dear lady, come in. You look very beautiful today," said the king, taking her by the elbow. The room looked much as it had before, though the candles were not yet lit and the afternoon shadows played along the walls. She heard the sound of the lute coming from an inner room and knew Master Smeaton would be there. Somehow, the thought comforted her.

The king led her to a table filled with food: roasted duck, a suckling pig surrounded by stewed apples, loaves of white bread made with flour designated for the king and queen's use only. A bubbling hot blood pudding was next to various tarts and other subtleties. There was enough food to feed three large families. Madge wondered what would happen to that which she and the king did not consume.

"Sit, sweetheart. Eat your fill—I intend to do the same," said the king as he speared a piece of pork onto his knife. The meat was so tender it almost fell apart. The king picked up the droppings and ate each morsel, licking his greasy fingers one at a time. "Eat, girl—you will need sustenance—for I intend to ravish you this night," said the king, his red mouth shiny as he licked his fingers one more time, holding Madge with his eyes as he did so.

"Yes, Your Majesty . . . I mean Henry," said Madge, taking her own knife and slicing off a bit of duck. She forced herself to eat a reasonable amount but she could not indulge the way the king did—her stomach rumbled and turned.

After they had supped, the king took Madge by the hand and led her into the same room with Master Smeaton. Madge and Master Smeaton nodded to one another, each unhappy, though for different reasons. Their unacknowledged sorrow seemed to bind them together and they expressed themselves kindly to each other. After the king and Madge had danced three dances, the king dismissed Master Smeaton with his usual bag of gold. He smiled at Madge as he left.

"Now, lady, I shall have that for which I have long waited," said the king. He led her into the bedroom once again and quickly removed his clothing. Rather than wait for him to take her clothes off, Madge began to undress herself. Soon, she stood before him in her chemise while he was clad in his nightshirt. Madge saw he was aroused as he came to her.

"Ah, Pretty Madge . . . they all speak of you . . . my chamber men. Each would give his toes to have what I shall have this night. For you are a beauty and pleasing to me," said the king as he walked toward her.

Madge curtsied to him, keeping her head bowed low.

"You do me great honor, sire," she said. He lifted her and his strong arms embraced her.

"And now, my sweet, to bed," he said as he picked her up and carefully placed her on the mattress. The sheets smelled sweet, like cloves, and Madge blushed to think of some cleaning woman coming to prepare the room for her.

"I have noticed how the queen . . ." Madge started to say.

The king placed his finger over her mouth and shook his head. "You will not speak this night, lady. You will obey me in this—for tonight, you are here for my pleasure and it is my wish that you remain silent," said the king, not unkindly.

He began to kiss her mouth, her cheeks, her neck. His thick hands ran up and down her body, stopping to caress her breasts, then her belly. Slowly, he moved his way to her womanly parts and touched her gently through the chemise.

Though she tried to think of other things while he expertly maneuvered around her body, she soon could think of nothing but the feel of him against her. She tried to remember Arthur, how she loved him, but the king was very adept at touching her in ways that pleased her, though such pleasure was against her will. He slowly pulled her chemise up until it was bunched around her waist. Then, his heavy fingers began to probe her gently. She felt herself opening to his touch and soon, his fingers were inside her, making her tremble.

"There's a fine girl," said the king. "Yes, you like this, methinks. I shall take you gently, Pretty Madge. And you will like it."

She felt him enter her and soon he was thrusting. Though she tried to restrain herself for she did not want to betray Arthur by taking her pleasure with the king, she found she could not do so. Soon, she felt the same throbbing sensation Arthur had first brought forth in her and she sighed loudly. At that moment, she felt the king's member also pulsate and he collapsed with a sharp cry.

"Too soon! Too soon, my girl. I am sorry," said the king.

It was true that the lovemaking had not lasted long but Madge was glad. She began to cry, so ashamed was she of her carnal lusts.

"There, there, Lady Margaret. Do not cry. I did not hurt you, did I?" said the king.

"Tears of joy, Your Grace," said Madge.

"Like you some wine? Mayhap it will calm you," said the king as he pulled her chemise down to cover her. He then arose and brought two glass of red wine to the bed.

"Thank you, Your Majesty," said Madge.

"I will send you back to the palace this eve as I have important state business to attend. Do not worry, my Pretty Madge—I will call for you again. I find you bonny and buxom in the bed," said the king.

"Thank you, Your Majesty," said Madge, relieved she would not be spending the entire night with this man who repelled her, yet could bring her the same pleasure as her beloved. She did not understand how this could be.

For several days after her time with the king, Madge heard nothing. She had informed Her Majesty of the success of the evening, omitting the part about her own enjoyment. The queen was pleased but also jealous and Madge had to walk carefully around Her Majesty. The king then sent for her and, once again, he bedded her with great success.

The queen had planned a festive gala to celebrate the return of her brother, George, from his ambassador's mission in France.

She had purchased a particularly beautiful dress made of cloth of gold for the event. The bodice was cut quite low, almost showing the edge of her paps. She told Madge she intended to win His Majesty as she had done ten years earlier. She confessed part of what had attracted the king to her in those early days had been the attentions of other men: Lord Henry Percy, Sir Thomas Wyatt, Sir Pierce Butler. The king liked nothing more than to best the men around him, winning at everything, whether it be at the lists or in the bedroom. Her Majesty decided to play the maid once more, encouraging the men around the king to enter her service in the fashion of courtly love. In this way, she told Madge, she hoped to lure the king back to her bed and get a son. Though she invited Madge to the homecoming of Lord Rochford, she insisted Madge wear a dark gray damask with only a few dull citrines and garnets sewn across the square neckline. The dress had come from the queen's own closet, yet the fabric was worn thin in places and the color was dreary.

In many ways, since Madge's affair with the king had become a liaison in earnest, the queen seemed changed toward her. Though she had done Her Majesty's bidding, she often caught the queen glancing at her with evil looks. Her Majesty had little use for Madge these days, except to give terse instructions about how to keep Henry's interest and turn him back toward Anne herself. His Majesty did not call for Madge often, perhaps once a week, if that. He was not driven to her bed as Arthur was. Madge found herself with time on her hands. She and Shadow used the days for hiking in the woods, to that secret place she shared with Arthur. He would meet them there and many a fine afternoon was made finer by love.

At first, Madge was bothered by the idea of having two lovers. Such a condition was not something she had ever dreamed might happen. She had intended to keep her virtue until her marriage, as the queen had instructed all her ladies to do. After that first time, Madge did not enjoy the king's lovemaking. He did not take time with her as he had on their first meeting. Instead, he barely kissed her, entered her when his member was able, and did the deed quickly with little skill. Madge felt as if she were some common stew and steeled herself against the king. Bedding him became an act she must perform, but one which she could do while thinking of other, more pleasant things— like meeting Arthur later. She kept ideas about sin as far from her consciousness as possible.

Madge and Arthur often made use of the prayer book the queen had given Madge. Though she kept it on her person most of the time, in order to plan their assignations, she sometimes wrote a note in the margins, telling Arthur, in their secret poetic code, when and where she could meet him. She would then have Nan Cobham, a serving wench, carry the book back and forth, telling the girl Master Brandon was thinking of going into the priesthood. Since Nan could not read the scribbles anyway, it seemed a safe way to communicate.

On the day of the queen's celebration, Madge was in the outer rooms with Jane Seymour, Lady Rochford, Margaret Douglas, and others. The queen and her brother had been in the bedchamber the whole of the morning, having great discussions about Francis I and his plans regarding the princess Elizabeth. It was to be determined whether Elizabeth would marry the dauphin or another of Francis's sons. Madge could hear bits and pieces of the conversation when the queen screamed about Francis being a "popish devil" and a "cursed mongrel." Lady Rochford and Lady Seymour sat in a far corner in quiet conversation while they embroidered something on luxurious satin. Madge brought out her prayer book and began to write the rhyme that would let Arthur know when she could see him again.

The queen and her brother entered the outer rooms without much ado and Madge had not seen them. She was still writing. Suddenly, her prayer book was jerked out of her hands by the queen herself, who stood over her, her face blazing.

"How dare you write idle poesies in the prayer book I have given you! Is it not enough that you write them with Wyatt and the others? I cannot believe you would deface God's word with such wanton toys! Be gone! Be gone from my sight!" screeched the queen. Madge made a brief curtsy and left the room, her face burning. She wanted to retrieve her book, but the queen was in no mood to return it to her now. Madge had seen the look on Jane Seymour's face when the queen dismissed her, a puffed-up gloating look. Oh, of all the women in the queen's service, the Seymour wench raised Madge's hackles. Lady Jane thought so well of herself and her family—and imagined herself, Plain Jane, replacing the queen in the king's affections. Fool!

Madge stormed into Cate's room without knocking.

"Maddie-girl, what is wrong?" said Cate as she looked up from her stitching, her mouth gaping.

Madge told the story and cried the tears of shame she had held back while the eyes of the court were upon her. Cate held her and patted her back.

"She is jealous of you, dearie. She can see your beauty outshines her own. Though I have never approved of our queen, I'll give her this—she has the heart of a king! She fights for what she wants and does not give up! The folk of the castle have begun to change their tune about her—they know she is not to blame for all the burnings and hangings. 'Tis the king and his greed, that it is," said Cate.

"I have done everything for her! Given myself to the king! It is not my fault he . . . he . . . cannot always . . ." said Madge.

"Shush, girl! No one should know that secret," said Cate. "Now, how about some tea?"

Madge and Cate passed the afternoon, planning and talking about when Madge would be free of the king and allowed to marry Arthur. They spoke of returning to Great Snoring where they could raise pups and ride each day; where Madge and her parents could enjoy one another again, once they were relieved of their duties to Elizabeth.

Right before they were to go to the Great Hall to sup, a knock sounded at Cate's door.

Cate opened it and immediately fell down in a deep curtsy. Madge looked up and then did likewise. The queen entered and bid them rise.

"My dear Lady Margaret, here is your prayer book. I wish to tell you how sorry I am to have lost my temper with you. My brother had disturbing news from France and, as you know, I am fighting to win back my husband. I fear my troubles made me not myself. I hope you know how I value the services you have rendered and the friendship you have given me since I became queen. I also hope I can continue to count on your friendship and love," said the queen in a calm voice. Her manner was so sincere and gracious that Madge immediately forgave her in her heart.

"You will always have my love and friendship, Your Grace," said Madge.

"And mine," said Cate, though no one had addressed her.

The queen smothered a laugh and then hugged Madge. She left as quietly as she had come.

———

In the queen's chambers, musicians played and people danced. Wine flowed and great plates of food were brought in. The queen had invited the prettiest people at court, a crowd of energetic youths who could twirl and leap like stags. Poets and scholars and singers and jesters and lovely damsels and handsome gentlemen roamed the outer rooms, laughing and talking. At the center of the evening was the queen herself, resplendent in her cloth of gold. Madge felt a bit dowdy and her clothing certainly did nothing to inspire her to approach any of the richly clad ladies or gallants who wore only the finest silks and velvets and jewels. She stood by herself in a far corner and watched the queen.

Anne was surrounded by her usual admirers: Wyatt was kneeling at her feet, intent upon reading her a poem; Brereton, the most handsome man in the room, stood behind Wyatt; Norris knelt on one knee, gazing adoringly at the queen; and Francis Weston manned the rear. This was the scene the king observed when he entered the room.

"Well-met, friends! Ah, the music is a delight—shall we dance, dearest?" he said as he cut a swath through the gentlemen to Anne. She curtsied and accepted his hand. They moved to the floor as the other dancers stopped and made way for Their Majesties. Master Smeaton began a slow, dignified pavane. The queen had lost none of her grace and the king seemed enraptured. By the end of the dance, he had vanquished the others and sat beside his wife, eating, drinking, and making merry. It seemed to Madge that Her Majesty's strategy was working.

After that night, the queen invited the same group of courtiers to her apartments often. The king usually appeared at some point, saying he "knew where to find those who would spend

good pastime." Through the summer, the queen played him thus
and Madge watched as she lured him, slowly, back to her. Though
the king visited the queen often in public, he had not yet approached her bedchamber. Madge was there each night on the
trundle, helping the queen prepare herself for sleep.

"I have failed you, Majesty," said Madge, one night in early
July.

"How so, cousin?" said the queen.

"Though His Majesty still comes to my bed, he stays not
long after. I have little chance to speak for Your Grace. Often,
he places his finger across my lips and forbids me to speak at all.
I have tried as I can to fill his ear with good news about Your
Majesty, but I fear I am having no effect," said Madge.

"You are in Windsor Forest!" said the queen, laughing.

"I beg Your Majesty's pardon?" said Madge, confused.

"Oh, dear—'tis a saying limned by Wyatt—we use it when
we mean to say someone is lost and does not understand what is
happening! You, dear cousin, have done exactly right. The king
often fails with you, a young beautiful maid. I am certain such a
fault has humiliated His Majesty—I have seen how he sometimes turns his head away from you when you are in the room.
Such occasional failure will surely send him back to me—for I
have known both his failures and his glorious successes. Already, he attends me more than he has done in months. And I do
not see him going after the Seymour whore! I believe my
schemes will bring him to me soon," said the queen. "So off to
sleep—by our wits we will be saved."

By mid-July, the king had grown into the habit of calling for
Madge to come to his bedchamber, quickly having use of her
body and then sending her back to the queen's chambers. He

did not allow her to speak, nor did he show her any of his previous tenderness. As a result, she became colder and colder to him. One night, he sent for her in the early evening rather than in the deep of night.

"Lady Margaret, I have called you to my chambers this night to give you some bad news," said His Majesty. He was seated at his table fully dressed and looked busy with affairs of state. His quill pen perched on the desk atop a pile of papers.

"Bad news, sire? Has ought happened to my family?" said Madge, suddenly filled with dread.

The king laughed his great, hearty laugh.

"No, no, Pretty Madge—no such tragedy. I wanted to tell you I will no longer see you. 'Tis no fault of yours, dear lady. But my queen has been wooing me back into her good graces and I mean to spend myself on her—I need to get a son and she has become a delight to me. I see how the courtiers flock to her apartments and how her beauty and wit enthrall them. I wouldst reclaim my wife, Pretty Madge. For the good of the kingdom," said the king.

Madge struggled mightily to keep a grin from exploding across her face. She tried not to let the sigh of relief escape her lips and so was silent for a moment.

"Do not dismay, sweetheart. You must have known this day would come—I tire of women so easily it seems. And the queen has spirit and all the graces I could desire. You cannot expect to win me from such a woman," said the king.

"Oh no, Your Grace. I am happy—for the kingdom—that you will turn your attentions to your wife. The country needs a prince and such I could never give you—but the queen has already given you one healthy child. A prince is bound to follow," said Madge, curtsying deeply.

"You are taking this news well, sweetheart, and I am glad of it. I tire of women's tears and tantrums. But my queen has been so gentle of spirit lately, it is my hope she will oppose me no more," said the king as he took Madge's hand and raised her up. He then kissed her cheek tenderly and led her to the door.

"Fear not, Lady Margaret. You shall see some benefit from our love affair—I shall find you a husband who will treat you more kindly than Norris—in time," said the king.

"I require nothing from you, sire. But such a change would be most welcome," said Madge. Then, she walked out of his chamber and down the corridor, her heart once again light and free.

As the princess Elizabeth's second birthday approached, the king and queen were planning their autumn Progress, though the season was wetter than usual. His Majesty had told the court that he wished "to make myself and my queen known to my beloved people" and all the courtiers were to ready themselves. The queen was busy ordering new clothes for her daughter, as the child was growing quickly and, as princess, had to be properly attired. She kept Madge busy looking at fabric and laces. The queen spared no expense when ordering items for her child and expressed great joy to think the Progress would stop for several days at Eltham to visit Elizabeth, whom she had not seen for several weeks.

While preparing to go on Progress, Madge had little time for Arthur. Recently, his father had asked him to come home to Guildford Palace in Suffolk to help with the family farms. They met one final time before his departure. Nowadays, no one took notice of Madge's comings and goings as they had when she had been the king's favorite. She did not miss the attention— even Norris kept away from her once he saw the king no longer acknowledged her. Norris was ever aware of which way the king's wind blew and followed it with gusto.

Madge had almost become a nonentity at court, except for the queen who continued to shower her with kindness. Lady Seymour no longer bothered to nod to her at all. Madge did not care. The queen's winning ways had finally brought His Majesty to her bed again. In the last week, he had visited her three times, though Madge had been excused from the queen's bedchamber each night. The king seemed happy again with Anne and the whole mood of the court seemed lighter.

On her way with Shadow to their meeting spot for their farewell, Madge noticed the beautiful blue sky, with not a cloud in sight. The green fields had begun to fade and the trees, though not yet turning, hinted at the coming change in season. Madge had turned eighteen and felt the future would be bright indeed. She hummed a ditty she'd heard Master Smeaton playing on his virginals and skipped with Shadow across the meadow. The dog knew the way to their place and eagerly ran ahead since Arthur always had a big bone for her to chew.

"My love! I have been waiting it seems forever!" said Arthur, handing the bone to Shadow so he could embrace Madge.

"I have not been long in coming, dearest! Surely, you have not had that long to wait," said Madge, kissing him.

"I will miss you, Pretty Madge! I do not know if I will be able to bear any absence from you," he said.

"You will be so busy working for your father, you will have no time to think of me. And do not let those pretty shepherdesses lead you astray!" said Madge.

"No one could lead me from you, sweetheart," he said, kissing her again and again. He spread his cloak upon the ground and they lay together, anxious to be as one. Afterward, he looked at her with a furrowed brow.

"I must speak to you of some unpleasant news," he said.

"Oh, dearest, let us not hear of it now—let us savor this last meeting before we must part," said Madge, kissing his hands.

"This I must tell you—it is of great import. I was in the privy chamber and overheard Master Cromwell telling Ambassador Chapuys that the queen was much angered with him—he did not say why. She told him she would separate his head from his shoulders if she so desired. But Cromwell said to the ambassador that, 'I trust so much on my master, I think she cannot do me any harm.' I fear Cromwell is turning further from the queen," said Arthur.

"Mayhap 'twas just an argument—the queen has a temper as well I know. Master Cromwell has been her man all along, except regarding the monasteries—why should he wish to turn from her now?" said Madge.

"I am not sure but I have heard much talk about the emperor coming to the aid of his aunt, the dowager princess. Master Cromwell would befriend Charles the Fifth if he could, but because of the queen, such a friendship is not possible. I have also heard scuttlebutt about the king's need of more money and Master Cromwell's plan to dissolve *all* the monasteries, not just the ones found guilty of abuses. The queen wishes to save those which are pious and which do not fool the people with relics and such other falsities," said Arthur.

"I do not believe such things can touch Her Majesty—she is but a woman! She is the king's wife and only wishes to bear His Majesty a son," said Madge.

"You do not understand—everyone wants power—to touch it, feel it, hold it like a flame in their own hand. And these cursed knaves will do what they must for just a moment of such power. Tell the queen to beware—her troubles are not yet over," said Arthur.

"You put too much credence on these gossips—the king has been coming to her bed with great regularity. We shall have a prince soon enough!" said Madge. "Now, come kiss me again—our time is short!"

On the night before they were to leave on Progress, Madge and the queen retired early. Madge had told the queen of His Majesty's decision to "spend himself" with the queen only and since that time, Madge had been invited to return as the queen's woman of the bedchamber. She slept again on a pallet beside the queen's enormous bed. The preparations for the Progress had tired both women and soon, Madge was sleeping soundly.

A strange sound awakened her. She thought she had heard a door scraping against the stone floor but such a thing was impossible—no one could enter the queen's bedchamber without permission.

Then, she heard whispers. She froze, fearful that some murderer had somehow made his way to the queen. She readied herself to call out for the guards and pounce upon the varlet.

"Harry? Dearest?" said the queen.

Madge could hear the rustle of the bedclothes and the sound of someone joining Her Majesty.

"'Tis I, my love," said the king.

Madge remained still and tried to calm her heart, which beat against her ribs like a wild bird in a cage. She kept her breathing steady to simulate sleep.

"You have not used the secret passage since before Elizabeth was born," said the queen.

"I wanted no fanfare—I desired only to be an Englishman bedding his wife this eve," said the king.

"'Tis late. But I do find it pleasant to be so taken by surprise," said the queen.

"I could not sleep, Anne. My mind was troubled," said the king.

"What troubles you, dearest? Perhaps I can ease you in some way," said the queen.

"I have been coming to your bed for near two month and still there is no babe. I fear my seed has grown weak and old, as am I," said the king, his voice dull.

"Oh dearest, take heart—we do not know the ways of God, nor what His plans may be for us. Such things are in God's hands, not ours. Our duty is to do as He commands, which is to be fruitful and multiply. We are doing our best, my love," said the queen. Madge could hear her move on the bed and imagined she was moving closer to the king. She heard them kissing.

"But I am no longer young—you know that better than anyone. Often, I cannot . . ."said the king.

"My sweetheart, such things are only to be expected. We cannot retain our youth forever. I grow sad when I think of my beauty fading but then I realize that though the hot passion of youth will dissipate, something gentler and stronger will take its place. As we grow old together, my love, we shall grow in kindness and true affection, rather than be driven by our lesser nature. I have seen such in my own parents, their tenderness toward each other," said the queen in a low, soft voice.

"But we must get a prince—the stability of the country depends upon it. If my seed has become weak, what then? What if I can no longer father a child?" said the king in a whisper.

"I have heard of men of great age still fathering children, Harry. Methinks you worry overmuch. Give us time, beloved. Give us time and a relief from the burdens of the state. We shall be together on Progress, hunting and sporting day and night. You will see—a babe will come," said the queen.

"I wonder if God is again displeased with me—for we have lost a son, just as Catherine and I did. Could we have offended the Lord with our marriage? Breaking from the church? All those who I have burned—could this be God's judgment against us?" said the king.

"No, dearest. We have a healthy daughter who is smart and full of promise. God is obviously pleased that you are no longer living in sin with your brother's wife. If you will but love me true, Harry, I will give you your long-awaited son," said the queen.

Madge turned away from the bed and put her pillow over her ears, for she did not wish to hear the sounds of their lovemaking. But the flow of the king's mind disturbed her—was he thinking of putting away his queen?

Thirty-two

*T*he Progress was one of great happiness for the king and queen. They traveled west from Windsor to Reading, Ewelme, Abingdon, Woodstock, Langley, and Sudeley Castle. They lodged at Painswick Manor to take advantage of the excellent hunting and then moved on to Berkeley Castle. In September, the progress returned to the Seymours' Wulfhall, where the king and queen hunted and made merry. However, they were not at Wulfhall long before a messenger came from London with news for the king.

The emperor had defeated the infidels at Tunis, which was happy news for all of Christendom, though such news did not find a welcome from Their Majesties. With Charles V no longer engaged in war, he was now free to come to the aid of his aunt and bring England back into the church at Rome. Suddenly, as Madge listened to the queen's explanation of the situation, she understood the great danger the dowager princess Catherine posed to the entire country. After receiving this message, the king and queen stayed only a few days at Wulfhall and quickly left for the parliament at Winchester. Again, Madge observed how merry Their Royal Majesties seemed, especially when Anne discovered she was once again with child. Surely, this would be the prince for which the entire country longed.

"Lady Margaret, we must make sure this babe arrives alive and well—I fear my life, and maybe your own, will depend upon it. I shall rest and take good care, even more so than last time. We will to bed early each night and rise early, eat healthy foods. Dame Brooke has told me of some herbs that will help the babe to grow and give me strength as well. We shall get hold of her once we return," said the queen as the two women lay upon the bed set up for them on their last afternoon at Wulfhall.

"We shall take the greatest care, Your Grace. And the babe will be full of life," said Madge.

"I fear for us if things do not go well. Henry is capable of ridding himself of me and bringing great ruin to all my family—I have seen such coldness in him before, though I never dreamed I would have to fear it. But fear it I do," whispered the queen.

"He seems quite merry these days and is evermore kind to Your Grace. Surely, you are safe," said Madge with what she hoped was conviction.

"He is happy, yes. But I stand in his way for friendship with the emperor and he blames me for his excommunication and the break with Rome that tears our land asunder. Much could be solved if he puts me away. We must tread with great care," said the queen.

"That we shall do, Majesty. But now, you need rest and so

does the babe. Let us get a nap while we can for we travel on the morrow," said Madge as she yawned and felt her eyes grow heavy.

Upon their return to London, the queen began preparing for her son. She and her ladies sewed tiny gowns embroidered with golden thread. Booties for little feet were crocheted and soft warm blankets cut and sewn. The king took all his evening meals with the queen in her chambers and Madge thought His Majesty looked tired on many of their evenings together. As was his custom, the king stayed away from the queen's bed because she was with child. Though he did not come to her at night, the king spoke with her often about the goings-on in the realm. Madge overheard him say that the dowager princess was quite ill, though she continued to write to her nephew, urging him to take the English matter into his own hands.

As the queen's belly grew, she became irritable and difficult. Rumors flew about the king and his revived interest in Mistress Seymour. One afternoon, the queen rounded on the king in her apartments.

"What have you to say, Henry? What have you to say?" the queen shouted after she had accused His Majesty of infidelity. Madge could not believe her ears as the queen continued to heap abuse on the king. She noted his face was red and his nostrils flared but he said nothing in return.

Then the queen moved to stand in front of Mistress Seymour.

"How dare you dally with my husband the king! I shall box your ears, you harlot!" said the queen as she beat Mistress Seymour about the head.

"Anne! Anne! Get hold of yourself. Do not forget our son!

For if you are upset, he will be, too!" shouted the king, holding her arms to her sides and indicating with a nod of his head for Mistress Seymour to leave.

The queen collapsed in tears against the king's broad chest and sobbed uncontrollably.

"I cannot bear it, Harry, I cannot bear for you to be with another," cried the queen.

"Believe me sweetheart, I have not been with another. I merely walked in the garden with Mistress Seymour. Her family is one of old greatness and I have promised her father to look after her. Be of good cheer, Anne. You are my queen and you are the one to give me a son! Now, try to tame your wild fancies. And take care of my boy," said the king in a soft voice. Though he spoke tenderly to the queen, Madge saw the flinty look in his eyes. The queen then told His Majesty he should be bound to her above all women because she had delivered him from living in sin with his brother's wife. The king drew his mouth in a tight line.

Not only did the queen upbraid the king, she also lost patience with her father, Lord Wiltshire, Master Cromwell, the duke of Norfolk, and a host of others. To Madge, it seemed that daily the queen grew more and more irascible. By All Hallows' Eve, the king had not supped with the queen for three days. Madge gathered her courage to speak to the queen about her behavior.

That evening, the queen had arranged for music and dancing, as she had before. Though several of those invited showed up, a few did not. Lady Jane Rochford and Lady Seymour were not in attendance, nor was Sir Brereton. Wyatt sent a note saying he was ill and could not come. Though not all her favorites were present, the queen played the hostess well and made merry with great gusto. At midnight, the queen sent them away.

"I am so very tired, Margaret. Will you get a bowl of water for my feet? They feel hot and I fear they will swell," said the queen as Madge and another lady of the bedchamber, Bessie Holland, removed the Queen's outer garments.

"Yes, Your Grace. If you like, I will rub them with scented oil when you are abed," said Madge.

"That would be a blessing from the angels," said the queen.

By the time Madge had found the proper sized bowl and poured the water, she and the queen were alone. Madge helped Her Majesty onto the bed and put the basin on the floor. The queen placed her narrow feet in and sighed.

"I must soon stop my dancing—I no longer have the strength for it, Margaret. Being *enceinte* is no easy thing. I fear it makes me quick to anger and slow to forgive," said the queen.

"Your Majesty . . . dearest cousin . . . I am filled with concern that the king has not supped with you these past three nights. There are tales once again about him and Mistress Seymour," said Madge.

"I have heard these stories and think they are true enough. The king seeks to go where he will and he has chosen one who will not argue with him as I have done. Nor will she do any of the things I have done to please him," said the queen with a strange look. "He will tire of her quickly, I'll warrant. You are much more beautiful than she and you have a mind and charm. She is as dull as dishwater. Yet, the king tired of you quickly enough."

Madge did not speak her anger at the queen's words.

"Jane has no beauty, that is certain. Yet, those who tell the tales say it is her virtue the king admires and her quiet serenity," said Madge.

"Virtue? Ha, he has played that game before! He will come back to me—I know it. I shall win him as I did before—my apartments will be filled with gaiety and laughter and music. He will want to be here, mark me," said the queen.

"Of this I have no doubt . . . but dearest Anne," said Madge in a whisper, "mayhap you should guard your temper with him just a little. Be sweet to him and win him with your kindness."

The queen removed her feet from the basin and Madge dried them on a nearby cloth. Then Madge cupped her hands and poured in the scented oil. She began to rub the queen's feet.

"Sweetness is not the only way to the king's heart. I know a secret way," said the queen in a whisper. She looked at Madge and spoke again, "Will you swear on your prayer book never to breathe a word of what I am about to tell you?"

"Yes, Majesty—I do swear never to tell, if they draw and quarter me," said Madge.

"Even so, perhaps I should not spill this news—I scarce know what to think of it myself," said the queen, her eyes staring into the firelight.

"Please, dearest cousin, do not tell me anything untoward," said Madge.

"No—I *shall* share it with you, for I know not what to make of it," said the queen. Her Majesty took a deep breath and continued. "Do you remember when last the king came to my bed while we were on Progress? We were at Sudeley Castle and had the entire second floor to ourselves," said the queen.

"Aye, I recall it well—you sent me down to the kitchens several times in the early evening to fetch food and drink. I remember traversing those steep stairs!" said Madge.

"After I sent you to sleep with the rest of the ladies, the king and I began to kiss and fondle each other as in days of old. He was breathing hard, panting really, and was eager to begin the act. I, too, was ready for him. We crawled into our bed and he then had his usual trouble—the same trouble he had with you," said the queen, her cheeks red.

Madge continued rubbing the queen's feet and her delicate ankles. She did not wish to hear any more about the private acts of Their Majesties.

"But I was not willing to give up this chance for my son, so I employed one final trick I learned in France," said the queen.

"How could there be any more devices for love than those Your Grace has already shared with me?" said Madge.

"I had heard this long ago while I was at the French court, but I never dreamed I would use such means to get a babe," said the queen. "As you know, Francis the First is a lecherous, pox-ridden man but he has a terrible secret vice. I learned of this from Madame Beauforte, one of Queen Claude's ladies."

"I knew you served the virtuous queen Claude, Majesty. What did you learn from her woman?" said Madge, whose curiosity was now alive.

"Madame Beauforte knew Francis's mistress, Mme. Anne de Pisseleu d'Heilly. She has kept the king's interest for almost twenty years. He made her the wealthiest, most powerful woman at the French court," said the queen, turning over to lie on her side while Madge continued to rub her feet. "It is said that men would sell their souls to have a night with her, such are her skills at lovemaking." The queen smiled at Madge.

"I suppose having that kind of talent is something one is born with—like the gift of music or beauty," said Madge, feeling suddenly inadequate.

"Do you not wish to know what her secret is, cousin?" said the queen.

"Only if Your Majesty wishes to tell me," said Madge, half-afraid.

"I do wish to tell you. There may come a time for you to use this hidden knowledge," said the queen.

"Majesty, I can only hope my charms will be enough for my husband," said Madge. The queen gave her an evil look and Madge realized that for some men, no matter how well-endowed their wives with wit and beauty, they would always need perversity in the act of love.

The queen yawned and then continued her story, "Mme. d'Heilly has a silken cord with nine silken tails at one end. When she meets with the king in one of his houses arranged for such a purpose, she takes the reins of power from him. Now, it is *she* who must be obeyed on pain of, well, a lashing with the silken whip. She commands the king and he obeys her every wish. It is said he parades on all fours like a horse, with nary a stitch of clothing upon his back. Around and around the room she drives him. If he does not gallop fast enough to please her, she flails him. She is rumored to have forced him to please himself in front of her, and to eat gruel from a dish set upon the floor. Some say she even places a strand of pearls in his nether regions and slowly pulls them out, to his great delight. Such treatment builds a wild frenzy in him until he can bear it no longer. Finally, she allows him to satisfy himself with her, often telling him to take her the way a stallion takes a mare," said the queen.

"I have never heard such . . ." said Madge with her mouth slightly open. She thought of the miniature she had seen of Francis I and could not smother a laugh.

"Nor had I—and it seems such a humorous picture I can scarce believe it. But the wench swore on the Holy Bible 'twas the truth," said the queen.

"If such methods would work on the body of an anointed

king, I cannot imagine how a mere yeoman might react," said Madge. "I would never have the courage to begin such a game."

"I would never have thought it myself. But I know I must bear a son to the king if I am to survive. So . . . I did try the same with my Harry," said the queen in a hushed tone.

Madge could not believe what she heard. Yet, she would hear more.

"What happened, cousin? How did the king like such sport?" said Madge.

"I will tell you, Margaret, our king was so amazed at my handling of him, he knew not what to do at first. But soon, he took to the game and I built a passion in him I had not seen before, nay, not even on the night in Calais when he took me for the first time. He was filled with rage and the devil knows what else. I brought out the young man in him that night. When the time came, he took me the same way Francis took his concubine—like an animal," said the queen.

"And did he fall in love with you again? Was he pleased?" said Madge.

The queen turned her eyes to the floor and spoke very softly.

"Nay, I think not. Afterward, we lay together and he was still panting. His face was flushed and he arose to gather his clothes. He said to me, "Madame, I know not where you have learned such sport but 'tis not fitting for a king—you will breathe of this to no one!" He then left, ashamed methinks. For my Harry is clean in all his habits and full of dignity. My game disturbed him deeply, I fear," said the queen.

"Do you think it is the memory of that debased night that keeps His Majesty from you?" said Madge.

"Perhaps. To recall all I made him do would bring shame to any man worth his blood. But Margaret, you should have seen him prancing on the floor, his belly hanging lower than his manhood—I had to bite my cheeks to keep from laughing," said the queen.

"Thank God you did not laugh," said Madge. She was amazed at what the queen had disclosed.

"No, even I know better than that. I had hoped such play would lead Henry back to me, begging for more, as Francis is said to do," said the queen.

"From what I know of His Majesty, such a stunt would work only once—you are lucky to have escaped with your head!" said Madge.

"You have taken his measure quite right. I sought to bind him to me, but it seems I have driven him further away. Now, I fear only the birth of a prince can save me—I see how he looks at me sometimes, when he does not suspect I am watching—it is a look of such coldness I can scarce bear it," said the queen.

Madge was suddenly sorry for His Majesty and for the queen as well. How strange a thing it was to be married to a king.

Madge fell silent and so did Her Majesty. Soon, Madge heard the soft familiar snores from the queen. At least the queen had gotten what she wanted—a babe growing in her belly. The king would have his son and the queen would be safe. And England would be free from another civil war. Maybe such rewards were worth a bit of debauchery.

As the weather grew more chill and the first snows began to fall, Madge longed for Arthur's return to court. She had received two letters from him, each one encouraging her to wait for him, bespeaking his love in plain terms. She had sent one letter in response but was carefully circumspect in her own admission of her feelings in writing. She had learned the ways of the court too well to commit anything of import to the page.

Each day, the king and queen attended matins, the Mass, and compline together. To the court, His Majesty showed the queen every consideration. But Madge could see the strange look that came to his eyes when the queen turned away from him to speak with a courtier. She also noticed the king no longer kissed his wife, except on the hand in greeting. Though he was always the gentleman with the queen, he had not yet come to sup again. Madge could almost feel the tension in the air at court and worried how such strains would affect the queen's unborn child. Each night, she prayed for the safety of both.

The winter winds blew fully as the Advent season approached and Greenwich buzzed with preparations for the twelve days of Christmas. Madge enjoyed the activity and the building excitement. She thought of the Blessed Virgin and how she, like the queen, awaited the birth of her son. With the changes in the service, Madge was able to hear preaching that forced her to think about herself and God in ways she had not considered previously. As she observed the intrigues at court, she saw she was in a hotbed of corruption. No one could be trusted, it seemed. Those who treated you most kindly one moment could cut you the next. One day, the Lord Privy Seal; the next day, one's head on a stake at London Bridge. As the queen continued to fall out of favor with the king, the court reflected his attitude. The king had almost strangled his fool, Will Somers, when he jested that the queen was a "bawd" and the Princess "a bastard," and banished him from court. Yet, few courtiers were as solicitous of the queen's comfort as they had been three years ago. They were, however, full of courtesy, for who knew when the king might return once again to his wife's arms.

Madge thought of these things and realized nothing at Court was secure; everything—the gold, the jewels, the merrymaking—was in flux, here one moment and gone the next.

"Lady Margaret, I have a message for you," said Nan Cobham, holding a folded piece of parchment in her hand.

"Thank you, Nan. Happy Christmas!" said Madge, handing the girl a small coin.

She carefully broke the wax seal and read the contents.

> Dearest Pretty Madge,
>
> I am to come to court by Christmas Day. I will meet you at Cate's.
>
> Love,
>
> Arthur

Madge folded the note and tucked it into her bodice. Her whole body trembled with excitement. Only two days until she could hold Arthur once more! Two days!

The queen was napping and had left instructions for no one to enter her bedchamber so Madge waited in one of the outer rooms. She picked up her sewing to divert her mind while she waited for the queen to arise. Several of the other ladies were similarly occupied, though Jane Seymour was not there. Madge wondered if she were with the king. Madge heard a commotion in the hallway and a handful of gentlemen entered the queen's apartments. Immediately, Madge saw Sir Norris and looked down at her sewing.

"My Pretty Madge, how now?" he said as he bowed to her.

"Good day, Sir Norris," said Madge.

"You will be happy to know I spoke to the king this very morning about our nuptials. He has given his royal permission for us to marry when the robin builds its nest," said Norris.

"I am surprised you would mention such a frivolity to His Majesty. Surely, the king has more important issues to concern him," said Madge.

"Your joy at the thought of our wedding is overwhelming, Pretty Madge. I think you love me not," said Norris.

"You have done little to earn love from me, sir. Methinks we should forgo this match and find love in another," said Madge.

"Mistress, I would have you—I care not a whit for love. You are young and fit, the prettiest girl at court. And I *will* have you," he said.

"If that be so, then tell me, sir, since you have the king's ear, how fares the queen in his affections?" whispered Madge.

"I can barely hear you, mistress. May I sit down so we can speak of this matter plainly?" he said.

Madge patted her hand on the bench beside her and Norris plopped down. He sat very close so that they rubbed thigh to thigh.

"As you may know, mistress, I am a great friend to Her Majesty. I would see her content on the throne for many a year to come. But the king has no stomach for her these days, though I know not why. He pulls a face when he must be near her and spends much of his time with the lady Jane. I know not what his intentions are, but if you have any sway with the queen, tell her to be humble and obedient to His Majesty. Beat Mistress Seymour at her own game," said Norris.

"I will tell her. And Sir Norris, thank you," said Madge.

"Anything to please my lady," said Norris, without his usual irony.

"When do you think he will arrive, Cate? It seems we have been waiting for hours," said Madge as she paced the short length of Cate's room.

"How should I know the hour he will set foot in the castle? Am I a soothsayer? Do I read the tea leaves? Sit down, Maddie-girl! You are making Shadow a nervous Nell," said Cate.

"Methinks it has been long since I have seen him!" said Madge, alighting on the edge of Cate's pallet. However, she could not stay seated. She resumed her route, back and forth, back and forth. Before she could make another round, she heard a soft tapping at the door. She flung open the heavy door with the vigor of two men.

"Arthur!" she cried out as she rushed into his arms. He quickly pushed her away.

"Inside, inside!" he said, closing the door behind him.

Once safely in Cate's room, they embraced and kissed for many minutes while Cate averted her eyes and petted Shadow. Finally, she spoke.

"I think 'tis time for me to gather some greenery for my room to give it a bit of Christmas cheer," she said.

Arthur broke his embrace and took Madge by the hand, leading her to the pallet.

"Prithee, wait, good Cate. I have news I must spill to both of you. You will like it not," he said.

"What is it?" said Madge.

"'Tis about the queen and our country," said Arthur.

"Then tell us quickly," said Madge.

"My father has let slip many things whilst we worked. First, the emperor threatens. Francis the First maintains close relations with the pope. Paul the Third has tried to gather a coalition against Henry, and Catherine still calls on her nephew, the emperor, to invade us. The common folk dislike Queen Anne as much as ever and there is disquiet across the land. The people do not like the changes Henry is making in the church and they blame everything on Her Majesty," said Arthur.

"But this seems much as it has always been," said Madge. "There are ever wars and rumors of wars."

"There is one change which you will not like," said Arthur.

"What is it?" said Madge.

"The king is thinking of putting away his wife. He is enraptured of Jane Seymour and with her brother, Edward, now a groom of the king's chamber, Mistress Jane waxes while the queen wanes," said Arthur.

"We know about the king's harlot," said Cate.

"He will tire of her, I am sure. And you forget, Arthur, the queen is with child," said Madge.

"He tires of them all, does he not? The queen's child can save her if it be a boy. Another girl? I believe His Majesty will find a way to rid himself of her," said Arthur.

"I hope you are mistook," said Cate.

"Let us speak no more of this—come, dearest, I have prepared food and ale for you. You are tired from your journey," said Madge.

"Let me feast on you, sweetheart—that is all I need of food and drink," he said.

IV

1536

👑

These Bloody Days Have Broken My Heart

—SIR THOMAS WYATT,
FROM A POEM OF THE SAME NAME

Thirty-three

O ne week after gifts were exchanged on New Year's Day, news came that the dowager princess Catherine had left this earthly existence. Madge was with the queen and king in the Great Hall when the courier arrived.

"God be praised that we are free from all suspicion of war!" shouted the king when he heard the news. The messenger then handed him a letter from Catherine's own hand, but the king did not open it. The queen and all her family were much relieved at the news, and Madge heard the queen's brother say, "Let her daughter join her!" Madge was shamed when George said such a cruel thing, and she felt sorrow for the lonely death of Queen Catherine, who had been Henry's loving wife for twenty-six years.

The next day, a Sunday, the king and queen appeared dressed

in yellow, the color of mourning in Spain. The king wore a white plume in his hat. Even Elizabeth was clothed in a gown the color of egg yolk. After they had attended church, the king took Elizabeth to the Great Hall and paraded her around for all to see. There was much dancing for several days to celebrate the death of the former queen. After the dancing, Henry decided a joust was in order and appeared in the tiltyard, paying his respects to Lady Jane, who gave him an embroidered handkerchief to wipe his brow. Though he was her champion for the joust, he was careful to insist the queen take an afternoon's rest before the tilt began, so as not to endanger the babe. Her Majesty did not see his public display of courtly love to the lady Jane, but Cate saw and reported it to Madge.

"Methinks His Majesty believes he is still young! Tilting at his age—he will soon be forty-six and his pate is balding, his belly growing. Such foolishness! Yet, ever such folly is found in man," said Cate.

"Aye, he does play the fool where his age is concerned—I am grateful he came to no harm," said Madge. "And let us keep this news from Her Majesty—it will not help her," said Madge.

"It is shameful the way he flaunts his new mistress for all the world to see—all the world except the queen. He did the same when you were his mistress, as you recall. He has no honor in him," said Cate.

"Have a care, milady—such talk is treason in these times. Say naught of that but to me," said Madge. "Now, let us go to the queen to see if we can ease her—she has been sick of the stomach again."

"'Tis natural—your own dear mother could not keep anything in her belly but you for many months!" said Cate.

The queen was still abed when Madge knocked gently on the door to her chamber. Her Majesty often wished to be alone these days and had sent her ladies out of doors, though the weather was cold. The queen believed brisk air would do them all good and was healthy for the soul as well as the body. She had explained such things to Madge many times.

"Enter," said the queen.

Madge went in first and gave the queen a deep curtsy with Cate behind her, doing the same. The queen was sitting up in her bed, leaning against several large pillows. Her color was better, pale roses blooming in each cheek. She smiled at both her servants.

"You are most welcome, ladies. I have rested well and feel like taking a stroll, perhaps even out to the herb garden, though there be little growing there at this time," said the queen. "Help me with my dress, will you?"

"Yes, Your Grace. But I would caution Your Grace, the wind blows chill this day. You will need your velvet kirtle and the ermine mantle for your heavy cloak. 'Twould not do to catch the ague," said Madge.

"Maddie's right, Your Majesty. 'Tis that season, after all. Will you drink a cup of tea ere you go?" said Cate in a soothing voice.

"No thank you, Mistress Cate. You are kind to offer it, though. I am glad you have come with Lady Margaret—I see you are a woman of great good sense," said the queen.

Madge turned to look at Cate and saw her flush with pleasure.

The queen was now ready for Madge to comb her hair and pin it up so it would fit beneath her hood. Madge noticed the queen was still very slim and delicate. She had not begun to add the usual plumpness of being with child, but then, the babe was barely begun. Madge did worry that the strain the queen endured was harming Her Majesty's health.

"Dear Cate, will you see to Urian? He is lazy and has not been on a run for many days. The lady Margaret will walk with me," said the queen.

"Certainly, Your Majesty," said Cate and tugged at the old dog until he finally rose and followed her out.

"Come, Lady Margaret, I feel so much better than I have for weeks. Let us be merry!" said the queen as she stepped into the outer rooms. A few of her ladies remained there, sewing or playing dice. They curtsied as the queen walked past.

"I am glad Your Grace is feeling better—'tis a good sign that all is well with you and the babe," said Madge.

"Yes, I thought I felt a flutter this morning, though I cannot be certain. Too early to be sure it was the babe and not indigestion," said the queen.

"Did you know His Majesty has planned a grand jousting tournament and a feast at Greenwich on the twenty-fourth of this month? I did not know if he had told you about it, as you have been unwell," said Madge.

"Oh yes, Harry explained it all. He wanted me to come to Greenwich, but I told him I would have to see how I am feeling. I may prefer to stay here, at Whitehall. I will take no chances with this babe," said the queen.

As they worked their way to the entrance near the kitchens, they heard giggling and a low male voice. Madge realized immediately the voice belonged to His Majesty. The queen stopped in her tracks to listen. When Madge started to speak, the queen put her finger to her lips and shushed her. The more they listened, the clearer it became that the voice was, indeed, Henry's.

The queen tiptoed to the half-open door into a small cellar. She stood in the archway for a moment, then pushed the door fully open. She gasped and then ran toward the figure sitting on His Majesty's lap. Madge followed her inside and saw that the woman in question was Mistress Seymour.

Madge had never seen the queen so angry. She flew at Mistress Seymour and began pulling her hair and slapping her about the head and shoulders. The king pulled her away and commanded Jane to leave immediately. Jane's usually pasty face was bright red as she swooshed past Madge without even looking up. Madge froze, too terrified to move.

"Henry, how could you? You promised!" screamed the queen, falling to her knees and sobbing.

"Sweetheart . . . dearest, do not take on so. Forgive me. If you wilt forgive the one who serves you still, you will have no cause to complain of me in this way again. Be of good cheer," said the king.

He pulled the queen to her feet and embraced her. Carefully, he wiped her tears and then sat down, gently bringing the queen to sit on his knee. Madge watched as the queen struggled to regain control of herself. Madge admired the way the queen retained her dignity.

"Harry, my love—don't you see—my great love for you is not like Catherine's—I cannot abide you loving another. We are made to be together, dearest. You have moved heaven and earth for me and I worship you for it," said the queen.

The king kissed her then, full on the mouth.

"All shall be as you wish, my sweet. Have no fears," said the king.

The king rose and walked with the queen to where Madge stood at the door. Madge curtsied to His Majesty, a deep blush filling her cheeks as she recalled the night he had pleased her and the many nights he had failed her. How odd to remember such things when one curtsied to the king.

"Lady Margaret, take care to see the queen back to her bed-chamber. She is in need of rest," he said.

Madge and the queen walked back to her apartments and Madge helped the queen into bed. The entire event had exhausted Her Majesty and set her nerves on edge.

"He is a monster to treat me thus—a monster! One minute kind, the next cruel. He has put to death his dearest friends—Sir Thomas More, Wolsey, all those men of the cloth—he will not hesitate to do away with me as well. I mean nothing to him now," fretted the queen.

"His Majesty is mercurial, 'tis true. And full of power. But you are his anointed queen and nothing can change that. You are to have his child—once the bonny prince is born, we can all rest with our ease," said Madge. "Now calm yourself and drink this." Madge had brewed chamomile tea with honey while the queen worried herself. Her Majesty sipped it and eventually fell asleep.

A few days later, Arthur met Madge in Cate's room.

"Will you come to the festivities the king has planned on the twenty-fourth?" she said.

"Yes. My father has told me I need not return home until early spring when the fields will need plowing and the spring lambs birthing. I am to oversee all such work along with my brothers. My father grows too old to attend to such things," said Arthur.

"He is older than the king, is he not?" said Madge.

"By almost ten years. So, yes, my love, I shall be at the festivities!" said Arthur.

"I think we should be seen together—we should dance and watch the jousts. The queen is not yet ready to make her request known to His Majesty, but if we are seen together, the court will become used to the sight. When Her Majesty does bring it up, the king will be more amenable," said Madge.

"Methinks you see the bright side of the sun. I see the dark side of the moon. I fear His Majesty might become enraged and toss us both to the wolves," said Arthur.

"Perhaps His Majesty has more on his mind than the actions of two insignificant people like us," said Madge, laughing.

"Let us hope so—dearest, let us hope so," said Arthur, kissing her.

The day of the great festival arrived, with the jousts beginning after the midday meal. The queen was in her bedchamber, once again unwell. Madge and Bessie Holland had been serving her all morning, attempting to find food she could stomach. Madge expected to meet Arthur as they had planned, in spite of the queen's indisposal. She would have to ride up the Thames to Greenwich in one of the boats for hire—she had hoped to find someone to ride with her, but Cate had refused.

"Your Grace," she said softly so as not to jar the queen, "I should like to see the tournament with your permission—I hope to meet Master Brandon at the lists."

The queen was reading her Bible. She looked at Madge for a moment as if studying her.

"Still fond of Master Brandon? Yes, yes, I can see you are. Go along then. Mistress Holland shall take care of me," said the queen.

Madge smiled and thanked the queen.

"I shall return as soon as the lists are over—I shall not stay for the dancing!" said Madge.

"Oh stay! You are young—life is a brief candle! You may as well burn a little," said the queen.

Madge grabbed her cloak and hurried to the river where she caught a boat to Greenwich. She quickly reached the spot where she and Arthur planned to meet. He was already there, a head taller than many of the men around him, almost as tall as the king himself. He led her by the hand and they made their way to a place in the stands for a better view. Arthur ran the lists himself at his father's manor house in Surrey, but at court, he had not yet been invited. Like his father, he was quite good at it.

"They say the king himself will joust this day! What a man is our liege lord! I hope I will do the same when I am old," said Arthur.

"If you are my husband, I will not allow it, sir! You could fall to your death at such an age. And look at the king's armor—it must weigh as much as a behemoth! 'Tis too much danger for a man of years," said Madge.

"Humph! Already you tell me what *you* will or won't allow? I think not, woman!" said Arthur, putting his arm around her shoulders. At first, she resisted, afraid of who might see. But then she remembered her thoughts on the matter and settled into him easily.

The first tilters were her cousin George against Henry Norris. Madge hid behind several tall men so Norris would not see her and ask for a token. She was quite surprised when he rode over to Anne Zouch and held out his lance for *her* token.

The trumpets announced the arrival of the king and all stood in his honor. The horses and riders were in place and the king gave the signal for the joust to begin. Thundering hooves cut the dirt track as the men raced at one another with frightening speed. The clatter of their lances against armor made more ruckus. Neither man was unseated, so they began once more.

Norris won in the second run, unseating Viscount Rochford rather easily.

Several more knights tilted against one another as the afternoon sun made its way across the winter sky. Madge and Arthur drank some ale and bought some roasted chestnuts from an old woman pushing a cart. Suddenly, the trumpets blared again and the king stood. The crowd grew quiet.

"My good people! Ye have come to see a jousting tournament and so ye have seen. But what is a tournament without your king! We would have you know us as not only the head of the church but also as head of our armies, a warrior in battle!" shouted the king. The crowd cheered as Henry left the royal box and donned his armor. Then he mounted his favorite steed, Trojan, who had been suited for the joust. The king called for Sir Henry Norris to run against him.

"He is too old to run against such a fine young man as Norris," said Madge. "I fear for him."

"Pshaw. He is the king—his skills are as good as ever. Let him be a man," said Arthur.

The horses raced at each other and the king almost knocked Norris from his saddle but he righted himself. The knights rode at each other once more and the king's lance was shattered but he was still sitting his horse. His page handed him another spear and they galloped their horses full-speed toward each other once again. Three times they raced together; each seemed hell-bent on unseating his man. Still, the king kept his horse as did Norris.

On the fourth run, Norris glanced a blow to the king's midsection with such force the king fell from his horse, though not from the saddle. Horse and king went down together and there was a gasp from the crowd. For several seconds, the horse lay upon the king and when the horse arighted himself, the king lay still as death.

Shouts echoed through the crowd.

"Fetch Dr. Linacre! Quick, man, quick!"

"Pray God he live!"

"No male heir—only princesses!"

"God save the king!"

Madge felt dizzy with fear. Arthur had left her to see if he could be of service. The first thing Madge thought to do was to go to the queen. But what would she tell Her Majesty? She did not know if the king lived or no. She decided to wait with the onlookers until she knew for certain about the king's condition.

She saw the queen's uncle, Norfolk, riding quickly away from the crowd. She could not know he was going to the queen immediately, before he knew the state of the king. But off he rode, cropping his mount until the horse could go no faster.

When Madge returned to Whitehall some hours later, the queen was pacing the floor, wringing her hands. She kept talking to herself, mumbling about what would happen if the king should die. Madge tried to comfort her and once again brewed tea. But the tea had no effect. Eventually, Madge called for Dr. Butts, one of the king's new physicians. He reassured the queen once more that His Majesty was safe and would see her soon. Dr. Butts had instructed His Majesty to rest at Greenwich for a day or so. He gave the queen a draught to calm her and, finally, she slept.

Five days later, Madge awoke to screams from the queen.

"Nooooo! Noooooo! It cannot be!" shouted the queen in a voice that would raise the dead.

Madge jumped up immediately and saw the blood soaking Her Majesty's bedclothes.

"I'll fetch Dame Brooke," she said as she ran to the door leading to the queen's outer rooms.

"Hurry! Hurry!" the queen screamed.

Madge ran as fast as she could to the lower rooms of the castle—she knew her way by now. She could feel her legs trembling as she made haste to find the midwife—everything depended upon the queen's delivering a fine, healthy son. Surely there must be a way to keep the babe within until the full time of fruition.

"Dame Brooke, quick—'tis the queen! She fears she is losing the babe," said Madge as she grabbed Dame Brooke by the arm and pulled her through the door of her small room.

"I need my kit, girl! 'Tis there by the trestle table—bring those clean cloths stacked nearby!" said Dame Brooke. Madge handed the kit to Dame Brooke and picked up the stack of cloths. Together, they hurried up the three flights of stairs to the queen's apartments.

The queen's bed was covered in blood and Her Majesty lay sobbing, holding her belly.

"Mary Mother of God! 'Tis a great deal of blood! The babe is lost but now we must save Her Grace," said Dame Brooke as she grabbed the cloths from Madge and began wiping away the blood from Her Majesty's legs and lower parts. "Get a serving wench to remove these bloodied sheets and put clean linens on the bed—hurry!"

Madge went into the outer rooms and called for help. The queen's women moved into action, one going for the maids, one bringing water, another sending for Dr. Linacre. Madge returned to the queen.

"Is he lost? Is my prince lost?" said the queen, her voice tight.

"I fear he is," said Dame Brooke. "Now we must work to save Your Grace."

"I am done for—do nothing to save me. Let me die! Just let me die!" screamed the queen.

"Get that vial with the greenish liquid—'twill calm her down.

If she continues to be overwrought, I'll never get the bleeding to stop," said Dame Brooke.

Madge found the correct vial and brought it to the queen.

"I'll have none of it! None! I wish to die! Oh please Jesu, take me now! I cannot face Harry for I have failed him yet again! Oh let me die!" sobbed the queen as she pushed Madge's arm away.

"Force it in her mouth—get in here, ladies, and hold Her Grace down while Madge pours the liquid down her throat," said Dame Brooke. The ladies did not move. Madge knew they were afraid to lay hands on the queen.

"Do it!" commanded Dame Brooke in a voice that dared disobedience. The ladies flocked to the queen's bedside and held her while Madge poured the syrup down her throat.

"I wish to die—I wish to die!" the queen continued to say, though soon, she slept peacefully and Dame Brooke was able to staunch her bleeding, but not before she pushed on her belly to remove all of the fetus.

Thirty-four

S ip a little of this broth, Majesty. It will help you get your strength," said Madge as she edged the soup closer to the queen's mouth. Dame Brooke and Dr. Linacre had instructed her to feed the queen as much as she could—Her Majesty had lost the babe and was close to death herself. The king had not yet come, but had sent word he would appear that afternoon. Madge shuddered to think of him here, in the sick room with the queen as white as the pale winter moon.

"Please, Anne, dearest cousin. Just one sip," said Madge.

The queen stirred but did not open her eyes. Tears seeped out from under her lids and ran down her cheeks. Still, the queen refused. The midwife and other ladies hovered around. The fetus had been wrapped in silks and taken to Dr. Linacre for examination to determine the cause of the miscarriage, if such a thing were possible. Madge thought the queen might respond more if the room were cleared of her serving women.

"Good ladies—the queen wishes you to leave the bedchamber at once. She needs quiet," said Madge in an authoritative voice. To her surprise, the ladies curtsied and obeyed. The nurse had taken out the bloody sheets and other soiled garments. Madge checked the rags that had been placed between the queen's legs to staunch the bleeding. They were secure and did not need changing yet.

"Dear cousin, we are alone. The ladies are gone. Please wake up and have some broth," said Madge.

The queen slowly opened her eyes and looked at Madge. Immediately, the queen burst into brutal sobs. Madge held her and said, "Let it out, Your Grace. Let it all out. I know your heart is broken."

Madge had no idea how long the queen cried in her arms. Only that Anne shook with grief. Her tears wet the pillow and the front of Madge's dress. When Madge thought there could be no more tears, the queen continued to shed them. Madge could not help but add her own sobs to those of the queen.

Finally, Her Majesty found the end to her tears, at least for the present moment.

"Oh Margaret, another son lost! No little one to hold and love, no dear little fingers to count or tiny mouth to kiss. I shall die, too. I shall join my son in heaven this day," said the queen.

"Do not speak so, dearest Anne. Do not speak so. You have Elizabeth to think about—she would be lost without you! Who would look to her care and love her if not Your Grace? You must not think to die but to live," said Madge, truly frightened that the queen *would* die, that she would will it so.

"I do not wish to live—except for Elizabeth. She is my heart!" said the queen.

"Will you have a bit of broth now? Please?" said Madge.

"I have no stomach for it ... but because you ask it of me, I shall have a spoonful," said the queen.

Madge managed to get two spoonfuls down before the queen closed her mouth firmly against her.

"The king will visit this afternoon," whispered Madge.

"Oh no! I cannot see Harry—not now! You must keep him away," said the queen.

"Anne, dearest, you know I can do nothing to stop His Majesty. He is still limping from his fall and they say he has a thunderous headache," said Madge.

"I am sorry for it. His wrath will be roused because I lost our boy. I fear what he will do," said the queen. "I think it best that I should die now. I am ready for it."

"Do not speak thus. The king will not harm you, madame. He is your loving husband and cares much for you. This I have seen with mine own eyes," said Madge, though she worried the queen was right. She began to fear for her own life, too. Why would the King spare *her* when he was so disappointed in the queen? She was, after all, the queen's own blood.

"I will sleep now, Margaret. Then, before His Majesty is to come, you will pin up my hair and add some color to my cheeks," said the queen, who seemed quite tired.

As always, Madge heard the king before she saw him, the trumpets heralding his approach. Even in such a private moment, the queen was forced to share her most intimate experiences with the court.

The king had cuts and bruises on his face and hands. His color was off and, though he tried hard to correct his gait, he limped. He strode quickly to the bed and gazed down at the queen, who seemed almost tiny as a child lying among the large pillows. For a moment, he did not speak, just stared at the queen, who feigned sleep.

Even though she was pale and tired, Madge still thought her lovely.

The king bent down and gently took her hand.

"Anne . . . Sweetheart . . .'tis your Harry," he said.

The queen's eyelids fluttered and she stirred slightly.

"Sweetheart—awaken for I am here," he said.

Anne's great brown eyes opened and she saw the king staring kindly at her. She immediately began to cry, though not sobbing as she had before. Instead, the tears came quietly, running like a slow-moving river, spilling over her chin onto the bedclothes.

At the sight of her tears, the king sat on the bed and held her in his arms. Thus they stayed for a long while. Finally, Anne's tears stopped and the king released her.

"Harry, forgive me . . . I fear the news of your fall gave me such a fright that I have lost our son. I am so full of grief," said the queen, crying once again.

"There, there. No more tears. There will be others, sweetheart. Do not concern yourself," said the king.

"I fear there may not be, Harry. This is two sons lost to us!" said the queen.

"I see God will not give me sons—not yet. Let us wait upon the Lord," said the king.

"Perhaps if you would not vex me so when I am with child with your amours, I could bring a son to term," said the queen in anger.

The king's face reddened and he rose.

"I will speak with you again when you are well," he said and left the bedchamber.

For a fortnight, the queen stayed in her bedchamber, slowly regaining her strength of body if not spirit. She would not allow Madge to leave her side and sent the other ladies away. The queen neither dressed nor combed her hair nor bathed. She ate little and had to be coaxed to it. Finally, her bleeding stopped, though her skin was still pale and she looked unwell. The king had come to see her twice, each time ending in her tears. But there were no more harsh words between them, for which Madge was glad.

During Shrovetide, the king returned to London, for the Reformation Parliament was meeting to pass the bill for the complete dissolution of all monasteries with all monies and property going to the Crown.

"I shall return soon, Anne. But this matter is of great urgency—I would do away with those corrupt monks and nuns who hide the bodies of babes in their cloister walls, and I fear Parliament will not pass this bill unless I show them my kingly person," said the king.

"You do not mean to destroy them all, do you Harry? Surely, this would be an error. They do much good, especially for the poor," said the queen.

"Madame, you would do well not to meddle in my affairs. You are a mere woman and your duty is to bear me sons. This sacred duty you have failed to fulfill thus far. I think you will get no more sons by me!" said the king as he turned on his heel and left the queen's bedchamber.

The queen shook her head and then lay back down to nap. It seemed to Madge the queen cared for nothing, least of all the king.

The queen did no celebrating during Shrovetide; she did not leave her chamber. Madge tried to get Her Majesty out of bed, if only to take a turn around the bedchamber, but the queen refused.

She cried a good deal of each day and nothing Madge could do seemed to help.

Finally, three weeks into the Lenten season, the queen called for Madge early in the morning.

"Lady Margaret, I would bathe and dress this day. I wish to hear the Mass and make my confession," said the queen.

Madge immediately set out the queen's black damask gown and went about preparing her bath. As she bathed Her Majesty, she saw that the queen had lost much of her flesh and her hair lacked luster. She washed the hair with soap and then rinsed it with olive oil to restore its shine. Once the queen was dressed, she returned to lie on her bed.

"Lady Margaret, even this small action has tired me. I must rest a while. You may see to your own body and change your gown," said the queen. Madge had not had a change of clothes nor had she bathed since she had been attending the queen. She did as the queen commanded and tried to make as little noise as possible. She selected one of the queen's russet gowns, the color of which almost matched her hair.

When the bells rang, she and the queen rose and attended Mass.

After this, the queen seemed to regain some of her old spirit. Though the court was keeping Lent, the queen invited several courtiers to her apartments for Bible reading and music. She called for Master Smeaton often, as well as Weston, Brereton, Norris, and Wyatt. Her ladies returned and she set them all to sewing furiously in order to have many shirts and gowns completed for the Maundy, as the queen wanted all the poor women and children of London to have something from her own hand. The gentlemen fell quickly into their old manners, bantering

and laughing with the women, fawning over the queen especially. Madge found herself once again sharing the spotlight
with the queen.

"Ah, Sir Thomas, have you penned any poems for me of late?
Or has your affection for your queen grown cold?" said the
queen to Thomas Wyatt, who was kneeling to her.

"Good my queen, you know my heart should never grow cold
to Your Grace. And yes, I have scribbled a few lines in tribute to
your beauty. Would you care to hear them?" said Wyatt, now
rising at the queen's command.

"Perhaps in a little while, Tom. Methinks I am of a mind to
dance—Master Smeaton? Could you strike up a fine tune?" said
the queen. Madge noticed Master Smeaton did not seem his
usual self—that look of sadness sat upon his features. The queen
must have seen his low demeanor for she approached him.

"Dear Mark, you must not look for the king nor me to
speak with you as we do the others, for you are of low birth,"
said the queen in all kindness. She took her fingers and raised
his chin so she could gaze into his soft brown eyes.

"No matter—a look sufficeth," said Master Smeaton.

Madge was glad the queen had taken the time to speak to
Master Smeaton as he had been ever kind to all. He strummed
a lively tune and the queen took Sir Weston's hand and began
to lead him in a merry dance. They moved well together and
Madge thought the queen looked better than she had in a long
while. Her high spirits seemed to bring her back to her old self.

For much of the time, the king remained sequestered with
Master Cromwell, discussing alliances with the emperor, the
German states, or Francis I. They debated whether or not the
pope was going to succeed in gathering the Catholic countries
to mount a campaign against the English king, who had broken with Rome over a mere woman. When His Majesty did

visit the queen, he discussed all these things with her and
Anne gave him her opinion about which path to take. Madge
listened but did not understand half of what she heard—such
talk bored her and she often fell asleep hearing the voices of
Their Majesties discussing matters long into the night. Madge
did not ever hear them speak of the loss of their boy, nor did
she perceive a cross word between them.

Arthur had returned to his father's lands in Surrey and she
missed him. She had no one to explain all she overheard from
the king and queen, but that was not what she missed most.
She desired his kisses and his strong arms around her. Some
days, she felt as if she would burst with such needs. Arthur managed to send her a letter once in a while, promising his love and
letting her know he should be able to return to court by Easter.
The Lenten season seemed especially long.

Though Madge missed Arthur, she discovered she enjoyed
the attentions of the courtiers as they gathered in the queen's
chambers. Sir Francis Weston had been paying her court, saying he should be her servant and asking for a piece of her clothing to carry with him. He was married and Madge knew it, but
such flirtations helped to pass the dull time of Lent, when few
activities were allowed. Besides, in the tradition of courtly love,
married men often served other mistresses—such play did not
harm one's standing but rather enhanced it. Madge observed
how the queen delighted in the game and felt she was following
in Her Majesty's steps. There was a tinge of danger to the play
between the men and the women. Only when the flirtations
became real did the gossips wag their tongues.

The queen also seemed to delight in the company of the
courtiers, though her manner had changed since her miscarriage. Her laughter had once again grown shrill and unseemly,
as though she forced mirth from deep in her belly. She laughed

often. Just as frequently, those around her did not get the joke. She seemed to have forgotten her own edict regarding the proper behavior of her ladies and often went beyond what she had previously allowed. To Madge, the queen seemed out of balance, as though the gaiety she exhibited did not belong to her somehow. One evening, when Master Smeaton was singing a love song, the queen turned to Norris.

"When will you marry my cousin, Lady Margaret, Sir Norris?" said the queen.

"I would tarry awhile," said Norris. He smiled at her in a most suggestive way.

"Humph, you look to fill dead men's shoes! If aught were to happen to the king, you would look to have me!" said the queen.

Norris blanched and immediately refuted her accusation.

"No, madame, no such thing!" he said and then the queen ordered him to leave.

Madge could not believe her ears—it was treason to even think of the king's death, much less say the words aloud. She glanced at the queen who was still angry at the way Norris had spoken to her.

"Majesty, perhaps you should send Sir Norris to your almoner to swear to your virtue," Madge suggested quietly.

"Yes. Yes, that is a good idea, Lady Margaret. I do not know what comes over me these days—I am not myself," said the queen. Then, she clapped her hands for everyone to leave her presence.

Just a few days later, Sir Weston brought Madge a gift of green silk, enough for a bodice. Madge accepted it with grace, knowing full-well they were simply playing the game. Weston would serve her for a while and she would pretend to welcome his attentions. He would give her gifts and she would allow him some token to wear near his heart. That would be the end of it.

He bowed as he presented the gift and Madge smiled up at him. The queen rounded on Weston.

"Francis, why come you so often to my apartments? Are you paying court to Lady Margaret? Get thee home to thy wife!" yelled the queen.

Weston seemed at a loss for words. Finally, after stuttering, he said, "I come for another even more fair."

"And who might that be?" said the queen.

"It is yourself," said Weston, still trying to play the game, though now with the queen.

"Be gone—and come not back until I call for you!" said the queen, still angry.

For the remainder of the Lenten season, the queen foreswore all companionship and spent most days reading or in deep discussion with Bishop Parker. During the afternoons, she took Urian for long walks and Madge accompanied her with Shadow.

As Holy Week approached, Viscount Rochford was quite visible at court and was awarded several properties, as was his father, now made Earl of Wiltshire. The queen also received property that had belonged to the king's son, the duke of Richmond, because the boy was quite ill and no one expected he should live beyond the spring. His illness placed even more pressure on the queen to bear a son.

One afternoon, as the queen prepared to attend the Mass, someone knocked.

"See to the door, Lady Margaret. Let naught but my brother have entrance," said the queen as she rose from her prayers.

"Mistress Mouse! I have been so busy with court business I have not seen you in some time—you grow more beautiful each day," said Rochford, breezing by her to see the queen.

"Dear sister, I would a word with you—privately," he said.

"Dearest brother, I trust our cousin in all things—you may speak freely," said the queen.

The queen and George sat beside each other upon her bed. Madge picked up her sewing.

"Sir Edward continues making troubles for you, Anne. Not only is he parading his sister to the king, coaching her to protect her vaunted purity, he is collecting friends from all those who support the pope and the lady Mary. I fear Master Cromwell has joined his faction," said George.

"I have known for some time Cromwell is no longer my own man, though it was he who found the way for Harry and me to marry. He could easily turn against us," said the queen.

"Madame, I have it on good word that Master Cromwell wishes to pillage every monastery in the land to fill the king's coffers," said George. "He has bragged that he will make Henry the richest king in Christendom!"

"I am still amazed Harry and I have often discussed the need for *reform* among the nuns and monks. I have been to Syon myself to scold them into better behavior. But I still cannot believe Harry would rob the church to fill his coffers!" said the queen.

"Master Cromwell has his ear in this. Edward Seymour has his ear in the other matter. We must gather our friends and fight them, or they will be the death of us," said George.

"Always the actor upon the stage, brother! You puff up our danger. I shall speak to Master Cromwell myself," said the queen.

"Have a care, sister. He is a snake in the grass," said George.

They rose and the queen kissed her brother on the tip of his nose, thanking him for his help. He walked out, bowing most courteously to Madge.

"Come, Lady Margaret, I must ready myself to meet with Master Cromwell after church," said the queen.

Thirty-five

Madge and the queen strode briskly to Master Cromwell's offices. Madge waited on the bench outside his door while the queen entered unannounced and sent his pages, scribes, and petitioners outside. At first, Madge could hear nothing, but as they continued to talk, she could hear the queen's voice raised in anger. Master Cromwell was almost shouting. This argument lasted well over half an hour and without warning, the queen marched through the door and motioned for Madge to accompany her. They walked out into the spring air and covered ground so fast, Madge felt as if she were floating.

She noted the new growth around her, pale green buds on the trees and the fields turning from stubble to grass. The sun, having been a stranger for many months, now shone boldly as if to reclaim the sky. The queen seemed to take no notice of the delicious spring but carried on as if driven by a whip. Finally, well away from the roar of courtiers and the goings-on of the parliament, the queen stopped short.

"Lady Margaret, as sure as I know murder is a sin, I am wroth enough to commit it!" she said breathlessly.

"Your Grace, what is it?" said Madge.

"That scoundrel . . . that varlet Cromwell is going to take *every* monastery in the land to make it property of the state—he does indeed mean to make Henry the 'richest prince in Christendom!' I will not have it—monies that could feed the poor or send a brilliant young lad to university! I will not have it!" said the queen.

"But madame, what can you do?" said Madge.

"'Tis Easter time, when men must consider the condition of their souls. Our dear Christ was betrayed and died on the cross for such as we. Will we then raid His church to make ourselves the richer? Will those who have much be granted more while babes and mothers starve? I will go to my almoner, Master John Skip, and ask that he preach a sermon on that holiest of days, a message that will remind men of their duty to God. I will sway His Majesty's conscience to oppose Master Cromwell," said the queen with great authority.

"Is that not a dangerous course, Majesty? I have heard it said that Master Cromwell does nothing without the consent of the king," said Madge.

"My course has been filled with danger at every turn, Margaret. Will I turn my eyes from that which I know to be sin? Did our Lord run from Judas? Did he call down His angels to lift Him from the cross?" said the queen. She looked out over London from the top of the hillock on which they stood. Her eyes were wet and there was passion in her voice.

"I know you do not understand me, Margaret. I may do

things which seem terrible—but I do them to survive! For if I survive, I can protect those evangels who wish to bring the word of God to all of England. If I survive, I can work for the good—the king needs someone who will tell him the truth, someone he can trust, someone who loves him as a man rather than as the fount of power and wealth. If I survive, I can still give England a son," said the queen.

Madge saw the color flooding Her Majesty's cheeks and knew she spoke from her very soul. The queen softened and continued, "All I do is to this end, Margaret. God has raised me to the very throne. I am expected to bring the new religion to all," said the queen.

"Is your faith so important to you? I am confused by the strength of faith shown by those who burn. I am not sure I would adhere to any belief if I were to die by the fire," said Madge.

"When I was your age, dear cousin, I did not understand such things either. My head was full of thoughts of love and pretty dresses and dancing until the dawn. Oh, I read many forbidden books while I was in France, but only to be fashionable and a bit rebellious. But now, as Harry and I have traveled across this land, I have seen how our people struggle. I have seen how they look to us for guidance and succor. In these days, I have come to treasure my faith above all else. The Blessed Virgin has been my comfort for I know that she, too, lost a son. No matter what happens, Margaret, remember these things about me," said the queen.

"I hope to find faith, though I have had only an inkling of God's presence," said Madge, suddenly shy.

"You will find it, dear cousin. And I shall pray daily that faith will come soon," said the queen. "Come, I have much to do."

———

On Easter morning, the queen and her ladies went to chapel dressed in fine clothes, ready for the noonday meal, which would boast many delicacies. They desired rich food since they had dined simply during Lent. The queen and king sat together in the royal closet where they could listen and participate in the Mass in comfort. Madge sat in the general area on a simple bench with several other ladies. When the time came for the homily, Almoner John Skip rose with great solemnity. He admonished those in the congregation, especially the royal counselors, to quit advising the king in the direction His Majesty was inclined to go. He instructed them, instead, to give the king wise counsel that would lead to the good of the country. He said, pointedly, that "nowadays many men . . . rebuke the clergy . . . because they would have from the clergy their possessions." Skip could not have aimed his arrows more directly at Master Cromwell if Cromwell had been pinned to a target bushel. He then told the story of Esther, who countermanded King Ahasuerus's head counselor, Haman, and saved the Jewish people. The point could not be missed as he said, "there was a good woman (which this gentle King Ahasuerus loved very much and put his trust in because he knew she was ever his friend) and she gave unto the king contrary counsel (from Haman's)."

By the end of the Mass, the entire court knew of the break between the queen and Master Cromwell because the almoner would never have preached such a controversial sermon without the queen's explicit permission. Madge took note of the talk and the astounded looks of many of the courtiers as they walked out into the fresh air. She watched as the king and queen left their closet. Madge searched the crowd for Cate so they could eat together in the Great Hall, but did not find her. She decided to go by herself to sup and was hurrying along, when she saw Arthur rushing to her.

She moved toward him as best she could and finally they stood facing each other.

"You came! I worried you had been delayed with some problem or other. I would I could kiss you right here," said Madge. She had to clasp her hands together to keep from hugging him. His face looked haggard and Madge knew immediately something was very wrong.

"I would speak with the queen," said Arthur in a whisper.

"Now?" said Madge.

"As soon as possible—I have important news," he said.

"Tell it to me then," said Madge.

"Nay, 'tis for the queen's ears first. Take me to her," he said.

"She and the king are dining. They cannot be disturbed. Shall we eat first and then see to them?" said Madge.

"Aye. My news is *not* for the king," said Arthur.

By midafternoon, the king had left the queen's apartments and Madge felt it was safe to bring Arthur to her. She entered the outer rooms and Madge was disturbed at the way Anne Zouch and Bessie Holland smiled and curtsied to Arthur. Even the cold Jane Parker seemed to warm to him. She was almost afraid to leave him with the ladies while she went in to the queen, but she had no choice. When she returned, all the ladies circled Arthur like a pack of wolves around a lamb. Madge cleared her voice.

"The queen will see you now, Master Brandon," she said.

Arthur bowed to the ladies and took his leave. He entered the queen's bedchamber and Madge closed the door behind him. He bowed low to the queen, who was resting in her bed.

"Welcome Master Brandon and happy Easter!" said the queen.

"Thank you, Your Grace. I wish you the same," he said. Be-

fore the queen could say anything else, Arthur fell to one knee
at her side and looked at her.

"Majesty, I have news. I have already heard of the uproar
Almoner Skip has caused and that you and Master Cromwell
have argued. What you need to know is that the lady Jane Seymour is housed in Master Cromwell's home. There is a direct
tunnel from there to the king's inner apartments. His Majesty
has been visiting her every night and Cromwell has joined forces
with Chapuys, the emperor's ambassador, to convince Henry to
make an alliance with Charles the Fifth. However, the emperor
will not agree until the lady Mary is promised the succession
over Elizabeth. Thus far, the king has refused this adamantly,
but there has been much talk about the king putting you away
to marry that curd-faced Seymour," said Arthur.

The queen said nothing. Arthur did not move and Madge
seemed frozen, too. After a few minutes of silence, the queen
spoke.

"Thank you, Master Brandon. You have done me a great
service. I have tried to fight Cromwell, as you heard in church
this day. I shall fight him still. As for the king, I have failed him
twice—Catherine failed him many more times than that. Perhaps he will not be so quick to put me to shame," said the queen.
She looked very tired.

"Majesty, I know you are exhausted and this is not a good
time to ask it, but I must know if you still plan to help Arthur
and me," said Madge.

"I am not sure I can help myself, much less two lovebirds.
Methinks you should not count on me. Perhaps another way
will appear for you," said the queen. She looked at Madge's downcast face. "I am sorry, cousin. I truly am."

Madge knelt beside Arthur, reached for the queen's hand,
and kissed it.

"Leave me," said the queen.

Arthur and Madge rose to go, but the queen then changed her mind and commanded Madge to stay a while. Madge returned to her pallet and waited for the queen's instructions.

"If Harry does put me away, methinks he will allow me to go to a nunnery. That is what he offered Catherine at first, but she refused. I should like such a life, I believe. I could read and study, sew for the poor, and I would still have a few ladies to attend me—do not worry, Margaret, I will not ask for you! I know you wish to be wed soon enough! I have had all I would ever want of married life—to be married to Christ would be a welcome relief," said the queen.

"Would you not miss life at court? A nunnery would seem quite dull after such as this," said Madge, indicating all the fine things in the queen's room.

"I am glad to have had my time here. I have enjoyed the love of several good men and I have held onto a mighty king for ten years. I bore a beautiful daughter and still count a few good friends who are loyal and true. I believe I would find the peace of a nunnery soothing to my spirit," said the queen.

"I will pray with all my being that it will not be thus. I will pray that the king comes to his senses and returns to you, Your Grace. And, God forgive me, I will pray that the strumpet, Mistress Seymour, gets the pox!" said Madge.

"My, my, my! I do believe it will be impossible for Mistress Jane to get the pox—her virtue, dearest—her precious virtue!" said the queen. They both laughed but then the queen gave way to crying. Madge sat with her until she fell to sleep.

"Dearest Margaret, you must listen! I beg of you, come away with me. We can ride out today as if we were going on a picnic—then, we can just keep going. I shall take you to Guildford Palace and we shall marry. We can live happily there in one of my father's houses. Our children can run in the fields and hunt in the forests. There is bounty and goodness from the fresh earth—come, let us leave this vile place and be together in safety and peace," said Arthur, while Madge sat upon his knee.

"How can I leave the queen now? When her future is not clear? This is the time she needs her friends—and I have noticed how they have become fewer and fewer. She is my cousin and, more importantly, she is my friend. I will not leave her," said Madge.

"Foolish, foolish woman! I tell you, as long as you stay at court, you are in danger! Have you not seen the burnings and the hangings this king of ours has wrought? He and Master Cromwell? These are treacherous times, my love. You must come with me," said Arthur. He turned her face to him and kissed her.

"Such kisses will not change my mind," said Madge and playfully chucked him under the chin.

"Then how about this?" he said as he put his hand beneath her skirts and began to stroke her thigh.

"Nay, sir. I will not be swayed. But I must ask you, will you be returning to Guildford or will you stay on a while?" she said, her breath coming more quickly now as he touched her.

"I will leave a week from this day. My father has sent word I am to return to help build a new barn. I wish I could stay, but I must do as he bids me," said Arthur.

"I suppose that in a week's time, you expect to win me to your way of thinking. You think I must go with you after having loved you for one full week," said Madge.

"I think if you love me at all, yes, you will go with me," he said.

"You know that I love you with all my heart—but I will not change my mind. I am determined to help the queen—it is the right thing for me to do," said Madge. "I will not run away from this unpleasantness like a dog with its tail tucked. I will face whatever is to come."

"Then face my kisses for they are here at this instant," said Arthur.

Thirty-six

Madge was worried. Since sitting together in church on Easter Sunday, the king had not been to see the queen, nor had anyone heard what events were happening. Mistress Seymour had left the queen's service abruptly, claiming that her father needed her at Wulfhall. She declared he was very ill. The queen had no choice but to allow Mistress Seymour to leave, though she knew Jane was living in Cromwell's house under the supervision of her parents and enjoying nightly visits from His Majesty. The queen tried to remain lighthearted, chattering about this and that. She busied herself by planning for Elizabeth's education and continuing to buy the child expensive clothes. She also purchased tassels of gold for the draperies of her bed and bolts of expensive silks and velvets for new gowns. Madge thought to herself that for a woman who was content to go to a nunnery, the queen certainly intended to live sumptuously now.

Madge and the queen were concerned that her brother, Viscount Rochford, had not been selected for the Order of the Garter, an honor that he coveted and that the queen believed should have been his. Instead, Sir Nicholas Carew received the Order, though he had been a strong supporter of Catherine and continued to defend the interests of the lady Mary as best he could.

"'Tis a slap at me," said the queen, after they had heard the news from Master Smeaton, who was one of the few people who still came when the queen requested it. Many of the others claimed illness or "the king's business" in order not to be seen entering the queen's apartments.

"If it be a slap, let it be. You are still queen and, though the king is enthralled with dough-faced Jane, they cannot harm you more than this," said Madge. She said it with great enthusiasm but in her body, she felt fear begin to take hold.

"You are right, Margaret. If the king is intent on making Jane his wife, I shall go to a nunnery without any argument. I have learned from my predecessor that obstinacy against His Majesty is not the answer. I shall agree to whatever the king might wish—I know I have lost his love, but perhaps I can retain his friendship," said the queen.

A couple of days after they had heard the news regarding the appointment of Sir Carew, Madge and the queen, along with a few of her ladies, were diverting themselves with cards and dice. There was a loud knock on the outer chamber door and one of the guards announced that a Master Brandon wished to speak with the queen. Madge stood up and started to the door but the queen spoke quickly.

"Please show Master Brandon to us—Margaret, will you

set up refreshments for the gentleman? The rest of you may leave us," said the queen.

Madge did as she was instructed, pouring a large mug of ale for Arthur and cutting some chicken from the bone. She placed the meat on a plate and tore off a chunk of bread to accompany the fowl.

"Master Brandon," said the queen as she rose to give Arthur her hand. He knelt and kissed it. She bade him rise.

"Madame, I come with a warning I hope you will heed. I fear Master Cromwell has hatched a plot to ensnare Your Grace. He, along with your enemies, Sir Carew, the Seymours, Exeter, and Sir Francis Bryan, have persuaded His Majesty to approve an inquiry into treasonous acts. His Majesty is unaware that you are to be one of the targets of this inquiry, along with your supporters on the privy council. No one knows what Master Cromwell is up to exactly, but I would warn Your Majesty to be circumspect in all your actions. God save Your Majesty!" said Arthur.

"Thank you for this unwelcome news, Master Brandon. Now I shall retire to my bedchamber. You must stay here with Lady Margaret and refresh yourself after your long journey," said the queen. She then turned and walked through the rooms to her private chamber, leaving Madge and Arthur alone.

"I did not think to see you again, my dearest," said Madge as she ran into his arms.

"Nor I you. But when my father told me all he had heard from his spies, I had to warn the queen. And, most especially, you. Sweetheart, I fear for everyone surrounding the queen; anyone who has ever been her friend is in grave danger," he said as he held her close. "You must come away with me this night. I fear if you do not, you will be caught in Cromwell's web."

"How I wish I could ride away from it all. But you know I

cannot. The queen believes she will go to a nunnery and when she does, I shall be free of her service. She has told me thus. Then, my love, I will send for you and you can carry me away to your peaceful haven," said Madge, kissing him.

"Prithee, mistress, think you we can persuade Mistress Cate to abandon her room for one afternoon? For it has been long since I held you and I would once again ere I depart," said Arthur.

"I shall command it!" said Madge.

"Soon we shall lie together on a proper bed rather than this lumpy, narrow pallet," said Arthur as he helped Madge to the floor. "There now, better?"

"I would lie with you on a pile of rocks, my love," said Madge as she stretched out her body.

"Let me look at you—I want to remember you as you are at this moment. I have never seen a woman so shapely or with skin so fair. How have I come to win such a prize?" he said.

"You were born under the proper star, I reckon. Now, kiss me ere our time run out," said Madge, holding out her arms to him.

As they kissed, Madge could feel him against her, every part of him hard and strong. He touched and kissed her on her mouth, her neck, her ears, her hair, and then continued to kiss her entire body. He worked slowly, building her desire as carefully as a man would build his own house, taking diligence over every square inch. When he gauged she was ready, he began to apply his usual protection.

She caught his hand and pulled the linen sheath out of his grasp.

"No, dearest. Not this time. For soon, I believe we shall be wed. If a child should come, I will be happy!" she said.

Arthur quickly obliged her.

Later that day, Arthur took his leave with many kisses. Madge wept as he departed, promising to go to Guildford Palace with him when he returned for her in the early summer.

"I beg you one last time, my beloved—come home with me now," said Arthur from atop his horse.

"Soon, my love, soon. Until the queen's business is settled, I will not abandon her. But we will be together by winter, when your own duties will be lessened and we will be able to marry," said Madge.

She watched as he turned his horse and rode out of the gates, stared at him until he was lost in the crowded London streets. Her eyes watered and she knew many months would pass before he was free to come to her again. And when he did return, she would follow him home to Guildford and become his wife.

When she returned to the queen's quarters, Her Majesty was dressed regally in a green gown that set off her complexion. Several of her ladies were sewing and Master Smeaton entertained them with his lute.

"Lady Margaret, will you accompany me on a walk to the gardens?" said the queen.

"Of course, Majesty," said Madge as she followed behind the queen.

They walked from the queen's apartments through the Main Hall where the courtiers waited to be admitted into the king's presence. Even Sir Carew bowed as the queen passed. But Madge noticed a great silence fell among those gathered as the queen approached. This quiet lasted until Madge and the queen were well down the hall. Then Madge heard the buzz of voices start up, louder than before.

"'Tis a lovely day, Margaret. See! The tulips are budding and will soon be in bloom, the daffodils sprinkle droplets of sunlight across the lawn. His Majesty and I are to go to Calais after the May Day. It should be lovely this time of year," said the queen as if nothing were amiss.

"Have you had a message from the king?" said Madge, hope rising in her heart.

"Nay. 'Tis a trip planned for some time," said the queen. She stopped at a bench hidden partially by the hedge. She sat and told Madge to sit next to her.

"I have decided that remaining in my apartments is not a good idea. Henceforth, I intend to be out in full view of the court. Those who are mine enemies will still have to show me courtesy, and my presence will reassure my friends. I shall act the queen for as long as I am able. Perhaps the king will see me and be reminded of all that we have been to each other. I shall send for Elizabeth and show her to His Majesty as well. Surely, he cannot think to take a mother from her child," said the queen.

"These are wise decisions, Your Grace. If His Majesty can be reminded of your beauty, surely he will leave the dough-faced Jane!" said Madge.

"Mistress Jane-Dough! 'Tis true enough! Yet, 'tis cruel to make such fun. I shall try to be kind, even to Mistress Seymour," said the queen.

"I have no such kindness in me," said Madge.

The evening before the May Day celebrations, the queen attended a dogfight. Madge, having no stomach for such diversions, invited Cate to play cards in the queen's apartments. When she rapped on Cate's door, she heard crying.

"What is wrong?" said Madge, going to her knees to comfort her friend.

"They have taken Shadow! Taken her clean away! They said she was banned from court and should have been removed months ago. She is to be placed with the king's dogs and I shan't see her again," wailed Cate.

"How can this be? This law they spake of is well over three years old. What nonsense is this?" said Madge.

"Master Cromwell's man came to get her. He was rough and without sympathy," said Cate.

"Have no worries, dearest. I shall bring this matter before the queen. She will see we get our Shadow back," said Madge. She did not tell Cate of the fear that made her hands tremble and her stomach sour. "But now, let us ease ourselves and gather the early flowers—we shall cheer your room with a hundred bouquets!"

"I will not be cheered until Shadow returns but I shall help you gather flowers, for our time is short, with fewer and fewer springs in which to enjoy the blooms," said Cate.

When Madge returned to the queen's chambers later that afternoon, she was surprised to find Her Majesty in excited spirits.

"The king has asked me to join him at the May Day jousts on the morrow! We are to sit together and I hope to use this time to bring us into accord again. After so many weeks of not seeing my Harry, I am overjoyed that he will set me before all the nobles of the realm and claim me once again as his queen," said the queen, her face filled with joy.

"That is, indeed, most welcome news, Your Grace! How shall I help you?" said Madge.

"First, I will need to bathe and then if you will get me some rosewater and cinnamon to mix together—I would smell as the king should remember. And my hair, I shall wear down— will you pluck out the few strands of gray? And my cloth of gold dress with the long strand of pearls. Will you see if it is presentable? I shall wear flowers in my hair and you shall weave them down the entire length of it. I shall look like a girl on the morrow and so shall win back my king," said the queen, and Madge thought she did look almost girlish once again.

Madge busied herself at once, helping the queen prepare. Later that evening, while the queen and her ladies were dancing, more troubling news came to them. When Mistress Anne Zouch returned from dining in the Great Hall, she was full of the latest gossip.

"Majesty, they say Master Smeaton has been arrested this very day!" said Mistress Zouch. "Some charge of treason is leveled against him—they have taken him to the Tower where some say they will rack him."

"Mark? He is not guilty of anything lest it be buggery. He is a gentle soul full of kindness and sorrow," said the queen. "I cannot believe this report—has the whole world gone mad?"

The queen's spirits fell at the thought of Master Smeaton suffering in the Tower. Madge tried to cheer her, but Her Majesty removed to her bed, bidding the ladies to dance as long as they liked.

"Majesty, 'tis May Day! Awaken and see the blue skies and hear the songbirds calling to their mates," said Madge softly in the queen's ear. "His Majesty has sent word he will call for you in a little while, and the two of you will process to the tiltyard together." Madge thought this would awaken the queen and cheer her after last night's unpleasantness.

"Thank you, Margaret—I see you have opened the draperies and let the sun warm the room. Aye, 'tis a lovely day at that," said the queen.

Madge pulled back the coverlet and helped the queen to her feet. Then, as the queen washed her face, Madge began to lay out her clothes. She had taken care to brush the queen's gown and sprinkle it with rosewater and cinnamon so no foul odors followed the queen. After the queen had put on her shift, Madge combed out her hair and plaited it with daisies and tulips. Then, she helped the queen with her stomacher and her kirtle. Finally, after the queen was dressed, Madge applied rouge and kohl to her Majesty's face.

"You look better than you have in some time, Your Grace. Your color is good and the gown becomes you. I think you have fleshed out since the loss of the child," said Madge.

"I am feeling better, especially today. I am cheered that His Majesty wishes to sit with me. Perhaps he tires of yon Jane," said the queen.

"Let us hope so—she has nothing to hold his interest in comparison to Your Majesty," said Madge.

"Ah, she is younger and, if she is to be believed, a virgin. There is a certain appeal in that for His Majesty, though I cannot comprehend why. Methinks he loves the chase more then the kill—oh well, enough of such chitchat. His Majesty should arrive momentarily. Lady Margaret, you may join the rest of the ladies—I would be in the Royal Box alone with His Majesty," said the queen.

"Yes, Your Grace," said Madge.

Madge continued to assist the queen, fastening the strand

of pearls around her long, thin neck and placing many rings on her fingers. Never had the queen looked so regal.

The fanfare announced the arrival of the king and Her Majesty glided to meet him, as graceful as any swan. When he entered the outer room, the queen curtsied all the way to the ground and kept her head down until the king took her hand and bade her rise. Madge watched as the queen smiled at him, took his arm, and chattered gaily, as if he had done nothing to offend her and she was still his sweetheart.

Madge and the rest of the ladies followed at some distance. Cate joined the group of ladies.

"Have you told Her Majesty about Shadow?" said Cate.

"Not yet. The time has not been ripe. Her Majesty has a great deal on her mind and I would not burden her. Worry not, Cate. I will speak with her and we shall have Shadow back with us soon. Now, put away your long face and smile—'tis May Day and we have much to look forward to! Let us hurry so we can find a good spot to stand. I would wish to see the jousts," said Madge.

They nudged their way into the crowd of commoners, who gave way with much grumbling as they recognized Madge as a person of importance. She and Cate found themselves directly across from the Royal Box and Madge could see the king and queen sitting together. The queen seemed to be trying to talk with His Majesty but from what Madge could see, the king did not look at his wife. Instead, he focused on the crowd and waited for the jousting to begin. The first contest was to take place between Sir Norris and Sir Nicholas Carew. Madge watched as Norris lost control of his horse and the king directed that one of His Majesty's own be provided. Madge hoped Sir Nicholas would unseat Norris in the first round, but after three attempts, it was Norris who unseated Sir Nicholas.

As the tournament continued, all seemed as usual. Madge saw a messenger approach the king and whisper in his ear. The king rose and left with only six attendants, motioning for Norris to come along. The queen looked puzzled and the king spoke not a word to her. She was left to watch the rest of the festivities alone.

Thirty-seven

I am mystified by Harry's abrupt departure this afternoon. I cannot imagine what has happened! Has war come upon us?" said the queen as Madge rubbed her back.

"I would be the last to know such a thing, Your Grace. Whatever the reason for His Majesty's actions, you can be assured it was of great import. How liked you the May Day celebrations?" said Madge.

"Aye, it was good to be outside and among my people. And to be with Harry, though he spoke very little to me. I took Elizabeth to him yesterday while he was with Master Cromwell, but he took no notice of me or the princess. Surely, there must be something of grave consequence on his mind," said the queen. "Once, I would have been his closest advisor and confidante— those days are over. At least for a while."

"Majesty, I have a small problem which I hope you can

solve. They have taken Shadow from Cate, saying the law will not allow dogs of size in the palace. I do not know why they have chosen this moment to enforce such a rule. Shadow has lived here these three years with no interference. I would wish to have her back," said Madge.

"This is most strange—I gave specific orders when you first arrived that Shadow would be exempt from the law. Of course, my Urian is large, too. I have not seen him of late, though he usually stays curled in the outer rooms near the fire. I shall check on this in the morning, Lady Margaret. Have no fear—I shall get your Shadow for you," said the queen.

On the morrow, the queen kept her word and walked with Madge to the king's kennels. There they found both Shadow and Urian. The queen spoke to the master of the privy hounds, Humphrey Rainsford.

"On whose authority have you taken Urian, Master Rainsford?" said the queen.

"On Master Cromwell's orders, Your Majesty . . . I assumed Your Grace had requested these dogs be removed from the palace," said Master Rainsford.

"I will take both dogs at once and please do not bother them in future," said the queen, more warmly than she had spoken at first.

"Yes, Majesty, I shall bring them to you immediately," said Rainsford.

"There you go, Margaret. You shall have your Shadow and I shall have my Urian," said the queen as Master Rainsford brought the hounds on tethers. Madge leaned down to welcome Shadow into her arms while the queen did the same with Urian. They thanked Rainsford and walked the dogs back to the palace. Madge had never seen Cate so happy as when Shadow jumped into her arms, covering her with licks.

The queen then invited Madge and Cate to watch a tenes match that morning to be played between Brereton and Sir William Sidney. The queen had placed a bet on Brereton and hoped to collect a fine winning.

Madge had never been in the Royal Tenes Box before and admired the lush seats and the damask-covered walls. Servants had left ale and delicacies on a table for the queen's refreshment and Cate made quick work of most of the food. Her Majesty was intent on the play when six armed yeomen entered the royal box. One of the men opened an official-looking document and read in a loud voice:

"Queen Anne Boleyn, you are hereby ordered to report this afternoon to the king's Privy Council at the hour of one after the noon hour by order of His Majesty, Henry the Eighth, King of England." The guards then turned and left the Royal Box. Madge went to the queen who had paled and seemed about to faint.

"First the news of Mark's arrest and now I am to appear before the Privy Council—what is happening, Lady Margaret? What is happening?" said the queen as Madge led her to her chair.

"Prithee, I know not, Your Grace," said Madge, whose whole body buzzed with fear. Cate took hold of the queen's other arm and held onto her as she lowered herself into her seat.

"It has come—it has come at last! The king and Cromwell have found a way to rid themselves of me! What I have feared all along has come to pass!" said the queen with breathless voice.

"Let us not borrow trouble, dear cousin. Let us becalm ourselves and think what best to do," said Madge. She looked at Cate and even staunch Cate was pale, brows bunched up with worry.

"Methinks we should go to the queen's apartments and help her prepare to meet the council," said Cate.

"Yes, good Cate, that is wise counsel indeed. Come, Your Grace, arise and bear yourself as worthy of a queen. We are going to your apartments now," said Madge.

The queen arose and walked with confidence from the Royal Box, across the lawns, and into her apartments. Only Madge knew her hands trembled as she took each slow step.

Once in the queen's apartments, Madge and Cate sought to gird the queen's loins for her battle with the council, for they all knew a fight was to come, a fight for the queen's very life.

"Which gown, Majesty?" said Madge.

"A solemn day must needs a solemn gown—the black silk and I shall wear the matching French hood. And my pearls, which speak of purity. Oh Margaret, my heart beats so fast! What is to be done? What will happen to me?" said the queen.

"I cannot know, Your Grace. But try to keep your spirits up and keep your wits about you. Do nothing to offend His Majesty or Master Cromwell for they hold the reins, I fear," said Madge.

"And remember, Your Grace, you are an anointed queen— not all the waters of the sea can wash that away," said Cate.

A few minutes before the appointed hour, the queen departed under guard for the Privy Council. Madge and Cate could do nothing but wait. They busied themselves, tidying the queen's bedchamber; when there was no more to do, they took up their sewing.

They did not have long to wait. Within the half-hour, the queen returned, obviously shaken to her core.

"What happened? What is it all about, Your Grace?" said Cate who could not keep still once the queen entered her bedchamber.

"I can scarce believe it myself—they left me speechless, nor could I form one word of response to the charges, I was so amazed," said the queen as if in a trance.

"Tell us, Majesty. What is happening?" said Madge.

"I was met by mine uncle, Norfolk, and several other grim-faced men. They admonished me to stand to hear the charges against me. Then, they accused me of having committed adultery with Sir Norris, Master Smeaton, and several others. They said all had confessed against me and I was to return here, under guard, until they decided what to do with me," said the queen, her voice a monotone.

"It cannot be—I have been with Your Grace every eve and no one but the king has come to you—I know this! How could those dastardly cowards confess to such a crime?" said Madge.

"I know not—I know not! This is Cromwell's doing . . . and the king's. It gives them both reason to be rid of me. But queens have been found guilty of adultery before and have not died. Surely, Henry seeks to send me to a nunnery. Then he can say he married a nun," said the queen, bursting into wild peals of laughter.

"Get ahold of yourself, Majesty. Such cackling is unseemly," said Cate.

"I shall pour you some wine—that will help. There now, drink up. Let us calm ourselves with sewing—look, cousin, I have begun a new chemise for my trousseau," said Madge.

Before the women had time to thread their needles, Norfolk, Cromwell, and the lord chancellor Audley, along with several others, knocked upon the door. The queen herself rose to let them in.

"Why have you come, good gentlemen?" she said.

Her uncle, Norfolk, spoke from a scroll he held in his hand. "We come to conduct you the Tower where you will abide during His Highness's pleasure."

"If this be His Highness's pleasure, I am ready to obey," the queen said, her voice strong now. With that, the men led her away.

"Wait! Wait! Surely you will allow the queen to have her ladies with her," said Madge.

"His Majesty has appointed four ladies already, mistress. Now, out of our way," said Norfolk.

"Where is His Grace? Where might I find him?" said Madge, standing her ground.

"He has retired to his bedchamber for these recent events have sickened him mightily," said Master Cromwell. "He is not to be disturbed."

Madge curtsied to the men and let them pass.

"Quick, Cate, I must get me to the king before Master Cromwell returns. I must plead for Anne—I must make His Majesty see the error of his ways," said Madge in a whisper.

"He may put you in the Tower as well, Maddie-girl. This is foolhardy—I forbid you to go!" said Cate, holding Madge's arm.

"I fear I must disobey you in this. I *will* get to the king," said Madge as she jerked her arm out of Cate's grasp and hurried down the hall toward the king's apartments. However, as she reached the outer room of the queen's apartments, she saw the queen's ladies gathered in clusters of twos and threes. The women were abuzz with talk.

Madge approached Bess Holland, who stood talking with Mistress Maude Lane.

"What know you of these unseemly events?" said Madge.

"I have heard the queen is accused of treason," said Bess, who had been crying.

"And they have arrested her brother as well as Master Smeaton," said Maude.

"Are they all accused of treason?" said Madge.

"Aye, and the court is filled with fear as to who might be next. Master Cromwell is sending the Royal Guard all over, methinks," said Bess.

"I am amazed to hear these tidings," said Madge. "Who might have more news?"

"I know not. I fear rumors are running amuck and who knows what is true?" said Bess.

"What are we supposed to do now? Where should we go? Think you Cromwell will have us arrested? We are her ladies—it is possible," said Maude.

"Nay, do not give over to fear. This is a net to catch a queen and those men who support her. We have no power so we should have no fear," said Madge.

"Pray you are on the mark, Lady Margaret—for you are the queen's cousin and perhaps still a threat to Master Cromwell," said Bess.

"Mistress Holland, know you where I might find the king?" said Madge breathlessly.

"Why would you wish to search out His Majesty when he is having so many arrested, even the queen herself? Are you mad?" said Bess.

"Perhaps. But I would speak with him as soon as is possible. Master Cromwell has told me the king has taken to his bedchamber, sick with grief at the thought of the queen's treachery," said Madge.

"Aye, that may be. But I know that each evening for the last week, His Grace has sailed in his barge up the Thames at dusk when few would see him. It is said he goes to sup with the Lady Jane Seymour in a lover's nest," said Bess.

"Then I shall find him thus . . . thank you, mistress. You have been of great help to me," said Madge.

"I hope you do not end up in the Tower, Pretty Madge. Have a care," said Bess.

The afternoon was at its zenith with several hours to wait until dusk so Madge tried to gain information from every person she met on her way to Cate's room. When she reached the door, she knocked and Cate cracked open the door just enough to see who was there.

"Ah, Maddie-girl, come in—quickly!" said Cate, shutting the door the minute Madge squeaked in. Shadow licked Madge's hands while Cate sat upon her stool near the fireplace. A small fire was burning in the grate and Madge could see Cate's hands shaking. She took hold of them; they felt like ice.

"What are we to do? What are we to do?" Cate said over and over. Madge patted Shadow absentmindedly on the head and poured two mugs of ale from the ewer on the table.

"Drink this—it will help," said Madge, handing a mug to Cate, then quaffing down the contents of her own. She hoped the drink would quiet her stomach, which sloshed around and gurgled most unpleasantly.

"We must think! She would have us clear-headed. They have taken her to the Tower along with several others: Weston, Brereton, Norris, Lord Rochford, and Master Smeaton. They are all accused of carnal knowledge of the queen—all of them!" said Madge.

"'Tis ludicrous, impossible. Why, anyone who knows Master Smeaton knows he loves the king, not the queen! I'll warrant he has never even been with a woman," said Cate.

"He has confessed it, though they say he was racked for hours before he conceded the truth of it. Cromwell is responsible for this—Her Majesty warned us of him and I believe she was on target—he is power-mad!" said Madge.

"Think what you will—I believe it is done so His Royal Lechery can take that Seymour wench to wife! He is nothing but a murderer! The good monks and priests! Sir Thomas More! Now his own wife!" said Cate.

"Bite your tongue, woman!" said Madge. "Think you he will not touch those near the queen if he catches wind of any treachery? Such talk is treason! Get yourself in hand!" said Madge.

"Forgive me, Maddie—I am full of fear," said Cate.

"As am I, but more for Her Majesty than for myself," said Madge. She looked out the window in Cate's room and saw the sky was growing dark.

"I am going to find the king—no, no, I will not be dissuaded. I must go to him, reason with him, beg him for mercy. I shall return anon," said Madge.

"I know you too well to try to stop you. But take care, girl. He is a monster!" said Cate.

Madge made her way outside and moved with stealth to where the king's barge was moored. She knew the path well and hid herself in a copse of trees, waiting for the king. As she stood behind the enormous trees, she prayed for courage. Soon, she heard footsteps and saw the king, with Sir Edward Seymour, and several Yeomen of the Guard approach. There was little talk among them. She noticed the king did not wear his crown and his balding pate shone in the moonlight. Otherwise, he was dressed in his finest jerkin, cloth of gold with slashes of silver in the sleeves. Sir Seymour was also arrayed in the best money could buy and Madge realized the king had already been generous to him, paying him for the few charms his sister held.

When the group had moved close enough for her to catch the king before his guards could lay a hand on her, Madge saw her chance and flew to him, prostrating herself on the damp grasses in front of him. The guards moved to grab her but the king motioned for them to desist.

"What is this? Lady Margaret?" said the king, not unkindly.

Madge did not look up but spoke with the same courage she had seen in the queen.

"I beseech Your Majesty to grant me an audience. I beg as your humble and obedient servant who prays for your health every night. I beg as one who has enjoyed your royal presence and one who has sought nothing but to serve Your Grace," said Madge.

"Arise, Margaret—let us go into my barge where I can sit down—my leg aches and I am weary," said the king. Madge followed him back into the barge, remembering how regally it was appointed. The king sank down upon a large pillow and sampled one of the small tarts laid out for him. Madge knelt at his feet.

"Oh great and merciful king, I come to testify for the queen, your good wife. I would beg you to pardon the queen. I have been with her these many months, night and day, as thou dost know well. She is innocent of the crimes Master Cromwell has found against her. She has never known another and I believe you know in your heart that this be true. You, who are the fount of all justice in this land, I beg you, have mercy," said Madge, keeping her head down, but her voice full and strong.

"You are either very brave or very foolish to appear before me, Pretty Madge. I could have you arrested on the spot as her accomplice, the one who procured for her," said the king.

Madge trembled but she did not stop.

"You could do so if you desired, but such a deceit would

disturb your conscience because you know such a thing is not true," said Madge. "And I know you to be a good and wise king who obeys a tender conscience."

"Stand up, mistress. Look at me," said the king, helping her rise by taking her elbow. "You are a lovely creature still, Lady Shelton. I believe I granted your last request—you wished to have your contract to Norris rendered null and void. I have done so," said the king, smiling.

"I cannot thank you for your favor—I would not have wished even Norris thrown in the Tower," said Madge, her voice growing angry.

"You like me not, mistress. I see it in your eyes," said the king, studying her. She noticed how fleshy his face and figure had become and how wrinkled his face. He was an old man. "I will not honor your request—the queen must die and that is that."

"If you will not grant her pardon, then please allow me to go to her in the Tower. She has need of those who love her. I beg of you, if there was ever any tenderness in your heart for me, allow me to go to the queen in her hour of need," said Madge, locking eyes with the king, hating him with every cell in her body.

"Guards! You heard the lady—take her to the Tower at once! I am, as you say, wise and merciful," said the king as he motioned for two of the guards to lay hands on Madge. The others began to push the barge from the shore. The king looked out to the river, but then turned again to Madge. "By the way, your mother is also with the queen—I sought to surround her by her kinswomen so they could comfort her. May you bring her what solace you can," said the king.

Madge did not respond but gave the king the foulest look

she could muster. He then turned his back to her once more and sailed away. She let out a deep sigh and realized she had not breathed while she had been in his presence.

"Come along, mistress. To the Tower you go," said the tall guard on her right. Both men held her by the upper arm and fairly carried her from the king's barge to a small wherry. "Get in, mistress. You shall follow your queen all right. Straight to the Tower."

Madge suddenly was filled with fear. Did the king intend to send her to her death, along with the queen? Had he remembered his many failures in her bed? Did he wish to remove such a reminder of his own mortality from his sight? Her legs began to shake and she felt very hot. A strong hand pushed her down upon a hard seat in the smaller barge and she watched as the boat left the shore and made its way to the Tower. She began to cry though she made not a sound. Every bone buzzed with terror.

The trip down the Thames took little time and soon Madge saw the outline of the Tower against the night sky. The building looked ominous and very, very dark. When the guards rowed the barge ashore, they were met by Constable Kingston, a man of about sixty who had been taking care of prisoners for many years. It did not shake him to see a young girl brought to his jail, Madge thought.

"Who is this and why is she coming to me without warning this late?" said Constable Kingston.

"The king sent her to wait upon Her Majesty—it was her own desire, which His Majesty graciously satisfied," said the tall guard, pushing her toward Constable Kingston.

"Well enough, but who is she?" said Kingston.

Madge drew herself to her tallest height.

"The Lady Margaret Shelton, cousin to Her Majesty, Queen Anne."

"Come with me, Lady Margaret," said Kingston.

The constable led her to the queen's apartments, the same apartments where Her Majesty had been housed prior to her coronation. He tapped on the outer door and a plain-looking woman opened it.

"This is Lady Margaret Shelton here to serve the queen," he said.

At those words, Madge sighed, realizing, finally, that she was not under arrest but was, indeed, here because she had requested to be with the queen. The king played no treachery this time.

"Come in, Lady Shelton," said the woman who introduced herself as Lady Lee, Margaret Wyatt, sister of the poet.

"You are well-met, Lady Lee. Your brother is a dear friend of mine," said Madge.

"Margaret? Dearest Margaret! Come in where I can see you," said a familiar voice.

"Mother!"

Madge embraced her mother and they kissed each other on the cheek. Her mother looked worn and Madge bade her sit on one of the nearby benches. The room was not unpleasant, certainly fit for a queen. Fine tapestries hung on the stone walls and fresh rushes had been scattered on the floor. There were several stools and benches and one fine chair covered in purple velvet. A golden ewer with several matching goblets was on a small table covered with a fine carpet. Madge noticed the familiar smell of roses and cinnamon and began to cry.

"Dearest daughter—I know. We have shed enough tears to flood the Thames. But let me see you—how you have changed these three years—you are all grown and more beautiful than I could have imagined, though you were always a pretty girl," said Lady Anne Shelton.

"I do not feel pretty nor do I believe there is any beauty left in this horrid world. I have seen enough of mankind and sin to be happy to leave this life," said Madge.

"Do not speak so. You are yet young. Though these are dark days, you have much ahead that will bring you joy!" said Lady Shelton.

"Where is Father? Is he safe?" said Madge.

"He is with dear little Elizabeth. When we discovered what was happening, we feared the henchmen would come for us, too. But no one arrived until yesterday when the king's men knocked on the door of Hatfield and commanded me to attend the queen in the Tower," said Lady Shelton. "Your father stayed on at Hatfield to care for Elizabeth and make certain no harm comes to her. And I was escorted here."

"How does the queen?" said Madge.

"Not well. She collapsed when she first arrived and asked Constable Kingston if she was going to the dungeon. When he told her she would be staying where she was lodged for her coronation, she cried and said it was too good for her. Then she laughed hysterically and said, 'I was received with greater ceremony the last time I was here.' And so it has been—laughter and tears, tears and laughter. The first thing she did when she arrived at her rooms was to ask for the Sacrament to be brought to her so she could meditate on it day and night. That is what she is doing now," said Lady Shelton.

"I will let Her Majesty know I am here in case she has need of me," said Madge.

She tapped gently on the door to the queen's bedchamber.

"Enter," said the queen.

Madge walked into the tiny room and ran to the queen, who was kneeling on a pillow in front of the Sacrament.

"Margaret! Oh, the king has sent you! He is ever kind and good to me, is he not?" said the queen, rising to embrace Madge.

"Your Grace," said Madge, hugging the queen. The two women looked at each other and embraced again. "How fares Your Majesty?"

The queen laughed hysterically, grabbing her sides as she chuckled too hard.

"Well, if they think of a name for me in the years to come, it shall be Queen Lackhead!" said the queen.

"Majesty, think not such thoughts! You may yet come through this," said Madge.

"'Tis true. Perhaps the king wishes only to test me, to see if I can love him even after such a horrid move on his part. That must be it, surely," said the queen.

"I know not how the king's mind works but let us keep cheer in our hearts. There is always hope," said Madge.

"Ah, hope. I fear there is none where this king is concerned. He has given me you and your mother and dear Margaret Wyatt. But he has also sent snakes into bed with me—the horrible Lady Kingston and Mrs. Cosyn. They have been my enemies always and I fear what they may do—poison my food perhaps?" said the queen.

"Come, let us join the others in the front room. It is too gloomy in here," said Madge.

"I suppose I should at least play the good hostess, eh? 'Tis my party, after all," said the queen.

As the two women entered the outer room, Constable Kingston knocked on the door, opened it, and brought in a great dinner for the ladies. The queen thanked him and then ate heartily, talking the whole time.

"Kingston, know you why I am here?" the queen said.

"Do you not remember the charges against you, madame? You are accused of adultery with many men—they have added yet another this day and Sir Norris has confessed his guilt," said Kingston.

"Norris? Dost thou accuse me, too? I can say no more than *nay*, without I should open my body," said the queen and with a dramatic gesture, she pulled open the overskirt of her gown.

"Majesty, do not forget yourself," said Madge.

Suddenly, the queen fell to her knees and began to weep. "Oh my mother, thou wilt die of sorrow," she said. "And what of Elizabeth? What of my baby?"

After Kingston left them, the queen continued her talk, wondering who else might accuse her and on what evidence these charges were based. She told of her conversation with Norris where she accused him of wanting to fill the king's shoes and she blathered about Master Smeaton, how she only meant to comfort him when she spoke kindly to him. On and on she prated, giving Lady Kingston much to report to her husband.

"Your Majesty, you must stop this at once! You are giving them tools to use against you! Get yourself in hand, please," whispered Madge in the queen's ear as she lay prostrate on the floor. At that, the queen turned her wild, red-rimmed eyes on Madge and told her to ask Constable Kingston for a sleeping draught. Madge complied and soon the queen slept peacefully.

For the next fortnight, the queen's behavior remained much the same—one minute tears, the next laughter. Madge tried to console Her Majesty in every way she could think of, but the queen was beyond consolation. She spent most of her days and nights in her chamber, in prayer and supplication. As the days

passed, the women learned from Constable Kingston that Wyatt and Richard Pace had also been arrested and all the accused
men were lodged in the Tower. This thought seemed to comfort the queen but she worried that innocent men might die
because of her. On May 12, all the gentlemen except Lord Rochford were tried and found guilty. Rochford would be tried on
the fifteenth, the same day as the queen.

Madge thought the days sped by, though the hours were
long and dreary. It seemed no time before Brereton, Smeaton,
Norris, and Weston were executed and the queen was brought
to the bell tower so she could watch them die. She stared as
each of her former friends went to the block. She could hear
them as each made his last speech. Norris, in what was his finest moment, declared the queen innocent of any wrong. Yet,
Smeaton said he deserved his death. When the queen heard
him, she said, "Oh Mark, alas, I fear thy soul will suffer punish-
ment for thy false confession!"

When it was over and the queen returned to her chambers,
Constable Kingston and Madge had to help her walk. She had
lost use of her legs. Madge asked Kingston for an extra strong
sleeping draught for the queen on that day, as Her Majesty had
begun screaming and ranting once she arrived at her bedchamber. Though Madge tried, there was no consoling her.
When Kingston brought the medicine, the queen was on her
knees in prayer. She grabbed him about the legs and said, "Oh
Constable Kingston, am I to die without justice?"

Kingston shook her off and said in a flat voice, "Madame,
the poorest subject of the king hath justice."

At that, the queen laughed again in that hysterical way of
hers, cackling and groaning, her large brown eyes unfocused
and wild-looking. Constable Kingston administered the draught

himself, while Madge and her mother held the queen down. Madge was glad the draught worked quickly.

Finally, the day of the trial arrived and Madge accompanied the queen, along with the other ladies. The first thing she saw was the enormous crowd that stood on the hastily erected stands that were said to hold two thousand people. The Duke of Norfolk represented the king, assisted by Cromwell and his justices. The twenty-six peers were seated in a semicircle, with Norfolk perched on a high bench above them.

"Her own uncle," whispered Margaret Wyatt.

"He cannot be human—he is a devil," said Madge.

The gallery grew still as Lady Kingston and Lady Boleyn led the queen into the chamber, with Madge and the other ladies following behind. The queen made her way to a single chair set on a stage in the midst of the justices. Madge drew in a quick breath. Her Majesty looked quite small in the large rooms of the Great Hall of the Tower. She had selected a crimson gown edged in ermine and a matching French hood. Madge thought her choice inspired, as she looked as queenly as Madge had ever seen her. She moved with a somber gait as the ladies escorted her to the chair. Madge and the rest stood at the edge of the crowd. Seated, the queen took her oath to tell the truth and she listened to the charges against her. With great dignity, she answered each charge with clarity and confidence, proving herself an anointed queen with each reply. Madge could hear whispers among the onlookers that surely, she would not be found guilty, so wise and honest were her words. However, when the time came for judgment, each justice stood and said the word "Guilty." The verdict was unanimous and Madge realized there could be no saving the queen now. At this point, the queen rose to speak once more:

"O Father, O Creator! Thou who are the way, the truth, and the life, knowest that I have not deserved this death!

"My lords, I do not say that my opinion ought to be preferred to your judgment; but if you have reasons to justify it, they must be other than those which have been produced in court, for I am wholly innocent of all the matters of which I have been accused, so that I cannot call upon God to pardon me.

"I have always been faithful to the king my lord; but perhaps I have not always shown to him such a perfect humility and reverence as his graciousness and courtesy deserved, and the honor he hath done me required. I confess that I have often had jealous fancies against him which I had not wisdom or strength enough to repress. But God knows I have not otherwise trespassed against him. Do not think I say this in the hope of prolonging my life, for He who saveth from death has taught me how to die, and will strengthen my faith.

"Think not, however, that I am so bewildered in mind that I do not care to vindicate my innocence. I knew that it would avail me little to defend it at the last moment if I had not maintained it all my life long, as much as ever queen did. Still the last words of my mouth shall justify my honor. As for my brother and the other gentlemen who are unjustly condemned, I would willingly die to save them; but as that is not the king's pleasure, I shall accompany them in death. And then afterwards, I shall live in eternal peace and joy without end, where I will pray to God for the king and for you, my lords."

As Madge and the other ladies led the queen back to the Tower, Madge heard again much mumbling against the king. While Madge had been waiting with the queen in the Tower, the king had been sailing up the Thames at night, surrounded by a bevy of beauties, singing and parading about under cover of darkness. The queen had acquitted herself so eloquently and with such conviction that Madge heard many say they believed her completely innocent of any wrong. As they moved through the throngs of people after the verdict was given, Madge heard many comments and complaints.

"The king's barge sails upriver every night to where the mistress Jane is housed . . ."

"I have heard the king makes merry with his paramour since the queen's arrest . . ."

"What has happened to our Bluff Prince Hal?"

"The poor queen, back in the Tower where she was just three years ago . . ."

"She has been kind to us, giving alms and sewing shirts . . ."

"What will happen to the evangelicals now? There'll be no good queen to protect them . . ."

The queen, Madge, and the others had to wait until Constable Kingston returned from the trial to learn of Lord Rochford's fate. The constable related it eagerly to his captive audience.

"First, Norfolk called Lord Rochford into the court. Rochford appeared calm and was dressed somberly. As the accusations were read against him, he answered each in turn. His comport was dignified and persuasive. Many believed they would find him not guilty after such a defense. He spoke so well each word declared the deceit in the accounts. But then, he cooked his own goose," said kingston.

"How so?" demanded the queen.

"All was going well. Lord Rochford even answered the accusations in a letter from his accursed wife . . . but then, Cromwell handed him a piece of paper and warned him not to spill the contents. The letter made mention of the king's inability to complete the act of love—and Rochford read it aloud—'tis that which condemned him. When the justices were paged, each gave the guilty verdict. He shall die on the morrow."

"Oh my brother—my brilliant, funny brother—who could love life more than thou?" said the queen, collapsing once again.

"If the king has willed them to die, die they shall," said Madge, hatred burning in her ribs.

By the next day, everyone knew the queen was to be executed in three days, and that the king had sent for a special swordsman from Calais, an act of mercy. "So the queen will not suffer," the king explained. His wish was that the execution be quick and relatively painless. Madge thought of the queen's own words: *He is ever good and kind to me.*

Thirty-eight

I n the few days that followed the execution of her brother and friends, the queen changed. Rather than giving in to hysterics, she seemed to have come to grips with her fate. Archbishop Cranmer visited with her several times and comforted her. Madge admired the way the queen regained her dignity. On the night before she was to die, Madge accompanied her into her bedchamber for the last time. She was going to rub her back once more, as she had done in happier days.

"How does Your Majesty?" Madge whispered, not knowing if the queen wished conversation or not.

"I am bound to die on the morrow. I have faced Death over and over since they brought me here. I believe I have made Him a friend. I no longer fear Him—I almost long for Him. When He takes me, I shall fly to heaven to be with the True King of all the heavens and the earth," said the queen.

"I am much aggrieved at what Cromwell and the king have done—I can scarce speak. There is no justice in this realm— they are . . . they are . . . murderers," said Madge, tears rolling onto her cheeks. She swiped her arm across her face to wipe them away.

"Hush, child. To speak such is treason, and there is still one among the ladies who is not my friend. I fear she reports all we say to Master Cromwell. So have a care," said the queen.

Madge rubbed the queen's thin shoulders until all the knots were released. She was at a loss for words—what could she say to a woman who was going to be executed in the morning? How could she bring comfort?

"I want you to promise me something, cousin," said the queen.

"Anything, Your Grace," said Madge.

"First, you must pledge your troth that you will look after my dearest daughter. She will be in great danger for all of her life, I fear. She carries the royal blood and there are those who would use her for their own ends. Swear to me that you will do all in your power to love and protect her," said the queen, her face full of sorrow.

"I swear it, Your Grace. Elizabeth will always be able to count on her kinsmen," said Madge.

"Now, one more promise—after it is . . . over tomorrow, you must leave court never to return. Your mother is riding to Great Snoring immediately after she is finished taking care of what is left of me. You must pledge to go with her," said the queen.

"But Your Majesty, I would wait for Arthur to return to London—we are planning to run away and be married in Surrey. We shall live at Guildford Palace with the duke," said Madge.

"The duke is too close to the king—he and his boy will not stay away from court for long. They are both ambitious. No, for you, dearest Margaret, I would wish a peaceful and happy life—a long life! Such as you will find at your home. I will insist on your promise," said the queen.

"Then you shall have it, Your Grace. I will do as you command," said Madge.

"I am hardly in any position to *command*, dearest! But I have asked for your word and you have given it," said the queen.

They sat in silence for a while, each lost in thought. Madge heard talking in the outer room.

"Ah, the constable with his nightly elixir. Thanks be to God for it. Yes, come in, Sir Kingston. I will gladly swallow your poison," said the queen, laughing.

"Madame, there is no poison in what I have brought—just a sleep help," said the constable.

"You see, Margaret, Kingston likes not my humor! There, one for you as well, cousin. To the king's health!" said the queen and quaffed hers down. Madge did the same. "Good night, sir—I will see you, no doubt, in the morning."

Kingston walked somberly out of the room and the queen looked at Madge. They both laughed.

"He is the right man for the job," said the queen. "He is as somber as Death itself."

Madge rose and mocked the way Kingston walked, much to the queen's delight.

Soon, Madge began to feel the effects of Kingston's brew. Her eyes grew tired and her limbs heavy. She lay on the bare floor next to the queen's bed.

"Margaret, there is one more thing I would ask of you," said the queen in a groggy voice.

"Yes, Your Grace?" said Madge.

"I would beg forgiveness for the vile sin I urged you to perform with the king. And for the unkind way in which I treated you, after you had done as I asked. I have begged God's forgiveness and know that my soul is pure from His generous mercy, but I would have your mercy as well," said the queen. The queen reached out for Madge's hand.

"I forgive Your Majesty with all my heart," said Madge, unable to stop the catch in her voice.

The execution was to take place at nine A.M. However, Kingston came early to tell the queen that the swordsman had been delayed and would not arrive until noon.

"I am sorry to bring you this delay, madame. But they say he is an excellent swordsman," said Kingston.

"So I have heard—and I have but a little neck," said the queen, ringing her fingers around her neck and laughing.

The constable seemed flustered and made a quick retreat.

"They shall soon call me Queen Lack-a-Head!" said the queen, still laughing, trying to cheer her ladies.

With yet more time to wait, the queen returned to her prayers and the ladies sat quietly in the outer room. As the hours passed, the tension grew until Madge could no longer stand it. She was about to go into the queen's room when the constable entered once more. He went in to see the queen and Madge followed.

"Madame, I regret to tell you that the swordsman is still delayed. We will put off the execution until tomorrow morning," said Kingston.

"I am sorry to hear it, sir. I had hoped, by now, to be past my pain," said the queen.

Madge asked the queen if she wanted company but the queen declined. Later that day, Archbishop Cranmer came to hear her last confession. She called Kingston in to witness it. In front of all her ladies and the two men, she confessed her innocence before God. She then received the Sacrament. She and the archbishop remained together for most of the afternoon. Thankfully, that evening, Kingston came again with his sleeping potion. Madge drank hers quickly, eager for escape from the torture they all endured.

The next morning was sunny and bright. Though the sound of the scaffold being hastily constructed had been bothersome for the past two nights, Kingston's potion had helped drown out the hammering. But now, the structure was complete.

The constable brought a hearty breakfast of which the queen ate a generous portion.

"I might as well enjoy what Kingston has brought—I will not eat again," said the queen. Madge could not force a bite down her throat. After her repast, the queen asked Madge and her mother to help her get dressed.

"I shall wear the gray damask gown with the crimson petticoat. And the ermine mantel over it. We shall put my hair in this linen cap so the tresses will not impede the sword. And I shall wear my English gable hood over the cap," said the queen. Madge combed the queen's long hair for the last time, her tears dropping onto the locks as she fit them into the embroidered cap. Lady Shelton helped the queen into her gown and laid the mantel across her shoulders.

"Majesty, you look beautiful," said Madge, still sniffling.

"It is my soul which must be pleasing now, dearest. I would please God above all else," said the queen. "Remember your promise—take care of Elizabeth and leave this den of iniquity."

"I shall, Majesty—you have my solemn word on it. I do love you so," said Madge, embracing the queen, unable to staunch her tears. The other ladies were crying, too.

"Take heart, friends. I shall be in heaven soon," said the queen.

At that moment, Kingston knocked on the door. He entered. "Madame, the time is come," he said, offering her his arm.

"Thank you, Master Kingston. And God's blessing on you," she said as she stepped into the sunlight, followed by her ladies. Madge and her mother were the last. Slowly and with great dignity, they walked toward the scaffold, which had been draped in black material. Fresh straw had been strewn over the stage to catch the blood. Rather than execute the queen in public view, as Cromwell had planned originally, the king commanded she be killed on the Tower green with fewer people in attendance. It was said that the king feared what Anne might say on the scaffold, and he was anxious about the reaction of the crowd to the execution of a woman.

As the queen climbed the steps to the scaffold, followed by Madge, Lady Shelton, and Margaret Wyatt, the swordsman was already standing on the stage in view of the witnesses to the queen's execution. Madge looked out into the crowd. She saw Cromwell and the king's son, Henry Fitzroy, duke of Richmond. Then she gasped as she saw the steely face of the duke of Suffolk. Brandon glanced at Madge and turned his head.

The queen mounted the platform and a great silence fell on the crowd. The queen spoke out in a strong, calm voice:

"Good Christian people, I have not come here to preach a sermon; I have come here to die, for according to the law and by the law, I am judged to die, and therefore I will speak nothing against it. I am come hither to accuse no man, nor to speak of that whereof I am accused and condemned to die, but I pray God save the king and send him long to reign over you, for a gentler nor a more merciful prince was there never, and to me he was ever a good, a gentle, and sovereign lord.

"And if any person will meddle of my cause, I require them

to judge the best. And thus I take my leave of the world and of you all, and I heartily desire you all to pray for me."

Madge watched as the queen then stepped back and Lady Lee, Wyatt's sister, removed her headdress. Her pearls and her Book of Hours she handed to Lady Lee. She looked at Madge, motioned her forward, and embraced her. Madge felt her place two rings into her hand and a small locket. Madge held her close, breathing in her fragrance, feeling once more the delicacy of her bones. When the queen released Madge, Anne stared directly into Madge's eyes and whispered, "Remember your promise, dear cousin—and remember me to my darling Elizabeth." Then, Her Majesty turned to the French swordsman and forgave her executioner. She placed a sack of gold coins into his hands, paying him for his work.

At that moment, the queen sank to her knees to await the blow, all the while saying, "To Jesus Christ, I commend my spirit. Lord, have mercy on me. Lord Jesu, receive my soul." Madge heard her repeat the words until the swordsman called for his sword, a ruse so that the queen would not look behind her. He smote off her head in one blow, then held the head up by the hair to show the crowd. Madge thought she could see the queen's lips still moving as he held the head aloft.

The cannon fired three times and Madge felt the vibration in her belly. She felt she would be sick at the sight of the queen's blood and bits of bone and gore smeared across the platform and spattering those who stood closest to the front. She watched as they wiped the queen's good blood from their faces with white handkerchiefs. It had happened so quickly, after all the long hours of waiting. Now, it was over and Madge knew the queen was in the hands of God even at that moment. She did not cry but moved to the business at hand—her last service for her queen.

The crowd began to disperse.

"Shall we tend to her body now?" asked Lady Lee.

"No. Let us wait until all have left. We will then give her the tender care she deserves without the prying eyes of the onlookers," said Madge.

As the people slowly left the scene of the execution, Madge saw a familiar shape make its way to her.

"Oh Maddie! My heart is sore broken. She died with such courage," said Cate, hugging her friend.

"She died well—that is true. But I shall never heal this wound in my heart—though I know she is now in heaven," said Madge, bursting into tears at the sight of her nurse.

"No, our hearts will wear this scar forever. But surely, we will know joy again someday," said Cate.

"Only seeing Arthur could ease my pain. But he is not here. And I cannot wait for him. I promised the queen to go to Great Snoring with my mother this very day. Her Majesty had fears that the king's killing spree might not be over. I fear as much myself," said Madge.

"Master Brandon should be here! Only a great coward would stay away from you at such a time," said Cate.

"Arthur is no coward—I do not know why he has not come. I shall be at your room as soon as we are finished here to pack what clothes I can. And you pack your things, too, dearest Cate, for you must come home with us," said Madge.

"I have been waiting to hear those words, Maddie-girl. And 'tis like music!" said Cate, hurrying off. "I shall be ready—have a care, Maddie. Danger still lurks near."

The stands had emptied and only the queen's ladies remained. Madge and the others tended to the queen's body, wrapping it in white cloth and placing it in an arrow chest, as the king had not provided any sort of coffin. The chest was not long enough to replace the queen's head onto her shoulders so they tucked the bloody parcel in the queen's arms.

"I cannot believe our charming Queen Anne has come to this," said Lady Shelton. "I remember her as a child—bright, happy, so very smart. Oh, this is too gruesome an end for such as she." Madge held her mother as she cried softly.

"Come, come. Let us bury her so she can be at rest," said Mrs. Orchard, Anne's nurse from childhood who had been brought to her on her last night. They struggled to carry the body to the Chapel of St. Peter ad Vincula, the same place the guards had taken her brother. They lay the queen beside George in an open grave and Madge thought it a comfort that brother and sister would be together for eternity.

"Hurry child—we must leave at once!" said Lady Shelton to Madge after they had finished their business with the queen.

"I am to meet Cate in her room—she is packing our things. Where shall we meet you?" said Madge, fear mixing with anger in her bosom.

"I shall be at the east gate. And Margaret, let no one see you. We can hope that the king is busy elsewhere and our danger is less than it was. But no need to remind His Majesty that we are the queen's dear family," said Lady Shelton.

"I shall take the greatest care, Mother. Have no fear," said Madge as she kissed her mother's cheek, which was still wet with tears.

Madge took the easiest way to Cate's rooms, remembering with each step her first time to Hampton Palace, how clumsy she felt, how out of place. Now, the rooms were familiar and felt like home—except the heart of that home no longer beat. The palace was oddly empty. All the queen's ladies had been dismissed and

Madge was surprised to see her gold plate had been cleared out, as well as her gowns and jewels. Madge felt in the pocket of her petticote for the rings and locket, thanking the queen silently that Her Majesty had thought to give her a remembrance. She shook her head to clear the threatening tears from her eyes.

She made her way quickly to Cate's room and opened the door without knocking.

"You scared the life out of me! Methought you were a guard come to get me!" said Cate, whose face had blanched. Even Shadow seemed terrified for, rather than jump into Madge's arms, she cowered behind Cate's pallet.

"I am sorry, dear. The castle is so empty of people, I thought you would know 'twas I," said Madge, going over to Shadow to lure her out.

"I have packed all your gowns—I thought you would not wish to leave them," said Cate as she pointed to an enormous chest.

"Dearest, we are running for our lives—I fear that trunk would be far too heavy for us to carry. And remember, we do not have His Majesty's permission to leave court. We are escaping! Let us bundle up a few things and be on our way," said Madge.

"I so hate for your to leave these exquisite gowns—you are unlikely to ever have anything so fine," said Cate.

"I care nothing for them—they remind me of all the greed and ambition here at court. I am happy to leave it all behind. If only I could get word to Arthur or at least know why he has not come to me," said Madge.

"That I do know, Maddie," said Cate.

"How could you know such a thing? Tell me—tell me all!" said Madge.

"After I left you, I went in search of Suffolk—I had seen him at the queen's execution and I would speak with him," said Cate.

"Mad, mad woman! To take such a chance!" said Madge.

"I felt I had enough to do with His Grace that he would speak with me . . . and he did. He told me your Master Brandon had been hot to come to you the minute they got word the queen had been taken. But the duke refused him. It seems Master Brandon raised his hand against his father and the duke had him bound and stowed under guard at Guildford Palace. He is under guard still and will remain so until the duke is convinced the young man will no longer pursue you," said Cate.

"But why? Why is the duke against me? Arthur is merely his natural son . . ." said Madge.

"The duke said even a son born on the wrong side of the bed was above a wench that came from a disgraced family, with a cousin who was the biggest whore in Christendom," said Cate.

"Damn him. So now, *Arthur* is too good for *me*! How the world has turned upside down!" said Madge. "Now my heart is doubly broken—I have lost my queen and dear friend—and my own true love!" Madge found she had no more tears but felt a heaviness settle around her heart.

"I am sorry to bring such sad tidings—but there is still hope. He cannot keep his son under guard forever . . . and now, I hear footsteps! We must go. I have bundled a few items and some food. Let us be off!" said Cate.

Thirty-nine

A s they had planned, the very afternoon of the queen's demise, Madge, her mother, Cate, and Shadow left London. Her mother had procured a horse and wagon in advance, sending payment and arranging a meeting place through one of Sir Kingston's servants. She feared any friend of the queen might still be in danger, even though most of the queen's supporters had been killed along with Her Majesty. But who could know how far-reaching the king's wrath might be? And who could feel safe while in close proximity to His Majesty?

Though Madge hated to leave without sending a message to Arthur, she had no choice. Not only had she promised the queen that she would leave court, her mother was insistent that they depart immediately. And so, Madge found herself heading north to Great Snoring, going, finally, to the place she had so longed for when she had first come to court.

The ride home was long, bumpy, and uncomfortable. Madge sought what solace she could in the beauty of the hills, the pastures dotted with new spring lambs, the tiny villages with their whitewashed walls and thatched roofs. The journey took six days, with Madge's mother driving the wagon as best she could. Their meager food ran out after three days and they were forced to buy what they could from farmers along the way.

When they approached the familiar grounds of Great Snoring, Madge had a brief moment of happiness, for the place looked much as she remembered and her childhood memories brought her joy.

But Madge soon discovered being in her old home gave her no real solace. Her grief for the queen and her hunger for Arthur mingled to form a dark place in her heart. For many weeks after the queen's death, Madge could not find reason to rise in the mornings. She was tired to her very bones and no hope filled her spirit. She missed the queen and thought she would never get the picture of the execution from her mind. Each time she thought of it, she sickened. All that blood, all that red, red blood. Such thoughts often made her gag. When she remembered the queen's beautiful hair, falling free of its cap, bits of bone and gore besmirching those long tresses, Madge literally became ill.

Not only was she heartsore about what had happened to the queen, Madge was furious at the injustice and cruelty exhibited by the king. Even in Great Snoring, she heard gossip from the court.

"They say he is betrothed to Lady Jane Seymour—that they plighted their troth the very day after good Queen Anne was killed," said one of the neighboring milkmaids to Cate. Of course, Cate repeated everything she heard to Madge. By June, Henry and Jane were wed and readying themselves to go on Progress. Madge became weary with her hatred of the king.

As the summer solstice passed, Madge grew more and more lonely. She had hoped Arthur would come for her, but now, she wondered if he would ever find her. If he had come to court, as he had said he would once the summer arrived, he would not have found her there. She had told no one of her plan of escape. Her mother had cautioned her to keep silent and she had had no opportunity to leave word for him. The more time passed, the more she began to doubt him. Perhaps he no longer loved her. Perhaps he had found another maiden to bed, one with more of a dowry than Madge could now hope to have. So many evil thoughts grew in her mind that Cate and her mother became worried about her. They both tried to give her comfort, but there was nothing that eased her.

As the weeks passed, Madge began to worry. She had been so ill, unable to hold much food in her stomach, and her monthly flow had not come. At first, she put the cause of her squirmy stomach to the ordeal she had witnessed. But, as the days continued, she feared she was to have Arthur's child. As the fear grew, Madge thought more and more about the man she loved. She did not know what to do. Her father would surely disown her if she were to give birth to a bastard. He would throw her out to live among the common folk or to die among them. Her mother would be of little help; she would rant and cry. Madge decided to wait a while before confessing her fears. Perhaps she was not with child after all. Time would tell.

It was Cate who drew the secret from her lips.

Madge invited Cate to walk among the rolling hills one sunny afternoon. They took Shadow and enjoyed a silent stroll to the first summit. There, beneath a large oak, the two women sat on a coverlet and admired the view.

"You are not looking quite so peaked as when we first arrived,

Maddie-girl. Though you are not eating much, your figure has filled out," said Cate as she spread the material, smoothing any wrinkles.

"I am still tired—still sick of heart, methinks," said Madge. "I miss Her Majesty and I keep seeing her death, even in my dreams."

"Aye, that was a vision no woman could forget. But we must go on, Maddie. Life continues," said Cate.

"I guess my own life must continue without love. I had hoped my dear Arthur would have found me by now," said Madge.

"Who knows how long the duke will keep him imprisoned? He is probably trying to escape or convince the duke he no longer loves you so he can find you. He's not the sort of man to give up the woman he loves," said Cate.

"But does he love me still? How can I know? And I am to have . . ." said Madge.

"What's that, girl?" said Cate, suddenly sitting up straighter.

Madge could hold it in no longer; she confessed her condition to Cate.

"Saints and angels! What are we to do?" said Cate. The two women sat side by side, looking out over the vast lands surrounding Great Snoring. Madge was moved by the beauty of her homeland and the memories of childhood games played among the woods and meadows. Suddenly, everything converged and Madge began to cry.

"No tears, Maddie-girl. Too late for tears now. You will have to tell your mother. She will know what to do," said Cate.

"I cannot! She will tell Father and he will throw me to the wolves! They will think me a common strumpet! I cannot tell them," said Madge.

"You might be surprised at the way your mother would accept

such news—I do agree that to spill the news to your father might not be wise. But your mother is a most remarkable woman," said Cate, putting her arm around Madge.

"But what could she *do*?" said Madge.

"Your mother is a capable woman, aunt to a queen. Do not forget what runs in the Boleyn blood—blood which is yours. Courage and dignity, a fighting spirit and a keen mind. Your mother will help you, Maddie-girl," said Cate.

"Think you so, dear Cate?" said Madge.

"Yes—you must tell your mother," said Cate.

The next morning, Madge was determined to confess everything. She expected great chastising, and was surprised when her mother said nothing accusatory. Instead, her mother frowned and kept silent. Madge did not move while her mother mulled over the news. Then, a slight smile twitched the corners of her mother's mouth.

"Leave everything to me, Margaret. We will solve this problem and your father will never know about it. Now, go down to the groomsman and have him saddle my horse," said Lady Shelton.

"What are you going to do, Mother? I don't understand. Where are you going?" said Madge.

"Why, to get you a husband, child! Where else would I be going?" said her mother.

"But I want the father of the baby—Master Arthur Brandon, natural son of the duke of Suffolk. His father keeps him under guard because the duke finds our blood distasteful after the queen's shameful demise. Arthur cannot yet come to me. But I know he will find me—I just know it!" said Madge.

"You will not have time to wait for your true love to rescue you, my dear. We must get you a husband now! And that I shall do. Out of my way!" said Lady Shelton as she wheeled around and headed downstairs.

Lady Shelton was gone for three days. Madge and Cate worried that robbers had attacked her, but decided to wait another day before sending a groomsman to look for her. Later that evening, Madge heard a horse galloping into the yard. She looked out the window and saw her mother was dismounting. Madge ran down the stairs to greet her.

"Ah, Margaret. I have fixed everything!" said Lady Shelton.

"How so, Mother?" said Madge. Her mother put her arm around Madge and led her into the kitchen where she immediately had the servant prepare a cold plate of venison, gooseberry tarts, and ale. Lady Shelton gobbled the food and gulped the ale. Then she indicated she wanted another mug. She drank that quickly, too.

"Now, I'm fit for talk—come Margaret, let us walk for a while in the garden," said Lady Shelton.

Madge followed her as she walked far away from the house. It was obvious Lady Shelton did not wish their conversation to be overheard. Finally, she sat down on a bench and told Madge to sit, too.

"I have found you a husband," she began.

"But Mother, I am with child. How can I marry anyone but the father of the baby? And that would be my dear Arthur," said Madge. "We are promised. You must help me find him! I know he is searching for me."

"Hush, girl. You will do exactly as I say—I'll hear no more about it. You are to be married next Sunday, here in our chapel. I have already arranged for the priest to come and have even sent for cloth to make you a pretty gown. I shall have plenty of flowers from the rose garden and Cate can stand up as one of your maids, along with your sisters. We shall invite the whole parish. Let's see, I have plenty of ale and wine—I'll have to get the baker for the wedding cake . . . I simply will not have time to do the baking," said Lady Shelton.

"Stop! Stop this talk! I am not going to marry anyone but Arthur—it would be wrong to wed another—I love only Arthur. Please, Mother try to understand," said Madge.

"I do understand—I understand you have gotten yourself into a mess and you need a way out of it, if you are to have any sort of life. If your father knew the truth, he would toss you out on your ears. No, I will brook no argument from you, young lady!" said Lady Shelton.

Madge knew her mother was correct on all points—she was in a mess, her father would rid himself of the mess and she would have no chance at life if she did not take the one currently offered. She did not speak for a long time while her mother continued to make plans. Finally, Madge spoke.

"But Mother, who am I going to marry?" said Madge.

"Oh yes. I almost forgot . . . He is our neighbor to the east, the first son of Sir Philip Wodehouse—Thomas is his name," said Lady Shelton.

"I do not know this man," said Madge. "How can you force me to marry a man I do not know?"

"Dear, most women do not know their husbands. We marry who our parents tell us to marry. Do you think I knew your father? Of course not!" said Lady Shelton.

"But what if I cannot love him—and I cannot, since I love another," said Madge.

"You will find that love and marriage have very little to do with one another. Only the peasants can afford to marry for love. Love is greatly overrated, dear. Sir Thomas's family holds vast properties which, as first son, he shall inherit. But the most important thing is, he understands your condition and is willing to claim the babe as his own," said Lady Shelton.

"How can this be? Why would he do such a thing? Will he not hate me for such?" said Madge.

"I told him that St. Joseph in the Bible did as much for the Blessed Virgin. I persuaded him that he would be performing Christian charity, helping a poor girl who had gone wrong. I told him God would bless the union. I also reminded him that you were cousin of the dearly departed Queen Anne and kin to the princess Elizabeth, who may yet sit on the throne one day," said Lady Shelton. She continued writing down her plans on a much-used piece of parchment.

"These are slim reasons for marriage, Mother," said Madge.

"Oh, and I paid him," Lady Shelton continued.

"That makes it clear. This man is easily bought and sold," said Madge. "I will have none such for a husband—why, he is no better than a common bawd!"

"Nonsense. He wanted to make a good match—I shall remind you as I told him—you are cousin of the queen, God rest her soul. Elizabeth may be queen someday, you never know. He will be marrying up and you will be well provided for. And your bastard will have a name. Not bad for three days' work— even the Good Lord took longer to fix His world," said Lady Shelton.

Madge was silent. She knew her mother had performed a minor miracle and yet, she could not be thankful for it. She wanted Arthur and no one else. The idea of sharing her bed with a perfect stranger made her shiver with disdain.

"I have much to ponder, Mother," she said finally and rose to walk again. She moved quickly so as to leave her mother behind. She did not want company.

The days before the wedding passed in a blur, as all of Great Snoring was busy preparing for the nuptials. In spite of her disdain for the marriage, Madge got caught up in the festive mood, though she held onto her misgivings. She selected a pale green silk for her wedding gown and talked with the cook about which foods to serve. Her mother gave her several gold plates and goblets while Cate worked on embroidering her trousseau. Her sisters, both of whom were married and lived nearby, brought linens and coverlets for her new home; and the simple farmers who worked her father's land gave her sacks of flour, skeins of wool, casks of ale, and great bowls of butter. Some offered cherry tarts and the sight of these made Madge remember Queen Anne and how she had loved cherries in any form. She remembered the queen's coronation and how they had prepared for it. At those times, Madge would retreat from the hustle and bustle of the manor house and walk up and down the hillsides, sometimes crying but sometimes praying. In her prayers, she begged for Arthur to come to her and carry her away to Guildford Palace where they would raise the babe in her womb and have a great family of sons. She often beseeched the Good God to bless the queen who was now with Him in heaven. And she prayed for the safe delivery of her own child, the child of her love for Arthur.

Before she knew it, Sunday had arrived and Madge was bathed, combed, clothed, and ready for her wedding.

"Come, come, Margaret—take off the long face. Your groom will not like to see that frown on the day of your wedding," said her mother as she helped her with her dress.

"I do not care what the groom will or will not like. This is what I am and he must learn to accept me as such," said Madge, feeling once again like a child who was being punished. She could not stop the pouting of her mouth.

"You had better have a care, mistress. You must be pleasing to the youth or he might decide not to go through with the marriage. Then we would both be in a hot stew. Your father would discover our secret," said her mother.

Her father was still serving Elizabeth at Hatfield, having not yet been dismissed, as they all had expected. He would not attend the wedding, nor would he ever guess Madge's condition. Her mother had figured it all out—they would explain the haste of the marriage by saying they feared the king's retribution upon Madge for her faithful service to the queen. When the babe came early, Lady Shelton would say it was a fault of nature. Hopefully, Sir Shelton would still be housed at Hatfield and would never know the size of the child when it arrived in this world. The lie would be safe.

As Madge stood in her room, looking at herself in the glass, she thought she could see a little pouch where Arthur's child lay. She cradled her belly with her hands. She thought of Arthur, who would be so proud to know he was going to have a little one—how often they had talked about what sort of family they would have. But Arthur had not found her; perhaps he had not even looked for her. She shook her head to rid herself of thoughts of her beloved. She rubbed her hands over her belly and thought how she loved the babe already. Feeling such love, she felt sorry once more for Anne, the queen. Anne, who had lost her babes; Anne, who had lost the man she loved. Madge hoped she would be able to bring this child to term and that she might find, again, her own love.

She heard the sound of a carriage and saw, from the window, people walking toward the courtyard. The carriage must belong to her intended. The people on foot would be the simple folk who lived in the small cottages of Great Snoring. Madge did not wish to go down the stairs just yet. She sat on her bed and Shadow nudged her with her nose.

"I shall not cry again, old girl. I shall not shed a tear. I shall meet my destiny with as much courage as Queen Anne faced hers. We do not know what the world will throw at us, Shadow. It does not matter. What matters is how we manage those things God sends to us. I would manage mine own life with dignity and I shall walk into the future with my head held high," said Madge. She took a lacy handkerchief, a gift from Cate, and wiped her eyes. Then, she pinched her cheeks and lips, wishing them to look rosy for her soon-to-be husband.

"Margaret, come meet Sir Thomas—he is waiting for you," her mother called from downstairs.

Madge gathered herself, remembering how Queen Anne had walked to the scaffold full of poise and grace. Madge wanted to walk down the steps in the very same way. Slowly, with the eyes of the entire household upon her, she glided down the stairs. As she reached the bottom of the steps, she curtsied to the young man who stood waiting. He bowed gallantly to her. When she looked up into his face, she found his eyes to be kind. He was not handsome like Arthur but he was pleasing enough. She watched as his face turned pink and, for some reason, his blush made her feel tender toward him. He took her by the hand and led her to where the priest stood waiting.

Forty

*M*adge sat on the edge of her parents' great bed, an enormous carved headboard with four large posts to support the goose-down mattress, which was covered with red and pink rose petals and smelled of roses and lavender. Though not half as big as the king's, this bed seemed almost sacred to Madge; none of the children had ever been allowed to crawl upon it, nor could they join their parents beneath the coverlet. Her mother had been inordinately proud of such a bed and now, as Madge twisted the linen sheet in her hands, she found it hard to believe she and her new husband would spend their wedding night here, in her parents' most private place.

The wedding had taken place hours ago with much fine food and ale: several coneys stuffed with pepper and currants; a dozen capons spiced with nutmeg, sugar, ground almonds, and garnished with prunes; venison roasts; spring salat made with asparagus to "renew love," bugloss to say "I am pleased with you," and rosemary flowers, meaning "I accept your love." The wedding cakes were gingerbreads gilded with gold. The ale and wine flowed without limit and the guests reeled and laughed, taking great merriment from the special occasion. Madge had danced with every man who asked for her hand, no matter how rank his odor or how drunken his manner. After eating and dancing their fill, the wedding guests carried Madge to the bedroom, then toppled Thomas onto her, all the while singing songs that caused the blush to rise in her cheeks. Finally, after much more singing and telling of bawdy tales, the villagers left, along with friends and family. Then, Thomas excused himself to the outdoor jakes and left Madge with much on her mind.

She could not imagine allowing this stranger to occupy her; the thought made her flesh creep and tears filled her eyes. Even when she had bedded the king, he was no stranger. He had saved her from harm, joked with her, danced with her. Allowing him to paw her body's intimate places had not been easy, but now, doing such with this new man—it was more than she could bear.

She heard heavy steps traveling up the stairs. She looked up and in the doorway stood her husband. He did not say a word but strode to her and sat beside her, taking her hand in his. Without thinking, Madge threw herself on the floor, grabbed his ankles, and spoke.

"My good lord, have mercy on me. I beg of you, delay for a while your pleasure. Let us grow to be friends so as to be at ease with one another. I fear if you meddle with me now, you will disturb the babe that rests within. I am at your mercy, my good husband," she said, not once raising her head to look at him.

"Prithee, arise, madame. Here, here," he said as he pulled her to her feet and patted the bed next to him. She sat a little way from him. Tears ran down her cheeks and her nose dripped. She could not stop either so she remained still, not sobbing or crying out.

"You give me pause, wife. I know I lack beauty but am I one to cause such dread? Eh?" he said, lifting her chin gently. A slight smile raised the corners of his mouth.

"No, my husband. You are kind to take such a one as I to marry. I am grateful," said Madge, finally looking into his face.

"I shall not dally with thee this night, madame. I know too well what danger such play is to the babe within. And though he be not mine, I would harm neither you nor him. We shall be chaste until he is born. And in that time, I hope to win you, as I would if you were a true maid," he said. "And now, let us sleep for I have drunk much wine this day."

Madge took his hand and looked straight at him.

"Kind sir, I thank you with all my heart. When the babe comes, I shall be as good a wife to you as you need—truly buxom in board and bed," she said.

Weeks passed and Thomas remained true to his word. He often returned to his home in Kimberly to oversee the care of his sheep, the running of the manor over which he would be lord someday. He told Madge about hunting the plentiful deer that roamed his forests and made humorous stories regarding the foibles of his servants. Because only his father, his two brothers, and he lived at Kimberly, Thomas believed Madge would be more at ease staying with her mother and family at Great Snoring. Sir Thomas rode to Great Snoring at least once a week and when he was visiting, he and Madge often walked the rolling hills, taking picnics by the creek and talking about the future. During his absences, Madge found herself with little to do except sew quilts for the coming child, along with caps, gowns, and booties. She took great pride in embroidering each garment with tiny violets and sprigs of lavender. She smocked the softest lawn available for the child's christening gown and attached fine lace around the collar and sleeves. She felt the babe quicken one day while she was walking in the garden to gather flowers. The almost imperceptible nudge within her caused her to smile with wonder, imagining the tiny babe she would soon bear for her beloved Arthur. Each time the babe kicked, it reminded her again of the man she adored and, often, she wept. Her sorrow and joy were so mixed, she could not tell where one stopped and the other began. Her heart carried a heaviness that nothing seemed to relieve as she slowly came to realize she would never see her darling Sir Churlish again.

All summer the weather had been unseasonably cold, with many cloudy days and much rain. Finally, the sun found his place once again in a cloudless sky and Madge wanted to soak up the warmth.

"Mother, I wish to accompany the washwomen to the hedgerows. I shall watch as they lay out the clothes to dry. The day is warm and I have been too much inside. I shall go mad if I have to stay so cloistered again," said Madge.

"'Tis warm enough, I gainsay. But have a care—place your feet on solid ground for a fall now could damage both you and the babe. And don't be gone too long—the afternoon turns quickly to eventide and the cold air will do you no good," said Lady Shelton.

Madge smiled at her mother and gave her a quick kiss on

the cheek. She called to Shadow and off they ran, following the washerwomen, who carried large baskets filled with wet sheets, nightgowns, and smocks. While the women laid the laundry over the hedges, Madge threw a small leather ball for Shadow to fetch. Tiring after a long game of it, Madge lay down on the warm grass, the sun on her face and Shadow's head on her lap.

"We be going back to the house, mistress. Will ye come along?" said Lucy, the chief washerwoman.

"No. Methinks to stay a while in the sun. I shall be along anon," said Madge, closing her eyes and flopping her arm over her brow to block the bright rays.

She could hear the women's voices growing softer as they made their way back to the manor. Soon, all she heard were the noises of the land: the lark's song, the chirp of the jays, the creak of the cricket. With the warmth of the afternoon came a peace she had not felt for many weeks. No thoughts of Queen Anne's execution troubled her, no dread of the king's wrath. Instead, she thought of Arthur, tried to remember the exact shade of his eyes, the shape of his mouth, the feel of him. She recalled the times they lay together and instead of feeling sad, the way such daydreams usually made her feel, she was happy to have known this love, happy to have his child in her belly. Soon, the sun warming her completely, Madge drifted to sleep with sweet thoughts of Arthur fluttering in her head.

"My love."

Madge heard his voice and she knew she must be dreaming still. For certainly, that was Arthur speaking. And it sounded as if he were lying beside her. She smiled and turned toward the sound but did not open her eyes. She did not wish to disturb this dream.

"You have never looked so beautiful."

Her eyes flew open at those words. She looked straight into Arthur's deep brown eyes.

"What? What is this? Enchantment?" she said.

"I am no phantom, my love," said Arthur, bending over her, taking her in his arms.

"How? What—"

Before she could say more, he kissed her, gently at first, then urgently. She responded to him without thought, still foggy from sleep, the sun striking her vision so that nothing seemed real.

Finally, she pulled away from him.

"Where have you been?" she demanded abruptly.

"My love, there is much to tell. I will shorten the tale as I am able. Come, let us walk along the hedgerow and I will make things plain," he said.

He pulled her to her feet and, arm in arm, they strolled while Shadow wove circles around their legs.

"When I discovered the queen was to die, I knew I must come for you—I knew you were in grave danger. My dear father knew my mind and had me bound and imprisoned in the barns at Guildford Castle. He did not wish for me to marry from such an evil family. He bade me eat once a day, bread and water, so my strength would ebb," said Arthur.

"How did you get away?" said Madge.

"I am not without certain, er, skills, milady," he said, smiling.

"Skills of magic? Ways to unbind yourself?" she said.

"The serving wench who brought my food was soon willing to bring meat and ale. After a time, she was willing to unloose my bonds," he said, still grinning.

Madge could feel her face burn.

"And how did you reward this wench? Did you bed her?" she said.

"You are a pretty one when you are angered! How your cheeks blaze! And your eyes are filled with passion! I wish to throw you upon the ground and take you, my love, right now!" said Arthur, pulling her to him.

"Not so, sirrah! You need explain yourself!" said Madge.

"Tut, tut. I did not bed the wench! But I did pack my horse and was ready to ride to London. I waited until nightfall, then led the horse out of the barn in all silence. But the wench must have spilled my plans to my father, for he met me in the outer yard," said Arthur.

"Oh no! What then?" said Madge, hugging him to her.

"When first I saw him, I feared for my life! He is not a man to be crossed. His sword was drawn and his face thunderous! He came at me and bludgeoned me about the shoulders with the blade flattened against me. Then, he took me by the ear and pulled me into the hall. He continued until we were in his privy chamber where there was set a table with meat and drink. He pushed me onto a bench and told me to stay put. Then, he poured us each a glass of Rhenish wine, thrust the cup at me, and commanded, 'Drink, ye lowborn son of a whore!' To which I drank," said Arthur.

Madge stopped walking and faced him. She reached her fingers to touch a bluish spot on his brow.

"How long did he make you suffer?" she said.

"He did not give me that blow—'twas from the horse. But pray, let me continue," said Arthur, kissing her fingers.

"I was used to name-calling so he did not get the rise from me he wanted. He ordered me to explain myself, and I told him once again of the great love I hold in my heart for you, my sweet. I allowed that since I was born on the wrong side of the bed, I owed him no allegiance and he had no right to keep me from you. To which he replied as my father, he had every right.

And then, to my astonishment, he pulled out a parchment and opened it. He had claimed me, had given me a small portion of his lands and gold, and all was signed by order of the king himself!" said Arthur.

"It is only right that he should do so, dearest! He should have done so long ago! I cannot help but think him a knave," said Madge.

"Nay, nay, sweetheart. He is the best of men. For he also gave his permission for me to marry to mine own liking—he said he did as much when he took His Majesty, the king's sister to wife—and he was none the worse for it. Then, we sat down together and drank more bottles of wine than I can remember," said Arthur, laughing a little.

"Oh, my love! I cannot believe this is true!" said Madge, throwing her arms around him.

"Take a look at this bag of coin if you do not believe me," said Arthur, taking a small bag out of his breeches. "And there is more in my saddle pouches, enough to buy a small house here. I thought we would settle near your own people, away from court and away from my father's wrath, should it roar up again," said Arthur.

Madge looked at the gold and burst into tears.

"What is this? Do you shed tears of joy to see such wealth?" said Arthur.

"No, 'tis nothing of that. But, how can I tell you . . . I am . . . I am . . ."

"What is it, woman? You are what?" said Arthur.

"I am married! And I am to have your child! Oh, all is lost and befuddled!" said Madge, crying harder now.

"What mean you? Married? How so? My child? Oh, 'tis glorious news! But the tale is muddled, I fear. Speak it plain, my love," said Arthur.

"My mother, when I told her I was with child and I had heard no word from you, she devised to help me. For surely, of all people, you know what happens to a woman who has a bastard child. My father, had he been home, would have thrown me out. So, my sainted mother found me a husband," said Madge between sobs.

"But how? And who? Who would marry under such conditions?" said Arthur.

"Sir Thomas Wodehouse. He is a neighbor and my mother paid him dearly for agreeing to the marriage. He is a kind enough man, though greedy. She gave him coin and land to take this babe as his own and to take me for his wife. We have been wed two months now," said Madge.

"And is there no way out? Can we not say we were precontracted to each other?" said Arthur, who turned away from her.

Madge could not think clearly. She longed to hold Arthur, kiss him, and make him her own again. She sensed he was angry and she knew he thought her false.

"I am sorry, dearest. I did not think I would ever see you again—I doubted your love. In this, I was wrong," said Madge. She felt the babe move, as if it, too, were sorry. She took Arthur's hand and placed it on her belly.

"Your son moves, sir," she said quietly.

"I feel . . . little bumps, kicks? Is that it?" said Arthur, his face aglow.

"Yes. He must needs walking. Let us continue," she said. She did not let go of his hand and he entwined his fingers with her own.

"Has the marriage been . . . consummated?" Arthur mumbled.

"Nay. Sir Thomas does not wish to disturb the babe and, as I begged him for time, he has agreed to wait until the babe is born," said Madge.

"So, he has not known you then?" said Arthur.

"No. All we have done is share a bed—for sleep, beloved. For sleep alone," said Madge.

"Then there is our answer. For a marriage can be annulled if man and wife have not known each other. My own father used such a ruse when he rid himself of his first wife. We must go to your mother at once. She will, mayhap, help you again," said Arthur.

He kissed her once again, deeply, a kiss that took possession of her, body and soul. Then, they walked back to the manor house.

"Madame? Madame? 'Tis he! 'Tis Arthur! Come, Lady Shelton! Come at once!" cried Cate as she stared at Madge and Arthur walking into the courtyard hand in hand. Her own heart was in her throat and she felt the flush of joy for her dear, dear Maddie.

Lady Shelton soon joined her, her sewing still in her hands.

"He is a pretty sight, is he not, milady?" said Cate.

"Quite manly and bold, too, to come here now. I see why my daughter would give herself to such a man," sighed Lady Shelton. "But he is come too late. She is wed to another."

"Surely, this can be changed, madame. Surely we can find a way to give my Maddie what she wants. She has suffered much, more than you will know, lady," whispered Cate.

"Let us remove from the door—we do not want them to find us gaping like sheep. Come, Cate. Into the sewing chamber. Let the serving wench lead them to us," commanded Lady Shelton.

The two women hurried to the sewing chamber where each sat on a low stool, bent over her work.

"I cannot keep my needle steady, my hand shakes so," said Cate.

"Hush! I hear footfalls," whispered Lady Shelton.

The women kept their heads down. Madge and Arthur waited for Lucy, the washerwoman, to announce them.

"Lady Wodehouse and Sir Arthur Brandon," shouted Lucy.

Lady Shelton rose to her full height and Madge noticed her mother looked as if she smelled something quite rotten.

"Mother, this is Arthur," said Madge as she curtsied to Lady Shelton.

"How is it he is now 'Sir' Arthur, rather than Master Arthur?" said her mother with venom in her voice.

Madge started to answer, but Arthur stepped up from his bow so that he stood between Madge and her mother.

"Lady Shelton, you have reason to be angry with me, for I know how this looks to you. But I assure you my love for your daughter is true and I wish to have her as my wife. We can claim a precontract—there is proof enough in her belly," said Arthur calmly.

"How do you imagine my daughter could be precontracted to a baseborn bastard?" said Lady Shelton.

"If this is your only objection, madame, I have the parchment to prove my father, duke of Suffolk, has now claimed me and made me part heir with my two brothers. This means I am to inherit one full third of his holdings. Lady Shelton, need I tell you such an inheritance will raise your daughter's status immensely. And that of your grandchild," said Arthur.

Madge's mother fell silent for a moment, then curtsied deeply to Arthur.

"My lord, you have astonished me. Forgive my impertinence," said Lady Shelton.

Arthur raised her up gently and smiled at her.

"It is I who should beg your forgiveness. I failed to come for my Pretty Madge when she most needed me. There is good reason for this but I shall save that tale for another day. I am here now and wish to claim my bride," he said.

"Hmmm. There *is* the precontract; but I have promised Sir Thomas both gold and land—he will not give these up, of that I am certain. And Margaret is a good match for him as well," said Lady Shelton.

"Mother, there is something you must know. Thomas has not bedded me," said Madge, her cheeks on fire.

"Why on earth not? He is no ganymede! And you are buxom enough!" said Lady Shelton.

"I begged him to wait until the babe was born. I told him I wished to know him a little before we . . ." said Madge.

"Ha! And he agreed to this?" said Lady Shelton.

"I told him such an act would endanger the babe and myself! He was kind," said Madge.

"What fools men be! Tut, tut. 'Tis good, though, for our purpose. What shall be done? Oh, what shall be done?" said Lady Shelton as she began to pace the room.

"Madame, if I may be so bold, this is between Sir Wodehouse and myself. I can handle him, even if I must draw my blade," said Arthur.

"Oh no, dearest! You cannot risk yourself so—I have only just found you! I would not chance losing you again!" said Madge, flinging herself into his arms.

"Have you so little faith in me? You think I would not best him? Pish! I would serve him carved in pieces!" said Arthur, pushing her away.

"My love, I meant only that I could not stand to think of such danger for you—I want our boy to know his father," said Madge, putting her arms on his chest. She then softly touched his cheek.

"You do know how to rule me, Pretty Madge. I shall use

reason on the man. And the force of gold rather than steel. Does this please you?" he said, placing his hands on her waist.

"Aye, my love," she said.

"By St. Anne, save your pretty words for the bedchamber," said Lady Shelton.

"If I may speak, sir?" said Cate.

"Good Cate! Forgive me! I greet you happily, my lovely!" said Arthur, turning to her and bowing.

"Pshaw! Enough of your shenanigans, Master . . . er, Sir Brandon," said Cate, turning red at his gesture. "Should you ride to Kimberly and speak man-to-man with Sir Wodehouse, a good end would come of it. Though his father and brothers be there with him, they are gentles, after all. With the right offer, Sir Thomas will agree, I wager," said Cate.

"What makes you so very certain, Cate? What do you know?" said Madge.

"I speak with his chief steward at chapel every Sunday. It seems there is a woman who caters to him, one he loves already. She is lowborn, so they cannot marry. But love her, he does," said Cate.

"This news explains much," said Lady Shelton.

"Methinks you have it by the right ear, Cate. I ride to Kimberly on the morrow," said Arthur.

That night, Arthur and Madge slept in the great bed, Madge in her gown of lawn with embroidered flowers on the neckline and lace at her sleeves. Her hair, reddish-gold in the candlelight, fell down her back in soft ringlets. Arthur wore his nightshirt and Madge could see his chest through the thin cloth. She lay against the pillows and watched as he crawled in beside her. He gathered her in his arms.

"I have waited long to hold you, my love. I will not be so easy to dissuade as Sir Thomas," said Arthur, kissing her eyelids, her cheeks, her nose, her ears.

"I do not wish to dissuade you, dearest. I have longed for you with all my heart," said Madge as she molded her body with his. She ran her fingers through his dark curls and circled his neck. She pulled him to her and sucked his earlobes while he nuzzled her neck, his beard soft against her. Soon, before she realized it, he was inside her, moving very slowly, incredibly gentle.

"I do not wish to rush this moment, my love. I have waited too long . . ." he said. He barely moved at all. So they lay together for such a time that Madge thought she had left the earth and its motions; that the moon no longer moved across the sky; that she and Arthur had lain like this for all eternity and would so lie always. She could feel the fire build in her belly and soon, it pulsed its way down through her womb to her womanly parts, pleasure immeasurable coursed through her body, until she thought she could bear it no longer, yet it continued, for what seemed like hours. Her body shook with it and she began to cry. Then, she felt Arthur's pulse as well as her own and once again, the pleasure released itself.

When it was over, they did not move, but fell asleep, Arthur still inside her. When they awoke to the bright sun, they made love again, waking the babe who kicked and kicked while his father spoke soft words to him and to his mother.

Reading
Group
Gold

AT THE MERCY OF THE QUEEN

by Anne Clinard Barnhill

About the Author

- A Conversation with Anne Clinard Barnhill

Behind the Novel

- Historical Timeline
- The Facts About Lady Margaret Shelton
- "What Should I Wear?"
  An Original Essay by the Author

Keep on Reading

- Recommended Reading
- Reading Group Questions

*A
Reading
Group Gold
Selection*

For more reading group suggestions,
visit www.readinggroupgold.com.

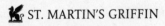 ST. MARTIN'S GRIFFIN

A Conversation with Anne Clinard Barnhill

Tell us about your background and how you decided to become a writer.

I've been telling stories since I was a little girl. I would entertain my cousins for hours outside my grandparents' house with ghost tales and funny, long jokes. I've always loved to read and, in college, the two loves merged into my desire to become a writer. I had to wait a long time to pursue my passion as I had to help support and raise three sons. I taught high school and college, assisted a dermatologist, worked in a jewelry store, counted billboards, and took various other part-time jobs to keep everything together, not to mention writing articles, book reviews, ad copy—anything to keep writing those stories that haunt me. Finally, at thirty-seven, I was able to devote much more time to writing. About fifteen years of hard work later, my first book was published. It's been a long road, but the journey has been worth every minute.

Who are some of your favorite authors?

I have a zillion favorites but I'll mention a few. For nonfiction about Tudor times, I love everything from Alison Weir, Carolly Erickson, Eric Ives, Anne Somerset, Sarah Gristwood, David Starkey, Tracy Borman, and Kathy Emerson's *The Writer's Guide to Everyday Life in Renaissance England*. There are really too many to name. For historical fiction, my first love is Jean Plaidy, who I devoured early on. Jeane Westin, C. W. Gortner, Alison Weir, Carolly Erickson, Sara Poole, Hilary Mantel, Diane Haeger, and others who can really take me to the Tudor world rank among my favorites.

For other kinds of writing, I love Fred Chappell, Robert Morgan, Marilynne Robinson, Elizabeth Berg, John Fowles, Dorothy Sayers, Tolkien, and most of the classics. And, naturally, Shakespeare.

"I had to wait a long time to pursue my passion. . . ."

Are there any historical figures you feel a particular affinity toward?

Anne Boleyn, of course—I do have the initials A. B., after all. She captured me early on and her hold on my imagination is still strong. I wish I could travel back in time and meet her. I'm not sure I would have liked her, but I feel very strongly she would have commanded my attention and admiration. And I'd love to know what she really looked like, too.

What was the inspiration for *At the Mercy of the Queen*?

My grandmother told me our family was related to the Sheltons and that those distant cousins were involved with Anne Boleyn and her court. That was around the same time I'd read my first novel about Anne and from that moment on, I grabbed every book that came along about the Tudors, always looking for information about the Sheltons. In one book, they were referred to as the "pesky cousins" of the queen. I read about Lady Margaret, Anne's first cousin, and her brief affair with the king. Some historians believe Anne put Margaret up to seducing Henry, in order to save herself. I just kept thinking about that, the moral implications of such an action, and the novel is the result.

Do you adhere to historical fact in your novels or do you take liberties if the story can benefit from the change? To what extent did you stick to facts in writing *At the Mercy of the Queen*?

I try to adhere as closely as possible to the information I have researched. I may change the dates, fiddle with the ages if that seems appropriate. But I want to stick to what we know as much as possible. History, especially Tudor England, is so rich in events and characters, it would be hard to top the reality of it by making any drastic changes. The "what if" question, though, makes me think about it in different ways. And, fictional characters seem to forge their way into every story, too.

In your research, what was the most interesting/ surprising/shocking thing you learned?

As I dug into genealogy online and continued to read, it seemed there was confusion among scholars about the lives of Margaret and Mary Shelton. Margaret did have a sister named Mary, who some believe wrote poetry in the Devonshire manuscript. I, however, think they are confusing *that* Mary Shelton with another Mary Shelton from Elizabeth's court. According to my family book about the Sheltons, passed down from my grandmother, Margaret was sent to seduce the king. And Margaret had a reputation for beauty; she was referred to often as "Pretty Madge," which also makes her more likely to have entranced the king.

The Mary Shelton with whom I think folks are confusing Margaret is famous for having had her finger broken by Elizabeth in a fit of rage over her clandestine marriage. I'm writing a book about her story as well.

Why do you think readers are so drawn to historical fiction?

First, historical fiction allows for exploration of themes that, for me, are more difficult to navigate in contemporary fiction. For instance, in those days, people were willing to die for their beliefs and took seriously the idea of heaven versus hell, good versus evil. That gives the idea of sin a reality and adds a layer of tension to any action a character might take. Secondly, the sumptuous lifestyles of the rich and famous are great fun to read about—their velvets and satins, gold plate and silver cloth—yet they had

"It's great fun to explore another time and place to imagine what our lives might have looked like then."

problems with fleas and bedbugs and a host of other scourges. All that money spent on show and they still faced the same problems as those who were less fortunate. And, since we only get the one life, it's great fun to explore another time and place to imagine what our lives might have looked like then.

Are you currently working on another book? If so, what—or who—is your subject?

Yes, I'm at work on Mary Shelton's story at the court of Elizabeth I. I've made some really neat discoveries that echo what I had in mind to begin with, so I'm wondering how my subconscious mind knew that stuff. I hope to show a side of Elizabeth that has not yet been explored and also to show how very treacherous those times were. There will be love, romance, intrigue, and danger.

January 1533	Henry VIII and Anne Boleyn are secretly married. Lady Margaret is called to court to serve the queen. Henry is declared Head of the Church of England.
September 7, 1533	Princess Elizabeth is born, much to the disappointment of her parents, who desperately needed a son and heir.
January 1534	Queen Anne is pregnant again.
June/July 1534	Queen Anne loses the child, though no one knows what happened.
1535	Henry and Anne's tumultuous relationship teeters first one way, then the other. Henry and Cromwell are destroying the monasteries to fill Henry's coffers.
November 1535	Queen Anne is pregnant once again.
January, 1536	Queen Catherine of Aragon dies. Henry falls during a joust and is unconscious for a few hours. Queen Anne miscarries.
May 2, 1536	Queen Anne is arrested.
May 19, 1536	Queen Anne is executed.

The Facts About Lady Margaret Shelton

When I read a historical novel, my first question is, "How much of this book is true?" Here is my answer to that question regarding *At the Mercy of the Queen*.

From the moment I first discovered that the Sheltons were my ancestors and served at the court of King Henry VIII and Elizabeth I, I have been scouring books to find mention of this relatively unknown Tudor family. I remember standing in bookstore aisles, scanning indexes for the Shelton name. If it appeared, I would immediately read that section, then buy that book. One book referred to Sir John and Lady Anne as those "pesky" Shelton cousins! They were so called because Sir John seemed to enjoy eating fine foods while Princess Elizabeth was under his care. Though the child was less than two years old, he insisted she eat in state so he and the rest of the courtiers in attendance upon her could feast on her leftovers. I did not find him a particularly endearing character. His wife, Lady Anne, became famous as the woman who kept Mary Tudor, daughter of Catherine of Aragon, and forced her to give precedence to her new baby sister, Elizabeth.

As I gathered information, I became fascinated with the daughter of Sir John and Lady Anne (Boleyn) Shelton, Lady Margaret, or "Pretty Madge" as she was often called. According to most historians, Margaret came to court when Anne Boleyn, her first cousin, was crowned queen. Though there is no definite birthdate for Lady Margaret, she is most likely much younger than Anne Boleyn, born around 1512 or 1513. Her claim to fame, however, is not her blood connection to the queen but her supposed affair with the king himself.

According to some historians, this flirtation lasted about six months in 1535, when the king's interest in his wife was supposedly waning. No one knows whether the affair was consummated or whether it was simply an episode of courtly love, where the king "served" an innocent lady and they flirted together. Some historians have suggested that Queen Anne put her cousin up to seducing the king, whose roving eye had landed on another. We will never know just how far this flirtation went, but certainly something happened.

We know Margaret was pretty—her nickname certainly would indicate that. There was also an instance later, after the death of Jane Seymour, when Henry was searching for a new wife, and considered Christina of Denmark, whose picture he had seen. When he asked if she were truly that attractive, an ambassador told him yes, she looked a good deal like Lady Margaret Shelton. Margaret was also described as having soft speech and a gentle manner.

"I have always loved to play dress up . . ."

In the last five to ten years, some historians have suggested it was Margaret's sister, Mary, who was the king's mistress. I disagree for several reasons. First, Mary was even younger than Margaret and I am not convinced she was even at court during this time. Many scholars, however, do believe Mary was at court and actively writing in the Devonshire Manuscript, a book of poetry in which several ladies and gentlemen, including the poet Thomas Wyatt, scribbled verses and copied older texts, such as one of Chaucer's tales. I believe Margaret was the budding poet, not Mary. Here's why: Names were often abbreviated. If Margaret shortened her name to Marg, it could be easily confused with Mary. Also, Queen Anne is recorded scolding Margaret for writing "idle poesies" in her prayer book, another clue that it was Margaret who enjoyed writing, not Mary. And the final reason I believe it was Margaret who caught the king's fancy lies in the *Shelton Family History* by R. Z. Shelton. This is an old book my

grandmother gave me and it mentions the story of Margaret's relationship with Henry VIII. We have no real stories about Mary at Henry's court, but many references to Margaret or Pretty Madge. Some historians believe they were one and the same person.

One possible reason for the confusion between Mary and Margaret Shelton is that there was another Mary Shelton who served at Queen Elizabeth's court. This Mary Shelton was quite well known as one of three very influential women who might sway the queen to grant positions and favors. This Mary Shelton was also the unfortunate lady-in-waiting who suffered the queen's disfavor after her secret marriage and the queen, in a rage, broke the lady's finger.

In any event, after the fall of Anne Boleyn and her family, Lady Margaret returned to Great Snoring and married Sir Thomas Wodehouse, giving him seven children, three of whom lived to adulthood. She lived to a ripe old age and did not return to court. She died on September 11, 1583.

Behind the Novel

An Original Essay by the Author

"What Should I Wear?"

I did not write *At the Mercy of the Queen* so I could justify having a Tudor dress made, I promise. But once the book was sold and I realized it would become a reality, I thought, Why not? Wouldn't it be fun to give readings dressed in period costume? Since I have always loved to play dress up, the idea seemed inspired.

But where to find such a dress? There are many places online where one could order a dress but I knew my body was, well, not exactly a perfect size. I would need someone who could measure me and then shape the dress accordingly. My dear friend from high school, Becky Nestor Thacker, could sew and we lived near each other. She was game to give it a try.

The first thing we did was find a pattern. Actually, two patterns: one for the undergarments, the other for the outerwear. We selected a dress in the style of Anne Boleyn's time rather than those battleship dresses Elizabeth wore. My hips are already quite wide enough without adding three feet of whalebone to extend them even more.

We chose material for the undergarments and Becky began to work her magic. Soon, I had a shift, the first article of clothing worn next to the skin. The shifts were made of finely spun linen called lawn, or silk if you were a queen. These garments were washable, as opposed to the outer clothes. This helped a little in the area of hygiene.

As I tried on the first draft, we both agreed the bodice was cut too low. I realize showing one's "dukkies" (nipples) is how the ladies of the day wore their dresses, but I could not imagine myself in the public eye showing, well, almost everything. Becky solved the problem by adding about an inch of fabric and lace. Then came the sleeves. Okay, I have

abnormally short arms—my sons call me T. rex. I warned Becky about this and she laughed it off, thinking I was exaggerating. Then, when the sleeves hung about five inches below my fingertips, she realized I was telling the truth. She shortened them accordingly and added more lace.

Next came the stomacher, something similar to a lace-up corset but prettier because it would have been likely to show. Often, these were embroidered in Tudor times, but mine is made of a silky red and black fabric with no extra decoration. Stays made of wood were used back then, but somehow, I could not imagine myself standing that straight and stiff, so Becky found something more flexible: plastic.

The contraption is hard to get on—I can't do it alone, and the first time I wore it, I thought I would never get it off. With my husband's help, we finally lifted it over my head.

The petticoat or slip will be next, red to match the stomacher. Red was also the color of martyrs and Mary, Queen of Scots, wore a red petticoat at her execution. Then, around the waist is tied a "bum roll," to help the skirt stick out.

So far, only the undergarments are completed, so I suppose I will be addressing audiences in my skivvies, basically. Rest assured, even the underwear is more modest than anything we wear today.

By the time the next book comes out, I hope to have the complete outfit ready, including velvet flats sewn with jewels and pearls. I already have my Anne Boleyn "A" necklace, thanks to theanneboleynfiles.com, and can't wait to struggle into the entire getup. I'll need several ladies-in-waiting to help me remove the garment or I just may be wearing it for a very long time indeed.

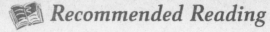 *Recommended Reading*

Nonfiction

Alison Weir
Henry VIII: The King and His Court

The Lady in the Tower: The Fall of Anne Boleyn

The Six Wives of Henry VIII

Eric Ives
The Life and Death of Anne Boleyn

David Starkey
Six Wives: The Queens of Henry VIII

Elizabeth: The Struggle for the Throne

Antonia Fraser
The Wives of Henry VIII

Derek Wilson
In the Lion's Court: Power, Ambition, and Sudden Death in the Reign of Henry VIII

The Uncrowned Kings of England: The Black History of the Dudleys and the Tudor Throne

Retha Warnicke
The Rise and Fall of Anne Boleyn

Joanna Denny
Anne Boleyn: A New Life of England's Tragic Queen

Fiction

Jean Plaidy
The Lady in the Tower (and all others)

Jeane Westin
His Last Letter

Norah Lofts
The Concubine

C. W. Gortner
The Tudor Secret

Diane Haeger
The Queen's Mistake

The Queen's Rival

Reading Group Questions

1. *At the Mercy of the Queen* takes place during Anne Boleyn's reign as queen. What did you discover about England at this time? Who were the major players and what were their motivations?

2. Anne Boleyn is one of history's most popular figures. Why do you think she continues to exert such fascination, so many years after her life?

3. How would you describe the character of Henry VIII? Was he a monster or a hero for religious reform?

4. Did Henry really love Anne? Do you think Anne truly loved Henry? What do you think went wrong in their relationship?

5. How was Madge, or Anne for that matter, different from other women of her era? Do you think she was "ahead of her time"? What do you see as her most and least admirable qualities? Take a moment to talk about women and their place in Tudor society.

6. How does Arthur's illegitimacy affect him?

7. Who was your favorite character in the book, and why?

8. Why do you think Anne Boleyn's plan did not work?

9. To what extent do you think Anne Clinard Barnhill took artistic liberties with this work? What does it take for a novelist to bring a "real" period to life?

10. We are taught, as young readers, that every story has a "moral." Is there a moral to *At the Mercy of the Queen*? What can we learn about our world— and ourselves—from Madge's story?

In her upcoming book, Anne Barnhill takes us to the court of Eliza-beth I. The queen finds herself betrayed by her ward, Mary Shelton, a young woman she has raised almost as her own daughter.

I shall have their heads! Traitors! To marry without the per-mission of one's prince is treason! Treason indeed! Heads will roll—the priest who dared marry them—the witnesses who ar-ranged the wedding! God's death! The Tower will be crowded with their stinking carcasses!

Parry, did she think her treachery would go unpunished? After our most kind treatment of the baggage! Oh, Parry, when I think of how she came to us, not much more than a babe in arms, how her chubby arms clung to my neck for comfort— God's blood, she shall pay! All I have given her—hearth and home! Food and drink! Satins and silks to show off her beauty! Rubies and pearls to sparkle in her hair and on her person!

Dear Parry, I gave her my heart—you know it is true! Does she put so little value on my love that she would turn traitor? I have cared more for her than I have for any man! A purer love. For she has been the daughter of my heart, if not my body! But she tossed my love back to me! Without a care!

No! I will not forgive her, Parry! She has gone too far! Un-grateful wench! I shall see her and that new husband of hers in the Tower! They shall suffer a traitor's death. I shall send for the guards this instant.